C0-AWJ-498

Theatrical Performance during the Holocaust

TEXTS | DOCUMENTS | MEMOIRS

PAJ BOOKS

Bonnie Marranca and Gautam Dasgupta
SERIES EDITORS

Theatrical Performance during the Holocaust

TEXTS | DOCUMENTS | MEMOIRS

Edited by
Rebecca Rovit and
Alvin Goldfarb

A PAJ BOOK
The Johns Hopkins University Press
BALTIMORE | LONDON

2 4 6 8 9 7 5 3 1

The Johns Hopkins University Press
2715 North Charles Street
Baltimore, Maryland 21218-4363
www.press.jhu.edu

Library of Congress Cataloging-in-Publication
Data will be found at the end of this book.
A catalog record for this book is available from
the British Library.

ISBN 0-8018-6167-5

To the memory of those artists
who performed during the Holocaust years

CONTENTS

II | Containment:
Performance in Ghettos and in Concentration Camps   91

ILLUSTRATIONS

| | | | | | | | | | | |

ACKNOWLEDGMENTS

THE MATERIAL FOR THIS BOOK could not be have been compiled, contextualized, and authenticated without the help of many people and institutions. First, there is a group of people whose inspiration, creativity, and experiences have helped to shape the soul of this book: the late Eike Geisel; Ruth Anselm-Herzog; Mascha Benya-Matz; Kurt Michaelis; Zdenka Ehrlich-Fantlová; Anise Postel-Vinay; Michèle Agniel; and Pierre Serge Choumoff. I am indebted to my family: Earl H. Rovit and Honey Weisenfeld-Rovit, for their encouragement and intellectual engagement; Robert Rohrschneider and Sarah Rohrschneider, for their very presence. I am also grateful to the American Council of Learned Societies and the Memorial Foundation for Jewish Culture for their support. Alvin Goldfarb would like to especially remember his family members who perished during the Holocaust and his parents, Martin Goldfarb and Shirley Dudelsak Goldfarb, who survived the Shoah.

Our access to archival materials was facilitated by Jürgen Wittneben, Akademie der Künste, Berlin; the staff of the Wiener Library, London; Jan Munk, Patmáník Terezín, Jana Vomácková, the Jewish Museum in Prague; and Marek Web, YIVO, New York. Special thanks to Joža Karas; Roy Kift; Volker Kühn; Sybil H. Milton; Alan E. Steinweis; Peter Rovit; Henry H. Remak; Ulrike Migdal; Henryk M. Broder; the Kramer family; Don Gilzinger Jr.; and Sol Shulman. We thank Bonnie Marranca, our series editor, for her helpful comments. Finally, we thank Georgia Bennett (Illinois State University) for her technical assistance and Robyn Jackson and Mary Ellen O'Hara at Illinois State University for their research support. Special thanks to Carol Zimmerman.

Theatrical Performance during the Holocaust

TEXTS | DOCUMENTS | MEMOIRS

Introduction

REBECCA ROVIT

It is the Past's supreme italic Makes this Present mean.
— Emily Dickinson

er pfeift seine Juden hervor läßt schaufeln ein Grab in der Erde
er befiehlt uns spielt auf nun zum Tanz
[he whistles his Jews out in earth has them dig for a grave
he commands us strike up for the dance]
— Paul Celan[1]

AS WE EDGE into a new century and a new millennium, what is surely among the most horrendous atrocities of history still lingers: the systematic murder of European Jewry by Nazi Germany. The Holocaust has scarred our memories, challenged our consciences, and left in its wake major complexities for scholars to record and for survivors to contest, as their remembered "lived" history and the flood of documentation converge. Some nations commemorate the Holocaust in memorial services or through monuments and museums for the victims and for those who survived. Other countries that perpetrated crimes against the Jews or collaborated with the Nazis strive for communal atonement, while trying to move beyond the past. Yet that past continues to resurface, calling these peoples to account, as in scandals of hidden bank accounts or the courtroom dramas of aged high officials belatedly brought to trial. The actual voices from the past have not yet been silenced. Archivists collect and catalog oral testimony. Meanwhile, filmmakers have turned aspects of these terrible events into riveting film material that sometimes has educational value and sometimes reaps great financial profit.

The Holocaust has become a universal symbol of evil. Its very notoriety has made it a marketable commodity. And yet, the tendency to commercialize the horrific past may serve one meaningful purpose: to attract a new generation of audiences with a true story that must never be forgotten. But stories require writers, translators, interpreters, and—for a potential film audience—media consultants. Inevitably, then, standards of strict accuracy are often undermined by the more primary urge for sensation, cathartic release, and satisfaction of one's own emotional or financial investment. In fact, cinematic, theatrical, or literary works inspired by the Holocaust more often than not have been first shaped out of our present-day culture and then honed according to the historical past. This too often results in representations only loosely based on the facts of the Holocaust.

This anthology focuses on past culture, specifically as expressed in the theatrical performances by Jews within the Third Reich and during the years of the Holocaust, 1933–45. But to create the full sense of theatrical activity within these years, also included are reports on theater staged by non-Jewish political prisoners in concentration camps, which is in keeping with how Sybil H. Milton suggests we review Holocaust art in the final essay of this collection. We also broadly interpret the term *theatrical* to encompass a variety of performative activities like storytelling and musical and dramatic recitation.*

The book is divided into three sections, interspersing past accounts from Nazi-occupied Europe with studies by cultural scholars and historians who—like Alvin Goldfarb and I—are committed to analyzing the past through Holocaust-related materials. The essays provide at once a chronological and factual context within which to view these documents and an exploration of themes of community and ideas of creative resistance. Above all, they wrestle with the most disturbing question of all: How could Jews have created art and attended performances while encompassed by unspeakable adversity? As unlikely as it may seem, cultural activity by Jews—as well as by non-Jewish prisoners—took place in situations of deprivation, torment, and death. Documents from that past, eyewitness memoirs, and critical essays provide a complex of description and analysis about a phenomenon that existed across Nazi Europe—in German cities, in Eastern ghettos, and in concentration camps. The theatrical performances were varied. Some were initially clandestine, undertaken at great risk; others were largely self-directed enterprises as in the Jewish Kulturbund within Germany. To boost morale, ghetto elders or *Judenräte* (Jewish self-administrators and councils) encouraged and even sponsored cultural activities and contests for ghetto Jews. The Nazis themselves also managed theatrical and musical performance; for their own pleasure and power,

---

*Unless otherwise credited, translations and notes are by the author (R.R.).

they forced inmates of camp orchestras to play jazz or classics at Westerbork or Belsen or to accompany public hangings at Mauthausen, for example. In the Czech ghetto, Terezín (Theresienstadt), Nazi commandants eventually patronized the well-known cultural program of *Freizeitgestaltung* (organized leisure time activity). This was particularly striking during the "model" ghetto's "embellishment" phase in 1944, when Red Cross representatives visited the "beautified" camp to watch children perform Hans Krása's popular opera, *Brundibár*.

There have only been a few books dedicated to the specific art created by Jews during the Holocaust. Janet Blatter and Sybil H. Milton's seminal anthology of artwork from the Holocaust provides us with reproductions of actual drawings and paintings rendered in ghettos and camps (1982). Mary Costanza provides an additional selection of the visual art created in camps (1986), while the pictorial collection of *Spiritual Resistance* displays selected pieces now housed at the Kibbutz Lohamei Haghetaot in Israel (1981). Joža Karas's scholarly examination of musical performance (including cabaret) from Terezín remains an exemplary study. Karas himself, as translator, conductor, and musician, has preserved some of this music, while London's Decca Records' music series *Entartete Musik* (*Degenerate Music*) concentrates on music banned by the Nazis. Recent recordings have also been made of songs written in the ghettos as well as at Terezín.[2]

In general, however, books related to the performing arts during the Third Reich—particularly the theater—tend to reflect the trends and practices of Aryanized theaters in Germany, with little or no mention of Jewish performances or the Jewish Kulturbund.[3] Books on the history of European Jewry and culture immediately prior to or during the Holocaust years do not focus on the theater arts at all, except for accomplishments by Jewish artists in exile. There is no English-language equivalent to Joseph Wulf's multivolume collection of documents related to theater, music, film, and the visual arts during the Third Reich.[4] Nor does a survey text or critical assessment exist that relates to theatrical activity during the Holocaust years. Even Wulf's invaluable collection lacks a critical commentary of the anthologized documents. Except for Karas's book, the work of Volker Kühn (virtually untranslated), several books and articles from the past two decades, and Peter Jelavich's excellent postscript discussion to *Berlin Cabaret* (1996) on cabaret in concentration camps, no author to date has combined historical documentation of this subject with critical analysis.[5]

On the other hand, many authors have been concerned with questions of representation and the Holocaust. Using Holocaust history as a departure point, such scholars as Lawrence L. Langer, Alvin Rosenfeld, Geoffrey Hartmann, and James Young have discussed the inadequacies of cultural memory, the post-Holocaust literary imagination, and "writing" the Holocaust. Robert Skloot, Elinor Fuchs, and Michael Taub have anthologized international plays that deal with the Holocaust, although none of the featured plays was actually written during those dark years. Langer's recent anthology, *Art from the Ashes* (Oxford University Press, 1995), chiefly presents examples of how the Holocaust has been represented in various genres, with an emphasis on testimonial writing. The book includes poems by individuals like Paul Celan, Abraham Sutzkever, and Don Pagis, incarcerated in ghettos and camps, but the anthology's sole example of drama is Joshua Sobol's play based on documents from the Vilna ghetto, *Ghetto* (1986). Meanwhile, dramatic criticism of plays related to the Holocaust and the theory of fascism are increasingly common.[6]

The proliferation of such books suggests that the topic of the Holocaust continues to arouse significant interest and curiosity. Why then has theatrical performance during the Holocaust received less scholarly attention? It is not difficult after all to understand the scarcity of research in this area. It defies our understanding to imagine concentration camp inmates singing, playing classical music, and dancing on makeshift stages or in crowded barracks, at the same time that cattle cars transported their fellow inmates toward Auschwitz. The grotesquerie of such events suggests frivolity and even sacrilege. If people could act in plays and create art while facing death, that would have to mean that life in the camps could not have been so desperate. But the inmates knew that the camps were evil. And we know that they were very evil. And we now know that people sang and danced in spite of and because of the Nazi hell and the murderous "Final Solution."

We do not wish to champion or to judge morally the practice of artistic creation and theatrical performance by inmates during the Holocaust, nor do we feel we have the right to evaluate the artistic quality of productions by Jews in Nazi Germany or the creative impact of orchestral arrangements in ghettos or of cabarets spawned in the camps. This book presents firsthand accounts about performing artists — primarily Jews — whose lives and careers were fatally bound to the Nazi-directed horrors. Therefore documents and essays are grouped into sections that more or less span the years from 1933, after Hitler's takeover in Berlin, through the 1940s in various ghettos and in selected transit and concentration camps. There is some historical overlap in the events we present in the book's three sections. The first concentration camps near Berlin like Sachsenhausen and Oranienburg were established in the early 1930s. The ghettos in Eastern Europe were established at the same time that camps like Westerbork and the Terezín (Theresienstadt) ghetto came into existence. One may perhaps see the book's divisions as an attempt to mark the Nazis' gradual determination through cultural and physical ghettoization to limit the Jews' repertories, resources, and ultimate capacity for making art; this can especially be seen in the case of the Jewish Kulturbund, which prescribed specifically "Jewish" art — whatever that was. The restrictions on the Jews' cultural activities increased with the outbreak of World War II as the Nazis accelerated their actions to deport and incarcerate the Jews of Western Europe in labor and concentration camps, and in such Eastern ghettos as Kovno, Warsaw, Riga, and Lódz. What kinds of performances were possible for artists under such conditions? Can something like a spiritual or creative "resistance" be suggested in an art that may have helped inmates retain their sense of humanity amid the most inhumane of circumstances?

The essays in this book provide a context within which to better understand the significance of the documents chosen.* In Part I, Alan Steinweis's essay on SS Commandant Hans Hinkel describes the Nazi apparatus that was created to oversee Jewish cultural activity in Germany. My essay on the only legitimate cultural organization for Jews, the Jewish Kulturbund, and Volker Kühn's essay on cabaret artists at the Kulturbund and at the Westerbork camp examine the options and dilemmas faced by Jewish artists who wished to continue performing and therefore had to participate in Hinkel's cultural empire. I include two narrative interviews from the late 1990s with former artists who worked within the Jewish Kulturbund. Their reminiscent voices may be compared to documents written during the 1930s and early 1940s, which show the fragility of life and the confusion of identity for Jewish artists who stayed in Nazi Germany, in spite of restrictions on repertory choices and programs. Managing theater directors like Kurt Singer and Fritz Wisten did not have the hindsight, alas, that we readers possess. And in their letters, reports, and final postcards, there is a poignancy of hope and a dedication to art and survival — perhaps, we may say now — against overwhelming odds.

The excerpted accounts from the ghettos in Part II attest to communal efforts by ghetto leaders to record the then-present for posterity's sake so that the Nazi criminals might be exposed someday with documented crimes. Avraham Tory succeeded in doing this with his Kovno diary, for example. At the same time, Tory's description of a Zionist holiday commemoration within the ghetto indicates the significance of communal efforts to maintain a spiritual and cultural life even while mass murder occurred at the infamous Ninth Fort. And even in the shadow of the notorious Ponar Wood massacres, the Jews of Vilna's ghetto attended lectures, composed music, and organized cultural per-

---

* Corrections to minor errors in already published works have been made "silently."

formances. Turkov shows how Lithuanian deportees brought with them to the Riga ghetto Yiddish song and culture, while later, inmates at Auschwitz subtly sustained some form of culture. Moshe Fass surveys an underresearched area: theatrical performances by Jews within Polish ghettos before their dissolution.

Part II also offers a grim look at the performances within various concentration camps as participants in cultural activities and surviving eyewitnesses describe performances. Alvin Goldfarb's and Samuel M. Edelman's sobering overviews of theatrical performances within various camps question whether "creative resistance" and spiritual survival through theater art was possible — however temporarily. The reports and reported memories from the concentration camps invoke rare moments of *communitas* and efforts to create meaning in a surreal nightmare existence. At the same time, writers like the Dutch journalist Philip Mechanicus have indicated the disturbing contradictions of death and the creative life of performance. In his diary from the transit camp, Westerbork in Holland, Mechanicus refers to an "atmosphere of painful melancholy and suffering" by the inmate audience at a theatrical revue; he writes: "Silently protesting, they give way to the vital demands of life. And the performers who laugh and flirt on the stage feel their acting blood stir within them, but offstage they too have to bear their sorrows. Man wants to mourn with those who have been struck down by fate, but he feels compelled to live with the living."[7]

We should recognize that within the vast network of concentration camps — labor, transit, and death camps — gradations existed in the severity of living conditions for Jewish inmates and non-Jewish political prisoners. Prisoners could retain their civilian clothes at some of the camps; books were permitted at Terezín and Dachau, for example. Yet writing paper and pencils were forbidden at Mauthausen and Ravensbrück. So too must we keep in mind the years in which prisoners were incarcerated. For example, surviving the gas chambers of Mauthausen, Ravensbrück, and other camps was obviously a daily preoccupation. At Westerbork, living from Monday night to Monday night without a deportation summons for the inevitable Tuesday morning transport eastward sapped inmates — even the cabaret artistes — of vital energies needed to survive the next week. At the same time, Madam Ehrlich-Fantlová suggests of her years of incarceration, transport, and survival, "when you live it day by day, you don't view your life as tragedy. Hope was our weapon; it was uplifting."[8] This is the spirit which she attributes to the art created at Terezín — hope, not despair.

Victor Ullmann, who left Terezín for Auschwitz on the same transport as Ehrlich-Fantlová (16 October 1944), said that the will to create was the will to live. He never returned. And yet, in order to sustain life, inmates resuscitated hope. Even for the "Nacht und Nebel" ("night and fog" political prisoners, considered to have virtually disappeared from life) at Ravensbrück, the "terrible struggle to live" did not stop inmates from stealing paper and pencils at the risk of severe beatings. Although books were forbidden, a tiny library of French and Czech verses and handmade books circulated in Block 32 and were hidden under the straw bedding. A leading figure of the camp's small Resistance movement, Germaine Tillion, became a fugitive within the camp's barracks. Protected by her comrades, Tillion hid in a large packing crate and wrote upon stolen paper an operetta styled in the verse of La Fontaine and parodying Glück's *Orpheus in Hell*. Called *Le Verfügbar aux Enfers,* Tillion's unpublished work describes and sings the living hell at her disposal, right outside her packing-crate refuge.[9] Tillion's close friend from Ravensbrück, Anise Postel-Vinay, told me of this "formidable moral effort," in which Tillion sought "to make fun of ourselves. This was typically French, to succeed in keeping [our] taste for laughter and farce."[10]

Evidently, the separate German-speaking and Czech-language theatrical cabaret troupes of Theresienstadt also retained the ability to "make fun." Part III is devoted to the "cultural ghetto" par excellence, established by the Nazis in Terezín, the eighteenth-century garrison town of central Bohemia. Many well-known cultural elites from Germany, Austria, and Czechoslovakia — including several from the Jewish Kulturbund — found themselves part of the *Freizeitgestaltung,* the cultural program led (and described) by Rabbi Erich Weiner. Accounts by the late Aaron Kramer and musicologist Joža Karas describe the translation and adaptation of operas written and produced in Terezín. Roy Kift's adept cabaret translations direct our focus to the musical performances of Theresienstadt, the camp which the Nazis exploited shamelessly for its cultural programs. Finally, Zdenka Ehrlich-Fantlová and Mirko Tuma recount their active participation in Terezín's Czech theater. Ehrlich-Fantlová's invaluable memories of specific colleagues, actual play line readings, and even costume details provide a rich immediacy of events lived as they were "on the inside." Those artists on the outside — a poet, a musician, and a playwright — have infused such Terezín documents as a foreign-language libretto, an original musical score, and comic verse with new meaning for post-Holocaust audiences. From a practical viewpoint, they have transcribed and interpreted the documents, making the original texts accessible to artists and scholars. They and the other contributors to this volume helped to reveal and sustain the heritage of the art created and played out within the Holocaust years.

Lucy S. Dawidowicz has written on the need to study Holocaust documents with special care. She warns us that Nazi German records deliberately mask language and obfuscate real issues. Documents we have from Jewish sources of the times, on the other hand, also conceal meaning because of official censorship and self-censorship.[11] The researcher must try to contextualize each document judiciously, understanding what may be omitted from the document and what meanings may be veiled. Prior to a tightening of censorship on outgoing mail from Westerbork, Etty Hillesum, for example, instructed her correspondents of a coded language she would use to ask for specific items in the succeeding weeks: "So, let's agree now, for example: book = butter, writing = jam," she wrote in July 1943.[12] As incomplete and enigmatic as such documents may be, they are as essential in recording and preserving history as are an eyewitness's imperfect and self-selective memories. As Dawidowicz declares, "Documents by themselves are no substitute for history, though history cannot be written without them."[13] And historians have preserved the history of the Third Reich and its consequences, compiling and cataloging volumes of "imperfect" documents from the Third Reich, available to us in archives worldwide as well as in published books. In addition to Dawidowicz's anthology, Henry Friedlander and Sybil H. Milton have edited a comprehensive multivolume collection of documents. Michael Berenbaum has recently written the introduction to a reader of documents related to the Nazis' persecution of Jews.[14]

In the epilogue to this volume, Sybil H. Milton eloquently sums up the vital significance of archival research dedicated to the Holocaust and its legacy. With the end of World War II and the subsequent division of Europe, sensitive documents from the Nazi Propaganda Ministry were divided among the war's victor nations and overseen, for example, by the American military in Berlin until the early 1990s. The collapse of the Iron Curtain has further complicated the potential search for archival materials. Those involved in personal research or professional studies related to the Holocaust, in general, and in art, more specifically, may now encounter new bureaucratic and linguistic obstacles to their searches for information. While archival centers, museum libraries, and memorials across the world may be more easily accessed now by local and foreign scholars, such logistical problems as updating cataloging techniques, translating indices, and creating Internet Websites still prevail. Milton touches on some of these problems as she examines the archival heritage of German Jewry and its link to Holocaust history and to cultural activity by Jews incarcerated by Nazi Germany.

Who were some of these artists? What choices if any did they make to create art? How was it possible for people to produce—and even enjoy—theatrical and musical performances amid a Nazi-supervised camp or ghetto? We hope to engage interest about such questions which have been debated since the Shoah and which understandably resist definitive answers. Some of those who "came back" like Primo Levi and Paul Celan and wrought meaning from the meaningless, eventually committed suicide in spite of their literary spirit. Others like Viktor Frankl, Bruno Bettelheim, H. G. Adler, and former members of the French Resistance like Germaine Tillion have emphasized the necessity of that spirit, linking a sense of human dignity and self-esteem to day-to-day survival.[15] We of a later generation can rely only on the testimony of "those who were there" to imagine the "unthinkable." We understand creativity as being born from spirit and thus we are inclined to grasp onto the evocative, yet vague notion of a kind of "spiritual resistance" and find it attractive. One cannot attribute any such notion to the so-called *Muselmänner* (walking corpses) of the camps, whose existence was marked by indifference to life or death. One has to wonder whether those people who found a temporary reprieve in a lecture, poem, play, or song were not involved in a kind of suspended life-affirming process, enabling them to retain a link to humanity. One has to wonder whether the act of performing art—whether theater or music—may be accompanied by a wholeness of self that transcends time and place and creates a buoyancy of mood and spirit. By engaging an audience who needed something emotionally meaningful to hold onto, perhaps they temporarily sustained the will to live.

In the early 1940s, Hermann Kruk—the Vilna ghetto diarist—implied that one should not create art in a graveyard. This idea recurs in other diaries such as in Youth Welfare director and avowed Zionist Egon "Gonda" Redlich's accounts of Terezín (January 1942–June 1944). The juxtaposition of life and death, of play and prayer, in the same halls confused him, although he acknowledged on 22 February 1942 that in a children's play, there were "great actors, and I liked their songs," especially the Zionist anthem.[16] By the start of his second year in the camp, Redlich had written his own play, *The White Shadow*, which dealt with assimilationism. Gradually, he reported enthusiastically about theater events, admitting, "Yesterday for the first time, I attended an experimental theater: The performance took place in an attic. You can learn a lot here."[17] The dilemma is clearly a moral one and it is twofold: Ought one to have produced art in the dire circumstances of the Holocaust, and was this art more than merely an expression of what was taking place around the artists? Can art be created under such perverse conditions?

Rainer Maria Rilke once wrote: "Surely all art is the result of one's having been in danger, of having gone through an experience all the way to the end, where no one can go any further."[18] According to those who were "over there," "là-bas," "dorthin," no one appeared to weigh the moral reasons for or consequences of making art, singing words of comfort, or writing prose in an atmosphere of death where people disappeared daily. The basic need to commune and converse necessitated the procurement of writing utensils, stories, and song, even at the risk of severe punishment. The need may have sprung from despair, but the creation itself did not. We who are fortunately on the outside may find it difficult to accept this contradictory and unsettling possibility. Even Tillion decided not to publish her operetta lest her motivations and creation be misinterpreted by the public. Postel-Vinay recalls, "She never wanted to publish it, never dared to, because she thought the public would not understand. She always said, they will believe we amused ourselves greatly at Ravensbrück; and in fact, this [operetta] was written under great risk."[19]

Throughout the 1980s and 1990s, scholars like Langer have written about what they claim to be a misguided notion of heroic "spiritual resistance" that many attribute especially to the martyred Jews, in spite of—and because of—their art (the Terezín Painters scandal, for example). In hindsight, it is easy to be cynical, particularly given the minuscule survival rate of those heroic resisters. But for the artists and community leaders whom we feature in this book, and according to those who have since researched their creations, there appears to be a consensus—however ambivalent: Musical and theatrical creation seemed to give people some sense of humanity—as ephemeral as it may have been. Langer has aptly rephrased the controversial idea of creative resistance to suggest that this activity may have been a resistance by inmates to "cultural genocide."[20] Perhaps we may consider the words of Postel-Vinay for whom the very act of having preserved one's ability to laugh and hope at Ravensbrück embodies a "profound form of resistance, an affirmation that one stays human," even when such "Judeo-Christian values [as] pity and compassion were abolished, because they had no place in the Third Reich."[21] This book is dedicated to a tenacious affirmation of spirit even as the flesh so cruelly perished.

I

Identification

Jewish Theatrical Performance in Nazi Germany

ESSAYS

ESSAYS

| | | | | | | | | | | | |

Hans Hinkel and German Jewry, 1933–1941

ALAN E. STEINWEIS

My research on Hans Hinkel originated as part of a larger project on Nazi cultural policy. Almost everywhere I turned, the name "Hinkel" kept coming up, yet the existing scholarly literature contained practically nothing about him. Why had he been overlooked by historians?

I think there are several explanations. First, Nazi cultural policy did not attract the attention of serious historians until very recently, and Hinkel's value to the Nazi movement and regime lay in his abilities as a cultural administrator. Second, research on anti-Jewish policy in Nazi Germany had tended to focus heavily on the makers of policy rather than on the Jews affected by it. While it was well known that Jews had been purged from the German artistic-cultural professions early in the Nazi regime, the existence of the Jüdischer Kulturbund, *in which many of the ostracized Jewish performers took refuge, went unnoticed even among scholars specializing in the area. Hinkel, who supervised the Kulturbund, was therefore overlooked as well. Third, Hinkel's very versatility as a Nazi functionary has made him a moving target for historians. Between 1921 and 1945 he carried out a wide variety of assignments at the behest of several top-ranking Nazis. The big picture of his life and career has consequently been ignored, while historians of propaganda, press policy, theater policy, film policy, and anti-Jewish policy have provided snapshots of Hinkel's activities in specific areas.*

In the realm of cultural life, no Nazi official other than Joseph Goebbels himself made as large and direct an impact on Jewish life in Nazi Germany as did Hinkel. My essay is an attempt to examine Hinkel's activity as the overseer of the Jüdischer Kulturbund *within the broader context of his Nazi career. — Alan E. Steinweis, 1997*

IN EARLY 1960, Hans Hinkel died in Göttingen at the age of fifty-eight. The death received little attention in the German press. Several newspapers noted that Hinkel had been an important official in the Reich Ministry of Pro-

Originally published in *Leo Baeck Institute Yearbook* 38 (1993), 209–19.

SS Commandant Hans Hinkel. Courtesy Alan E. Steinweis and the former Berlin Document Center (now part of the *Bundesarchiv,* Federal Archives, Germany), undated

paganda and Public Enlightenment in the Nazi era, and that he had served as a Reich Culture Manager (*Reichskulturwalter*) in the Reich Chamber of Culture (*Reichskulturkammer* [RKK]). To one newspaper, however, Hinkel's death possessed a far greater significance. The *Allgemeine Wochenzeitung der Juden in Deutschland* published a detailed obituary, recounting aspects of Hinkel's career that had been curiously omitted by other papers.[1] As the "Aryan" supervisor of the *Jüdischer Kulturbund,* the *Wochenzeitung* pointed out, Hinkel had been the regime's chief overseer of Jewish artistic and cultural life in Germany during the National Socialist era. The *Wochenzeitung* also deemed it significant that Hinkel had joined the NSDAP [Nationalist Socialist Worker's Party] * in 1921, early enough to receive Party Number 287.[2] These were hardly trivial details in Hinkel's twenty-four-year career as a National Socialist. The *Wochenzeitung* speculated that the silence over Hinkel's past reflected the dismal failure of German society to come to terms with its history. Even lesser figures of the National Socialist leadership like Hinkel served as unpleasant reminders of a past most Germans were unwilling to digest fully.

* Editors' note: Bracketed interpolations are by the general editors, not the contributors, unless otherwise indicated.

Several recent scholarly and popular treatments of the *Jüdischer Kulturbund* have underscored the importance of Hinkel's role in the Nazi era.[3] They have, however, done little to examine Hinkel's activity as cultural overlord to the Jews within the context of his long career as a National Socialist and antisemite. The motives and personality of a figure who so profoundly influenced the lives of German Jews during the Nazi era require closer examination than they have received.

Hinkel was born into a Protestant family in Worms, in the Rhineland, on 22 June 1901. The son of a successful businessman, he grew up only a few minutes' walk from the old Jewish neighborhood.[4] Defensive about his middle-class origins, Hinkel preferred to depict his father as the antithesis to the "dizzy, mentally sluggish, effete bourgeois type" that dominated Worms society. Among the "effete" bourgeoisie that the young Hinkel had often encountered in Worms were many Jews. Hinkel later recalled that his Jewish neighbors had treated him politely, albeit with condescension.[5] According to the recollections of Herbert Freeden, a Jewish cultural official who had contact with Hinkel in the 1930s, some of the better students in the young Hinkel's school had been Jewish, and Hinkel had both resented and admired their success. Freeden claims that Hinkel carried forward from his youth a highly ambivalent attitude toward Jews. In the 1930s, Hinkel could indeed exhibit a surprising degree of respect toward individual members of the German-Jewish community.[6] Yet in his memoir (as in hundreds of other places), Hinkel reserved his worst epithets for the Jews. "The Jew," the memoir asserted, is "the eternal parasite and homeless master of lies."[7]

Although too young to have fought in the Great War, Hinkel shared in the bitter disappointment over Germany's defeat in 1918. Like many contemporaries, it was easy for him to conclude that "Jewish internationalist money powers" in cahoots with Marxists, Freemasons, and Liberals had stabbed the Fatherland in the back.[8] While pursuing university studies in Munich (which he never completed), the disillusioned twenty-year-old fell under the spell of Adolf Hitler and joined the Nazi Party. As a member of the *Bund Oberland Freikorps* unit, Hinkel participated in the ill-fated putsch of 9 November 1923. After the second founding of the Nazi Party in 1925, Hinkel became an effective Nazi organizer and publicist in southern and central Germany. In 1927 he collaborated with the Strasser brothers in the founding of the *Kampfverlag*, which quickly emerged as a leading National Socialist publishing house. In 1930, after Hitler had forced a split between the Strasser brothers and brought about the dissolution of the *Kampfverlag*, Hinkel accepted the position of press chief of the Berlin *Gau* of the Nazi Party. The move to Berlin marked the beginning of the association between Hinkel and Joseph Goebbels. In Berlin, Hinkel helped edit *Der Angriff*, the official *Gau* organ, and also served on the editorial staff of the local edition of the Party's national newspaper, the *Völkischer Beobachter*.

In Berlin, Hinkel was active not only in political organizing and propaganda but also in cultural agitation and mobilization. In 1930, he founded the Berlin branch of the Nazi-affiliated *Kampfbund für deutsche Kultur*. As leader of the local *Kampfbund*, and as editor of the *Kampfbund*'s organ, the *Deutsche Kultur-Wacht*, Hinkel established himself as a leading NSDAP spokesman on artistic and cultural matters. Yet he possessed no artistic training or special experience in cultural affairs. Whether he was a "philistine," as one historian has alleged,[9] is a matter of interpretation, but there was certainly little in his experience to qualify him for the decisive role he would be called upon to play in German artistic and cultural life after 30 January 1933.

During the first three months of Nazi rule, two official appointments empowered Hinkel to supervise the artistic-cultural purge in the German state of Prussia. On 30 January 1933 Bernhard Rust, the new Nazi Minister of Education and Culture in Prussia, appointed Hinkel special *Staatskommissar* for the *Entjudung* of cultural life [de-Judification]. In April 1933, in the wake of the passage of the notorious Civil Service Law (*Gesetz zur Wiederherstellung des Berufsbeamtentums*—BBG) of 7 April, Hermann Göring named Hinkel head of the Prussian Theatre Commission, a body charged with monitoring personnel policies of theaters, orchestras, and opera companies. Aside from these state positions, Hinkel retained his post at the head of the Berlin branch of the *Kampfbund*, whose size and power had been greatly enhanced by the Nazi seizure of power. So influential had Hinkel become in these early months of the Nazi regime, that one Nazi activist observed that Hinkel was the de facto Minister of Culture in Prussia.[10]

Hinkel's triple portfolio placed him at the center of artistic-cultural *Gleichschaltung* [political synchronization or transformation within new government] in Prussia in early 1933. Numerous cultural associations and interest groups declared their loyalty to the new regime, and placed themselves at the disposal of the *Kampfbund*, which many mistakenly expected would evolve into a permanent institution. By issuing statements of official approval, Hinkel prompted the process by which the boards of directors and executive staffs of such organizations were "purified" of ideologically objectionable persons, be they Jewish or Socialist, and reorganized according to the National Socialist leadership principle.[11]

Even more important was Hinkel's role as coordinator of the regime's early purges in Prussia. In February and March 1933, only generally applicable emergency decrees provided legal cover for moves against Jews, Communists, and other "unwanted" persons in the cultural sphere. The BBG, which stipulated the dismissal of most "non-Aryans" from government positions, simplified the assault on Jewish artists employed by state-run cultural institutions. Systematic mechanisms for artistic-cultural censorship and personnel screening were instituted only in the second half of 1933, concentrated mainly in the new Reich Ministry of Propaganda and its subordinate mass organization, the RKK. Consequently, during the key phases of artistic-cultural *Gleichschaltung* in early 1933, activists such as Hinkel had to rely by and large on improvised methods, at times exploiting intimidation provided by National Socialist thugs.

The cases of the conductors Bruno Walter and Otto Klemperer exemplify both Hinkel's technique as well as the general environment in which the early purges occurred. In a *Frankfurter Zeitung* interview of 6 April 1933, Hinkel attempted to place the new regime's domestic and foreign image in a better light by explaining why Walter and Klemperer had disappeared from the German music scene. He claimed their concerts had not been canceled by the authorities, but rather by their own producers on account of insufficient security at the concert halls. "German public opinion," Hinkel asserted, had long been provoked by "Jewish artistic bankrupters." The SA and SS, "whom we need for more important things," could not be spared to protect Walter and Klemperer as a by-product from the "popular mood." [12] This attempt to characterize the measures against Walter and Klemperer as a by-product of a popular uprising, in which the government only passively participated, arose from the absence of a legitimate legal justification. Once the BBG had taken effect, Hinkel no longer needed to fall back on such manipulations, and could turn his attention away from celebrated personalities such as Walter and Klemperer and to the far larger number of more or less anonymous Jewish artists employed by the state in Prussia. Ironically, Hinkel's extensive powers to purge Jews from artistic-cultural institutions led to his long involvement with the *Jüdischer Kulturbund,* the Nazi regime's organizational ghetto for Jewish cultural life.

The Kulturbund originated in the spring of 1933 as an initiative of Jewish civic leaders, including Leo Baeck, who sought relief from the economic and spiritual deprivation many Jewish artists felt as a result of the mass dismissals. Their plans envisaged an officially tolerated cultural association that would provide employment for Jewish artists and entertainers, and would serve as a source of cultural enrichment for the Jewish population. In May, Hinkel was approached about the idea by Dr. Kurt Singer, a physician whose interest in music had impelled him to become manager of the Berlin City Opera (which had "released" him in March 1933). After securing Göring's consent, Hinkel approved Singer's plan for a Kulturbund in Berlin that would operate one theater, employ only Jews, and perform before audiences composed exclusively of Jews.

The plan appealed to Hinkel for several reasons. It encouraged Jews who had been dismissed from state cultural institutions to seek employment with the new Kulturbund rather than with other private theaters or orchestras, which were not covered by the BBG and, therefore, had not yet been legally closed off to Jews. A Jewish cultural organization would also provide grist for the German propaganda effort abroad, which needed ammunition to counter allegations about mistreatment of Jews. Finally, Hinkel recognized the plan as an opportunity to expand his own authority. Here, his instinct proved particularly keen. After the experiment of the Kulturbund had proved successful in Berlin, many additional local branches began to spring up. In March 1935, the forty-six existing local organizations were placed under a supervisory umbrella agency, the *Reichsverband der jüdischen Kulturbünde*. By 1937, the organizations supervised by Hinkel had grown to encompass about fifty thousand people.

Much of the impetus for the creation of the *Reichsverband* in March 1935 had come from Joseph Goebbels, and the assignment to supervise the organization opened a new phase in Hinkel's relationship with him. Since the creation of the Propaganda Ministry in March 1933, Goebbels had been steadily consolidating his grip on power over cultural affairs. The creation of the RKK in September 1933 as a subsidiary of the Propaganda Ministry had represented a victory for Goebbels over Robert Ley, who had wanted to organize the artistic-cultural occupations in the *Deutsche Arbeitsfront*. Also, owing to Goebbels's steadily increasing influence, the *Kampfbund für Deutsche Kultur* had been pushed to the margin of German cultural policy by the end of 1933, despite its instrumental role in *Gleichschaltung* earlier in that year. By mid-1935, the numerous Jewish cultural associations throughout Germany stood conspicuously outside Goebbels's empire. Moreover, Goebbels had been growing increasingly frustrated with the existing leadership of the RKK, which, the Minister believed, had been too tolerant of modernism, and had been equivocating on the expulsion of Jewish members.

Goebbels turned to Hinkel, his former employee, for assistance. Hinkel possessed the experience, skills, and knowledge needed by Goebbels to stake his claim to jurisdiction over the Jewish cultural organizations, and his dynamic role in the *Gleichschaltung* of cultural organizations in 1933 made him a natural choice to force through organizational and policy reforms in the RKK. In May 1935, Goebbels appointed Hinkel one of the triumvirate of *Reichskulturwalter* in charge of the RKK. Several weeks later, Goebbels added to Hinkel's responsibilities the special task of supervising "non-Aryan" culture. Hinkel received the formidable title of "Special Commissioner for the Supervision and Monitoring of the Cultural and Intellectual Activity of All Non-Aryans Living in the Territory of the German Reich."

For this second office, in particular, Goebbels had based his choice not merely on Hinkel's obvious qualifications, but also on the fact that Hinkel had already attained the rank of *Sturmbannführer* in the SS. The *Sicherheitsdienst* [security forces] (SD) of the SS had recently begun to express close interest in the regime's management of the "Jewish Question." The SD favored ghettoization of Jewish cultural-intellectual life, believing it would discourage assimilationist optimism among Jews and thereby promote emigration. Goebbels, a virulent antisemite in his own right, probably had few grounds for ideological disagreement with the Jewish experts in the SD. He probably recognized that coordinating policy with them would preclude interference from those quarters.[13]

Hinkel did not wait long to make his presence felt in the Propaganda Minister's empire. In the spring, summer, and autumn of 1935, Hinkel implemented a thoroughgoing purge of the RKK bureaucracy, in many cases replacing Conservative Nationalists with Nazi *Alte Kämpfer* like himself. Simultaneously, he engineered sweeping organizational changes resulting in a far more centralized, authoritarian system in the RKK, essentially ending the professional self-administration that had characterized the Chamber during the first two years of its existence.[14] In addition, Hinkel oversaw the final stages of the mass purge of Jewish members from the RKK, which had begun earlier in 1935. Goebbels was impressed by Hinkel's energetic measures, but reservations about Hinkel's ambition and lack of loyalty persisted. "Hinkel works well, but he is not personally reliable," the Minister recorded in his diary in September 1935.[15] Several days later, Goebbels's patience had worn thin; now Hinkel was a "born intriguer and liar."[16] Although Goebbels's doubts about Hinkel's character would never be calmed, Hinkel stayed on in his important positions, and would even receive several promotions from Goebbels.

Once he had completed the shake-up of the RKK, Hinkel devoted most of his energies to the solution of the "Jewish Question" in the cultural sphere. In the RKK he concerned himself primarily with eliminating Jews, offspring of Jews in mixed marriages (*Mischlinge*), and persons related to Jews (*Versippte*), who had remained in the Chamber with "special dispensations" beyond the great purge of 1935. Hjalmar Schacht, the Finance Minister, had repeatedly intervened with Hitler to prevent the RKK from moving against economically important book, art, and antique dealers. Goebbels had little patience for Schacht's financial calculations, and urged Hinkel to press forward with the expulsions as fast as economic circumstances would allow.[17]

Hinkel's supervision of the increasingly ghettoized Jewish cultural life formed a logical complement to his overseeing of the RKK expulsion process; in effect, Jews who were purged from the RKK were transferred from one sphere of Hinkel's jurisdiction to another. In the fields of music and theater, the Hinkel-controlled *Reichsverband* provided the sole refuge; the Jewish press and publishing industry, although not formally incorporated into the *Reichsverband,* also gradually came under the direction of Hinkel's office at the Propaganda Ministry, the so-called *Büro Hinkel.*

Hinkel's office exercised "comprehensive prophylactic control" over the content of Jewish artistic-cultural programming.[18] In practical terms, precensorship was carried out by Jewish officers at the *Reichsverband* level; the *Büro Hinkel* exercised a veto power, and made decisions in questionable cases. For the Jews involved, the stamp of approval from the *Büro Hinkel* could be used as protection against police officials, the Gestapo, and other government and Party agencies that may have wished to prohibit *Reichsverband* functions.

The censorship policy of the *Büro Hinkel* toward the *Reichsverband* constituted an effort at enforced artistic-cultural dissimilation, intended to negate the German component of German-Jewish identity. From the very beginning, the repertoire available to the Jewish cultural associations had excluded the works of German romantics such as Wagner, and those of composers particularly valued by the regime, such as Richard Strauss. With the passage of time, Hinkel's office steadily restricted the range of possibilities. The works of Goethe and other classics of German literature were added to the blacklist in 1936; Beethoven's turn came in 1936 as well; Mozart and Handel were added relatively late in 1938. Works by non-German authors and composers were generally tolerated, provided they were not objectionable on political grounds. The *Büro Hinkel* particularly encouraged the Jews to perform pieces by Jewish authors and composers. Thus by the late 1930s, the *Büro Hinkel* was seeking to enhance a stereotyped (hence ahistorical) Jewishness, while systematically eliminating ostensibly purer artistic manifestations of Germanness.

In speeches and publications, Hinkel frequently tried to interpret this progressive ghettoization as evidence of the regime's enlightenment and magnanimity. In effect, he argued, the Jews had been granted special recognition as a minority, entitled to cultivate their own cultural heritage. "Jewish artists are working for Jews," he pointed out in a speech in 1936. "They may work unhindered so long as they restrict themselves to the cultivation of Jewish artistic and cultural life, and so long as they do not attempt, openly, secretly, or deceitfully, to influence our culture."

Furthermore, Hinkel asked, how could foreigners criticize measures that had received the blessing of the Jews who were most directly affected? "The leadership of the *Reichsverband der jüdischen Kulturbünde* has repeatedly assured us," Hinkel claimed, "that the measure we have taken is a humane one," both "for Jewish artists and for the cultivation of Jewish art." At the same time, Hinkel covered himself against accusations of deviationism from Nazi hardliners: The *Reichsverband,* he emphasized, was a "practical solution to the Jewish Question in National Socialist cultural policy entirely consistent with the basic principles of National Socialism."[19]

Such propaganda highlights what may well have been one of the most profound consequences of the Kulturbund's existence. Among German Jews, as well as "Aryans," the *Jüdischer Kulturbund* served as a mechanism for psychological accommodation to Jewish cultural disenfranchisement. By providing Jewish artists and audiences with an outlet for creative expression, the Kulturbund rendered Jewish existence in National Socialist Germany somewhat less desperate than it otherwise might have been, thereby lulling German Jews into a tragically false sense of security about the future. Similarly, "Aryans" who found the regime's antisemitic measures distasteful could reassure themselves that Jewish artists were at least permitted to remain active in their chosen professions.

Hinkel's own comportment may have contributed to the illusion. In an interview in 1960, Hinkel attempted to advance the notion that he had actually been a protector of the Jews, who shielded them from the designs of radically anti-Jewish elements in the regime.[20] Although this contention, when considered in retrospect, is absurd, Hinkel's defense of the Kulturbund seems to have won him a measure of reluctant gratitude from the leaders of the Jewish artistic and cultural community. According to Herbert Freeden, for example, German Jews connected with the Kulturbund saw Hinkel as both promoter and oppressor, protector and tyrant. On the negative side, Hinkel most directly personified for German Jews their own cultural disenfranchisement. On a less symbolic level, in the late 1930s Hinkel presided over a steady tightening of the artistic restrictions governing Jewish artistic and intellectual activity. On the positive side, however, Freeden recalls Hinkel intervening on behalf of the Jews when police or other local officials attempted to prevent Kulturbund productions from taking place. Hinkel also seemed to have had genuine respect for the Jewish officers of the Kulturbund, especially Kurt Singer. Freeden describes Hinkel's demeanor in the presence of his Jewish underlings as polite, even considerate.[21] This image of Hinkel as a paternalistic dictator attained wide currency among Jews in Germany after the war; even the obituary in the *Allgemeine Wochenzeitung der Juden in Deutschland,* which otherwise stressed Hinkel's function as an "outspoken Jew hater," felt obliged to mention Hinkel's strange benevolence.[22]

In the wake of the *Kristallnacht* in [November] 1938, the Propaganda Ministry ordered Hinkel to close the *Reichsverband* and all Jewish cultural activity with it. But as the foreign policy implications of the brutal pogrom and its attendant repressive measures became clear, the Ministry reversed its decision.[23] On 12 November, only two days after the violence, Hinkel convened a group of Jewish leaders and ordered them to resume their cultural program. So urgent was this matter that Hinkel had to pull strings to arrange for Jewish performers to be released from the concentration camps to which they had been dragged only a couple of days earlier. Nevertheless, after November 1938 Jewish artistic-cultural life continued on a much narrower basis than had been the case before the *Kristallnacht.* The mechanism for more intrusive official supervision was set in place in January 1939, when the *Reichsverband,* which had been essentially an umbrella organization for the local associations, was dissolved and replaced by the *Jüdischer Kulturbund in Deutschland,* a single, centralized organization.

In general, the *Kristallnacht* had spurred a radicalization of the regime's policy toward the Jews. The opportunistic Hinkel experienced little difficulty in adjusting to the new conditions. He had come to be widely acknowledged as one of the Propaganda Ministry's foremost experts on the "Jewish Question." Hinkel seemed to savor this reputation and did much to enhance it. In 1939 he edited and published *Judenviertel Europas,* a collection of essays about "the Jews from the Baltic to the Black Sea."[24] Hinkel's own contribution to the collection, "Germany and the Jews," contained the familiar vitriol and stereotypes, although it also emphasized the vitality of the cultural life that the Jews had been permitted to pursue in Germany since 1933. Yet, Hinkel claimed, the Jews had exhibited little gratitude for the regime's generosity, as evidenced by the Jewish murder of Ernst vom Rath. Writing as though he had been personally betrayed by his Jewish wards, Hinkel concluded his piece with the observation that "the present struggle of World Jewry against National Socialist Germany as the heart of Europe is nothing more and nothing less than a struggle against the thousand-year-old culture of the West!"[25]

This post-*Kristallnacht* propaganda was designed to accompany and to justify intensified anti-Jewish measures. As the Propaganda Ministry's foremost Jewish expert, Hinkel inevitably became involved in the formulation of these measures. In 1938, Hinkel had emerged as an intermediary between the Propaganda Ministry and the SS-SD. The Propaganda Ministry had been confronted by the threat of the SS-SD's aggressive campaign to monopolize authority over Jewish policy. To protect the Propaganda Ministry's position, Hinkel opened negotiations with the SD's *Referat* II 112, which specialized in Jewish matters, in May 1938.[26] Despite the institutional rivalries, the liaison offered practical advantages to both sides. Hinkel provided the SD with sensitive information about Jews, homosexuals, and other ideologically tainted persons still active in the cultural sphere; in return, Hinkel hoped for SD assistance in racial and political investigations of RKK members and applicants. A factor allowing for cooperation between the two rival agencies was that both favored an accelerated purge of the vestigial Jewish presence in German public and economic life.[27] Hinkel certainly showed little personal resistance to cooperation with the SS; he encouraged his immediate staff to join the SS, and he himself met Himmler on several occasions in order to discuss censorship and personnel policy for the RKK.[28] For Hinkel personally, the liaison with the SD may have helped advance his ambitions for promotion within the SS. In September 1940, Himmler approved Hinkel's promotion from *SS-Oberführer* to *SS-Brigadeführer*.[29]

Goebbels had often expressed frustration with what he saw as the slow pace of the *Entjudung* process.[30] The outbreak of war presented new opportunities. In July 1940, bolstered by the recent humiliation of France, Goebbels who in addition to being Minister of Propaganda and Public Enlightenment was also *Gauleiter* of Berlin, directed his chief assistants at the Propaganda Ministry to expedite planning for the evacuation of the Jews of Berlin to German-occupied Poland. "Within a period of at most eight weeks immediately after the end of the war," Goebbels hoped that "all 62,000 of the Jews still living in Berlin" would have been deported to the east. The report of this meeting then goes on to state: "Hinkel reported on the evacuation plan already worked out with the police. It should make certain above all else, that Berlin would be first in line to be purified (*gesäubert*), as the Kurfürstendamm will retain its Jewish face . . . until Berlin is really free of Jews. Only after Berlin will the other Jewish cities (Breslau, etc.) receive their turns."[31] At a meeting of Goebbels's staff on 6 September, Hinkel issued an updated report on evacuation plans for both Berlin and Vienna. He noted that while good progress had already been made in Vienna, there were still 71,800 Jews in Berlin. Hinkel assured those present, however, that 60,000 Jews would be removed from Berlin to the east "within four weeks" of war's end, while the remaining 12,000 "would also disappear within an additional four weeks."[32] Except for the records of these conferences at the Ministry of Propaganda, documentation is lacking on the nature of Hinkel's involvement with these plans. The precise numbers cited in his presentations suggest that his involvement was more than casual.

Hinkel's most thorough briefing for his colleagues at the Ministry (including Goebbels) came at a conference on 17 September 1940. Hinkel supplied a demographic breakdown of the "72,327 Jews still in Berlin," as well as more general statistics on the 4 million Jews living in German-occupied Europe. Hinkel then reported on the so-called Madagascar Project (as submitted in detail by the *Reichssicherheitshauptamt*—RSHA), which envisioned the transfer of "about 3½ million Jews" to the remote island in the Indian Ocean.[33] It seems likely then that Hinkel had been assigned the task of maintaining contact between the RSHA and the Propaganda Ministry. Unfortunately, the available documentation tells us little else about Hinkel's role in these events.

In 1940 and 1941, constraints on Kulturbund activity intensified considerably. In September 1941, the Gestapo dissolved it. With the onset of the mass murder and deportation of the German Jews the Kulturbund lost its utility to the regime.

Hinkel's special role in Jewish affairs essentially came to an end. By the time of the Kulturbund's demise, Hinkel had already turned most of his attention to other priorities in German cultural policy. While continuing to preside over the racial and political purge mechanism of the *Reichskulturkammer*, Hinkel undertook a succession of special assignments from Goebbels, the main purpose of which was to prepare and mobilize the German cultural establishment for war. Among Hinkel's responsibilities was the organization of extensive entertainment programs for German soldiers. During a tour through Poland in 1942, Hinkel took several of his entertainers on a sightseeing visit through the Warsaw ghetto. Looking at the dreary scene through the windows of the sealed bus, Hinkel demonstratively voiced his contempt for "God's chosen people."[34] In contrast to his polite demeanor in the presence of Kulturbund officials in earlier years, Hinkel now seemed determined to emphasize his antisemitic credentials. The one-time "protector" of the Jews was now viciously ridiculing them on the very eve of their annihilation.

As the supervisor of Jewish cultural life and as a central figure in the *Reichskulturkammer*, Hinkel had become one of the Propaganda Ministry's most powerful and prominent officials. His main responsibilities prior to the outbreak of war underscored the duality of Nazi artistic-cultural policy. On the one hand, Hinkel purged German cultural life of Jews and other "undesirables." On the other, he helped implement a variety of RKK measures that aimed at ameliorating poverty and unemployment in the artistic-cultural occupations.

In a very real way, Hinkel had come to occupy a central place in a system designed to address the problems of which he first became conscious during his student days in Munich in the early 1920s. No longer would the German government take its artists for granted; and no longer would it tolerate Jewish domination of artistic-cultural life.

After 1945, Hinkel faded into obscurity, a broken man.[35] Unlike many physicians, jurists, civil servants, and artists, who encountered little difficulty in making the transition from the Nazi era to postwar conditions in West Germany, Hinkel led a fruitless life after the demise of National Socialism. He possessed no technical skills or special talents that made him indispensable. Despite his experience in cultural administration, he had never been anything more than an energetic dilettante. He had known little in life other than National Socialism. Having embarked on his National Socialist career in the early 1920s, convinced that his generation would save Germany, he was rendered an anachronism by the ending of National Socialism. When Hans Hinkel died in 1960, the national memory had little place for this *Alter Kämpfer*. It is, therefore, with some degree of ironic justice that the rediscovery of Hans Hinkel's role in history comes as the result of recent endeavors to reconstruct and understand the lives of his Jewish victims.

An Artistic Mission in Nazi Berlin

The Jewish Kulturbund Theater as Sanctuary

REBECCA ROVIT

> The economic crisis, this primadonna of public interest . . . is with
> all its pomp, so far ahead of events, so distorting that it hides its true
> supporter . . . our most dangerous enemy: the crisis of the spirit. This
> complicated collaboration has produced in a people an agony that incites
> lunacy. Today's theater? Its content? Its actor? The mirror and the
> abbreviated chronicle of our times.   — Fritz Kortner, 1932[1]

THESE REMARKS made by the actor, Fritz Kortner, stem from a 1932 book in which the leading stage performers of the Weimar Republic portray themselves in photographs and through their own words. In response to the editor's questions, Kortner — among other artists — analyzes his role as an actor within Germany's greater cultural and historical context, linking the crisis in theater to existing economic and intellectual crises. Given the unstable socioeconomic situation at the end of the Weimar Republic, the cultural years ahead looked particularly grim. The actor's commentary reveals the vulnerable situation of German theater in a country on the brink of dictatorship.[2]

Kortner's premonition of a collective "madness" takes on special significance in historical hindsight if we consider that scarcely one year after his photograph was bound in the volume of national German stars, both he and at least half of those actors pictured and interviewed — who happened to be born Jewish — were ousted from the spotlight. With Hitler's ascension to power,

Originally published in *Theatre Survey* 135.2 (1994), 5-17. The ending has been slightly revised for this anthology.

Jewish performers who once shared the stage with fellow Germans were denounced as Jews and their performances were deemed "harmful to the national sentiment."[3] Such actresses as Elisabeth Bergner and Grete Mosheim, who, respectively, once identified themselves with the German stage and with Goethe's stage heroine, "Gretchen,"[4] had little choice in 1933 but to accept their fate as "polluters" of the new German stage. And while such non-Jewish stars as Käthe Dorsch and Gustaf Gründgens recognized the link between their pure-blooded Germanness and their success as legitimate stage representatives for Nazi Berlin, Bergner, Mosheim, and Kortner emigrated within the first years of the new Reich. But not all Jewish performers chose to leave Germany. Indeed, some of them were so rooted in German tradition that they sought to merge their national sense of self with an artistic mission, in spite of the worsening social conditions for Jews in Germany.

A Jewish Theater in Nazi Germany: An Introduction

This chapter probes how a group of Jewish artists in Germany after 1933 reconciled themselves as German Jews *and* performers within a sociopolitical system that was gradually depriving them of their civil and cultural rights. Using the extraordinary example of an all-Jewish subscription theater in Nazi Germany's Berlin, I will examine the social and artistic objectives toward which the Jewish performers strove as they sought both theatrical representation and personal preservation. These artists belonged to the *Jüdischer Kulturbund Deutscher Juden* (the Cultural Association of German Jews), later renamed the *Jüdischer Kulturbund*, whose nationwide network of theaters was more or less organized, sponsored, encouraged, and even protected (until 1941) by the Nazis.[5] An ongoing scholarly debate — begun in the mid-1930s — questions whether the Kulturbund actors truly represented Jewish culture and high art or were instead shamelessly exploited by the Nazis for political purposes. A review of this debate will reveal the complicated nature of the German-Jewish cultural association, particularly in light of new testimony from surviving Kulturbund theater members.[6]

Describing the effect of the Jewish theater's 1933 inaugural production of Lessing's *Nathan the Wise* on weeping spectators, the significant Kulturbund performer Kurt Katsch — who played Nathan — recalls: "It wasn't theater anymore; it was an almost religious experience in its intensity. One believed one was in a temple, not on the stage. . . . I extinguished my private life. I had only the feeling that I must fulfill a mission. I felt myself to be more like a priest than an actor."[7] To what extent does Katsch's self-described onstage mission symbolize the Kulturbund actor as a cultural crusader who, by countering spiritual crisis through art, provided audiences with a sense of belonging? Given the curious historical situation of the Kulturbund, Katsch's testimony is especially poignant. For the performance of Lessing's classic German play about a sympathetic Jew by an all-Jewish cast for an all-Jewish audience reveals both a historical and a theatrical irony. Lessing's protagonist advocates the idea that humanity precedes any religious label, whether Gentile or Jew. Once Hitler gained power, however, the majority of Berlin's Jews—although still assimilated—were losing their rights precisely because they were Jews.

The Kulturbund: Its Ideals and Identity

Yet, in spite of the laws against Jews in Germany, the Kulturbund's principal founders, musicologist and nerve specialist Dr. Kurt Singer and stage director Kurt Baumann, upheld German-Jewish identity as they envisaged their organization's tasks to serve social, ethical, and instructive purposes for Jews: to provide work and the will to live, to promote pride and unity among Jews, and to teach and to learn through art.[8] The association's call to prospective members, meanwhile, reinforced the primary desire to lead an "intellectual life open to the human ideals" nurtured from German classics, while developing a connection to the "spirit and being of Judaism."[9] And stressing what *he* saw as the identity of those actively involved in the theater and the largely acculturated community-at-large, the theater's main dramaturg, Julius Bab, proclaimed: "We will create a Jewish stage, which, at the same time, will be a German one; it will stem from these double roots of being which nourish us German Jews and from which we cannot be severed." Bab's pledge to turn to plays of Jewish and East European origin was balanced by his commitment to great German and other European playwrights.[10]

But the Nazi government's agenda obviously restricted the cultural organization's autonomy as well as its freedoms, threatening those people rooted in German culture. Only Jews were allowed to be Kulturbund members and attend events. The Jewish press alone could advertise and review the performances. Strict censorship regulated the programming. Many of the initially proposed German plays—including *Nathan the Wise*—were eventually forbidden. And by 1938, not one opera, symphony, or theatrical work by non-Jewish Germans and Austrians was officially permissible. The directors felt increasingly compelled to fill the gaps in their repertory with works by Jewish composers and playwrights.

The artists of the Kulturbund found themselves in a situation shaped largely by the Nazi agenda, which had swiftly redefined race and cultural identity according to body and blood. In fact, looking back to 1933, Nazi SS-Commandant Hans Hinkel—responsible for Jewish cultural affairs—reports how his office successfully "cleansed [German] cultural institutions, particularly the theater, of all representatives of the Jewish race."[11] Hinkel's primary objective was to ensure the purity of German cultural life. But this also meant concerning himself—at least outwardly—with those unemployed Jewish artists who did not leave Germany. As a liaison between the Kulturbund directors and his Nazi superiors, Hinkel was instrumental in establishing the governmental contact that the Kulturbund needed in order to exist.[12] And with the creation of the Jewish organization, Hinkel could proclaim: "What once seemed incomprehensible and even unnecessary, proved itself over time to be right and organic: The Jews in Germany can [now] nurture their Jewish culture within their own circles . . . as long as they do not directly or indirectly influence German cultural life."[13] By declaring Jewish culture as separate and identifiably Jewish, the Nazi state thus tried to force a Jewish identity on the Jewish artists regardless of their religious feelings and racial self-conceptions. But in spite of such external pressures, as well as demands from the Jewish community, which eventually compelled the Kulturbund actors to use the stage to present themselves as Jews and to instruct their audiences in Jewishness, these performers retained a sense of themselves as German citizens and artists.

An Artistic Mission:
Representing German-Jewish Cultural Identity

The Kulturbund symbolizes the complexity of the theatrical phenomenon and underscores the dilemma of identity that the performers faced. In a situation where the Nazis promoted caricatures of Jews, the Jewish artists had to determine first, within the limits set by the Nazis, how they as German Jews should present themselves offstage, and second, how they might portray their Jewish roles onstage. To complicate this issue of self- and staged representation, the actors had to balance demands from the various liberal and Zionist groups within their community for specific cultural representations.

The Kulturbund representatives knew, for example, that the assimilated majority was not interested in specifically Jewish themes and had little desire to join an exclusively Jewish cultural club, while the Zionists preferred cultural events based on Hebrew or Yiddish sources.[14] And the Nazi overseers like Hinkel also wanted to see the Jews produce Jewish art. How could one appease all factions within the Kulturbund audiences? While the assimilated Jews could agree that Lessing's play represented high ideals of humanity in the best German tradition, Jewish newspaper editorials saw the play as "a text of the times," demanding months before the premiere that the production depict the current "situation" of Jews realistically, instead of "spinning a world of illusions" around them.[15] And referring to his role as Nathan, Katsch recalls how Lessing's words of tolerance allowed him to express the emotions he had felt since being dismissed from the German theater.[16] This brings us back to his performance of the wise Nathan. Should the stage figure of Nathan, for example, embody the assimilated Jew, the religious Jew, or the Jew whose racial characteristics separated him from others?

Such varying stage interpretations were, in part, rooted in the long-standing debate on the biological and cultural status of Jews in Germany. The discussion, begun by both German nationalists and Jewish intellectuals at the turn of this century, incorporated race theory, which used anthropological sources to endorse negative, antisemitic views. These views implied that Jews were biologically different from Germans and, in fact, a separate race.[17] While German Jews were assimilated within German political culture, they were, at the same time, subject to antisemitic measures within Germany.[18] In order to cultivate positive images of themselves as a group, the Zionists, in particular, countered racial antisemitism with arguments similarly steeped in popular race theory. This included stressing unique Jewish physical attributes as well as focusing on the contributions Jews had made to German culture; in this way, Jews tried to combat the looming threats to "Jewish" life and art, whatever that might entail. A common response among even the more assimilated German Jews—especially after 1933—was "to look inward at a Jewish interior landscape that had long ago grown barren."[19] Nonetheless, German Jews remained equivocal about their place and role in German society, especially in light of antisemitism.[20]

As a consequence of both their ambivalent "spiritual stance" and the political atmosphere they lived in, the Kulturbund performers faced the problematic question of what exactly *was* a "Jewish landscape" and *how* they might convey this culture to their audiences. Such Jewish newspapers as the *Israelitisches Familienblatt* and the *Jüdische Rundschau* tried to shape Jewish cultural and religious awareness and to encourage readers to identify with their Jewishness. In regard to the theater's emblematic production of *Nathan,* Jewish newspapers noted that the choice of Lessing's play was suitable as long as the production would be an artistic rather than a political one.[21] The all-Jewish premiere of *Nathan,* however, soon became a politicized event whose directors catered to the various contingents of Berlin's prospective audience: liberal Jews, Zionists, and Nazi censors. First, a rabbi delivered a pre-performance prayer to an audience whose guests included high-ranking officers of the Gestapo seated in the mezzanine. And not only were Jewish audiences requested to comport themselves "inoffensively" on opening night, but the evening's program notes suggested that they "refrain from any political discussion during the performance."[22]

The government laws against Jewish artists and their work impelled Kulturbund production teams to emphasize Jewish themes onstage. In *Nathan the Wise,* for example, Katsch as Nathan hummed Hassidic songs, murmured Hebrew, and prayed at his Oriental home pulpit that was adorned by a Star of David and a menorah. For the Zionist newspaper reporter, the Kulturbund ending to the play depicted "Jewish fate" by emphasizing Nathan's exclusion from the group.[23] Such praise, however, was not unanimous. Apparently, the majority neither identified with such a representation of Jewishness, nor with this interpretation of Lessing's play.[24] The theater's initial tendency to suggest Jewish culture through externals — setting, props, and head coverings — is interesting in light of the Nazis' crude concept of Jewishness, which suggested that Jews could be easily identified through visible means like physiognomy, gesture, clothing, and material symbols. It is indeed ironic that both the performers and the intended recipients of such a "Jewish culture" were, for the most part, accustomed to the language and setting of Western, specifically German, culture and therefore generally unmoved by the theater's designers' and directors' attempts to infuse overt symbols of Judaism into productions.

So steeped in German tradition were the actors that they were unable to dissociate themselves from that culture in order to craft a separate Jewish stage culture. Their persistence in adhering to the belief that their theater was a German one rather than a solely Jewish one reveals the perplexing difficulty that the performers had in identifying with their Jewishness and with Judaism. For their art depended on the written German word — not Hebrew or Yiddish; their repertories consisted of classic German dramatists like Goethe and Schiller.[25] And the designers relied on West European stage models. This obviously created problems for the theater directors especially as German plays became increasingly taboo as potential staging possibilities. By late 1936, when an article in the German *Frankfurter Zeitung*[26] announced the need to reclarify the distinctions between German and Jewish cultural life, the Kulturbund artists held a national conference to recast their artistic objectives vis-à-vis the problem of Jewish content.[27]

The conference encapsulates the crucial problem for these German-Jewish artists whose struggle to define Jewish content persisted as long as the theater endured. How could Jewish content be related to culture? And how might performers be retrained to represent Jewish culture onstage? The Kulturbund theater opted to introduce pedagogical methods for actors (including classes in Hebrew and Yiddish inflection) by which they might enlighten their audiences about Judaism.[28] As a result of the conference and increased pressure from the outside — government officials like Hinkel, Zionist organizations, and Jewish representatives of the German Reich — the theater pledged to adopt a stronger Jewish representation in its programming. That same year (1936) Herbert Freeden, who directed the cultural sector of the Zionist Union in Germany, joined the theater as chief dramaturg and program adviser. His main task was to steer the theater onto a more conscious Zionist course. Over the next three years, Freeden worked on translations from Yiddish of works by such East European Jewish writers as Nathan Bistritsky (*Schabattai Zwi*), Sholom Aleichem (*Amcha*), and Halper Leiwik (*The Golem*) to add to a repertory that already included Scribe, Shakespeare, Molnár, and Ibsen. Nonetheless, not only have former actors admitted their inability to play religious roles, but the so-called Jewish events were also poorly attended. And audiences ostensibly remained largely unconcerned with plays featuring biblical themes or about Jewish life in Eastern Europe, Golems and all. In fact, the most successful play of the Berlin 1936–37 season was *A Midsummer Night's Dream*.[29]

Freeden recalls how difficult it was to find suitable plays written by Jews that might pass the government censors *and* be relevant to Jewish life. If a Jewish playwright had ever criticized National Socialism, his or her plays were automatically banned. In addition, "a play that referred in any way to the plight of the Jews in Germany would certainly have been prohibited."[30] There was one exception. A contemporary play by a female playwright from Palestine passed through the censors as late as 1938. *The Trial* by Shulamit Batdori dealt with the unrest among the Jews, Palestinians, and the British; at a time when emigration among German Jews to Palestine was on the rise, the play apparently appealed to the audiences who filled the auditorium for a four-week run in May. As Freeden puts it, "The events in Palestine were, at that time, central to Jewish interests; and we were successful in creating a realistic picture of those events."[31] Batdori focuses on Zionism in her portrayal of the three warring factions within Palestine. The play, originally written in Hebrew in 1936, captures the tensions of the times when Jews fought for the independent state of Israel. Radio broadcasts and a night raid on a kibbutz open the play. The play's "Speaker" narrates six episodes, while also interacting with the other characters. At the end of the play, a young British soldier, an Arab youth, and a Jewish settler question how they might co-exist peacefully. These young people must find a solution, for they are "our future," says the "Speaker."

The theater produced the play without incident, regardless of the parallels to the plight of Jews in Germany. Perhaps this was due, in part, to the play's didactic tone, the Middle Eastern setting, or the Zionist Organization's matinee introduction to Palestine prior to the premiere performance. While many of the plays performed by the Kulturbund provided audiences with metaphorical situations with which to identify—Stefan Zweig's *Jeremiah* (1934), Richard Beer-Hofmann's *Jacob's Dream* (1935), J. B. Priestley's *People at Sea* (1939)—no other production portrayed events that so directly applied to the contemporary situation for Jews as *The Trial*.

An Ongoing Debate on the Kulturbund

In spite of their attempts to create art within an atmosphere antagonistic to Jewish creativity, the Kulturbund directors persevered in their quest, but a recurrent question concerned them: Did their theater give its actors and audiences a false sense of reality, as if their situation were really better than it was? Did the theater enterprise impede emigration because the Jewish artists and technicians were unaware how severe the situation was? Participants contradict one another as they remember their past involvement with the Kulturbund: Freeden attests that during the mid- to late 1930s, "one knew what was happening outside the theater."[32] Yet the wife of one of the last managing directors of the Kulturbund, Dr. Werner Levie, says one could not see what was really happening "outside," because the theater became their whole life.[33] Within the small group of Kulturbund scholars, there are those who believe that the Jewish artists were manipulated by the Nazis as identifiable pawns in a grotesque game. These researchers conclude, with confident historical hindsight, for example, that the Kulturbund was a "calamitous misunderstanding in which Jews had been abused for the Nazi cause."[34] They suggest that the Kulturbund functionaries were "under the illusion" that they could co-exist with the Nazis and create a "Jewish State Theater."[35] This argument challenges the notion that the German-Jewish actors could be credible representatives of theater art, least of all ones of specifically Jewish culture. Given the aims of the Nazis to isolate Jews from German culture, true creativity would have been impossible to achieve. The measures taken by the Nazis against Jews required both artistic and political collaboration among the Kulturbund artists, causing them to compromise some of their artistic ideals. In sum, while all present research on the German-Jewish association at least indirectly questions the role of the artists vis-à-vis the Nazi government, some cultural historians prefer to report events historically, without having to probe the crucial relationship between culture and

identity as spiritual resistance to the Nazis.[36] The dilemma of how Jewish performers sought to reconcile themselves with their precarious status as artists
and German Jews in a regime hostile to Jews may seem trivial at first given the
basic scholarly verdict on the Kulturbund: the inevitable failure of an institution forced to exist and to promote a Jewish culture no one really wanted.[37]

But such bold pronouncements become problematic upon considering the
unusual testimony presented by ex-Kulturbund members about their theater.
In 1992, Berlin's *Akademie der Künste* sponsored an exhibition entitled *Geschlossene Vorstellung* [*Closed Performance*], which by presenting information
from the personal archives of former Kulturbund members, prompted a general reevaluation of the Jewish organization. Two edited publications now exist
that include interpretive essays, replicated documents, photographs, and firsthand accounts.[38] And the 1992 exhibition culminated in a roundtable discussion with the aging ex-Kulturbund artists who had reunited in Berlin to talk
about their one-time theater.

The artists' and members' conflicting views complicate the theater historian's task. For the voices in the present expressed disagreement about the past.
Among the speakers was Herbert Freeden. Until the exhibition, his 1964 book
(reprinted, 1985) had been the seminal source for information on the theater.
As a one-time participant in the theater, Freeden records an especially enlightening history, even though he lacks the critical objectivity of other cultural
historians.[39]

Freeden's recurrent thesis suggests that the Kulturbund Jews clung to their
German-Jewish roots, resisting a forced Jewish culture. He maintains throughout his writing (from 1964 to 1992) that the Jews strengthened their "mental"
resistance to possible ghettoization by performing classics by such authors as
Schnitzler and Shakespeare. Yehoyakim Cochavi, on the other hand, has recently suggested that the core of spiritual resistance for Jews was precisely
in constructing a new Jewish self-image.[40] Cochavi intimates that by embrac-
ing their Jewishness and seeking to embody it in art, the Kulturbund artists
were able to maintain their own self-esteem, revitalize Jewish culture, and
thereby provide audiences with a renewed sense of Jewish selfhood. From all
accounts, however, it remains questionable whether those artists were successful in strengthening their own Jewish consciousness, or in promoting a new
Jewish self-awareness in their audiences.

In fact, for Cochavi, the Kulturbund theater could only succeed in its mission if it truly became a "Jewish" ("German-Jewish") theater infused with a
humanism and spirituality specific to Judaism; then it might contribute to the
fight against an intellectual crisis and breakdown.[41] The majority of the sur-

viving performers who have recently voiced their opinions about their theater actually deemphasize the import that "Jewish" culture had on their artistic endeavors. But while they readily admit the general lack of understanding and success for the so-called Jewish plays, particularly those from East Europe, they do stress the importance of their theater work for their sense of selves and for their audiences, especially given the social circumstances for Jews under National Socialism.[42] Freeden concedes that while the theater was unsuccessful in actually creating Jewish culture, it did give the audiences a vital spiritual boost. Not only was there an intense craving for culture among Berlin's Jews, but "the people were concerned and desperate. . . . [Kurt] Singer's task was to offer them something spiritual to keep them from breaking down. . . . They applied everything [in a play] to their own destinies," recalls a performer.[43] And the actress, Ruth Anselm-Herzog, acknowledges, "I was never afraid; on the contrary, you had the feeling you were doing something and fighting for it."[44]

The actress has since elaborated on her participation in the Kulturbund: "Where could I have gone as a young person? . . . I wanted to be in the theater. It gave me time to develop my skills. Besides, we could not imagine, what the Germans had in store for us."[45] "We didn't really think of anything else but our theater work," admits another performer; "it didn't occur to us that the circumstances were so special until much later. Today, that's hard to understand, of course, but back then it seemed as though it [the theater] could just go on and on," she continues.[46] Both of these views can be corroborated by other Kulturbund performers, who claim (at least in retrospect) how grateful they were to work at all, and particularly to work in their theatrical "element."[47] Freeden has both criticized and praised the notion of apparent artistic and economic freedoms for performers at the Kulturbund. Besides referring to an institution where employment hindered emigration and safety,[48] he has also stated that "no one gave up emigration because the Kulturbund existed; no one was really fooled."[49] Practically speaking, for those Jewish artists who stayed in such German cities as Berlin throughout the 1930s, their work was a necessary means for maintaining economic security, which in many cases meant being able to afford emigration—especially after 1938.[50]

Fritz Kortner pessimistically identified a pervasive crisis of spirit as the great enemy to theater and its future within Weimar Germany. But Kortner was able to secure acting engagements abroad and thus could elude the bleak theater prospects he had foreseen. Other Jewish theater artists in Germany, however, either had no other work opportunities, or were unable—or unwilling—to leave their country. For some of them, the Kulturbund theater became a refuge where they could, at least temporarily, engage in their craft for the future of art's sake, as well as for their own sake—so as not to succumb to a personal crisis of spirit. In the early years of the theater, Kurt Katsch had attributed to his role as Nathan a missionary appeal both for himself and for his audience. More seasoned Kulturbund actors like Martin Brandt, however, who remained with the theater almost until its end (Katsch emigrated in 1935), have used somewhat less self-aggrandizing terms to explain how actors worked in the Jewish theater, despite a government increasingly bent on destroying Jews: "The Kulturbund was my spiritual salvation . . . the theater was our liberator . . . like an island. We had blinders on, because if we had known what was going on around us, we probably would've ended up in the loony-bin." [51] Brandt, like Katsch, ostensibly understood the primary need to use art in order to cope with—or to transcend—the grim realities of Germany in the late 1930s and early 1940s. His remarks suggest that some actors evidently were able to create meaningful theater art and thus avert potential spiritual crisis and lunacy. Whatever the personal motives or potential missions—for the community or themselves—that such actors as Katsch and Brandt saw as integral to their vocations of acting, the Kulturbund theater stage provided them with a sanctuary where they could find a reprieve from the ruthless conditions outside the theater. On the "Jewish" stage, they practiced their craft with intensity, transforming their anxieties into artistic energy for audiences eager for distraction and enlightenment. "We knew that this theater was like a moral anchor for Jews. They could forget everything for one evening and enter another world," Freeden recalls.[52]

The directors of the Kulturbund had often debated whether it was ethical under the worsening circumstances for Jews in Germany to work for or even attend the Jewish theater. Even a media debate within Jewish newspapers in Berlin amplified these private debates. Moral issues aside, however, it is certainly questionable whether the actors' efforts or the attempts by the theater's leaders to infuse the Kulturbund with a social purpose actually produced a stronger sense of Jewish cultural enlightenment for participants or spectators. Does this make the theater's preoccupation with questions of Jewish content and culture seem all the more futile? Our historical hindsight may lead us to judge the Jewish troupe's tactics as perverse, primarily dictated by the Nazi supervisors, and therefore doomed to fail. But may we not attribute to the Kulturbund performers' search for group identity and artistic representation a useful "mental" strategy against persecution? By exploring what Jewish culture entailed, the artists also engaged in a process of counteridentification, differentiating themselves all the more from their Nazi nemesis.

Such community cohesion may have strengthened some of those artists' resolve to use art to provide audiences with insight and comfort amid extreme circumstances. The unusually risky external situation for Jews in the Third Reich impelled these artists to focus on inner resources, developing an uncompromising sense of self through performing. Perhaps this explains, in part, how one musician made music while "sweating it out for six years" until he could emigrate, or how an actress at home in the glare of spotlights—even Gestapo interrogation lamps—played the role of her life, the "Idiot," to protect her real-life role in the Resistance. Perhaps this also helped the singer, Masha Benya-Matz, to keep "Jewish culture going after the destruction." So too did Fritz Wisten survive the war (his wife was an Aryan) to rebuild a postwar German theater in the spirit of the Kulturbund, even relying on some of the Kulturbund scripts during his new theater's first years. Lessing's *Nathan the Wise* was one of his first productions.

Among the programs of the Kulturbund orchestra, Kurt Michaelis has singled out the February 1941 performance of Mahler's Second Symphony—also known as "Resurrection"—as especially moving. The words of Mahler's choral finale resound with the bittersweet message of hope within an increasingly bleak time. These words suggest the spirit that made the Jewish theater what it was. A single soprano speaks to the chorus: "Oh believe. / Thou were not born in vain! / Hast not lived in vain. / Suffered in vain!" The chorus answers: "What has come into being must perish, / What perished must rise again. / Cease from trembling! / Prepare thyself to live!" [53]

Some of the Kulturbund artists never performed again after emigration: their accents too strongly Germanic or their musical instrument unconducive to chamber music; yet for others, those careers begun on the Kulturbund stage, in part, enabled them to start again—albeit on new soil: One artist established a dancing school, another plays concert violin; still another coaches well-known film actors. Those Kulturbund artists who fled and survived the Third Reich brought with them the fragments of memory that we on the outside must respect as we piece together the past.

"We've Enough *Tsoris*"

Laughter at the Edge of the Abyss

VOLKER KÜHN

NOVEMBER 1937. The daily situation on Berlin's streets: SA men riot through the city center. Whoever "looks Jewish" is vilified. Store windows are broken, graffiti on apartment house walls announce: "Juda drop dead!" The black and white of the newspapers in their *Stürmer* display cases declare: "The Jews are our misfortune!" And the official newspaper of the SS, *Das Schwarze Korps*, wages a vicious campaign against Jewish "germ carriers." The campaign makes clear that "this has nothing to do with the Jews 'themselves'; rather it is the spirit—or evil spirit—that they spread." One can already read between the lines what will later be referred to as the "Final Solution": "Unfortunately, it must be that . . . there remains a broad field of operation for an active antisemitism, even if not one crooked nose exists in the German Reich . . . We must exterminate the Jewish spirit."

At the same time in 1937, a master of ceremonies steps in front of an enthusiastic audience at Berlin's Brüdervereinshaus to speculate in his cabaret solo on the "necessity of our situation." He chats, as one might expect from him—the friendly, charming conversationalist who has spoken of this and that for decades: for example, about humorists, who "for the most part, are comedians." And he chats about the task of fostering a "Jewish culture out of our own qualities and based on our own possibilities." Finally, the man speaks of Judaism "that neither had nor had known its own artistic creation in the sense that other peoples did."

In his amusing lecture, which has been previously submitted for approval

Originally published in *Geschlossene Vorstellung: Der Jüdische Kulturbund in Deutschland 1933–1941*, ed. Akademie der Künste (Berlin: Edition Hentrich, 1992), 95–112.

and censorship to Hans Hinkel, the chief of Jewish cultural affairs in Goebbels's ministry, the Jewish cabaret artist reflects on a chimera: namely, Jewish cabaret: "We have no experience in Jewish intimate theater or Jewish cabaret — a domain that does not exist. We can only try to find our own way by building on that which in the cultural tradition of Jewish cabaret-goers satisfied them. Because a cabaret of only Jewish artists with works by Jews for Jews is by far no Jewish cabaret." A Jewish joke? In his introductory remarks to his *Tourists — A Cabaret of Jewish Authors,* this evening on Berlin's Kurfürstenstrasse the professional cabarettist, Elow — who now must use the name Erich Lowinsky again — jokes about the joke itself to his Jewish audience: "The best is still this: One person meets another. The other says: 'I know. . . .' But the time for jokes is over. It is our duty to bring you joy and lift your spirits." And after a short pause, he resumes: "One can also take joy seriously." What sounds like a punchline is none.

Two years earlier in the *Monatsblätter des Jüdischen Kulturbundes,* Margarete Edelheim posed the fundamental question about mirth with proper seriousness: "Does Jewish cabaret exist?" This journalist continuously demanded in her reviews for the *C.V.* [*Central Verein der deutschen Juden*]*-Zeitung* that the Kulturbund stage reveal "Jewish content" and present the "lovely art of song in the East European Jewish tradition." What she could glean from her visits to cabaret performances "was not simply Jewish art"; rather, at best, folkloric East European images in the tradition of the *Blauen Vogel* [*The Blue Bird*] as staged in Berlin and Frankfurt by Nikolai Eliaschoff and based on the famous Russian cabaret of emigrés.

The first of these revue-like collages graced the Kulturbund stage in November 1934: *Berliner Bilderbogen-Östlicher Bilderbogen* [*Berlin Picture Album-Eastern (European) Picture Album*]. Berlin's troupe presented Eliaschoff's cabaret spectacle the way one knew it from the Kurfürstendamm — popular *Chansons* and seasonal hits from the studio of the unforgettable Hollaender's Tingel-Tangel club and the stylish Nelson-Revue.[1] Annemarie Hase, the robust "Diseuse" of the Wilde Bühne and the Katakombe, presented herself with solid Berlin dialect in tested showstoppers; and although the audience celebrated its darling, the press held back its praise for the prominent interpreter of Tucholsky and Kästner[2] ("runaway ballad-singer mouth and bleary-eyed") and likened her performance to "charming fun with Aunt Klara," concluding that "family evenings with Aunt Klara must cease."

The second half of the program, on the other hand, pleased critics because it "gave rise to the message from the land of our children and our hope. The old 'Blue Bird' rose; a series of medieval images passed; an eternal ghetto came to life; sweet Romantic conjured up a fairy-tale of the 'Nowhere King.'" That actually sounds like a new version of the *The Blue Bird*, known in Berlin during the 1920s as a product of the Russian emigré stage that once formulated its intentions in this way: "Tired of politics and daily life, the Russian went to his cabaret in search of a complete break from the reality of life and a cheerful escape from himself in music, color, and play."

And yet Eliaschoff's illustrated songs, which included the laughing rabbi, the little Jew with his little fiddle, and little Duderle "whose burdensome little pack almost pressed him to the ground," were enthusiastically received by the *Jüdische Rundschau* and perceived as a political event. "An awakening passed through the whole theater, and as if touched by some invisible hand, the people stood, clapped, shouted with joy, laughed, and wept. . . . Feeling is all. Names and ideas are immaterial. It was blessed to be connected to — no, to be part of a community — a people."

The hope that the cabaret stage might enable one to gain strength, self-revelation, or orientation soon proved itself misleading, especially since the expectations of audiences were as varied as the programs that the Kulturbund presented between 1934 and 1941. Eliaschoff tried a second time to offer a scenic blend of modern city life and East European Jewish ghetto folklore. This time the description of Berlin reached back to the turn of the century: variety theater, *Chansons*, Cancan, "Negro songs," and clichéd rhymed couplets about domestics.[3] There were songs about a wood auction in Grünewald and the beauty of May in Schöneberg before the old rabbi laughed again and the beautiful "Mädele" [young girl] turned to the Hassidic ways; still, at times, the critics indulgently noted something wrong with the Yiddish and they doubted whether the actors "had ever seen real Hassidim before." This time, too, the reviewers in the Jewish newspapers regretted ("if we had only these worries!") that the audience "gratefully used" the nostalgic Berlin happiness created by Eliaschoff "to escape from present times."

However, Jewish cabaret was no longer mentioned, not even when Eliaschoff staged a "new East European and Palestine collage" in Berlin's Bach-Saal in December 1935. Indeed, Arthur Elösser pointed out in the *Jüdische Rundschau* that in spite of the professionalism and the "improvised levity" of the evening, and "despite the Oriental hand-wringing," the "amateurs prove more powerful when they stamp on the territory of Eretz Israel which they too had prepared." Still, Elösser praised the Jewish humor, whose "fool's bells ring above the solemnity of suffering and seem to say to us: Even when we have nothing else, at least we still have ourselves."

Yet there remained an unease with what should be presented on the Kulturbund's cabaret stage which, after all, should offer something to the most people possible. "What does cabaret mean for us in our situation?" the *Jüdische Rundschau* asked itself two years later in regard to the expected premiere of *Tourists*. The answer may sound "rather primitive" to readers: "According to us, material for Jewish cabaret is everything that has to do with Jewish content, can be understood by Jews in Germany, and can—and may be—encapsulated in small form." As to how this could be accomplished, the same newspaper suggested: "One paints colored placards and sings folk songs in unison beneath them." Yet in the next sentence the writer cast doubt on these words, "How questionable that all is!"

In this way, Elow tried to incorporate relevant and timely themes in his *Tourists* program, all the while remaining true to his motto, "the cabaret is always the fool of its time." The one-time managing editor of the once-famous Berliner comic stage, the Namenlosen [Nameless] (which Erich Kästner made into a literary monument in *Fabian*), tried to delete what the Jewish press had criticized from the Kulturbund's cabaret beginnings as "reminiscences of an earlier, long gone time, . . . a mishmash of isolated Herrnfeld Theater[4] and stale Kabarett der Komiker," and finally as a "salad of very old Berlin N and Berlin W Remains" with the "ugly smack of unequivocalness and jabber."[5]

In *Tourists*, the opening address and the songs focused on "Goodbye 1937" and emigration, of a letter from the brother in Palestine, and a ship that will arrive. The program was mindful of a recommendation from the *Gemeindeblatt der Jüdischen Reformgemeinde zu Berlin* that cabaret "should not only stimulate the laugh muscles, especially in our situation," rather it should "take issue in artistic form with daily questions, daily concerns, and daily upsets, while lifting us beyond them."

And yet the reviewer had basic doubts. *Tourists* was in the well-established tradition of the comic stage (the program noted, "costumes: our own; scenery: none; beards: our property"). But while the production literarily tingled in front of an "audience laden with worry," according to the *Jüdische Rundschau,* it neglected to "criticize the weaknesses of Jewish life—which a cabaret is supposed to do"—in spite of "honest attempts and well-earned success." On the other hand, the introductory address "should have been less sharp" than it turned out to be. And although "the whole event maintained high standards and satisfied intellectual and artistic demands—combined with a natural need for entertainment throughout," there "are (and always were) experiences that are too serious to be expressed by a *Chanson.*"

Jewish cabaret? Even Margarete Edelheim concluded, "we cannot easily have Jewish cabaret. We will always perceive Hassidic dances, East European

Jewish folk songs, the song of the Rothschilds, the description of any New York ghetto scene, or a folk song from the Emek [East European region] as small slices of the reality which together present the diversity of Jewish life in the Diaspora and in Palestine. . . . Even so, however, we should not dispense with Jewishness in cabaret." What exactly that was, though, remained unclear: "Only the best, only true art and culture may be presented to Jews in the various Kulturbund theaters. What may not be shown are the rejected remains of an illusory culture of the metropolis—something we've been seeing in the cabarets of the last decades."

This required the "squaring of the circle": Laugh, but not too much; offer measured fun with profundity that distracts the audience. The discussion centered on a seemingly academic question, namely, whether there actually could exist what really was not supposed to exist. Obviously, this discussion drew its contemporary relevance from the tension between the Kulturbund's aims to "offer Jews relaxation and pleasure" and the increasing seriousness of the daily situation in which this task was to be fulfilled. The question of how Jewish the cabaret had to be—if even such a thing existed—pointed to the absurdity of the situation in which the question was seriously discussed. In practice, there was something much more fundamental to consider: the ambivalence of human beings' basic needs in no-win situations. The joke as a drug; satire and irony as harbingers of hope; the punchline as a weapon of resistance; fun as distraction; and laughter to document the will to survive—right there in places where laughter sticks in one's throat. This all marks an unsolvable problem with which those people who faced death on the ramp of Auschwitz had to deal.

The cabaret artists themselves wrestled with the question differently back then—in fact, more practically. Prominent artists still popular among audiences—blacklisted overnight—without a possibility to perform, grabbed any opportunity they could to appear onstage—regardless of the conditions. Erich Lowinsky's newly opened Künstlerspiele Uhlandeck in Berlin had just been closed. He received a "pink slip" just like his colleagues had: expulsion from the Reich Chamber for Writers, expulsion from the Reich Theater Chamber, expulsion from the Speciality Alliance of Varieté, Theater, and Circus Directors.

The application for readmission was rejected: "According to the will of the *Führer* and Reichs-Chancellor, only suitable and responsible fellow countrymen may administer German culture as indicated in paragraph 10 of the first ordinance for implementing the laws of the Reichskulturkammer. In light of the lofty relevance that spiritual and culture-creating work has on the life and the development of the German people, only those persons are qualified—without a doubt—to execute such a task in Germany who belong to the German race not only as citizens of the state, but also through their deep connection in manner and in blood . . . Because you are not an Aryan. . . ."

The existence of the Jüdischer Kulturbund would come to Erich Lowinsky's attention in a letter from the president of the Reich Union for German Artistry. The opportunity to appear before an audience in spite of the ban was for many artists a way out during a time without prospects. So they played on from 1934 in Berlin, in Frankfurt, Stuttgart, Cologne, Hamburg, and other places at first. In the beginning they played in special cabaret locales for Jewish artists like in Berlin's Café Léon on the Kurfürstendamm, Bühne und Brettl on the Joachimsthaler Straße, or in Brettl, im Zentrum, in the King of Portugal Hotel, which adorned its advertising sign with two Stars of David. Many prominent cabarettists performed there: the emcees Willy Prager, Willy Hagen, Alfons Fink, and Fritz Benscher; the "Diseuses" Dora Gerson, Annemarie Hase, Gertrud Kohlmann, and Rosa Valetti; those stars of recitation — Ludwig Hardt, Dela Lipinskaya, Karl Ettlinger, and Joseph Plaut; the comedians Max Ehrlich and Otto Wallburg; the music-hall impresario Willy Rosen; and the fife player Guido Gialdini. The Jewish newspapers announced guest programs by the prominent from the entertainment world: droll skits with Felix Bressart; grotesque dance with Valeska Gert; concerts with the "film and record star" Joseph Schmidt. At various places, Jewish cabarets were established where well-known artists participated and where unknowns showed off their talent: the Kunterbunte Würfel [Topsy-turvy Cube] in Frankfurt; Leo Raphaeli's Rosarote Brille [Rose-Colored Glasses] in Hamburg; Fred Wald's Bunter Karren [Colorful Wheelbarrow] in Leipzig. Even in remote Beuthen, an ensemble established itself in 1934 under the directorship of Willi Feuereisen. Committed to the Muse of Cabaret, the troupe performed cheerful revues year after year, creating the cozy atmosphere of club meetings in rhymed images.

At the same time, the actors, singers, and dancers of Berlin's Kulturbund stage created cabaret shows that they toured to the provinces. Cläre Arnstein, Jenny Bernstein, Alfred Berliner, Steffi Rosenbaum, and Fritz Tachauer soon became the stars playing the highlights of touring revues named the *Kunterbunt* [*Topsy-turvy*], *Quer Durch Ernst und Scherz* [*Traversing Seriousness and Jest*], or simply *Heiterer Abend* [*Cheerful Evening*], promising a "varied blend of cabaretic delicacies" until 1941. The repertory consisted of traditional, old numbers from the 1920s: songs by Tucholsky, Hollaender, Spoliansky, grotesque lyrical songs from Morgenstern to Ringelnatz; sketches by Molnár and Salten; numbers from operettas; and finally, original compositions with thought-provoking and cheerful undertones.

They performed afternoon and evening variety shows, at cabarets, and even for social evenings of the Jüdischer Kulturbund. For example, in April 1938, Camilla Spira and Max Ehrlich presented skits in between a dance competition and a raffle whose first prize was a trip to Palestine and a crossing to the United States.

Actors had to rely on their ability for improvisation — not only onstage, for a stage was not always available. Egon Jacobsohn reported in the *Jüdische Allgemeine Zeitung* (November 1934) on a variety show in Stettin that he performed with Camilla Spira, Erna Klein, Elsa Koch, and Wilhelm Guttmann. Just hours before the event began, they discovered that the Kulturbund hall was unavailable. And so they played in the synagogue although there was not even a curtain for the Torah. Jacobsohn reported how one was "gripped by an odd excitement upon entering the room and finding oneself before the Torah shrine. In the room — silence." Then the program began with skits and song. Spira recited cheerful verse and the audience — clad in hats and coats — was not stingy with applause. They "laughed, laughed a lot," concluded the report from Stettin as it marked "drowning applause … six hundred pairs of hands clap without pause."

The programs were strictly monitored. Gestapo reports noted the sequence of musical numbers, reactions of the audience, and whether or not there existed a "reason to object to the lectures." This was not usually the case; however, the texts were subject to strict censorship and had to be submitted to Hinkel's office for appraisal prior to performances. And just about anything that belonged to a cabaret critical of its times fell victim to Hinkel's red marker. The censor would find and strike allusions to the times, insubordination in tone and gesture, "between the lines," hidden meanings and messages within words, and double-entendres. Forbidden were parodying lines that referred to Heine's "Lorelei" or Goethe's "Erlkönig"; jests about baptism; jokes about ancestry, race, and the power of holy water; as well as allusions to what "kind of a grandmother one has." Any *Chansons* submitted by Dela Lipinskaja had no chance for acceptance — her "Lügenlieder," for example ("although they already are lying like troopers, accept my verse graciously")[6] or the poem by Bry about two trees in the forest, where some things are puffed up "in pride," such as "a large family tree which is essentially of the same wood as a small tree trunk."[7] Further, permission was denied those texts that dealt comically with the situation of the Jews — an example of which was written by Willy Prager — "What good is it if one is sad and no longer gay, because we're bankrupt anyway!"[8]

The censor was especially hard on Ludwig Hardt, banning his recitations temporarily because his "manner of speaking ridicules Germany and our goals in the coarsest manner" — so read a Gestapo report to Hinkel. Also scrapped often from Hamburg's calendar of events were Leo Raphaeli's revues for his cabaret ensemble. Known before the First World War as Willy Hagen of the Nelson-Stage, Raphaeli was now forbidden in his sketches to mention this long-faded time of glory. Nor did Willy Prager—once Raphaeli's cabaret colleague—receive permission for such reminiscences. Often, just the name of an unpopular or all-too popular author was enough to secure a ban from Hinkel. Consequently, Hedi Haas passed off as her own texts poems by Kästner and by foreigners, including the lascivious-erotic couplet "Der gute alte Ton" ["The Good Old Tone"], which was really "Die Dame von der alten Schule"—originally written in the 1920s by Hans Hannes for a Nelson revue. Haas, a Jew, would never have been authorized to perform Hannes's texts: Hannes alias Hans Heinz Zerlett had become a well-known writer and director of films that partly emphasized antisemitic themes.

At the onset of World War II, the Kulturbund's cabaret interpreters saw what a precarious situation they were in professionally; everything that was not expressly permitted was forbidden. In January 1940, the Reichsministerium für Volksaufklärung und Propaganda announced in a protocol note for Jewish masters of ceremonies what Goebbels would soon order for Aryan cabaret artists: a ban on all onstage addresses made by cabaret emcees. An instruction to the *Jüdischer Kulturbund* stated that "Before submitting requests in the area of cabaret, it is essential to prevent such sketches as those by Prager and Tachauer, in which . . . one cannot distinguish whether they are tasteless or brazen. All lectures, texts like Prager, Willi [*sic*] Rosen, Tachauer, and others will no longer be authorized."[9]

Censorship threatened the cabaret artists from the other side as well. The Kulturbund—more than once the target of its own cabaret's sport—did not even submit those self-mocking texts to the censor for appraisal. "Gute Verbindungen" ["Good Connections"] was one of the texts that made fun of patronage at the Kulturbund:

> Have you heard? Oh? Do you already know?
> Whosiwhatsit, the son of, you know, what's his name?
> The singer has no theater engagement anymore. What?
> What's he doing now? Well, you know,
> The boy is truly a genius.
> What? He should join the Kulturbund?
> Oh, Thanks! With *Eizes* I'm blessed
> Do put yourself in his shoes
> There one hears: *Nebbich!*[10]

Kurt Singer, who saw these lines first, noted in the margin on 8 September 1937, "Ill-spirited trash. Don't pass on!"[11]

In an article from 1935 entitled "A Jewish Theater in Berlin?" Hans Hinkel announced: "We have limited the Jews who have stayed in Germany to their own cultural circles and have with this condition created a German politics of culture." The NS-Reich's cultural representative continued his essay with pride, "'Jews work for Jews!' — With this motto I permitted the Jewish cultural organization to exist in the summer of 1933 and since then continue to ensure that this Jewish cultural movement — now extending across the Reich — fulfills its goals in accordance with our established guiding principles." In August of the same year, Kurt Tucholsky discouragingly commented on this process from far-away Hindås in a letter to his Swiss friend, Hedwig Müller: "Dear Nuuna . . . One ordered the German Jews to found ghetto-theater and cultural organizations and they do so. I can hear the know-it-alls with glasses and beards saying, 'And now we want to show them how we have the better theater — and recently, the aunt of a Stormtrooper was in our midst and she said it too: This is better than our own state-theater,' and with that, they all are satisfied. One should not disturb them." In another part of the letter, he summed it up: "The Kulturbund is really an opportunity to say *nebbich*."

One could have seen through the alibi nature of such a "cultural movement," along with Kurt Tucholsky (whose effective, popular texts belonged to the cabaret repertory for some time), but many of the actors and cabaret stars saw no alternative for themselves. At the mercy of the German language for better or for worse, they apparently found it more difficult to emigrate than other artists — painters or musicians, for example. Add to that, especially for cabaret artists, an astonishing naiveté and blindness concerning the political currents of those years: One did not take especially seriously the brown masses that marched through the streets at the beginning of the 1930s.

This is clear enough in a mini dialogue between professional cabaret stars of the times, Kurt Robitschek, who directed *KadeKo,* and the comic Kurt Lilien. When Robitschek spoke of the need to gradually look for exile, Lilien naively rejoined, "What do you mean by that?" And to the next question whether he had not read *Mein Kampf,*[12] Lilien answered, "I don't read bad books." The short exchange — almost a music-hall skit — does have its bitter point: Robitschek made it to America in time, whereas Lilien died in Auschwitz, having been discovered by the Germans in his Dutch exile.

Rosa Valetti was the grand old Dame of Berlin's theater — the actress with the unmistakable face of a bull who played the role of cabaret director in the film, *The Blue Angel.* She was also known as the surly and sharp-voiced

"Diseuse" who performed her songs and sketches in her own cabarets, the Rakete, Größenwahn, Rampe, and Larifari. Just before she left Germany in 1934, Valetti appeared on the Kulturbund stage in such Boulevard comedies as *Weekend* and *Sturm im Wasser.*[13] Her farewell to her audience, reported the *Gemeindeblatt,* took place amid "lively ovations," during a variety show, replete with *Chansons,* skits, and poems by Kästner and Kaléko.[14]

Other actors waited, hesitating to emigrate. In fact, homesickness urged some of the refugees to return to the German Reich from the safe havens to which they had fled. Opportunities to appear onstage at the Jüdischer Kulturbund, for example, played a significant role in luring actors home. Willy Rosen, for instance, had long since emigrated to Holland and become very successful as a touring artist; he kept returning to Berlin until 1936 to appear in the Kulturbund cabaret. In May 1935, he recorded four lively Rosen titles with S. Petruschka's "Sid Kay's Fellows" for Jewish LUKRAPHON labels. Among the recordings "that will give you pleasure"—so read the company's advertising brochures—were the tango "I Lost My Heart in Hawaii" and the waltz-like German carnival song "Gasthof zur goldenen Schnecke" ["Tavern of the Golden Snail"], "in which a piano stands in the corner."

At about the same time (1935), Dora Gerson also returned to Berlin to make a record. She fled to Holland in August 1932, after having been harassed as a Jew onstage at the Katakombe. She voiced her criticism at the microphone more forcibly than her male cabaret colleague. In addition to Endrikat's sailor ballad, "Backbord und Steuerbord," she sang Curt Bry's *Chanson,* "Die Welt ist klein geworden" ["The World Has Become Small"]:

> We are zooming over there on 1000 horsepower and cannot help doing so
> We sit inside the Tower of Babel and can only hate ourselves for it.
> We've created electric light, and yet cannot see ourselves.
> We've invented Esperanto and will never understand ourselves.
> The world has become vast, so horribly vast. And all our hopes
> are dreams. You became clever and have become ready to be but chaff
> on this earth.[15]

In November 1936, Gerson returned to Germany again to partake in a cabaret evening of the Jüdischer Kulturbund. She sang Mehring, Bry, Eliaschoff, and recited "Lottchens Beichte" ["Confessions"] by Tucholsky. Then she returned to Amsterdam, where she resumed her career in performing Nelson-revues at emigré cabarets. Five years later she died at Auschwitz, an early victim of the pogrom for which her ex-husband, Veit Harlan, had helped pave the way with his film *Jud Süß.*

Max Ehrlich also came to Berlin from Holland in the fall of 1935 to inaugurate his cabaret. Two years later he traveled to the United States, performed his best numbers for a theater agent, and, disappointed (the American was unimpressed), boarded the next ship for Hitler's Germany to resume his Kulturbund career.

Even Valeska Gert apparently could not live without her Berlin public. After a London performance in 1934, the temperamental grotesque dancer with a capacity for scandal, retracted her criticism to the British press on the situation of Jews in Germany. She suggested "misunderstandings," distanced herself from the interview, and hoped that "no objections will be made to my next appearance and my return." She would be "totally unhappy if I could not return to Germany," she wrote the Kulturbund from London. "The artist yearns to come home," Singer informed Hinkel.

Camilla Spira was much in demand for years as an actress and cabaret artiste. She won great acclaim as the blond innkeeper of the Rößl in the popular production by Charell. And on the occasion of the premiere of her film, *Morgenrot,* she received a laurel wreath, "To the Personification of the German Woman — UFA" — in the presence of those in power, Göring, Goebbels, and company. Nonetheless, like many of her colleagues, Spira saw herself — a half-Jew — become the victim overnight of a complete ban on all professional appearances. In September 1934, she made her cabaret debut at the Kulturbund in a program called *Freuden der Sommerreise* [*Joys of the Summer Journey*], dedicated to "those who stayed at home and those who have returned." The *Jüdische Gemeindeblatt* noted about Spira's performance: "light at heart and of hair . . . light in voice and mood — most effective, of course, was the song which could have been written about her: 'Mein Liebling ist so blond.'"

Willy Prager hosted the evening; Prager, an old master of the cabaret, had already enthralled listeners during Imperial Germany in Rudolf Nelson's Chat Noir. Even though "the audience laughed so that the rows of benches shook," the *C.V.-Zeitung* was concerned that the cabaret stars lacked the deep solemnity appropriate for the new situation: "Revealed here is the actual, even tragic difficulty of people who lack the profound Jewish security." The same might be said of the audience "that is obviously inspired by the dusty old jokes and art forms of a lost world." The reason for such harsh criticism was the fact that the program included "not only very old jokes, but some tasteless ones about Tel Aviv." Also, the "only thing Jewish" about a scene entitled "Simchat Torah at home": the "two silver candlesticks and the hand movements of Nelly Hirth." Moreover, a picture was drawn of "an unpleasant family, using very un-Jewish jokes, whose age cannot even be written with two-figure numbers."

Critic Margarete Edelheim called cabaret sketches like "Karriere" ["Career"] and "Ein Besuch im Kulturbund" ["A Visit to the Kulturbund"] an "embarrassing mistake"; it was incomprehensible "how even one Jewish hand could applaud." No indeed, it was concluded: Such portrayals were "neither Jewish nor German—not even culture or art."

Even those who applauded Willy Rosen, now an internationally renowned entertainer of the Kabarett der Komiker, at the Kulturbund's first cabaret evening were criticized. Neither were Rosen's talented new hits updated, nor did he modify his standard audience address, "Text and music from me!" In fact the numbers represented yesterday, because they "could have been sung in 1911 as well as in 1932—but in 1934? The audience, however, rejoiced and was happy."

The *C.V.-Zeitung* was not alone in reprimanding its audience or in challenging the Kulturbund repeatedly to turn from the "path that led into a thicket, not a free atmosphere." Indeed, the Kulturbund must "not react to the audience: It must educate it." The *Jüdische Liberale Zeitung* also responded vehemently against the aims and tastes of Willy Rosen's October 1934 performance. The cabaret star's finale especially "drew the audience into a 'strudel' of his powerful Berlin expressions."

The newspaper commented further on the presentation's lively mood. "In all understanding for the social needs of the actors, it must be said that the Kulturbund also has to fulfill tasks it established with the choice of its name." What could be meant by this could also be read in The *C.V.-Zeitung:* The Kulturbund must not be satisfied with "this kind of intimate theater; in spite of the great laughter-filled success" it must create "true cabaret evenings, so that one may at least sense that one is in a league of 'culture,' and not in one of the former theaters on the Kurfürstendamm."

Such objections all but disappeared when the much-criticized Kurfürstencabaret prominence actually did move into the Kommandantenstraße with Max Ehrlich as its director. In October 1935, Ehrlich—once the star of the world-renowned KadeKo—formed his own institution at Café Léon on the Kurfürstendamm, the "cabaret theater of the *Jüdischer Kulturbund e.V.*" The *Jüdische Allgemeine Zeitung* did comment on the occasion of the premiere: "Jewish cabaret—today: two words which do not connect well. Cabaret gains its true legitimization from reality. Jewish reality is sorrow, need, concern—appearances that in the cabaret's colored footlights would hardly make a good impression." In the end, however, the reviewer was also convinced by the concept Ehrlich had described in his opening address (grabbing the bull by the horns, so to speak). Among the many congratulations he had received since the cabaret's debut, one sentence was especially noteworthy. Someone had written him: "Be really funny. We've enough *tsoris* at home." This, said director Ehrlich, should be the motto of his cabaret.

His success proved him right. The press championed his "choral and creative art" evident both "scenically and musically in the polished, successful performance." The press also legitimized the needs of the enthusiastic audience "to allow themselves to be transported for a few hours from the darkened existence into the illusion of unburdened brightness." And indeed, the experienced professional, Max Ehrlich—well-versed in staging techniques—had arranged his show with a rapid succession of only those numbers whose success had been proven. And so with confident grandeur, the clever director offered his audience—so keen on distraction—a program unlike ones by his predecessors: a bouquet of joyous cabaret fun. "Mr. Honest will last the longest!" [16] called the *Jüdische Allgemeine Zeitung* to the man who for three years would give the light muse a lasting home during hard times.

His formula for cabaret was as simple as his tested entrance numbers and their capable scenic preparations. In front of [Heinz] Condell's fairly opulent, painted backdrops, Ehrlich always introduced scenes and sketches with the standard flourish "Just take a look at this!" The numbers ranged from "Gespielte Witze" to a new version of Wilhelm Bendow's skit, "Auf der Rennbahn" ["On the Racetrack"], to happy *Chansons* that reminisced about the good old days. And Ehrlich moderated brilliantly as a mimic in his "Parade" number, a parody of prominent artists, memorializing such recording stars as Richard Tauber, Marlene Dietrich, Al Jolson, and Fjodor Schaliapin.

Ehrlich brought his experienced cabaret colleague, Willy Rosen, back to Berlin for the second program. He staged one musical revue after another with Rosen on the Kulturbund cabaret stage: *Kunterbunt* [*Topsy-turvy,* December 1935]; *Herr Direktor—bitte Vorschuß!* [*Advance Payment, Please, Mr. Director!,* February 1936]; *Bitte Einsteigen!* [*All Aboard!,* March 1937]; *Gemischtes Kompott* [*Fruit Cocktail,* October 1938]. Rosen wrote the new musical numbers. Ehrlich arranged them scenically, added comic skits, and sketched in jokes; drawing on the rich repertory of cabaret, he dusted off old numbers that still made people laugh. Director Ehrlich himself embodied his own best stage actor—character actor, comedian, and emcee all in one person. He also proved capable of forming a talented cabaret ensemble. Ehrlich and Rosen were an unbeatable team that promised success. Willy Rosen had an unfailing recipe for their success: "One takes a thin comedian and a fat comic; one adds a few pounds of sex appeal; one adds a few comprehensible melodies which the audience can sing after the show; one adds a few old jokes from which you 'cut off the beards'; one takes a lot of new jokes, some ornaments; red, green, and blue light. Blend all of the ingredients well and the revue is done!" A series of successes emerged at the Jüdische Kulturbund. The Café Léon soon became too small for the throng of cabaret-goers; and the cabaret had to move to a larger hall.

Willy Rosen, a stage interpreter in Berlin until the fall of 1936, delivered his catchy melodies to Ehrlich's cabaret up until that time and later from Holland. The *Israelitisches Familienblatt* praised his *Chansons* in April 1937 as ones "which were immediately sung by the entire audience" from "Mandoline, kleine Mandoline," "Wenn du denkst, ich liebe dich" ["If You Think I Love You"], "Wolln wir heute abend mal ins Kino gehn" ["Shall We Go to the Movies Tonight"], to the "Postkutsche" ["The Stage-Coach"] number where Ehrlich (October 1938), dressed in nineteenth-century postillion, sang: "Slowly, slowly, always goodnaturedly, we're not in a hurry and we've plenty of time."[17] He sang it again in December after the notorious pogroms of *Kristallnacht* had raged. Five years later this song by the Ehrlich–Rosen team took on a frightening reality—before the camp wardens on the concentration camp stage of Westerbork.

Max Ehrlich, or the "Tausendsassa" ["devil of a fellow"—the affectionate name the press gave him], was inexhaustible. When a new program went well, he sought and found new tasks. He directed for the Kulturbund stage, acted in Shakespeare, Courteline, and Molnár, and hosted film premieres. And he was at home in "Fruit Cocktail." He brought two unmistakable boulevard hits to his cabaret stage: *Warum lügst du, Cherie?* [*Why Are You Lying, Darling?*—Hans Lengsfelder/Siegfried Tisch] and *Essig und Öl* [*Vinegar and Oil*—Siegfried Geyer/Paul Frank]. He had tested his effectiveness in front of audiences with *Vinegar and Oil* during the time of Max Reinhardt. In the "modern fairy-tale," Max Ehrlich played a fruit vendor who decides not to hang himself because he sells a girl the rope he had planned to put around his neck.

A metaphor? The allusions to the time in which Ehrlich learned to create good spirits are vague. Even the travel-revue, *All Aboard!* (March 1937) for which the director decorated both the auditorium and the stage as a train station, although signaling a major farewell, did not overstate the parallels to the times. Arthur Elösser commented in the *Jüdische Rundschau:* "We know that we'll have a good ride with Max Ehrlich. Among 23 stations there are surely several which aren't worth a stop; but with this conductor, derailments into platitudes are not to be feared. The journey with Ehrlich does not go far; it's a trip to familiar places like Leipzig, Finsterwalde, and especially Kalau:[18] Instead, the trip succeeds for a few hours in harmoniously relieving our cares."

When Ehrlich finally boarded the train for Amsterdam in the spring of 1939, leaving Berlin for good, the Jewish press devoted moving addresses to him.

Vinegar and Oil, cabaret sketch at the Kulturbund, Berlin — Max Ehrlich and Camilla Spira featured, 1937. Photo courtesy Akademie der Künste, Berlin

Julius Bab spoke of the "master of the art of masking," of his cabaret "works of art," and of the stage actor who "placed in the service of creative imagination his ability to develop characters."[19] Ehrlich's farewell show, the *Revue der Revuen*, had many repeat performances. The farewell revue of the star—already announced by the press as Max Israel Ehrlich—with the "seventeen most beautiful scenes from eight revues" played on 2 April for the very last time. The cabaret theater died on that day.

It would be revived not long after in the concentration camp, Westerbork—that "waiting hall of death." More than one hundred thousand Jews were rounded up there, among them the prominent cabarettists of Berlin and Vienna. These stars had fled Hitler after 1933 and gone to neighboring Holland: the masters of ceremonies Josef Baar and Franz Engel; the comedians Otto Wallburg and Hermann Feiner; the cabaret stars Chaja Goldstein and Alice Dorell; dancers and musicians like Otto Aurich and Erich Ziegler and the onetime stars of the legendary Nelson-revues Kurt Gerron and Camilla Spira. And finally, Ehrlich and Rosen.

The camp commandant at Westerbork, SS-Obersturmführer Gemmeker, was a friend of the light muse known as cabaret. He had a stage erected in the registration barracks, a building from where those consecrated to death were sent to Auschwitz and Sobibor. The stage boards stemmed from a demolished synagogue from a town in the nearby county. Instruments were carted in; expensive curtain material was requested from Amsterdam; and costumes were "put in safekeeping" in exclusive fashion houses.

The revues that Max Ehrlich and Willy Rosen brought to their "Camp Westerbork stage" from 1943 on, *Humor und Melody, Bravo! Da Capo!*, or *Total Verrückt!* [*Totally Crazy!*], gave the cheerless camp on the heath near the German-Dutch border the reputation of being the "stronghold of European cabaret." The programs contained songs from operettas, popular hits, moody skits and silly sketches, ballet numbers, and jokes. A reunion took place with familiar material that was no longer fresh even on Berlin's cabaret stage or Rosen's Dutch boards. And in the first row surrounded by his team of guards sat the commandant in a large armchair.

"The people laughed and clapped. It was as if we were in Berlin on the Kurfürstendamm," remembers Camilla Spira, who at Westerbork sang her successful songs from the Weißen Rößl [White Horse Inn]. "We were suddenly somewhere else. One can hardly imagine that. The people down in the audience forgot everything during those two hours."

They always performed when the transports headed for the extermination camps—cabaret as a mood drug to quiet the candidates for death. "My God,"

Program from Max Ehrlich and Willy Rosen cabaret revue, *Curtain Up,* Beuthen-Oberschlesien (Silesia) Kulturbund, 1938. Courtesy Akademie der Künste

wrote Etty Hillesum in her diary: "The room was full to a bursting point and one laughed tears, yes tears!" Philip Mechanicus noted shortly before his deportation: "We're all sitting here up to our necks in filth, but in spite of that, one chirrups. Psychological riddle. Operetta music at the opened grave . . . Amid jokes, they blow to death." [20]

Whoever appeared on Ehrlich's concentration camp stage saw a chance for survival. Willy Rosen, according to fellow inmates, for example, auditioned his songs for the SS-commandant: "He sang for his life, sang his lungs out of his chest." In fact, he even wrote new songs for the camp's stage: "If one is unlucky, then life has no meaning; if one is unlucky, then one slips and falls down. That's why I beg you, Fortune, to be true to me." [21]

Luck failed to appear. In the beginning of August 1944, it was time. Commandant Gemmeker dissolved the camp and sent his cabarettists on a transport; the "special trains" rolled by Theresienstadt to Auschwitz. Scarcely one of those who saw to the mood and good spirits of Westerbork escaped the gas chamber. Rosen and Ehrlich died in October 1944. A few lines written by Willy Rosen at his brief stop in Theresienstadt have been passed down:

> There's always someone somewhere whom one laughs about.
> There's always someone somewhere who makes the jokes.
> Someone is intended to play the fool.
> It lasts one's whole life and begins in school.
> Someone must wander through life — the eternal clown.
> Ach, people like to laugh, especially at the cost of another.
> There's always someone somewhere whom one laughs about.
> There's always someone somewhere who will play the POJAZ.[22]

DOCUMENTS AND MEMOIRS

Interview with Mascha Benya-Matz

REBECCA ROVIT

Mascha Benyakonsky (Benya-Matz) was an opera singer with the Kulturbund ensemble in Berlin from the spring of 1937 to October 1938. Benya-Matz describes Berlin in the early 1930s as an exciting place, particularly for a young vocal student at the Stern Conservatory of Music. She had no formal theater training until she became a lead soprano for the Kulturbund ensemble. When concert halls were unavailable to Jewish artists, she also sang at house concerts in private homes and synagogues. And she sang for Berlin's Zionist organization, singing Yiddish and Hebrew. She emigrated to the United States in December 1938.

Benya-Matz and the well-known musicologist, Dr. Anneliese Landau, traveled to a number of cities in the United States during World War II for the Red Cross, singing music by Jewish composers that was forbidden in Germany. After finding out what had happened to the Jews in Europe, Benya-Matz felt it was her "mission" to continue Jewish culture—after "the destruction." "If not me, then who?" she has said. In America, she sang for such Yiddish-speaking organizations as the Labor Union of Israel, as well as for English-speaking organizations like Hadassah, Pioneer Women, and Mizrachi Women. She had her own radio program in New York for three years. And she frequently sang for the Workman's Circle groups and radio programs. She has made many recordings of her music. After she retired from professional singing, she became a teacher of Hebrew, Yiddish art, and folk song. She taught until her retirement in 1995 at the Hebrew Arts School of the Elaine Kaufman Cultural Center for Music and Dance.

She is still active as a vocal coach, even over the telephone as cantors and singers from across the country call for her guidance in interpreting Hebrew and Yiddish song. She has obviously influenced many young students with her talents as evident on the day when I met her at her home in Queens. A student cantor interrupted our interview on 9 November 1996 to bring her homemade rugelah as they chatted

This interview has been adapted from conversations on 9 November 1995 (New York) and 15 July 1997 (telephone) and correspondence from the fall of 1995 to October 1998.

about a lesson she had previously given him. But perhaps her own most formative influences came from her parents.

MY FATHER was a Zionist, a "Musernik."[1] My mother was quite educated. At home, she instilled spiritual values in me. I was born in Lithuania—in Virbalis. At home we spoke Yiddish. We also spoke Lithuanian in general, and Russian. I spoke Hebrew at school. All subjects were taught in modern Hebrew. We had German in school, as well as a little English. Virbalis was 4 kilometers to the German, Prussian border. There in the East German town, Eydtkuhnen, I had a singing teacher who was a German Jew. I had a pretty voice, took piano lessons; I practiced in the saloon next door to my house, because we didn't have a piano at home.

My teacher advised me to go to the Berlin conservatory to study music. An uncle of mine in the United States sent me $100. That was a lot of money at that time. And I went to Berlin in about 1931. In 1933, when Hitler came to power, German Jews started emigrating to Palestine. I had a chance to teach Hebrew. Many Jews wanted to learn Hebrew. Young people. Old people. I taught the president of the Zionist organization and the wife of the editor of the *Jüdische Rundschau*.[2] I had lots of food. My mother used to send me food packages from Lithuania by people passing Berlin on the way to Palestine—that's what Israel was called then.

There were many artists in Berlin. I was great friends with Mascha Kaléko, the poet whose books were burned by Goebbels.[3] We called her the "Große Mascha" and I was the "Kleine Mascha." I'd never met people like that before. Maybe I didn't have any brains—personally I felt wonderful. We were young. In Berlin, Jews would sit in outdoor cafés in the afternoons and at night where non-Jews were, get beaten up and yet, go out again the next day. No one knew how long the Nazi dictatorship would last. But really, they believed it wouldn't [last].

I sang for presentations with Dr. Anneliese Landau on classical music tours before I became part of Kulturbund.[4] It was my friend, Mascha Kaléko, who first recommended me to the Kulturbund. But when I spoke to a clerk at the Kulturbund office about my Yiddish repertoire, the casting agent at the Kulturbund, said, "No one could possibly understand it; who needs that stuff?" That was in about 1935 or 1936, my first attempt. Then a friend, Chemjo Vinaver— a choral conductor—suggested that I try the Kulturbund again. He was a Pole, from a Hassidic family, a "typical Ostjude."[5] I auditioned in the spring of 1937 to fill the place of a soprano who was emigrating and sang two arias—one in

French. I was engaged almost on the spot. The next day, they called me to offer me the role of Norina in Donizetti's *Don Pasquale*. After that, I sang Neméa in *Si J'étais Roi* [*If I were King . . .*] by Adolphe Adam, and my last role before leaving Germany—Gilda in Verdi's *Rigoletto,* in October 1938.[6] All were sung in German! When I was engaged to sing, as a foreigner, I needed a special permit to work. The irony was, that just because of my Yiddish and Hebrew repertoire I was given that permit especially willingly. I was, so to speak, a persona grata to the Nazis.

The Nazis wanted to "impose" Jewish culture upon German Jews, who in general looked down on the Ostjude and his culture. Dr. Singer, the director, was an assimilated Jew. It was so tragic. He was betrayed as he believed that the Nazis would spare him because he was so German. All the German Jews were betrayed, because they felt they were more German than Jewish. They called themselves Germans of Jewish descent. Many of them committed suicide because of this. The assimilated German Jews felt superior to the Ostjude. Only the Zionist groups in Berlin really tolerated Yiddish art. Because many of them were Ostjuden. But there were also German-Jewish Zionists. They loved Yiddish and Hebrew of course too. There was the Berlin Zionist organization (BZV). I toured to Leipzig where I was in a music program. I also traveled with Anneliese Landau in the Rheinland, in the Ruhr Valley to perform at other Kulturbund branches in those cities.

There wasn't much Yiddish performed. In the beginning, they [Nazis] allowed the Kulturbund to perform German writers . . . later, the Kulturbund couldn't perform German authors or composers so they [artists] had to resort to translations or to originals. The Kulturbund put on Sholom Aleichem stories, *The Golem* by Leivick [1937]. There were many other shows by Hungarian Jews—Molnár, Kalmán, the Russian Jew, Dymov, who lived in America —*Bronx Express.* . . . and then they played operettas by Offenbach. Italians were also allowed, you see—Verdi's *Masked Ball.* . . . In September 1938, Vinaver conducted an original opera by Jacob Weinberg for the Kulturbund, a concert called *He Chalutz* [*The Pioneers*]. The concert was in German except that I sang the aria from "Song of Songs" in Hebrew with the orchestra. The concert took place in a temple.

I was asked to sing a Yiddish folk song at the Kulturbund house costume ball in [the spring of] 1938. There I was made up as a poor girl with an organ as an organ grinder. I learned it from Vinaver after he had visited Warsaw and came back and he sang it for me. I learned a lot from him, especially how to appreciate and interpret Hassidic music. [For my benefit, Benya-Matz mimes grinding an organ as she demonstrates and sings the one Yiddish role she played at the

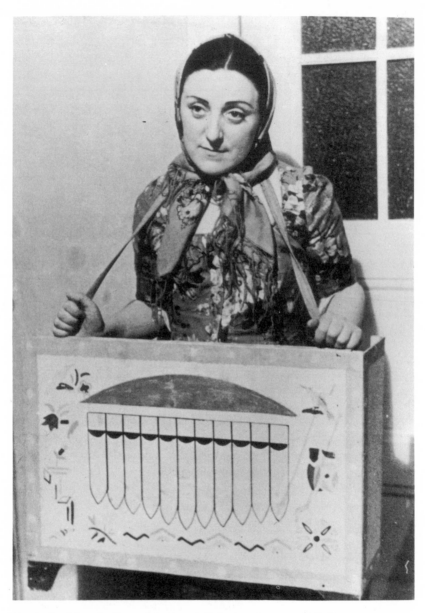

Mascha Benjakonsky (Benya-Matz), 1938, Kulturbund costume ball. Courtesy
Akademie der Künste, Berlin

Kulturbund. When I ask her to tell me more about her life in Hitler's Germany, Benya-Matz suggests the normality of her life in spite of the dictatorship.]

In those days I was probably stupid. When La Scala di Milano came to perform *Tosca*, I went to hear Gigli sing at the Städtische Oper [the City Opera] and Hitler was in the audience. On another occasion, I stood in line for tickets to hear Gigli and met a Jewish fellow buying tickets who would go every night to the opera.[7] Music students could buy tickets to sit on the stage. I looked out in the front row and facing me was Goebbels. I must have been a *meshugganah*.

I went to the Städtische Oper to see *La Bohème* on the evening of the day that the Germans reclaimed part of France.[8] The *Intendant* [managing director] came out on the stage. The audience was joyous and everyone stood up. He raised his arm in the *Heil Hitler* salute as did the entire audience. I stood up, but I didn't raise my arm. I looked around and noticed another man standing, who didn't raise his arm. We looked at one another with frightened eyes as if we were almost supporting each other. There were other Jews at the opera.

I can also remember walking on the Kurfürstendamm in early 1933 with a friend—a student from Palestine. We were speaking Hebrew and joking around. Suddenly, we were stopped by some "Brown Shirts" who thought we were speaking Russian. They accused us of calling "Heil Moscow," which was the communist greeting. This was one of the early *Einzelaktionen*.[9] We insisted that they take us to the police station, because the police were not so Nazified yet. So we went to the station on the Joachimthalerstraße. The Brown Shirts insisted that we were Communists. The police asked for our passports. I had an ID card from the music conservatory and a Lithuanian passport. My friend was from Palestine and had a British passport. So they let him go. But they kept me in order to be taken to the Central Police Station, which was frightening. You know, in those days that was Alexanderplatz, where people went but didn't come out. I had asked the man to get in touch with my Lithuanian friend, a librarian at the Lithuanian consulate. After everybody left, the policeman asked me, "What has really happened?" I told the truth—that we were joking around in Hebrew. And the policeman called the precinct where I lived and was told that I was registered as a music student. "Go home," he told me. As I was leaving, my librarian friend arrived in a taxi.

It is hard to understand why the Nazis allowed the Kulturbund to go on. Why? . . . Many people thought, including Vinaver, that the Kulturbund was doomed from the beginning.[10] But it was a good thing while it lasted. The Kulturbund was a godsend for artists who lost their work. Also for the German Jews who were afraid they were not welcome. The Kulturbund was also doomed. The Nazis wanted to show the world how good they were to the Jews.

In the prayer book on Rosh Hashanah and Yom Kippur, it is already decided who will live and who will die. They go to *shul*[11] to pray that the decision will be postponed. Some of the people who go to *shul* are already doomed, but don't know it. And they go home to eat. A people doomed but they go home to eat Zimmes and Kugel.[12] That's why the German Jews who went to the Kulturbund were singing, enjoying themselves, but they were doomed.

I have left out a very important fact, and that is that I lost my entire family, as well as all my friends, and all the people I knew as I was growing up. For years I was being tortured by feelings of guilt. What did I do to deserve being saved? Those very feelings had a lot to do with my decision to dedicate myself to Jewish music almost exclusively.

Interview with Kurt Michaelis

REBECCA ROVIT

Kurt Michaelis—German-born—joined the Kulturbund Berlin orchestra in 1937 as an English horn and oboe player. Michaelis emigrated to the United States in the summer of 1941 via a banana boat. Emigrating from Hitler's Germany was "not by choice, but if and when one could get an immigration visa after a long waiting time," he wrote me. Michaelis gave up playing the oboe in 1945. "You can't play alone—it's not like playing in a string quartet," he has said. His oboe is on permanent loan at the U.S. Holocaust Memorial Museum in Washington, D.C.

In the 1940s, he toured with the Ballets Russes de Monte Carlo for two seasons, where he played a forty-week season; played one concert of the "now defunct" New York Symphony under Bernstein, worked for G. Schirmer's, and then became Senior Manager of Orchestra Performances at C. F. Peters Corporation Music Publishing from 1947 to this day. He has translated biographies into German on Donizetti, Rossini, Bellini, and Tchaikovsky; also many texts from and into German.

Michaelis sees himself as an American patriot, "more so than other Americans," he acknowledged.

I STARTED as second oboist with the Kulturbund, since my mother was a friend of Dr. Kurt Singer since the days when they lived in Oppeln [Upper Silesia, then part of Germany]. You probably know enough about Kurt Singer who was an idealist (originally a neurologist and amateur musician), led the Doctors' Orchestra, then a choral group, thought up the idea of the Kulturbund and hoped that it would save some Jewish musicians and survive the Nazis! Before that, he was *Intendant* [general manager] of the Städtische Oper, and our family often got box seats for opera performances there.

This interview has been compiled from an interview on 12 August 1996, New York, and correspondence from the fall of 1995 to October 1998.

I started in 1937; later on when Mr. Bremer, the first oboist, left I played first oboe plus English horn, since the young second oboist did not have that instrument for doubling. The conductor, Rudolf Schwarz . . . made something out of us fifty musicians of no great distinction that we could be proud of. By the way, Kurt Singer of course got me the job in 1937 which was not too difficult, since naturally there was not a situation like today here when hundreds of applicants turn up for any orchestra opening, with hardly any chances to get the job. Still, it was the beginning of my lifelong career in music, and I have always been grateful, being able to do something with my life that I want to do and know best.

I trained privately, the only and actually hidden way to do so: with three excellent teachers who were all first oboists at the State Opera Unter den Linden, the Municipal Opera [Städtisches Oper], . . . and the Berlin Radio Symphony Orchestra. They were, of course, state employees and therefore members of the Party, at least the second and the third one. But while they had courage enough to help me, nothing fortunately happened to them. Except in my beginnings, we were no longer allowed to play non-Jewish German music and after the *Anschluß*, also Austrian. My first concert had the Dvořák Cello Concerto with Leo Rostal, the brother of the famous violinist Max Rostal, plus the Mozart Symphony No. 41 (Jupiter). But we [at Kulturbund] had fine programs, some operas, also chamber music concerts and recitals; the high points were the Mahler Symphonies No. 1 and then, repeated several times, the — because of the circumstances, most moving — No. 2, a miracle with such a small group [February 1941]. I never saw any Gestapo censors at orchestra rehearsals, but I understood that at every performance there was someone present.

Others have asked about how one could make music under the Nazis in the cramped circumstances at the theater in the Kommandantenstraße that served as our music center. This question only comes up in retrospect; we did not know what would happen, and being real musicians, we concentrated even when the theater was closed temporarily after the Paris murder of a German consular (?) officer [this reference is to the assassination of Grünspan and the beginning of Kristallnacht, 8 November 1938]. We just went on; I do recall spending once a night away from home when the Nazis called in the dark removing people. No one can understand what it was to play in an orchestra as if it were normal. It was a crazy time. I spent much of that time copying parts of an oboe repertory from Eulenberg miniature scores into parts which I extracted to be able to play from them, as I did with my colleagues in chamber music sessions at home (Mozart Divertimenti and Serenades; wind quintets; orchestra studies from the full repertory). Also there was a time much later when I received a summons from the labor office to appear for reporting for some menial work [with the beginning of World War II, all men under sixty-five were summoned to labor detail] (or being sent away?). Fortunately, I had a letter from Hinkel protecting me from that call which I presented just as the official thought to have finished with me — he was furious, and I was frightened and relieved.

I probably told you before that somehow there was just no choice; life went on from day to day; I had to prepare reeds for my oboe, a job which for any oboist takes up much time and distracts from other, even life-threatening worries.

Over the years I have learned that things in life develop much simpler than commentators, critics, *post festum* opinion-pronouncers, especially if they were not yet born or present on the occasions which they are discussing try to impress others with. Richard Strauss has been condemned for keeping music alive [during the Third Reich]. I don't like those sitting in armchairs and making pronouncements about the past. Tearing down, for instance, musicians and other artists who stayed in Germany during the Hitler years for various reasons: They are often condemned by unqualified people removed by several generations from that period ([Wilhelm] Furtwängler and [Herbert von] Karajan are just two examples). . . . Same with making pronouncements on recordings of music and not the real performance. The same does apply to much that is said about the existence of the Kulturbund. Without the cooperation between Kurt Singer and Hinkel, the Kulturbund couldn't have worked. "Nurturing his relationship with Hinkel" was a necessity. To keep your job, you have to find a way.

Kurt Singer. To get back to him once more, I cannot totally judge whether he "embraced his Jewishness"; I know that his family did, and I have no reason to doubt that he felt as Jewish as others, me included. Feeling German . . . was in all of us, having lived as Germans for many generations. You cannot say that it "sealed his fate"; he like so many others, my parents included, who met him in Theresienstadt again — and who . . . were among the 1,200 who were saved, by being transported to Switzerland [February 1945] — were subject to the same fate. He surely did not go to Theresienstadt voluntarily. Taking part there in the *Freizeitgestaltung* was one of those illusions created by the Nazis for the Red Cross visits and must have been either forced upon him or taken up like other artistic (futile) efforts.

You can't look into the future. We didn't know about concentration camps, but we knew about forced labor camps. Even if I barely remember, it's difficult even for me to understand how we could go through daily life with a middle name that wasn't our own.[1] We went on as if it was normal.

Recommendation for Kurt Michaelis, 1940. Akademie der Künste, Berlin: "Herr Kurt Israel Michaelis is the first oboist in the Jewish Kulturbund orchestra. His sounding and technical abilities are first-rate and will satisfy all the demands of opera and concert literature. What especially distinguishes him as a wind player is his great musicality and artistic sensibility. His phrasing is flawless and his playing in the best musical sense distinctive. His sense of responsibility and his conscientiousness make him one of the most valuable pillars of our orchestra." Photo/facsimile courtesy Akademie der Künste, Berlin

How can you explain the strangeness—you just go on living. If someone hits you, you get up again. And music is a different world—to a certain point.

Art here [the United States] is not important. These days music is boring. The good music is played over and over again. These are difficult times—then and now. Who knows about art? In Germany in the old days, music was taught in the school orchestra. It was customary to have a subscription to operas. Even the Kulturbund was in the same spirit. Singer's task was the need to keep musicians busy as long as it took to get out. To give people who lived under these threatening circumstances something to hold onto. It was a simple, decrepit house—the theater at Kommandantenstraße, fifty men. . . . [But] the spirit was there.

Correspondence, Julius Bab and Fritz Wisten

Before Hitler came to power, Julius Bab had established himself as a writer and lecturer of dramatic criticism and cultural history. In 1933, Bab became the Kulturbund's primary dramaturg and literary critic and, along with Dr. Kurt Singer, established the Kulturbund and hired its acting ensemble. Bab also headed the Kulturbund's lecture series. Bab received a visa to go to France in 1939 and later that year emigrated to the United States, where he continued to write. He is known for his book, The Death and Life of German Judaism *(German translation, Berlin 1988).*

Fritz Wisten was one of the ensemble's first actors (from the Stuttgart Theater), who became one of the theater's main stage directors. He succeeded Singer and became the Kulturbund's managing director in Berlin from 1939 to 1941, when the cultural organization was dissolved. During World War II, Wisten went into hiding and emerged after the war as a major director of East Berlin's Theater am Schiffbauerdamm (the theater Brecht eventually transformed into his Berliner Ensemble). Wisten died in 1961, before the Berlin wall was erected.

* * *

17 May 1933

Highly esteemed Herr Bab!

I heard from Emmy Remelt of your intention to found a Jewish theater in Berlin. I may understand in this, no doubt, your desire to bring together the now-unused Jewish workforce within the framework of a German-speaking enterprise.

Indeed, I need not stress that I will gladly make myself available for such a thing—a stage under your direction or at least under your patronage.

You know me both artistically and personally. The prospect of measuring my abilities against my Berlin colleagues is tempting enough.

From the archives of the Jewish Kulturbund, Akademie der Künste, Berlin. Fritz-Wisten Archives (FWA) 74/86/995; FWA 74/86/1002, FWA 74/86/1021.

I am skeptical only about the question of whether such an undertaking will be authorized, given the momentary attitude of the authorities.

I feel it is extremely comforting, that you, most esteemed Herr Bab, in the difficult situation in which you find yourself—as Emmy writes—still think of me. I can assure you that we thought often of you in recent times and that I would have liked to write to you, had not the manner in which I was dismissed sapped all of my emotional energies.

In order to counter the humiliations of the last weeks with something positive, I traveled here with my wife to the Riviera. Do not think of me as conceited when you read the postmark of Alassie. I will be back in a few days and would be pleased to find further information from you in Stuttgart. Until then, my very fond regards to you and your family,

Your
Fritz Wisten

* * *

7 July 1933

Dear Mr. Wisten!

Here comes the big news: After long and rather repugnant negotiations, the government made its decision yesterday: As a pure Jewish theater, we will *not only be tolerated, but even protected*. So begins our organizational and publicity work with the strongest tempo. Now without this most difficult obstacle, our theater is at least 90 percent secure. And you can consider yourself a member of this theater today with the same certainty.

We will not be able to make contracts, however, until the first half of August. And now at last to name a figure once more: You will, according to the estimation that I bring you—certainly receive the highest salary possible within our permanent Ensemble under the *very limited* possibilities for revenue of our association. But this ceiling will hardly reach M 6,000 per year and will certainly not exceed this [amount].

Write me a word or two, whether I may count on you. And accept my greetings to you and your wife,

from Your JB

Dieser Ausweis berechtigt zur Mitwirkung bei jüdischen Veranstaltungen. Der Inhaber ist zur Betätigung zugelassen, ohne daß der Reichsverband für eine Beschäftigung garantiert.

B. J. K.

REICHSVERBAND DER JÜDISCHEN KULTURBÜNDE IN DEUTSCHLAND

Ausweiskarte

Nr. E 604

für das aktive Mitglied

Edith
Vorname

Eisenheimer
Zuname

Sängerin
Fachbezeichnung

Frankfurt /M
Wohnort

Friedberger Anlage 28
Straße

Januar 1938 — Dezember 1938

4.53.55,2

Ich bestätige durch meine nebenstehende Unterschrift, daß ich Jude im Sinne der Reichsgesetze bin, daß ich die Bedingungen des Reichsverbandes für meine Mitgliedschaft anerkenne und daß diese aus triftigem Grunde widerrufen werden kann.

Edith Eisenheimer
Unterschrift

* * *

24 October 1933

Dear Wisten,

I believe that the office already notified you that we will play *Nathan* again on the 30, 31, and 1st [of November] and that we expect you here on Monday morning for a line read-through.

These performances will take place in the "Berliner Theater." Where we will play *Figaro* after that, we still do not know; nor where we will continue to play. The situation is indescribably intricate and difficult. Besides which, the higher authorities have denied us permission for a performance of [Emil Cohn's] *God's Hunt* [*Die Jagd Gottes*]. And with that, all of the casting questions have been resolved. After long deliberations, we have now decided to perform Hebbel's *Judith* first. This is also not certain, but rather probable. So you must come forth as Daniel—which is after all a nice thing—even though it does not satisfy your not unfounded desire for prominence. I assure you, however, that we will all be concerned to give you the honest to goodness leading role in the third play.

Best wishes to your wife and children; enjoy pleasant days in Stuttgart; and let me know, when you are back in Berlin.

Many greetings,
Your, JB

FACING PAGE: Facsimile of Kulturbund identification card for cabaret actress and singer Edith Elmer (née Eisenheimer), Frankfurt, 1938. Courtesy Akademie der Künste, Berlin. The mandatory identity cards required both a photograph and signature of the member. The text reads, "This identification card entitles participation in Jewish performances. The owner is permitted to participate without a guarantee from the *Reichsverband* [Reich Association for Jewish Cultural Leagues] for employment." The German next to the singer's photograph translates to "I hereby confirm with my signature that I am a Jew according to the laws of the Reich; that I acknowledge the conditions of the Reich's organization [of Jews] for my membership; and that it may be revoked for valid reasons." Eisenheimer, who also appeared with the Berlin cabaret ensemble, emigrated to England shortly after the 1938 season with the Kulturbund branch known as Rhein-Ruhr.

"Protocols," Nazi Propaganda Ministry

Sometimes as many as six times a month from late 1939 to September 1941, Kultur-bund artistic director Fritz Wisten or another Kulturbund director was required to meet with Nazi representatives from the Ministry of Propaganda to discuss devel-opments within the Jewish cultural organization. The so-called Rücksprache, *which actually translates as "talk back," was more of a one-way discussion whereby Hans Hinkel's staff might make clear to Kulturbund officials what was to be permitted or changed within the Jewish organization and its various branches all over the Ger-man Reich. Hinkel's staff members were all members of the SS except for secretary Fräulein Ursula Framm. None of them had any prior training in cultural matters.*

* * *

14 December 1939

Present: Herr Kochanowski, Herr Wisten

1. The general question of performing plays is especially addressed in connection with the ban on *The Pastry Chef's Wife* [*Die Zuckerbäckerin*] [1] [Molnár]. A basic rejection of theater performances is not planned.

Herr Kochanowski gives me general directions to adhere to; in par-ticular, he indicates that plays with an "assimilatory character" must be rejected from the start. Their program rejects the assimilation of the nineteenth century, etc.

I cannot see any assimilatory aims in the *The Pastry Chef's Wife;* how-ever, I will see to it in future submissions that I check against such ten-dencies. My will is strong; my spirit is weak.

Due to the layoff of our dramaturgical adviser, Leo Hirsch, a detailed check according to the wishes of the authorities is no longer necessary.

I touch on the question of the next play by suggesting an "Oriental evening" with *Judith* by Ettinger (Act 3) and *The Language of the Birds*

[*Rücksprache im Reichministerium für Volksaufklärung und Propaganda, Abteilung Be K A.*] Protocols from meetings between Kulturbund representative and official from Propaganda Minis-try. From Akademie der Künste, Berlin. FWA 76/86/5001, 21, 23, 75, 102.

[*Die Sprache der Vögel*] by Adolf Paul.² Before I officially submit the play, I must personally give him [Herr K] the script for perusal.

2. Lectures remain forbidden on principle. Upon my suggestions, Herr Kochanowski replied that permission may possibly be granted for politically objection-free topics that interest Jews today—emigration problems, for example, etc. I should discuss this with him before any submissions.

3. Performances may be produced in Bremen, Essen, Hannover if we are sent to these cities and the communities there take over the production process.³

4. Herr Kochanowski is making inquiries into the request for authorization for Cologne and Frankfurt/am Main; also about the rejection of the children's performance (proposal # 3712) on 9 Oct.; and finally, about the film list submitted on 9 Dec.: *A Visit to Tilsit* [*Eine Reise nach Tilsit*], *A Woman like You* [*Eine Frau wie Du*].

5. A new application need not be issued to obtain performance permission for the cabaret event (submitted 12.8.39), starring Messrs. Menu, Berg, and Grünne. Notification to the Propaganda office will suffice.

[signed] Wisten

* * *

5 January 1940

Present: Herr Kochanowski, a lady (probably Fräulein Framm) [Hinkel secretary, Ursula Framm], Herr Wisten

1. Herr Kochanowski issues new guidelines for future programming, as well as for theater, cabaret, and music.

a. Requests to perform German composers (except for German Jews) may no longer be submitted. Händel also remains forbidden from now on. However, requests to perform such Czechs as Dvorák, Smetana, all Italians, Old French, and foreigners in general, will be accepted.

b. Before submitting requests in the area of cabaret, it is essential to prevent such sketches as those by [Willy] Prager and [Fritz] Tachauer, in which—as Herr K. expresses—one cannot distinguish whether they are tasteless or brazen. All lectures, texts like Prager, Willi Rosen, Tachauer, and others will no longer be authorized.

c. On principle, theater is allowed. There are no reservations about Shakespeare. All authors of German descent or those who belong to the Reich Theater Chamber are excluded from consideration.

d. The authorization number must be submitted for approved texts, and the texts must be submitted once again for examination.

e. We must examine the submissions for *Winterhilfe*[4] events in strict concordance with the new regulations.

2. The question of page proofs must be resolved with Herr Kreindler;[5] on the whole, Herr K. confirms the need for a timely inspection into proofreading.

3. Herr K. will make inquiries again into the authorizations for the branches Frankfurt/M and Cologne.

4. The film *Mother Love* is not to be put on the list.

* * *

31 July 1940

Present: Herr Kochanowski, Wisten

1. Herr Kochanowski expresses his satisfaction that our performances are so well attended. He regrets that he cannot come to the performance of *The Imaginary Invalid*[6] on Thursday, the 15th of August; he is very busy with business affairs.

2. I tried to expand our options for shaping future programs, specifically in regard to authors and composers.

Beyond the guiding rules established in January, he authorizes such composers as Liszt and Sibelius, so now we may also suggest Hungarian and Nordic composers for consideration. Along the same lines, Molnár is not principally forbidden as a submission. Further, I may suggest Wilde (*Bunburry*) in the future. He would not recommend Henry Bernstein.

For all of the authors and composers whom I suggest for consideration, I must personally present him with a short commentary justifying the requests, along with some biographical details on the authors in question.

3. I may present the *Chansons* which I have examined, as in the case of Arnstein;[7] I am still fully responsible for an initial check into the qualifications [of the performers].

4. He will search again for the files concerning permission to hire Pollack.[8]

5. I convey Assessor Brasch's[9] desire to go on holiday on 5 August, and his request for me to represent him during this time in the general directorship of the Kulturbund.

Herr Brasch should call Herr Owens, now back from holiday, at 1 o'clock this afternoon.

[signed] Wisten

* * *

3 January 1941

Present: Herr Kochanowski, Wisten

1. I report on the planned performances for the employees of the Jewish organizations and about the rejection that occurred in December during Herr Kochanowski's absence. My request to offer a free performance of a closed nature once a month as a Sunday morning performance is approved.

The proposal should be addressed personally to Herr Kochanowski. I suggest at once 1.19 [19 January] for the first Sunday performance.

2. The comedy, *Thirty Seconds of Love* [*Dreißig Sekunden Liebe*] [10] must remain at the chancellory due to Fräulein Framm's illness. Herr Kochanowski wants to make inquiries and will give me an answer as soon as possible.

After that, I spoke of the difficulty in choosing a play that must follow the not very successful *The Virtuous Knight of Fortune* [*Tugendhaften Glücksritter*].[11] I ask for permission to submit Wilde's *Bunburry*. At the same time, I stress that Wilde is Irish and belongs to a past epoch so removed from us that the English atmosphere should not be able to cause offense.[12]

3. I report further on the planned exhibition of the *Reichsvereinigung*[13] [*der Juden*] and on my joining the committee of this exhibition. Herr Kochanowski agrees to the establishment of a separate division devoted to the Kulturbund and a review of its achievements since September 1939. I must keep him apprised of the current state of the negotiations and submit a list with the planned objects for the exhibition.

4. The events for the *Winterhilfe* no longer need be separated for approval. However, I must take on the entire responsibility for the programming myself. Here too, I must provide him with a list of dates concerning the events.

5. The petition for relocating the film projectionist, Hochheimer, of Breslau unfortunately still exists only as a single copy. Today between 3 and 4 a messenger will tender a duplicate for authorization.

6. Herr Hinkel himself will examine the lists of proposals for up-coming films, of which the first was submitted on 11.23. Because Herr Hinkel is out of town at this time, the authorization will be delayed. I point out how this makes it difficult to schedule films for the coming weeks.

Kulturbund Dramaturg Dr. Leo Hirsch

Leo Hirsch was the Kulturbund's dramaturg after the departure of Herbert Frieden-thal (Freeden), 1939. Hirsch reworked foreign scripts for the Kulturbund stage, including plays by Priestley and his own translations from Yiddish into German. During the last years of the Kulturbund, Hirsch was partly responsible for justifying the repertory choices. The following rationale for the performance of a new comedy by a Berlin Jew, Gordon Rogoff, suggests some of the difficulties the theater had in selecting plays for performance (i.e. censorship, basic morale of audience, royalty fees, and basic Kulturbund aims to present new work for the stage).

The play by Rogoff, Bob Is Honored to Introduce Himself . . . , *features a young playwright named Bob Young who with a script in one hand and a revolver in the other forces a failing theater director to consider his play for performance. The play within the play concerns four poor students (one of whom is the bright young Bob) who create an "idea factory" to make money during bad economic times. The series of comic scams include selling an ink remover on crowded streets to people whom the students have already sullied with ink. Bob and his friends are successful as they sell "ideas" to those who cannot think clearly. And the young playwright is also success-ful as his play receives its due premiere.*

The world premiere of Rogoff's own play received only three performances during May 1940. In spite of a small onstage jazz band, a light comic mood, and an over-all optimistic spirit, the play did not appeal especially to Kulturbund audiences. The play was originally set in New York with plentiful references to America, the land of unlimited possibilities—and money. However, in spite of an obvious American-ization of the characters and the overall atmosphere, all direct references to America have been deleted from the original director's script. Such deleted references include a song in honor of "the most beautiful country in the world, America. . . ." While an American ambience still pervades the script, the characters have been somewhat universalized.

Rationale for the production of Gregor Rogoff's *Bob beehrt sich vorzustellen . . .* (*Bob Is Honored to Introduce Himself . . .*). From Akademie der Künste, Berlin, FWA 74/86/5102.

WE NEED NOT SPEAK of the weaknesses inherent in Rogoff's play, on the one hand, because of questions of taste, about which it is futile to speak; on the other hand, because we were aware of these weaknesses from the beginning. In other words: It was clear to us that we did not have a patented or polished classic before us, nor a sophisticated or tightly constructed box-office hit of scenic perfection like the French or Hungarian Boulevard-plays. We are dealing here with a facile play, albeit one less mechanical and stereotypical—replete with fresh dialogue and a life-affirming spirit. This youthful affirmation of life, a kind of "in spite of" optimism—something that we all could use—was vital to the play's acceptance and it also justified the performance.

Second, a decisive factor in choosing this play was that it is a comedy. Allowances had to be made for the many objections by the audience to staging dramas and tragedies (one already has "enough worries anyway"); the result has been that we may be reproached again by others that it is most improper of us to offer comedies at this time. But finally such objections counterbalance one another so that their influence on the continuation of our work is negligible; and so, in any case, a play with positive tendencies may most easily be accounted for . . . considering perhaps the paradoxical nature of other comedies, operas, and such which are ill-equipped for and inapplicable to our lives. . . .

Third, the acceptance of the play was further endorsed by the fact that the author belongs to our circles. It need not be mentioned that it is impossible for us to perform practically anything from the entire modern theater literature. And this goes for German, as well as foreign plays—of which even most of the Jewish ones are out of the question for political, thematic, or technical reasons (i.e., currency-related, royalty transfer reasons). If however the Kulturbund has any cultural duties to fulfill, then above all these tasks: to help young, aspiring, *Jewish* talents who live here to attain the only publicity that still exists for them. In order to fulfill such a task, one may and must take weaknessess into account; and he who is in this or that detail weak, an unknown of today will then perhaps become the Molnár of tomorrow—not least of all thanks to the first performance with us. Indeed, we elected to perform the controversial play because it is by a young—and, in our opinion, talented—Jewish author who lives here. It should also be mentioned in passing that herewith we may also fulfill a duty to social justice.

It is clear from all of this that this is an experiment. Like most experiments, experiments in theater are not to be judged afterwards whether they "succeeded" at once; what is more, all criteria are absent except for the dubious criterion of an audience success. It is unquestionably of greater significance that we are now experimenting to bring about a world premiere of a contemporary Berliner and Jewish author than this justified decision or that misjudgment.

("If a head and a book knock against one another and it sounds hollow, must it a l w a y s be the book?") *

---

* Ironic inference that some of the time the "head" is to blame for thinking the play's bad.

Letter from Actor Kurt Suessmann
to Martin Brandt

The following is a letter from one young Kulturbund actor, Kurt Suessmann, to his fellow actor and dear friend, Martin Brandt, who emigrated to the United States in April 1941. The text suggests the preoccupation with emigration (affidavits and passage) that consumed those still awaiting quota numbers or the opportunity to leave Germany. Suessmann never managed to leave Europe, even though his friend, Brandt, tried to help him. Suessmann perished in a camp.

Brandt continued his acting career in the United States, specifically Hollywood, where he played film roles of Nazi officers, for example. He returned to Germany in the 1960s to continue his career as an actor. He died there in 1989.

The letter has been rendered without paragraphs to duplicate the German original.

* * *

Berlin-Charlottenburg 5
Suarez str. 15

26.4.41 [26 April 1941]
p. 1 (p. 2, missing)

My dear Martin,

I received your card on 4/22 and your air mail letter from Lisbon on 4/25. Both were awaited with longing and therefore, all were pleased when the letters arrived. Naturally, I reported the contents to all — uncles and friends. Aunt Elisabeth with Heni, Uncle Jochen warmly returns your greetings; Frobenstr. will surely write you himself. Aunt Elisabeth was very pleased that Mrs. Page's help was useful to you. The telegram was superfluous, alas, as it was clear from your card of 4/22, that you have already left Lisbon. I hope that you arrived safely yesterday, and all — Emmerichs — and I thought very very much about you. Hopefully, both

From Akademie der Künste, Berlin, Martin Brandt Archives, SJK 1.56.66.

of you bore the sea journey well.[1] You write that you received 2 cards and a letter from us in Lisbon, but there were more: Did you receive the one with the photos? Dear Martin, it's more than touching that you already tried to help me even before leaving Europe. By all means, I will write tomorrow to the Europeia as you suggest.[2] But what has changed a lot, though, and what you will have undoubtedly learned by now is that Portugal is closed until further notice. It is believed that this blockade is but temporary and that thereafter, all will resume as it was. In any case, it still inhibits one terribly. It is supposed that the reason for the block is a rampant epidemic in Spain, but one can't know for sure.[3] The affidavit from Landay has still not arrived and I am somewhat unsettled about it. I'll wait until the end of the month and then telegraph Jacobs. You will already have guessed how Mr. Guth or Miss Brandt reacted to my plea. But it is certainly a mistake for you to assume that "passage" is the main thing for the consulate. Affidavits and passage are equally weighted. The newest proof of this was supplied once more by Deutschkrons. Their brother, Mr. Laufer — who already had issued an affidavit for them — (or his representing lawyer) mistakenly put the names Max and Eva on the new affidavit. Even though all the rest was correct, the affidavit had to be corrected over there.[4] So you see that it is important whether the papers are there, sufficient, etc. I have but one explanation for Landay: that he needs a lot of time to assemble the supporting documents and perhaps could not get the tax papers together so quickly. The new possibility of passage is over Goeteborg.[5] However, the HV[6] could only obtain a limited number of places, since so many people would need transportation from there. At the moment, everything is in limbo again. That is why I would be happy if, in the meantime, I could finally overcome the problems with my affidavit. Well, I do have the best mediator working on this now and that comforts me. You just have to be able to let yourself be divided in two. What you wrote about Lisbon was extremely interesting; Luxi, by the way, thinks that you write good letters. 4/27/41

As much as I was loathe to, I had to interrupt this letter yesterday. The reason: 2 performances, shopping, etc. Today, I received a card from your uncle — a response to my letter to him — in which he wrote he had received no direct mail from you. Meanwhile, I had written to him a second time once your air mail letter arrived. I reported all to him, also about Lilli. Thanks so much for your regards to Hilde Sch. I enclose a letter for Martha and Hans. You can speak to them, so it saves postage. — As I found out yesterday, Portugal is only unofficially closed; it will be decided today whether this will continue or not. It would be horribly difficult to make it over Goeteborg, because the price of passage is $450 — Who indeed could raise that. — Some news in the Kulturbund. The sudden death of Wilhelm Guttmann has shaken me. He sang Thursday afternoon — three days ago — for a Winter Relief benefit performance, where he collapsed as he was singing: stroke, right side-total paralysis. He died at 10 P.M. — In the new play, *Señor Alan from Purgatory,* a modern Spanish comedy, I have a nice, small role: youthful, comic; Wisten plays the leading role. E's went yesterday to the current play[7] — a small boost that I initiated by buying tickets. You cannot imagine how desolate it has become there, even Lulu. . . .

Letter from Fritz Wisten to Max Ehrlich

Max Ehrlich was a vital force on the Berlin cabaret scene before the Nazi takeover. He was an important master of ceremonies and comic performer in the Kulturbund's own cabaret, which he helped to establish. He emigrated to Amsterdam in 1939, whereafter he co-founded a Dutch continuation of the Kulturbund, more or less— the Hollandsche Schouwburg. After his deportation to the transit camp, Westerbork, he performed on the camp stage as well until his final deportation in 1944 to Auschwitz, where he perished. For more on Ehrlich, see Volker Kühn's essay in this section, as well as excerpts from Etty Hillesum and Philip Mechanicus in Part II. The following is a letter to Ehrlich from managing director Fritz Wisten, not long after the dissolution of the Kulturbund by the Nazi authorities in 1941. It is important to remember that all letters in Germany and occupied Europe were subject to strict censorship, as was this letter.

* * *

10.7.41 [7 October 1941]

My dear Max!

I'm sorry that you have discovered things about Dr. L. that haven't been surprises to us here for a long time. For your sake, I'm sorry. — But perhaps it was destiny that you should recognize this ambiguous character through your own experiences with him.[1] You never really trusted the descriptions of others. As painful a disappointment as it is after such a long-term relationship, I believe that you may draw a lesson from this experience, that it may serve you in your future outlook toward people. — And so: Leave Herr Dr. L. to the rest!!!!!

Quite different worries oppress us at this time. Our Kubu[2] has been dissolved since 9.12 [12 September]. The undertaking that I was permitted to steer for two years past all obstacles under the most unfavorable conditions is no more! One cannot imagine Jewish life without this institution. And with one single stroke the establishment that we were allowed to co-

From Akademie der Künste, Berlin, FWA 74/86/053.

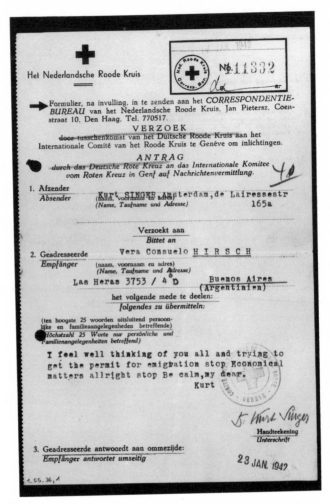

Postcard document 1.55.36, 1 from Kurt Singer, writing from his
Amsterdam exile. Courtesy Akademie der Künste, Berlin. It is
interesting that Singer chooses to write in English. Regardless
of the Red Cross's role in delivering mail during the war, censorship pervaded. It was not uncommon for letter writers to
use a foreign language.

create and build together has ceased to exist! You will understand what this means for us and what it means especially for me. I must forgo a detailed description of the circumstances. Your New Year's greetings[3] arrived too late, alas. What depresses me most is my concern for the people who acknowledge my authority. The majority will find work. But what will become of the old people, whom we brought along with us all these years, like Lupschütz, Berisch, Raden, etc. etc.???[4] Dr. L. made it easier on himself when he left us in the lurch in 1939. In the process, he did not leave a cash reserve of RM 170,000 behind either. Unfortunately, in practice, it amounts to the same thing; because in spite of our favorable financial situation, I still cannot help the people!

The little skit you sent has now missed its purpose. Thank you so much for it — that you thought of us. If I sent you only one typed page of *Jettchen Gebert*,[5] it was not because of unreflectedness or indifference. According to our information, it was forbidden to remit a whole book. I regret that this question too has now come to nothing, because I no longer have access to our library. I am mailing you back the manuscript of *Kleine Katharina*. The scene is very effective; and I see you vividly before me in the role of the Professor. I hope that you are successful in pursuing your plans further. Herr Dr. L. — whom I see from your newspaper — has become a cabaret manager, will hardly have the ambition to become an acting director! Or does he?

My family, about whom you ask, is well. The children are growing and are healthy, thank God. My wife slaves to maintain the household. These are all things which can't be different for you.

I wish you and your wife all the best for the coming year and for better times!

In old cordiality,
Your
Wisten

II

Containment

Performance in Ghettos and in Concentration Camps

"It's Burning"

MORDECHAI GEBIRTIG

Mordechai Gebirtig (born 1877), wrote this poem after hearing of a 1938 pogrom in a Central Polish village. The poem warns of the "dangers of passivity in the face of oppression," says translator Joshua Jacobson. The poem became one of the most popular songs in ghettos and concentration camps.

It's burning, dear brothers, it's burning!
Ah! Our poor, wretched town is burning!
Angry, raging winds are
tearing, breaking, blowing,
fanning the flames even stronger —
All around, everything's burning!
    You just stand and look around
    And wring your hands.
    You just stand and look around
    while our village burns.
It's burning, dear brothers, it's burning!
Ah! Our poor, wretched town is burning!
Tongues of fire have already
swallowed the entire village —
And the angry, raging winds are howling,
Our village is burning!
    You just stand and look around
    And wring your hands.
    You just stand and look around
    While our village burns.
It's burning, dear brothers, it's burning!

From *Hear Our Voices: Songs of the Ghettos and Camps.* HaZamir HZ 909, HaZamir, Transatlantic Music Publications. Translated by Joshua Jacobson.

Ah! The dreaded moment is approaching:
Our village, together with all of us
will disappear into flames,
What will remain — like after a battle,
only hollowed and blackened!

    You just stand and look around
    And wring your hands.
    You just stand and look around
    While our village burns.

It's burning, dear brothers, it's burning!
You alone can help yourselves.
If your village is precious to you,
take up arms, stop the fire,
Extinguish with your own blood;
only you can do it.

    Brothers, don't just stand there
    And wring your hands.
    Don't just stand there, extinguish the fire.
    Our village is burning!

ESSAYS

Theatrical Activities in the Polish Ghettos during the Years 1939–1942

MOSHE FASS

THE HISTORY of theatrical activities of the Polish ghettos may be divided into two main periods, each closely connected with the events of the times. The first period, which lasted approximately one year, began when Governor General Hans Frank ordered the establishment of the Judenrat[1] and lasted until the erection of the ghetto walls. The second period, which lasted over a year and a half, deals with the theatrical activities in the ghettos themselves.

Insecurity and anxiety characterized the first period. The Jewish population was subjected to constant persecution and to discriminatory measures designed to isolate it from the local inhabitants. Some of these decrees were aimed specifically against Jewish cultural life. In 1939, for example, Jews were reluctant to assemble in one place for fear of being rounded up for forced labor and to avoid arousing undue suspicion of political activities. Another characteristic of this period was the disintegration of the established cultural framework, which caused the more talented artists to flee to Soviet-occupied areas. "It is impossible to organize cultural functions. The departure of the leaders and directors has left institutions without guidance," stated Emanuel Ringelblum, the ghetto historian.[2]

After a short period, when this type of life became to a certain extent routine, a new social framework was developed and conditions permitted the resumption of cultural activities on a small scale in private homes. Two important factors contributed to this. One was the curfew imposed on the Jews, which forced them to remain at home at night. The other was the desire to provide financial assistance to the refugees who had gathered in the blocks of

Originally published in *Jewish Social Studies* 38 (1976): 54–72.

large houses as well as to the families that had became impoverished as a result of the war. The wealthier families would gather for an evening's entertainment provided by a performer who was in need of money. By the end of 1939 this had become a widespread practice. Jonas Turkow [Yonas Turkov] mentions the fact that prior to the establishment of the ghettos the first performance took place in a private home in Warsaw in November of 1939 with the famed actor S. Partel: "When it became known in the other homes [that Partel was performing] people tried to imitate this event by 'kidnapping' Partel. Because he had extensive invitations, however, they contacted other actors and singers. . . . Immediately, impresarios were born. They accepted invitations to perform in private homes."

Once these private performances had grown in popularity they came under the jurisdiction of the "House Committees," which were formed (primarily in the Warsaw ghetto) at the beginning of the war for civil defense purposes but now assumed new social functions. This practice became accepted and even popular. The House Committee would invite a performer for the purpose of collecting money.[3]

At the beginning of 1940, permission was granted to open a "café" with floor show entertainment. The financial success of this café-coffeehouse promoted the establishment of many other cafés, which were for the most part operated by members of the Judenrat and Germans who used their influence to secure the license. J. Turkow gives an account of the situation in his memoirs: "During the year 1940 many halls were opened, most of which were 'cafés' with artistic performances. This was so successful that every second house became a premise ["café" or restaurant]* with an artistic presentation. In the summertime there was a flood of 'summer-gardens' where musicians and actors performed."[4]

Individual performers began to rent halls and give one-man shows in order to support themselves. Here and there professional performers, and occasionally amateurs, would join to form entertainment groups. It was at this point that initial attempts were made to organize theaters on a commercial basis. However, most of these "theaters" operated under the most primitive conditions, in basements and attics, where actors performed secretly for fear of the Germans. The following is a description of such a theater in Warsaw:

On Walowa Street, next to the Franciscan Church, a theatrical troupe was organized at the beginning of 1940 that performed three times a week. The performances were held in an attic, where a stage was set up with a curtain. Pillows and table cloths were used as

---

* Brackets here appear in the original essay.

decorations with kerosene lamps for lighting. Benches were set up in the hall. In front of the entrance a table stood as a cashier's window, where a young lady sold tickets for the performance. In order to get to the house where the theater performed you had to pass through many side streets and rubble of destroyed houses. In order to let the public know the place of performance, guides would be stationed in many corners to direct the people. They would also see that no undesirable [German]* guests would come.[5]

This type of theater was designed especially for those people who could not afford the high prices of the coffeehouses and other expensive entertainment. At this time a large number of actors were employed by "Jewish Self-Help Organizations" (Yiddishe Sotsiale Aleyn-Hilf, J.S.H.) which were formed in each ghetto, though under different names, immediately after the German invasion in 1939, opening large, free kitchens that soon became centers of cultural and political activities. They employed many different actors for these purposes.[6]

In sum, this first year (1939–40) shows the creation of new theatrical forms to fill the vacuum caused by the disbanding of former cultural institutions. Turning theatrical performances into a profitable business was a factor that limited these activities to certain classes of the population, affecting the level of the performances as well as their contents. Another development was the use of theatrical activities to gain educational and financial help, with a similar effect on their caliber and content.

After the establishment of the ghettos the feeling prevailed among the Jews that this was to be a permanent way of life. This illusion of normalcy and the wealth of certain members of the underworld who made their money from black-market supplies combined to create an increased desire for ways to spend money. To this must be added the educational and psychological needs of the population. As a result, the theatrical institutions flourished. We shall deal with each of their three manifestations, small stages, "miniature" theaters, nightclubs and cafés, Jewish self-help organizations, and the legitimate theater.

Small Stages, "Miniature" Theaters, Nightclubs, and Cafés

Although the small stages were in existence before the establishment of the ghettos, it is only during the ghetto period that they were developed into an important means of entertainment. In places like the Warsaw ghetto the café acquired an atmosphere of vulgarity and triteness. Emanuel Ringelblum used the phrase *Das Ghetto Tanzt* (*The Ghetto Dances*) to hint at the famous description of the Congress of Vienna. J. Turkow in his memoirs states: "Almost every

---

* Brackets here appear in the original essay.

second house on Leszno Street (the Broadway of the Warsaw ghetto) and on the other streets became a café, restaurant or theater. . . . In the evenings, songs and music would be heard from the various halls."[7]

The fact that most of these clubs were opened with the help of Gestapo or Judenrat members strengthens the impression that the Germans were interested in encouraging the cheaper levels of entertainment in order to promote demoralization in the ghetto. The situation reached the point of absurdity when the "Jewish Cultural Organization" (J.C.O., Yiddishe Kultur Organazatsia, or, in Polish, *Zydowsky Culturna Organizatia*, ZYKA) applied for permission to organize cultural performances on its premises. Permission was granted on the condition that it would be organized as a café. All the free kitchens in Warsaw were turned into cafés so that the J.S.H. could get a license to perform.

The great number of cafés and nightclubs increased the demand for different types of performers: "Because the popular performers were always busy, they (the cafés) would take the first young pretty girls and youngsters who knew how to dance a step or two, or sing a song. Suddenly, there was a flood of new musical and dance performers."[8] These "performers" were subject to the whims of the café proprietors. The *Gazeta-Zydowske*, a Jewish Polish-language magazine published by the Germans for propaganda purposes, saw fit to mention this in one of its articles.[9] When these "performers" were not at the mercy of the proprietors they were most certainly at the mercy of the Germans.

Flooding the ghetto with cheap performances of all types lowered the status of the cafés. It cannot be said, however, that all the cafés and nightclubs were of the same kind or of a similar caliber. As in most places, they served as a meeting place for different types of people. Some cafés catered to men of a particular profession. It is known, for example, that a certain café was frequented by writers and journalists. Some of them attracted the Polish-speaking intelligentsia; hence, the clientele was above average. However, as time went on, there was a slow but marked decrease in the number of such places because of the pecuniary difficulties of their clients. In addition, wealthy members of the underworld drove away many of the former customers. In the second period of the ghetto, poverty increased and encompassed more and more sectors of the population. The underworld rule and strong-arm methods made the cafés a symbol of the ghetto in the eyes of the Germans and the Poles, and disfigured the image of the ghetto in the eyes of the Jewish public and religious leaders.

On Number 2, Leszno Street, there is now a cabaret called *Sztuka* [Art]. . . . In the ghetto, light was permitted until a certain hour. After that we had to sit around the house by the light of candles or kerosene lamps. When we reached the nightclub the street was dark.

My escort suddenly said to me: "Be careful not to step on a corps [*sic*]." When I opened the door the light blinded me. Gas lamps were burning in every corner of the crowded cabaret. Every table was covered by a white tablecloth. Fat characters sat at them eating chicken, duck, or fowl. All of these foods would be drowned in wine and liquor. The orchestra, in the middle of the nightclub, sat on a small platform. Next to it a singer performed. These were people who once played before Polish crowds. Now they were reminded of their Jewish heritage. When I came in, M.Z., the renowned Polish actor, played the role of a comic character, eliciting lots of laughter. Afterwards a singer, U.G., sang old Polish hits and romantic songs. The audience crowding the tables was made up of the aristocracy of the ghetto — big-time smugglers, high Polish officers, and all sorts of big shots. Germans who had business dealings with the Jews also came here, dressed in civilian clothes. Within the walls of the cabaret one could not sense the tragedy taking place a few yards away. The audience ate, drank, and laughed as if it had no worries.[10]

The virtual expulsion of the middle classes and the intelligentsia from the cafés forced them to look for new forms of entertainment. They founded clubs where they could meet, play cards, and attend the theater. During the two and a half years of the Warsaw ghetto's existence, October 1940–July 1942, according to Ringelblum, "the people of the ghetto enjoyed themselves, not only in the open premises whose number is continually growing, but also in the many gambling clubs which can be found in almost every house. . . . A short while ago there were over sixty clubs."[11] A description of the clubs is found in one of the underground newspapers, *Dror*: "In the clubs of the House Committee high-stakes tables often make as much as 1,000 *zlotys* and more in profit a night. . . . Card players in the clubs of the House Committees salve their consciences by [giving to charity] a small percentage of the stakes."[12]

These descriptions relate mainly to the Warsaw ghetto, which was the largest, and most of the information we possess concerns it. In the smaller ghettos, class distribution was not sufficiently differentiated to allow many nightclubs, or else sponsorship of the cabarets was not financially feasible. Instead there were private clubs serving the Jewish police and the ruling classes. In Lódz there was such a club for the police, called the Police Revue. In the Vilna ghetto there was also such a club called Di Yagedes in di Fass [The Youngsters in the Barrel]. A description of this club is found in the diary of Hermann Kruk. "The program: a full and good performance by some members, then a cheap imitation of popular cabaret jokes was followed by . . . vulgar dances performed by some cheap slut."[13] An article in the Vilna *Ghetto Yediot* [*News of the Ghetto*] alludes to the various forms of entertainment available: "Our lives have become more stable, our houses are a bit warmer and livelier and we spend more time at home. If we do not want to stay home we can sit in cafés." There is also a hint that a coffeehouse existed even in Radom, one of the smaller ghettos.[14] Despite all the negative aspects of the cafés it would be unfair not to mention their positive qualities. Many of the cafés and nightclubs were the only places where there could be satirical expression of the conditions of ghetto life because they were not subject to Judenrat censorship. They became a source of promising new talent. Talent contests were held in the cafés, where winners would receive cash prizes as well as further encouragement. The cafés also served as a stage for those actors of quality who preferred them to the inferior Yiddish theater, not to mention their advantage as a source of livelihood.

Jewish Self-Help Organizations

The second kind of theatrical institution, sponsored by the Jewish Self-Help Organizations, had a completely different character. Performances were given in the House Committees, free kitchens, and children's theaters. Everywhere, in Warsaw, Lódz, Cracow, and other cities, the kitchens were utilized for educational performances. The content of such performances was mainly of a national Jewish character; their goal was to educate and encourage those parts of the population whom the cafés and the nightclubs did not reach. The greatest effort was made in the area of children's theater as a supplement to the general education program in the ghettos. Paragraph 5 of the instruction manual prepared by CENTOS (Centrala Opieki nad Sierotaoni, the Organization for Protecting Orphans, established by the "Joint" in 1923) for the children's kitchens reads as follows: "Morning performances must be organized for the children in order to develop the individual ability and talent of the child. This should also include performances by artists."

The framework of J.S.H. employed many actors, but its greatest service was providing a stage for performances with a Jewish national content. The performances dealt with the holidays, tradition, and Jewish folklore, and included the works of such writers as Sholom Aleichem, Y. L. Peretz, and Mendele Mocher Sforim. Topics from ancient Jewish legends, and themes that dealt with the rebuilding of Israel and the hope for better days, were also presented. The J.S.H. performances constituted one of the most positive elements in the entire theatrical enterprise of the ghettos.

Unlike the other theaters of Warsaw, the J.S.H. theaters were under public control and not designed to make a profit. As a result the content of the programs was governed by educational aims. The J.S.H. theaters also reached a wider cross-section of the population than any other form of theater. The audience of the CENTOS productions in Warsaw included 25,000 children in 110 institutions and "food corners."[15] Support for this is found in a letter written by A.H. to the teachers of the ghetto:

In our kitchen we are producing a very lovely play which the teacher wrote for us. I play the role of a Jewish mother who tries to steal a piece of bread for her children from a passerby on the street. After that, we danced the "famine dance." But the sun shines for us. The Germans are kicked out and we Jewish children live to see a good life and a new era. This is how our play ends. When I am performing, I forget that I am hungry and I no longer remember that the evil Germans are still roaming about. In the morning, I quickly run to the kitchen and I wish the day would never end because when it is dark out we are forced to disband and go back to our homes.[16]

The Legitimate Stage

The third form of theatrical activity whose development started immediately after the ghettos were sealed off was the legitimate theater. By November 1940, just when the Warsaw ghetto was closed off, the Germans permitted the opening of its first theater, the Eldorado. The second theater, the Nowy Azazel, was opened about a half a year later in May 1941. In the same month a Polish-language theater, Na Piaterku (The Upstairs) was opened. June brought the opening of a second Polish theater, the Nowy Kameralni (The New Room), while in July 1941 a third Polish theater, the Femina, was opened. A sixth theater, Palac Melodia (Melody Palace), presented both serious programs and burlesque. These were privately owned theaters and the desire for profit influenced their content, the level of performance, and consequently the class of patrons they attracted.[17]

In the Lódz ghetto, for example, the Avant Garde which was established at the same time as those in Warsaw (October 1940) developed from occasional illegal performances into a licensed and publicly acceptable theater. In Vilna, the Vilna Ghetto Theater gave its first performance in January 1942. A Hebrew-language Vilna theater was founded in May of the same year. Sources pertaining to theaters in the other ghettos are meager. It is known that the first theatrical performance in Radom took place in December 1942 but the date of the second program is unknown. In Czestochowa two theater groups started to function immediately after the establishment of the ghetto. They soon merged and continued to function despite a German ban. There was one legitimate theater in Piotrkow and two in Otwock. However, the information available is insufficient to establish the nature of the performances or their exact dates.[18] No hard evidence is available for the existence of theaters in Szyolowiec, nor in Cracow or Kutno.[19] In this context, we must mention again the children's theaters supported by the J.S.H. Performances took place in "food corners" mostly in the Warsaw ghetto.

In Vilna, a Youth Theater was established by the Youth Club in October 1942. It gave its first performance in January 1943 and continued to perform regularly for the ghetto youth. A children's theater was also established in Lódz; it performed in the Children's Colonies of the ghetto. In Cracow, a children's theater was established by the J.S.H., while in Piotrkow it was under the auspices of the Judenrat. In Czestochowa it was created by TOZ (Towaraystwo Ochrony Zdrowia), an organization for the protection of the health of the Jews in Poland, established in 1921, and in Kovno by the Young Zionists. We do not know how long they survived nor the content of their programs, but it is reasonable to assume that since these theaters were established for educational purposes, they lasted as long as educational activities continued to be permitted in ghettos.[20]

Another form of children's entertainment was the puppet show. Its advantages were its moderate budget, its great mobility, and children's love of puppets. In Warsaw, there were four known puppet shows. One was in the Janusz Korczak orphanage. Two others—one that was performed in Yiddish and the other in Polish—were established under the auspices of CENTOS, while a fourth was established by a group of Lódz artists. In Vilna a puppet theater was established by the police. In Lódz the puppet group was called Had-Gadya. We also know of puppet shows in Czestochowa.[21]

The Theatrical Repertoire

Two of the five theaters in Warsaw performed in Yiddish, the other three in Polish. However, this does not mean that the Polish theater had a larger audience than the Yiddish theater. In fact, at the beginning, the very opposite was true. Most of the population of the ghetto spoke Yiddish, which is why the first two theaters were Yiddish theaters. It is interesting to point out that they were owned by a certain Judith, a woman who had connections with a German officer. Fearing competition, she saw to it that no other theaters were permitted to perform in Yiddish.[22] This was contrary even to official German policy, which ruled that all Jewish public activities must be conducted either in Yiddish or in Hebrew, but definitely not in an Aryan tongue.[23] "Jewish artists are not allowed to perform in Polish, but they do perform for bribe money," Ringelblum noted in his diary on 16 September 1940.[24] The two Yiddish theaters faced no competition. Since the audience came to performances in large numbers, and since the receipts were enormous, these theaters did not have to maintain high standards.

The Polish theaters, on the other hand, had to face stiff competition. Because of the language the audience was limited to the assimilated Jewish intelligentsia and to converts whose cultural level was quite high. The caliber of the actors was high because many of them were products of the prewar Polish theater.[25] Another reason for the higher standard of the Polish theater was the migration of many fine actors from the Yiddish to the Polish stage. As a result of these factors, the Yiddish theater sank to an unprecedented low level. Turkow recalled that they paid no attention to their potential talents, they did not even try to maintain any kind of standard. They kept going downhill, playing upon the cheapest instincts of the crowd.[26] Two stages of development may be discerned in the content of the Yiddish plays performed in the Warsaw ghetto: In the first stage, popular themes in the tradition of Eastern Europe, family tragedy, unrequited love, and the like, were presented. During the second stage, toward the end of the ghetto period, a certain standard was maintained and decisions were taken to improve the quality of the performances.[27]

Several reasons can be given for this rise in quality. The taste of the audience seems to have improved or else they tired of the long series of cheap tragedies and soap operas and sought something better. Another reason was the competition of the Polish theater.[28] Furthermore, the leaders of the communities fought for a higher quality of performance.[29] Perhaps most important was the task fulfilled by the theater as the mood of the population changed. In the beginning the theater had served as a means of forgetting one's plight but, toward the end of the ghettos' existence, when people became used to this mode of life, the artistic experience of the drama became an end in itself and not a means. This gave the Yiddish theater a new impetus.

The Polish theater was completely different from the Yiddish theater in the content of its performances. It assumed the responsibility of giving the Polish-speaking Jewish audiences classical Jewish works. Such was the case when the Nowy Kameralni presented *Mirele Efros* in Polish, as well as a long list of serious plays.[30] The second Polish theater, Femina, was unusual in that it presented satires on ghetto life and did not try to escape harsh everyday reality. The Zionist parties gave presentations on Jewish national themes.

Every theater changed its plays once a month. This leads to the conclusion that the theatergoing public was quite limited. Otherwise there would have been no need to change performances so frequently. Evidently one month sufficed for all potential customers to see the plays; it would be safe to assume that the total number of the theatergoing public was about thirty thousand.[31] The frequent changing of performances naturally caused a lowering of their level. To this may be added the objective conditions of the ghetto and the German effort at demoralizing the ghetto population. Turkow describes what went on: "It is difficult to say who is to blame for this. One thing is sure — that the essential guilt lay in the abnormal situation and circumstances thrown upon us by the execution of Hitler's orders. The Germans were interested in seeing that we cause our own demoralization, that we dirty ourselves, and eventually drown in our own filth." [32]

From the partial information available from the other ghettos it appears that the theaters gave performances of classical works as well as plays dealing with Jewish reality and life in the ghetto. The emphasis was on the revue. These theaters served the same function as the nightclubs of the Warsaw ghetto, relaxing tension and giving expression to the bitterness of the Jewish plight. In this respect the Vilna theater was exceptional in that it emphasized classical Jewish works that encouraged revolt. [33]

German Policy toward the Theatrical Activity

It is clear that the cultural activity of the ghettos and the policy of the German conquerors had an impact on each other, and here we find an interesting phenomenon. While in those areas of Poland which were directly annexed to the Reich all the discriminatory laws against the Jews, including the cultural laws, were enforced, in the remaining areas of the General Gouvernement no single statewide law dealt with Jewish cultural life. [34] The laws concerning the Jews were published as an appendix to general statewide orders in the *Gazeta-Zydowska*. For example, the nationwide order, *Über die kulturelle Beteiligung des General Gouvernement* (the official name of the territory which was left as part of Poland and was not annexed into the Reich), had a special order attached concerning the Jews. [35] Thus, it may be assumed that the policy relating to cultural and theatrical activities was left in the hands of local authorities. The fact must be emphasized that no orders were published which outlawed independent Jewish cultural activity. On the contrary, we see that the local authorities attempted to set up an organization parallel to the Kulturbund in Germany in order to have some sort of control over cultural activities. Even the *Gazeta-Zydowska*, which was under direct German control, published detailed accounts of the cultural activities of the General Gouvernement. [36]

Because the cultural policy in the ghettos was left to the local governors, it is easy to understand that there were many variations. In some ghettos the theater was outlawed; in others it was permitted and even encouraged by the Germans.

It seems that the policy adopted by the Germans was to encourage cheap entertainment that caused demoralization and distracted the people's minds from the fate that awaited them. In Warsaw expressions of this could be seen in the cafés and nightclubs. In Łódz the Germans objected to a Central Cultural Union (Tsentrale Kultur Organazatsia) that demanded high-caliber cultural performances, but they did not object to performances that could be characterized as cheap entertainment. Even in newly conquered Russian territories where the Nazis were less lenient, specific laws against Jewish cultural activities were enforced on the basis of the German practice in Poland. The Germans permitted the establishment of a theater in Vilna and they patronized it.[37] One of the founders of the theater remarked: "The Nazis were satisfied by Jewish interest in the theater. They thought that by this they could divert the Jewish minds from the hopeless situation of the ghetto and from the evil thoughts planted in the minds of Himmler's faithful messengers."[38]

Following are two quotations that will illustrate that the Germans were successful in their demoralization campaign: "Outside, the police guarded the entrance to the theater. Here in the theater hall it is as if nothing has happened. A premiere: The play went well, the performance was flawless. The decorations are nice, as if we were not in the ghetto."[39] And Ringelblum recalls: "I went to the Yiddish theater yesterday. . . . You are looking for an escape from reality. The hall is beautiful. For two hours you forget the bitterness of the wretched world around you."[40]

Generally, the Germans were lenient when theaters circumvented the law but, according to the regulations, all performances were to be approved by the German censorship board.[41] Only immediately prior to the destruction of the Warsaw ghetto, in June 1942, did the Germans enforce censorship strictly. Suddenly, notices were posted by the head of the Judenrat, the engineer Adam Czerniakow, to the effect that the Jews must respect the German law prohibiting the performance of any play written by a non-Jew and that they submit all performances to censorship. This was one of the signs of the ghetto's imminent destruction.

In conclusion, it can be said that the Germans did not formulate a unified and specific policy to regulate cultural activities in the ghettos. If there was German intervention at all it was slight. In theory all plays were submitted to censorship, but in practice circumvention was commonplace. The theaters had almost complete freedom and German interests were satisfied with encouragement of the cheaper forms of entertainment although there are no signs that the Germans interfered with quality performances. Therefore, it is an exaggerated claim that the theatrical activities were underground activities. Consequently, if one wishes to understand the reasons for the level, the form, and the materials of the theatrical performances, one must look not so much to a German policy of suppression, which was a minor factor, but to the ghettos' Jewish institutions.

The Attitude of the Jewish Institutions toward Theatrical Activity

The fact that the theatrical activities depend on Jewish institutions leads us to first examine the Judenrats since, as the autonomous ruling bodies of the ghettos, they were also in charge of cultural activities.[42] They set up cultural departments and controlled the theatrical activities in the ghetto. At the beginning, since the Germans were essentially concerned with pressuring the Judenrats to confiscate the ghetto population's possessions, they were powerless to do anything on the cultural scene. As a result, their cultural activities were weak or rather subsidiary to their other functions and those activities fell into the province of other public institutions. However, even in this period, the Judenrats sought to have theatrical performances legalized, claiming that this would provide work for the unemployed. On the other hand, they attempted to apply censorship to make sure that the plays would insult neither the Germans nor the Judenrats themselves. The constant fear of slighting the Germans forced the Judenrats to give preference to the musical variety revue. Another factor that tied the Judenrats' hands was the partnership of Jews with Germans in nightclubs or theaters; in these cases the Judenrats did not dare intervene.

The second period is characterized by the Judenrats' attempt to influence cultural activities as part of their general plan to control every phase of life. However, the success or failure of these attempts varied locally. In Warsaw, for example, where the Judenrat could not interfere with the activities of the theaters, nightclubs, and cafés, it did force itself upon the cultural activities sponsored by the J.S.H. In April 1942, the Judenrat ordered the Tzentrale Imprezes Komisye (Central Performances Commission) to disband, but it was only a formal order. In practice, performances continued until the ghetto's destruction despite interference by the Jewish police.[43] In Lódz, Rumkowski, the head of the Judenrat from its beginning in 1939, gathered all the cultural institutions into an organization which he controlled called the House of Culture (Kultur Hoys).[44] In Czestochowa, two departments of the Judenrat took care of cultural activities. These were the Labor Department, an underground anti-Judenrat group, and the Cultural Department, which attempted to control theatrical activities by obtaining permits from the Germans. The Germans refused to grant these however, and the Cultural Department's attempt failed. Activity continued under the Labor Department despite the opposition of the Judenrat.[45]

In Vilna the Judenrat initiated the cultural activities and subjected them to police permission; in this manner it succeeded in controlling them from the very beginning. As a result the police department became the patron of all cultural activities in the ghetto.[46] The more the Judenrat asserted itself, the more theatrical activities became dependent on its favors. On the one hand, the Judenrat attempted to spread its influence by making food grants and offering work permits (which constituted life permits under ghetto conditions) to the performers and by investing in scenery and costumes as well as halls. On the other hand the stage was exploited for Judenrat propaganda purposes, to offer free entertainment to reassure the population.

In Warsaw, Ganzweich, the head of the "Thirteen,"[47] as well as Cohen and Heller,[48] who were in charge of burying the dead, were also patrons of the theater. There were also individuals who sponsored and encouraged cultural activity, people of a special class or members of the underworld who had contacts with the Germans.

The many different authorities involved in the ghettos' theatrical activities influenced the performances, each in its own way. This caused a certain haphazardness in the content, quality, goal, and direction of the performances. The fact that there was no unified policy made it possible to present many colorful topics to suit the various classes of society. Unequal legal status was held by the various theaters in the different ghettos, and a theater's status was completely dependent on its sponsor. For example, the German-Jewish nightclubs and cafés had authorized status, the performances of the J.H.S. had a quasi-legal status, while the activities sponsored by the political parties were completely illegal.

Theatrical activities remained widespread until the beginning of the final "action" by the Germans. At its inception the theaters disbanded and the actors sought employment in commerce in an attempt to save their lives. Finally, like everything else in the ghettos, the theatrical activities ended in destruction.

Appendix 1 [original by Fass, related to theaters]

Theater performances in the Warsaw ghetto, January to November 1941, as recorded in the *Gazeta Zydowska* (*GZ*).

Eldorado

Di Mazeldike Khasene [*The Lucky Wedding*] 10 January 1941 (*GZ*, No. 3, 4).
Dos Dorf Moyd [*The Village Girl*] 12 February 1941 (*GZ*, No. 13, 9).
Di Komedyantke [*The Comedienne*] 28 March 1941 (*GZ*, No. 23, 3).
Rivkele dem Rebens Tokhter [*Little Rivke, the Rabbi's Daughter*] 2 May 1941 (*GZ*, No. 35, 3).
Tsipke fun Novolipye [*Tsipke from Novolipye*] 13 June 1941 (*GZ*, 47, 3).
A Heym far a Mame [*A Home for a Mother*] 6 June 1941 (*GZ*, 45, 8).
Unzer Rebenyu [*Our Beloved Rabbi*] 11 July 1941 (*GZ*, 57, 2).
Farkoyfte Neshome [*Sold-Out Soul*] 11 August 1941 (*GZ*, 70, 2).

Nowy Azazel

Motke Ganev [*Motke the Thief*] 6 September 1941 (*GZ*, 81, 2).
Hertser tsu Farkoyfn [*Hearts for Sale*] 10 July 1941 (*GZ*, 56, 4).
Got fun Nekome [*The God of Vengeance*] 1 August 1941 (*GZ*, 66, 3).
Der Dibbuk [*The Dybbuk*] 28 August 1941 (*GZ*, 75, 3).

Femina

Szafa gra Femina [*Szafa Plays in the Femina*] 18 July 1941 (*GZ*, 60, 44).
Od Geminy do Feminy [*From the Judenrat Office to the Femina*] 15 August 1941 (*GZ*, 72, 2).
Milosc i Mieszkanie[49] [*Love and Lodging*].

Nowy Kameralni

Mirele Efros.[50]

Theater Performances Given from December 1941 to June 1942[51]

Eldorado

Tsipke Fayer [*Tsipke Fire*]; *Frayleche Makhutonim* [*The Merry In-laws*]; *Shvartse Khupe* [*The Black Wedding Canopy*]; *Di Grine Kale* [*The Green Bride*]; *Urke-Nakhalalnik*;[52] *Shirhashirim* [*Song of Songs*];[53] just before the destruction of the ghetto, *Des Dorf Yingel* [*The Country Boy*].[54]

Nowy Azazel

Twvei Ganovim [*Two Thieves*]; *Ishah Raah* [*A Bad Woman*]; *Der Muskiter* [*The Muske-teers*]; *Shlomke Sharlatan* [*Little Solomon the Charlatan*]; *Libe un Pracht* [*Love and Splendor*]; *Shulamit;*[55] *Kliyatshke* [*The Little Mare*]; *Shmates* [*Rags*].

Femina

Two operettas: *Maritsa* and *Tshardash;* two plays: *Matura* [*Matriculation*] and *Mary Duggen.*

Nowy Kameralni

Gassen-Muzik [*Street Music*]; *Dr. Berghoff; Vilner Balabesel* [*Vilna Boss*]. The last show was *A Kish Far Shpigel* [*A Kiss Before a Mirror*].

Appendix 2

Performances in the Vilna ghetto by the "Ghetto Theater," 2 January to 19 July 1943.

First Performance — 16 January 1942

1. Bialik, *Se Glist Mir Tsu Vaynen* [*I Want to Cry*].
2. Folk-songs: "Eli Eli" ["Oh, My God"], "Zamd und Shtern" ["Sand and Stars"].
3. Parts of the play *Mirele Efros* by Gordin; *Goldene Kayt* [*Golden Chain*] by Peretz; *Rachel Imenu* [*Rachel Our Mother*] by Stefan Zweig.[56]

Second Performance — February 1942

1. Parts of *Ha-Golem* [*The Golem*] by Leivik.
2. Readings from the Bible (Isaiah).
3. Parts of *Bar-Kokhba* by Goldfadden.

Third Performance — 23 April 1942

1. Parts of *Shlomo Molkho* by Leyeles.
2. *Mazel-Tov* by Sholom Aleichem.
3. Light music played by "The Ghetto Orchestra."

Fourth Performance (a review)

Franke Koren un Vaytsene Teig [*Poor Corn and Wheat Dough*],[57]

Fifth Performance (a review)

Men Ken Gornit Vissen [*You Can Never Tell*].

Sixth Performance (a review)

"Pasah Marisha."

Seventh Performance (a review)

Moshe Halt Zich [*Moshe, Keep Strong*].

Eighth Performance — July 1942 (not a review but the first complete play to be shown by the troupe)

Greine Felder [*Green Fields*] by Hirshbein.

Ninth Performance — November 1942 (a complete play)

Der Mentsh Unter dem Brick [*The Man Under the Bridge*] by Oto Indi.[58]

Tenth Performance — March 1943 (a complete play)

Der Oytser [*The Treasure*] by Pinski.

Eleventh Performance — May–June 1943 (a complete play)

Ha-Mabul [*The Flood*] by Berger.

Rehearsals were begun on *Tevye, The Milkman* by Sholom Aleichem, but they were stopped in the middle because of the destruction of the ghetto.

The Hebrew Theater:

The Hebrew Theater prepared to present Bialik's *Yom ha-Shishi ha-Katsar* [*Short Friday*], but in the end performed *Ha-Yehudi ha-Nitshi* [*The Eternal Jew*] by Pinski because it was more representative of the general atmosphere of resistance in the ghetto. The play was first performed on 10 June.[59]

Latvia and Auschwitz

YONAS TURKOV

Yonas Turkov [also transliterated as Jonas Turkow] was born in Warsaw (1898). He wrote twenty books in Yiddish and Spanish. In 1919 he was drafted into the Red Army. He narrowly escaped from Germany during World War II and wrote a book about his experience. He was a well known actor on the Yiddish stage. He was the brother of Sigmund Turkov, a famous Yiddish actor, and the brother-in-law of the Yiddish star, Ida Kaminska. After World War II, he interviewed actors who had performed in the ghettos and camps. He then reconstructed their stories in Yidisher Teater in Yirope . . . Poilen.

Latvia

There were numerous ghettos in Riga. The Latvian Jews were in a separate section of the street. The German Jews who were deported from Germany were kept also in sections of streets, based on the localities from which they came, for example, Berlin, Köln [Cologne], Hannover. They had their own "governments" (Judenrat) and their own administrations. However, all of them were under the Judenrat from Köln — probably because Köln Jews were the earliest deportees.

In the Riga ghetto, there were also Jews from Czechoslovakia (Prague) and Austria (Vienna). They also lived in separate sections of streets. One needed a permit to go from one section to another. The ghetto was formed soon after the Germans occupied the city in 1941. During the years 1941–42, there were numerous artistic undertakings. There were many artists, theater artists, and musicians, and musicals from Germany, Austria, and Czechoslovakia. The dra-

From "Teater un Konsertn in di Getos un Konstentratsye Lagern," in *Yidisher Teater in Yirope . . . Poilen* (New York: Knight, 1968), 493–95, 500–502. Translated by survivor Sol Shulman.

matists put on the play *Jeremiah* [by Stefan Zweig]. And all subsequent plays were put on in the great hall of the "Köln" section of the ghetto.

In discussing the musical life, one must recall the ghetto jazz orchestra. There was a popular Riga saxophonist called "Johnny." Jews from different sections of the Riga ghetto came to the literary and artistic events that were held in the great hall of the Judenrat of Köln.

Lectures and literary discussions on various topics were held in the German-Jewish school. Concerts, readings, and plays were organized every Saturday and Sunday in the great hall or in other halls of the Judenrat.

The renowned Riga opera singer Jacob Yofi used to present a program of religious songs. The cantor Serenski used to sing folk songs and songs that he composed, for example, "Bombs, Bombs Are Dropping." Serenski wrote and composed another ghetto song, "There Go Canons and There Go Fatalities," which people sang solo and in groups.

The well-known Riga pianist Herman Godes also gave piano concerts. There were also a violin virtuoso and professor of cello, Metz and Temko. The concerts were also attended by the Germans from the *Kommandatur*.

The Riga singer Sheklan had great success with his renditions of "The Lithuanian Shtetl" and "The Bekher" ["The Baker"]. Chana Teitz also was popular with her renditions of folk songs. L. Burian of Prague sang from operas.

The German and Czech artists played and sang using the German language. When deportees from Lithuania started to arrive, the Yiddish language and Jewish song became more prevalent. This started with a boy from Kovno, Mapoo. He used to go from yard to yard and house to house singing sad songs which were written in the Kovno ghetto, causing many a tear. Such a very popular song was "It Must Be So, It Must Be So."

The deportees from the Vilna ghetto brought the songs "Ponar," "Vilnea," "Don't Say That You Walk the Last Way." The songs were also sung in the Kaiserwald concentration camp and others. The main singers singing these songs were Betty Segal, Peikele from Vilna, and Feygele Broydo.

The Germans ordered the formation in Riga of boxing groups and soccer teams. German and Latvian Jews were the participants. The artistic and sport activities existed during the life of the ghetto.

Auschwitz

This concentration camp was one of the most horrible camps constructed by the Germans. It was located in a small town that was known as Oswiecim.

Although there were also non-Jews in the camp, the Jews were treated the worst. The population of the camp consisted of people from European lands occupied by the Germans. Jews who were lucky enough upon arrival to the camp to avoid the gas chamber were utilized in various slave labor activities.

Even under the most horrible conditions in the camp Jews were able to organize cultural activities. They had several artistic and literary activities. A group of Jewish inmates organized Jewish poetry and music concerts in the camp, Buna-Monowitz. Among this group were the writers Yosef Wolf, Poldek Wasserman (from Krakow), an actor from a Vilna troupe, Moishe Potashinski, a Jewish-Hebrew teacher from Holland, Itzhak Goldman, the Jewish German journalist Shpiegel, Eisenberg from Belgium, Alfred Besserman, Yudl Korman, Dovid Rappaport from France, and others.

After a series of consultations, they decided to start cultural activities so inmates could hear a word, a good song, a recitation. The activities were organized in the blocks. Several academies were also established, for example, the Peretz academy. Typically the people would sit in cramped quarters and listen to the performer(s). For example, the actor Potashinski recited a program from Sholom Aleichem's *Tevye, the Milkman,* Chaim Grade's *The Crying from Dorot,* Moishe Kolbak's *The Bells Have Rung,* and sang Itzig Manger's "The Song of Rabbi Tam" and Mordechai Gebirtig's "It Burns" ["It's Burning"]. The whole tired and hungry audience participated in the songs.

Potashinski writes about these events in his memoirs: "The inmates stand around with tears in their eyes and thank profusely for the great joy." One of the prisoners writes, "Since we lived through to sing in the camp we will live to see the Messiah come." Potashinski writes further: "This was my first open concert in Oswiecim No. 3."

Potashinski also presented a program for Jewish doctors and helpers at the K.B. (Kranken-Ban), a sort of ersatz hospital. The secretary of K.B.—called Leizer—would introduce Potashinski to the audience and describe how important the Jewish theater in Poland was for Jewish life. Leizer would also describe the effect of Jewish literature and the rise of Jewish culture. Leizer gave summaries before each of the numbers presented by Potashinski so the doctors who did not know much about Yiddish and Jewish culture (they were mostly from France, Hungary, and Germany) could understand the meaning of the presentations.

Potashinski writes: "Through the barred window I see the electrified wire fences, the guard tower in which stands an SS man with a machine gun. I feel that here in the barracks there is a sorrowful solemnity . . . in the quiet solemnity I start with Y. L. Peretz's 'If Not Higher' and soon with Peretz's 'The

Student from Chelm.' The two Peretz stories had an exhilarating effect on the doctors. They became happy. It showed on their pale faces." Potashinski also recited for them Bialik's "I Want to Cry," and later humorous works of Moishe Nadir, Baruch Shefner, A. Lutzky, and finishing the program with Gebirtig's "It Burns, Jews, It Burns." After the program one of the doctors, Professor Weitz from France remarked: "We, the doctors, do not have the means to treat the sick, let the Jewish songs be their medication." Thus, there were other concerts, also in Block No. 6. The events took place on Saturdays, after work.

In addition to Potashinski, Abramovitch, David Bergholz et al., also gave recitations. There were other Jewish actors who gave concerts in different blocks. An actor from Gev. "Ararat" and leader of the Lódz ghetto theater organized a seven-member singing group. The program consisted of various folk songs from the prewar Revue Theater. Inmate actors from Lódz: Shmai Rosenblum, Weinberg, Numberg, Rothstein, and Nelkin, also sang in the choral group. The concerts took place in the block leader's barracks. A couple of cigarettes were the honorarium for the singers. Moishe Pulaver and Shmai Rosenblum presented programs at the "Canadiens." A table served as the stage for the two performers. The program consisted of songs and recitations such as Manger's "The Gold Peacock," Sholom Aleichem's "The Fire of Kasrilovka," A. Lutzky's "Waltz," and works of A. Sternberg and Moishe Nadir. The performers also gave recitals in the infirmary and Block No. 13. Their programs were very successful.

In the Women's Block No. 10 there was a young Jewish actress, Mila Veyslitz. A group of women from Belgium who knew her from the stage asked her to entertain the people with a Jewish word and song. Through the barred window in the block the wall of Block 11 was visible where executions by shooting took place. Through the barred windows one could also see the flames of the crematoria. Potashinski writes about this in one of his memoirs: "Mila (Veyslitz) gave her first concert, Yiddish word and song, in Block 10, in the shadow of crematoria. There was a mixture of young Jewish women and girls from Czechoslovakia, Poland, France, Belgium, Greece, Germany. And these women, who communicated in different languages, wanted to hear not only songs and light conversation, but also serious discussion in Yiddish, even though some of them did not understand Yiddish."

Mila Veyslitz, the wife of Moishe Potashinski, repeated several concerts and provided joy for the inmates. And it made them forget—albeit for a short time—the nearby standing crematoria.

Theatrical Activities in
the Nazi Concentration Camps

ALVIN GOLDFARB

AS CAN BE SEEN from the many essays and excerpts found in this reader,
theatrical activities survived in the Nazi concentration camps. While Part III of
this anthology reveals that there is an immense amount of writing about theater presentations in the model camp of Theresienstadt, there are also many
remarkable examples of activities in the transit camps, labor camps, and death
camps established by the Third Reich throughout war-ravaged Europe. Possibly the best way to survey these activities, especially since chronological
documentation is understandably sketchy, is to attempt to catalog the various
types of theatrical presentations that were organized.

The most common theatrical activity in the Nazi concentration camps was
the presentation of clandestine programs of songs and readings in the individual barracks. In Buna-Monowitz (Auschwitz III), a group of Jewish cultural leaders, including the author Joseph Wolf, the actor Moishe Potashinski,
and the Dutch, Yiddish, and Hebrew scholar Itzhak Goldman, organized such
entertainments. In his memoirs, Potashinski, a former member of the renowned Yiddish Vilna Troupe, describes a typical presentation. The audience
sat on their bunks; the performers recited fragments from Sholom Aleichem's
Tevye, the Milkman, Chaim Grade's *The City of Generations,* and Moishe Kolbak's *The Bells Have Rung.* They also sang Itzik Manger's "The Song of Our
Teacher" and Mordechai Gebirtig's "Our Town Is Burning," a song commemo-
rating a 1938 Polish pogrom in Przytyk.[1]

A similar production, staged in the Monowitz infirmary for the Jewish doc-

Much of the material in this essay originally appeared in "Theatrical Activities in the Nazi Concentration Camps," *Performing Arts Journal* 1 (1976), 3–11.

tors, was prefaced by a lecture discussing the contributions of the Yiddish theater to European theater. (Apparently, one of the most popular divertissements in the camps was literary discussion. Nico Rost notes that on numerous occasions in his Dachau barrack, he and compatriots discussed the dramatic works of Racine, Goethe, Mickiewicz, and Toller. One full evening was spent analyzing Stanislavski's production of Hautpmann's *Before Sunrise* and another devising a short play that dealt with what the reactions of the great German literati would have been had they discovered themselves in Dachau.)[2] Songs were followed by readings from Isaac Loeb Peretz, Chaim Nahman Bialik, Moishe Nadir, A. Lutzky, and Baruch Shefner; this program also concluded with the singing of "Our Town Is Burning."[3]

Similar concerts were organized in various other barracks in Auschwitz. Among the other performers who entertained fellow prisoners were David Abramovitsch and David Bergholtz. Some entertainers were able to earn necessities and luxuries by staging such concerts. Moishe Pulaver and Shmai Rosenblum, after entertaining "Canada" laborers, received cigarettes for remuneration. The Yiddish actor and theater historian Yonas Turkov, a survivor of the Holocaust, describes Pulaver and Rosenblum's presentation: "A table served as the stage for the two performers. The program consisted of songs and recitations . . . and works by A. Sternberg and Moishe Nadir. The performers also gave recitals in the infirmary and Block No. 13. Their programs were very successful."[4]

Similarly improvised entertainments were staged in Auschwitz's women's camp. The Yiddish actress Mila Veyslitz, the wife of Moishe Potashinski, presented programs of songs and readings in Block 10.[5] Kitty Hart, a survivor of Birkenau's female camp, was fortunate enough to be assigned to a comparatively easy work detail barrack. Here various impromptu entertainments were organized:

Supper over, then came entertainment. As a rule, the Greek girls had wonderful voices and their very popular sentimental song "Momma" made most of the others sob, for nearly all had lost their mothers. Then there were the Hungarians who could dance so well they dressed up in rags, and even on one occasion staged a complete ballet. There were also many gifted writers who recited their poetry. Comical acts were very popular, especially those imitating the SS.[6]

As in Auschwitz, artistic internees in various other concentration camps attempted to make their compatriots' existences more tolerable. Holocaust historian Dr. Mark Dvorzhetski points out that clandestine meetings, which included community singing and recitations, were held in the barracks of the Jewish Estonian camps, even though these were among the worst labor sites established by the Reich.[7]

In the Riga labor center in Latvia, the actress Musia Deyches often recited poetry and drama for fellow female prisoners. Sirele Lipovsli and the Czech opera singer L. Burian entertained the women who were laboring for the German Electrical Organization.[8] In the Malines transit camp in Belgium, Veyslitz and Potashinski, who were imprisoned in this camp before being transported to Auschwitz, organized clandestine entertainments. According to Turkov, the Nazis interned prisoners of French, German, Flemish, and Dutch origins in Malines, many of whom were theater artists. The SS exploited these performers for propaganda. The Nazis forced them to present "variety shows" in the camp yard on Saturdays and Sundays; reports of these productions would then appear in the Belgian press to allay fears of still hidden Jews and to counter rumors of German atrocities. At the same time, however, Veyslitz and Potashinski organized two surreptitious presentations in the camp barracks; thematically, the material selected dealt with the historical suffering of the Jews. Their second presentation, on 15 April 1943, was their last in Malines, for four days later all those imprisoned in this Belgian camp were shipped to Auschwitz.[9]

In the women's camp of Ravensbrück, French prisoner Denise Dufournier was asked to organize her barrack's spare time. "Travel talks, philosophical discussions, discourses on our folklore, alternated with the précis of one of Shakespeare's plays. . . . A revue of great originality was staged in twenty-four hours. Choruses were trained to sing classical music in perfect harmony. Poets were invited to read their verse."[10]

Corrie ten Boom describes similar concerts in the Dutch transit camp Vught,[11] as does Micheline Maurel in her reminiscences of Neubrandenburg. Maurel remembers one camp performer in particular: "Among the performers who joined us in the summer of 1944 was Fanny Marette, the comedienne, who amused us so greatly with her imitation of a man at the movies. She sat on a stool . . . pretending the bowl on her lap was the gentleman's hat."[12]

In Bergen-Belsen, Samy Feder organized the primitive attempts to keep theater alive, even when it meant making great sacrifices: "We had produced shows even in the concentration camp. We used to improvise a stage right in the middle of a foul barracks, make an old blanket into a curtain and put on a show, with myself as producer, for Chanukah, Purim, or whenever we felt we had a 'good' guard who would not be too harsh. Sometimes we paid for it with casualties, but we never gave it up."[13] Later, when Belsen was converted into a Displaced Persons (DP) camp, Feder helped establish the famous Belsen Katzet [Concentration Camp] Theater, which toured throughout Europe.

The diversity of the materials presented indicates that these clandestine programs of readings, sketches, and songs served various functions. The need for escapist entertainment accounts for the popularity of humorous works by Sholom Aleichem, A. Sternberg, and Moishe Nadir. The desire to cling to tradition resulted in lectures, like the one on the contributions of the Yiddish theater, and the reading of I. L. [Y. L.] Peretz, C. N. Bialik, and other noted Jewish authors. These surreptitious entertainments also functioned as outlets for resistance. Potashinski and Veyslitz chose works describing Jewish suffering. "Our Town Is Burning," sung at many of the Auschwitz gatherings, was probably meant not only to lament the current plight of the internees but to assure camp audiences that previous oppression had been overcome. The prisoners in Kitty Hart's barrack resisted by mimicking the SS.

Even more important, these minor theatrical activities aided some in surviving. Fellow prisoners frequently rewarded these performances with scarce necessities. On occasion, even the SS might reward imprisoned performers for entertaining them. For example, in Auschwitz and Majdanek, Nazi audience members provided extra rations to Greek singers and dancers.[14] Gisella Perl, who was an inmate-doctor in Auschwitz, relates the tale of a French actress who, in order to escape a gas chamber selection, "wandered from one block to another, singing her arias to obtain right of asylum."[15]

The Nazis frequently oversaw cabaret-like productions organized by prisoners. For the 1938 New Year, Buchenwald's camp commandant ordered the internees to give a week of "humorous" presentations. The essay by Curt Daniel, which is included in this reader, provides a detailed description of such entertainments.[16]

In Oranienburg, one of the early pre–World War II concentration camps, prisoners were given permission to stage shows once a month that were attended by the SS as well as the internees. The *Theatre Arts* essay, which is reprinted in this volume, describes the entertainments presented in this camp, including a subtle anti-Nazi cabaret sketch.[17]

In 1940, for Christmas and New Year's, the prisoners in the French Vernet concentration camp were allowed to organize entertainments in each of their three sections. Arthur Koestler, an inmate of this internment center, provides a lengthy account of these cabaret presentations in his memoir, *The Scum of the Earth*.[18]

In Buchenwald there was also underground cabaret, both of a political and nonpolitical nature; the nonpolitical performances were staged by professional entertainers, while the political cabaret was organized by amateurs. Writers interned in the camp, such as the Austrian poet and dramatist Jura Soyfer, authored these shows.[19]

Surreptitious cabaret presentations were also common in Dachau. Bruno Heilig, a Dachau survivor, presents a detailed description of the individual artists' contributions to this camp cabaret:

Every Sunday a cabaret performance was given by the artists in the camp. Fritz Gruenbaum, Paul Morgan, Hermann Leopoldi, and the Berlin singer Kurt Fuss. At first the idea of starting a cabaret in a concentration camp seemed to us absurd; but it proved a success. Crowds of prisoners attended the performances. Gruenbaum and Morgan gave their old sketches, which were uproariously applauded by their comrades. Leopoldi made a great hit with Viennese Lieder. Kurt Fuss sang sophisticated ballads about women and love. "From early youth the cunning band have had me on the string" — this song had not been absolutely the latest thing even when I was still a schoolboy, but in a concentration camp it is of no importance to hear only the latest popular favorites. These cabaret matinees gave us the illusion of a scrap of freedom. For an hour or two one almost had a sense of being at home.[20]

Many of the excerpted memoirs in this reader describe the cabaret presentations in Auschwitz, Westerbork, and Theresienstadt. According to psychologist Viktor Frankl, who was imprisoned in Auschwitz, a kind of cabaret was established in that camp in a temporarily cleared hut; programs of sketches satirizing camp conditions were produced. The Kapos and those prisoners not assigned to evening work details attended.[21] Similar presentations took place in Westerbork, a Dutch transit camp; Bruce Zortman notes that "camp comedian Max Ehrlich accompanied by Willy Rosen at the piano revived their revues *Vinegar and Oil* and *Mixed Fruit Cocktail* before meeting their untimely death."[22] A significant number of cabaret performances were staged in Theresienstadt.

The popularity and proliferation of cabaret was probably due to the ease with which productions could be mounted. Any available space could be transformed, as was done in Auschwitz, Buchenwald, Dachau, and Theresienstadt. It seems quite apparent that these cabaret presentations were acts of resistance and attacks on the Third Reich. The heavily satirical content of these entertainments has already been noted.

Cabaret was not the only popular performing art to survive in Nazi concentration camps. Probably the most unique theatrical presentation in an internment center took place in Kaiserwald, near Riga. A group of female internees, in the German Electrical Organization's block, decided to honor their lenient

Lagerälteste by organizing a puppet show for her birthday. The organizer of this project was a Flora Rome from Vilna; assisting her were Adela Bay, Musia Deyches, Regi Litvas, and the Kotik sisters. Rome authored the satirical program and supervised the construction of the puppets, which were made out of material cut from the prisoners' pin-striped uniforms and sewn together with thread from their kerchiefs. A bench was converted into a puppet stage and blankets employed as curtains. Serele Lipovski and Musia Alperovitsch spoke the text. Musia Deyches directed the production. Traditional songs, sung a capella, were included in the program. The presentation was so successful it had to be staged twice.[23]

Children's theater was also produced in some internment centers. Vittel, a French resort, was transformed into a camp serving as a way station for Auschwitz. Here Jews who had earlier taken refuge from Hitler in France were imprisoned until being deported to the gas chambers. Nevertheless, the Hebrew and Yiddish poet-dramatist Yitshak Katzenelson organized various cultural events, including a Hanukkah presentation for sixty interned children.[24] A Hanukkah entertainment implied an act of passive resistance. The festival, celebrating the Jews regaining control over the Jerusalem temple from the Syrians, glorifies active Jewish defiance even in the face of overwhelming odds. (It is no coincidence that Samy Feder remembered that the two holidays which inspired theatrical activities in Bergen-Belsen were Hanukkah and Purim. Purim also celebrates Jewish victory over oppression.) Probably the most successful production in Theresienstadt was the original children's opera *Brundibár*, composed by the Czech Hans Krása.

While the documents reprinted in this volume clearly describe the full-scale productions mounted in the Nazis' model camp, Theresienstadt, including operas and classical texts, there were also fully staged presentations in another camp: Czestochowa (Poland). The Czestochowa labor camp was run by the *Wehrmacht* rather than by the SS and, therefore, daily existence was comparatively more tolerable. Shie Tigel, a Warsaw Yiddish actor, a singer named Tisaman, and an amateur named Jacobovitsch organized the entertainments presented in this camp in early 1944. Going from barrack to barrack, they created an improvised traveling theater by placing a plank over bunks and employing a curtain of blankets sewn together. Since Tigel, the group's director, had a comparatively easier work detail, he was able to devote time to reconstructing theatrical materials from memory, while holding rehearsals in the evenings.

With the arrival of more Jews, including a complete sixteen-man band, Tigel's theater ensemble grew. Even more remarkably, "a special barrack for theater, with a stage, curtains, and light reflectors was constructed."[25] The first full-scale production, a classic Yiddish farce, *The Two Kuni Lemels*,[26] was presented four times with music arranged by the camp orchestra's conductor, Katershinski. Understandably, Czestochowa's theater became a popular institution, with performances given every Saturday and Sunday.

According to Tigel, the only damper on the holiday-like festivities was the presence of German observers. Other productions directed by the Warsaw actor included Goldfadden's *Hungerman un Kibtsnizon*, Lateiner's *Sarah Scheindel*, a musical entitled *I Am to Blame*, and a Yiddish version of Sergei Tretyakov's *Roar China*. For *Roar China*, intensive rehearsals were held, new scenery painted, new costumes sewn, and Katershinksi composed a new score. The only change in Tigel's adaptation of the Soviet propaganda play was that instead of the red banner being flown at the play's end, a green flag was substituted. At the end of 1944, when control of the Czestochowa camp was turned over to the SS, this short-lived, yet productive, theatrical venture ceased operation.[27]

Analyzing the varied fare produced under Tigel's supervision sheds more light on the functions of concentration camp theater. The Goldfadden plays and the Lateiner drama are all classics of the Yiddish theater; Goldfadden, for that matter, is considered the "father" of Yiddish drama.[28] The productions of these works indicate the desire to cling to tradition. *Roar China*, on the other hand, could only have been meant as propaganda.

Tretyakov's play deals with the exploitation of Chinese coolies by Western powers. When a Chinese boatman kills an American businessman in self-defense, retributions are demanded, including the execution of three innocent coolies. The final scene, however, depicts the successful beginnings of a revolt by the oppressed.[29] The parallels between the exploited Chinese and Jewish slave laborers in Czestochowa are quite obvious. For example, just as the boatman's act of self-defense resulted in brutal and arbitrary revenge, any act of resistance or attempt to escape usually culminated in the execution of innocent concentration camp prisoners. Therefore, in Shie Tigel's production, *Roar China*'s denouement may have been intended as an incitement for revolt. Tigel apparently realized how propagandistic his production was and, fearing German reprisals, he presented it only once.

Though accounts of the survival of theater in the Nazi concentration camps are fascinating, the more important question is why did the performing arts survive? Part of the reason, as has been indicated, lies in their being seen as acts of resistance. Satire was the main ingredient of the camp cabarets. The production of the propagandistic *Roar China* was an act of defiance.

These artists were also attempting to make their existences more bearable. Entertainment and escapism were key factors in keeping theater alive. Hence,

traditional dramas, comedies, and cabaret were the basic staple of camp productions. As art historian Paul Moscanyi notes in his general discussion of
culture in Theresienstadt: "All [the] . . . cruelty and sadism contrasted strangely
with the total indifference of the SS as to what was going on in the houses and
barracks after the doors closed for the night. Cultural life sprang up quickly
and spontaneously as a necessity for survival."[30]

Many contemporary historians and literary critics, including Lawrence
Langer, point out that acts of cultural resistance were ultimately futile. In addition, they correctly warn against the danger of creating an overly sentimental
portrait of Holocaust existence by focusing on such activities. That theater survived in the ghettos and concentration camps during the Nazis' war against the
Jews does not diminish the horror; for that matter, the cultural struggle against
the Nazis' death machine underscores even more sharply the abandonment of
Europe's Jewish population.

Still, the survival of theater in the Nazi concentration camps illustrates
novelist and camp survivor Jorge Semprun's observation that "in the camps
man . . . becomes that invincible being capable of sharing his last cigarette butt,
his last piece of bread, his last breath to sustain his fellow man."[31] If the outside
world provided no support or sustenance, theater was another attempt by the
victims to sustain one another and to try to preserve a semblance of normality
in an obscenely abnormal universe.

Singing in the Face of Death

A Study of Jewish Cabaret and Opera during the Holocaust

SAMUEL M. EDELMAN

THE ACT OF RESISTANCE suggests a reverse action on the course of events that affect individuals. When confronted with one force a second force will be used to counteract the first force to either place it in balance over and against the reaction or to overcome the original force. In the case of the Holocaust, Jewish resistance took a number of different forms. First, there was the armed resistance against the Nazis by the various Jewish partisan groups or in individual circumstances where arms could be constructed or purchased. Second, there was the physical resistance embodied in various acts of sabotage against the production of German war materials by Jewish workers. Third, there was, what many scholars have ignored, spiritual resistance or the active use of literature, music, art, and theater to react against the Nazi decrees and actions.[1] In the face of the Nazis' desire to dehumanize and eradicate the Jewish people from the earth, resistance was expressed in means other than physical. Words too could be actions. Symbolic behavior could mediate between people and achieve what force was not permitted to do. Without weapons or means of sabotage the victims could not stop the killing but they could act upon the attempted dehumanization. This was the tragic choice confronting the victims of the Holocaust—to die by giving up or committing suicide or to fight back with whatever means at hand. For some the only means at hand were rhetorical—to resist the dehumanization through art and literature. To understand the rhetorical nature of the use of spiritual resistance we shall examine some of

Originally published in the *Publications of the World Union of Jewish Studies* (Jerusalem: Publications of the World Union of Jewish Studies, 1986), 205–11.

the cabarets and operas done during the Holocaust and review the comments of two survivors who participated in these activities.

To understand how words could act as actions in the creation of new realities we must explore the idea of rhetoric and the rhetorical situation. The idea of the rhetorical situation is crucial to our understanding of the utility of cabaret and opera during the Holocaust. Lloyd Bitzer wrote a seminal article explaining the rhetorical situation. Bitzer explained that a situation became rhetorical when communication could be used to overcome a real or imagined exigence. Bitzer wrote that "a work of rhetoric is pragmatic; it comes into existence for the sake of something beyond itself; it functions ultimately to produce or change the world; it performs some task. In short, rhetoric is a mode of altering reality, not by direct application of energy to objects, but by the creation of discourse which changes reality through the mediation of thought and action."[2] The rhetorical situation only applies to those situations in which individuals can act upon the concern confronting them through communication of some sort.[3] What gives the creative residue of the victims of the Holocaust its rhetorical emphasis? Simply put, words could create actions and through words resistance could be taken. First of all the situation confronting the victims was one of violence and unrelenting horror which for the most part could not be met by force of arms or sabotage. Second, without arms the only recourse was to use discourse as resistance.

One of the most famous cabaret players in Europe was Willy Rosen. He was incarcerated in the Westerbork concentration camp in northeast Holland. At this camp the camp commander believed that plays and cabarets would be a means by which the prisoners could be kept calm until they were transported to their deaths. But for the prisoners the exigence confronting them was quite basic — the need to know what was awaiting them outside of Westerbork. To do that one needed information. Information was needed about their situation in the camp and also about the infamous transits. Most at Westerbork had no idea of what awaited themselves in Auschwitz and in the transports. Little was known of the outside world at all. Yet within the cabaret bits and pieces of information could be transmitted with small doses of implied warning to those who listened. Subtly, without calling attention to it, Willy Rosen was warning the members of the audience at his last performance that the transports meant no return. It was an act of resistance that many of us today may not perceive, but nevertheless it was there in this excerpt from a cabaret piece by Willy Rosen called "Goodbye to Westerbork," a monologue given the night before he was shipped to Poland.

"We're not in a hurry and we've plenty of time . . ." scene from Max Ehrlich's revue, *Humor und Melody,* 1943, Westerbork. The popular October 1938 cabaret number, "Stagecoach" ("Die Postkutsche"), featured music by Willy Rosen. Courtesy Akademie der Künste, Berlin

My beloved Westerbork, you and I must part,
And a small tear cannot be avoided.
Though you were often tough and unpleasant,
At times, you were almost peaceful.
My Westerbork, you plagued me a lot
And yet you had a sex appeal all your own.
And now softly I say goodbye, beloved boiler room.
One last toot on the whistle before I go.
Farewell my little room with your little carpet . . .
Farewell all you many beloved service reports,
I'm no longer compartmentalized.
I make place. I yield.
I've seen many a transport leave,
And now they are about to throw me on
the old iron.
Now I, myself, get on the train with my back pack.
If you ask me I think it's pretty nasty.

But I don't want pity, nor good advice,
I'll make it alright, I'm an old front soldier.
In Westerbork, nothing can happen to me anymore,
I am going where others are organizing things.
Give me my last time rations.
I depart with butter and a lot of experience.
I'll pack everything, leave nothing behind,
I'll even take my little wife, my best piece.
Adieu F.K.* and Y. Adieu to the laundry,
Today my laundry number will be available again.
Farewell dear JPA,** farewell it's time for me to go,
Tell your worries to someone else,
Farewell you old camp dwellers, dear Brothers,
Perhaps we'll see each other in this life again.
I can't send postcards from where I'm going,
So perhaps I can remain in your memories this way.
Now I am sitting in that compartment
And the whistle sounds
And I let my eyes wander across the area.
Now I realize what it means to say
Farewell my Westerbork, camp Hooghallen.[4]

The key phrase in this monologue by Rosen is the simple phrase, "I can't send postcards from where I'm going, So perhaps I can remain in your memories this way." The quiet implication here is to Rosen's future. One must understand the context for these two lines. Westerbork was a transit camp to the death camp at Auschwitz. The Nazis created a facade that Auschwitz was a relocation camp for people to start new lives. To help that myth continue they forced the victims to write postcards about how nice the camp was to their friends and loved ones left behind. The implication in Rosen's monologue is that he is going to his death and by extension so too are all the rest of the audience who will be transported. It is possible that everyone in the audience may have known about the reality of Auschwitz via the grapevine Rosen refers to. Nevertheless, the rhetorical nature of his action is that he stated his feeling in public even under the watchful eyes of the Nazis. He knew that the Nazis were listening and therefore his monologue was filled with statements and descrip-

* Original editorial note: F.K.: Fliegende Kolonne [Flying Brigade] — A group of internees who were in charge of putting luggage into the trains.
** JPA: Jewish Press Agency, that is, camp grapevine.

tions that formed a simple code about the camp and its everyday activities. His reference to the grapevine as the Jewish Press Agency and to the dispensary and to his giving up his laundry number all were poignant reminders of the Westerbork camp. All are also reminders to both himself and to the audience of the constraints that kept them from a greater range of decisions about their lives. The rhetorical nature of the Rosen cabaret monologue can best be seen in the final ironic line: "Now I realize what it means to say Farewell my Westerbork."

A second example of the rhetorical nature of resistance comes from the Auschwitz concentration camp. Max Garcia was sent to Auschwitz in 1943 from Holland. While there he joined up with a group of other Dutch Jews who had been involved in cabarets. Max's friends were able to persuade the SS to permit a cabaret to entertain the Nazis and the inmates. For some reason the Nazis permitted this event to take place. In the cabaret there was some singing and dancing, some reference to various German cabaret material, imitations of Maurice Chevalier and other famous performers and some comic routines were performed. The effect on the audience of inmates was understandably great. They responded enthusiastically. The cabaret returned to them a small sense of normality under the most abnormal of conditions.

Eventually, Max found himself working in the women's camp, Birkenau. While there the cabaret was performed for the Dutch women.

We had planned this, we had fun in doing it, we executed it and we realized that we had taken something on that was bigger than all of us there together. Because after the performance was over and after we had spoken, you know, as little as we could and as illegal as it was, we spoke with some of the Dutch women. Some messages were passed back and forth about those who might be alive or we know might have died and vice versa. We realized, on the way back, that what we had done, although good in heart, was a total failure in the sense that we could not cope [with] what we had awakened in the women and awakened in ourselves in the misery in which we were living.[5]

The cabaret created by Max Garcia and his friends in Auschwitz was a remarkable feat. Yet it gave them pain. For while the cabaret may have been a creation of fantasy, the harsh reality intruded. While Garcia and the men of the cabaret saw this as a defeat it was not. The pain they felt was a reminder to them all that they still were human and they still could feel pain. And that they would not succumb to the numbing failure of giving up.

Garcia clearly stated in interviews that his goal was to survive. Survival was the exigence confronting Max Garcia. He acted upon that exigence with whatever he had at his means. The cabaret acted as discourse upon that exigence within the severe constraints imposed upon Max and his friends and enabled them to avoid the incremental slippage of the victims into their own state of hopelessness. As Max Garcia has stated:

Now what I'm leading here to is that the resistance was there, the resistance was among the prisoners. The resistance was not just in the music, it was not in the joking, it was not just in anything else we did. It was in the refusal. It was in the refusal of becoming inhuman and to refuse them the chance of totally dehumanizing us, those who were still at that time surviving. Now mind you, we who were surviving at that particular time were a handful compared to all those who had arrived there. We were small in group, and yet we persisted because of what we had learned in our survival process, that there was a way in survival by defying.[6]

Another example comes from the Terezín concentration camp in Czechoslovakia. This camp probably more than any other was a cauldron of creative activity, first because the Nazis needed a showcase for world opinion and second because so many of Europe's Jewish elite were incarcerated there. Artistic works from the creation of painting and sculpture to the production of poetry, diaries, and journalism to opera and symphonic creativity were the hallmark of this camp.

Dasha Lewin was a survivor of Terezín and Bergen-Belsen. As a young girl in the Terezín camp she was gifted with an excellent voice. Because of her lovely voice she was asked by one of the artists to participate in productions of Verdi's *Requiem, The Bartered Bride,* and, most important, the famous children's opera *Brundibár.* Dasha Lewin described her situation in Terezín in an interview in this way: "And, at that time, we were told by the elders that anything could prevail and people with strong beliefs and good causes will always survive and for us it was much stronger than just the children doing something for their mother—it was for us the hope that we could survive." The idea that anything could prevail with people who had strong beliefs and good causes is a rhetorical strategy of great strength. The children were imbued with an idea of moral superiority and thus given a sense of hope however unreal it might have been. Certainly, in the case of Dasha Lewin that sense of hope enabled her to survive the war.

The play did another very important thing for the children and the adults both that we have not discussed as yet—it made them forget where they were for a few moments. That ability to disappear into a fantasy world for even a short time was very important. It enabled both adults and children to strengthen themselves for the traumas in front of them. The tragic choice for Terezín and Dasha Lewin was that there was no other means of escape. There was only the fantasy.

It meant much more than just a play. Somehow it got our mind off the daily tragedy of people being sent away and our friends being pulled apart from us and sent to other camps. We did not know really exactly what Auschwitz was, what horrible situation and the conditions were there. I'm sure our elders protected us from it. But we knew that we were departing and being torn apart from families and friends and this music and this loving care and this make-believe which all the elders created around us made us forget many times those ordeals. . . .

I think, looking now as much older than then I think it gave us an idea that we could achieve almost anything. Also, it was entertainment because life there was horrible and boring and sorrow and threats and departures. Then it was like living in another world when you can spend a couple hours listening to something as beautiful as music. For us children, it was certainly entertainment. It was a world of make-believe. We did not realize that we were in Terezín. We were on a national Prague stage; singing and being part of the lives there.[7]

One cannot fathom the pride and hope unless one sees the words themselves in this excerpt from the opera:

> We won a victory
> Over the tyrant mean,
> Sound trumpets,
> beat your drums,
> And show us your esteem!
> We won a victory
> Since we were not fearful,
> Since we were not tearful,
> Because we marched along
> Singing our happy song,
> Bright, joyful and cheerful.
> He who loves his dad
> Mother and native land,
> Who wishes tyrant's end,
> Join us hand in hand
> And be our welcome friend![8]

The ability to resist or to escape, even in fantasy, was developed by the rhetorical creation of cabarets, operas, and plays. One was able to hold on to one's sanity just a little bit longer—to hope just a little bit more—to remember for just a fraction more time that one was truly human. This was the exigence and the outcome for those who participated in the cabarets and operas of the Holocaust.

In conclusion, *Brundibár,* the cabarets, other operas, and creative work taught the victims who participated in them necessary survival lessons as well as an understanding of the evil around them. These creative acts were focused toward either making a statement against the Nazis or in recording the hopes and aspirations of the inmates of the camps for their future lives. Most of all, these works of art were used as creative fantasies to permit the victims to disappear from their starvation and torture for a brief time to another world of music and voice far removed from the concentration camps. For the survivors described in this chapter, their only means of resistance was in words and art. The time has come for scholars of the Holocaust and Jewish culture to begin to analyze the vast amount of surviving cultural materials to begin to understand the reactions of the victims more clearly. That exigence is left to us as the survivors of the Holocaust. It is the rhetoric of our own tragic choice.

DOCUMENTS AND MEMOIRS

Cultural Activities in the Vilna Ghetto, March 1942

THE NUMBER of cultural events in March [1942] was exceptionally high, because all existing suitable premises in the ghetto, like the theater, gymnasium, youth club, and school quarters, were used. Every Sunday six to seven events took place with over two thousand participants. At the end of the month the Culture Department had to give up to the incoming out-of-town Jews a number of premises like the gymnasium, School No. 2, Kindergarten No. 2, and a part of School No. 1.[1] This will greatly affect the work of the schools, the sports division, and also the theater, which had to take into its building the sports division and the workers' assemblies.

(1) School Division

A disruption in the regular school activity occurred 24 March because of the occupation of the above-mentioned part of the school premises. School No. 1 had to shift its two upper grades (6 and 7) to afternoon session. School No. 2, which occupied the upper story of the school building on 21 Niemecka Street, also had to shift two classes (both 6th grades) to afternoon session. Kindergarten No. 2 moved into the quarters of the Children's and Youth Club. School No. 3 gave up half its quarters to School No. 2 and shifted all five high school classes to afternoon session. All these changes are an impediment to the work of the schools, and, if at all possible, the schools should be returned to their premises as soon as possible.

At the start of the month, the schools conducted several more morning programs (see report for previous month). On 7 March, School No. 3 invited all parents to a school program in the theater. School No. 1 presented a morning program on 14 March by the younger classes in its own quarters. On 21 March

From *A Holocaust Reader,* ed. Lucy S. Dawidowicz (New York: Behrman House, 1976), 208–18. Translated, with notes, by Adah B. Fogel.

(Purim), special children's celebrations were held in all classes without exception. The children received a gift from the Food-supply Department — *hamantaschen*.[2] Kindergarten No. 1 and School No. 2 presented morning programs that day for the parents.

The Children's and Youth Club, beside its regular activities, organized special projects every Sunday. The History Circle presented a trial of Josephus Flavius, which was on a high scholarly level; the Literary Circle — a Yehoash evening with a rich program.[3] Besides that, the club prepared a Purim entertainment and a recitation contest. In connection with the Yehoash program, the Club set up a Yehoash exhibit, which later remained open to the public for two weeks. The older classes of the schools also visited the exhibit with their teachers.

High school teachers have completed their work on the curriculum of the high school classes in the ghetto.

On 11 March a discussion evening was held at the Ghetto Chief's on the education of the young people in the ghetto. Several dozen teachers, writers, and communal leaders were invited.

On 12 March a Sutzkever evening was held at the Teachers' Association.[4] The poet read his latest poem, "Kol Nidre." The Music School continues regularly.

(2) Theater Division

Two important premieres took place in the theater this month. On 13 March, the symphony orchestra, under the baton of W. Durmashkin, presented its fifth program: Beethoven's Leonore No. 3, Chopin's Piano Concerto in E Minor, and Tchaikovsky's Fifth Symphony. The youthful orchestra surmounted the great difficulties of the program and the performance was satisfactory. On 27 March, the opening of D. Pinski's *The Treasure* took place.[5] The play's text was significantly abridged and considerably revised by the director, I. Siegel. His conception was to turn the play into a musical comedy. Original lyrics were written by Leib Rosenthal. Musical accompaniment was by M. Wechsler. Opening night was a great success. A number of writers, teachers, and cultural leaders attended a general rehearsal (a day before the opening), of which they spoke favorably.

Because of preparations for the two openings, there were only twelve events during the month. There were four performances of *The Treasure*, two of *The Man Under the Bridge* (for the fifteenth and sixteenth times; the play is still a success), two performances of the review *You Never Can Know* (the nineteenth and twentieth times, a special matinee performance for residents of the Káilis blocks);[6] the program of the symphony orchestra was repeated three times, and a literary-musical evening was held once, with a mixed program. . . .

On 30 March the theater celebrated the fortieth anniversary of actress Esther Lipovska's stage career. *The Treasure* was given and appropriate speeches were made. The guest of honor was awarded all receipts.

The theater's gross receipts for March totaled over 4,300 marks. Of this, the Communal Relief Committee and Winter Relief received about 2,000 marks.[7]

For April, fourteen events in the theater are planned. Because of the small number of events in March (only Saturdays and Sundays), there was no free performance. In April one free performance is being planned for the Brigadiers Council and one free concert for the Social Welfare.

(3) Library, Reading Room, Archives

During the month the library lent 13,500 books (an increase of 2,800 over the previous month), 65 percent of which were for adults and 35 percent for children. In March 100 subscribers were added and by 1 April the library had 2,592 readers. On 12 March, the Ghetto Chief ordered the ghetto population to return to the library all books (except textbooks and prayerbooks). By the end of the month 1,750 books had been returned. On 25 March the ghetto court tried 15 readers who had not returned books. The court sentenced them to one day conditional arrest and a fine.

An average of 206 persons visited the reading room daily (155 in February), as hitherto, a maximal number.

During the month the Archives collected 101 documents. Besides that, 124 folklore items were assembled.

(4) Sports Division

The Sports Division, which resumed its activity only at the beginning of February in the room at 7 Rudnicka Street, had to give up the space on 24 March and is once again without quarters. This is a great loss, because in a short time the Sports Division had attracted 415 active members, acquired considerable equipment, and developed exemplary activities. When the premises were closed, 2 groups had been organized for gymnastics, rhythmics, running and jumping games, and boxing, with 637 members (many members are registered in two or even three groups). Besides the usual program of the sports groups in March, sport competitions were held every Sunday, namely, a contest of running and jumping games between the "Káilis" and the ghetto teams; a five-player team for men and a three-player game for women, and a basketball tournament.[8] In the mornings the ghetto schools held their gymnasium classes on the sports premises.

In April it is expected that Sports Division will move to the lobby of the theater. The quarters are small and the Sports Division will have very few program possibilities.

(5) Art Exhibit

On 29 March an art exhibit of paintings, sculpture, graphics, etc., opened in the lobby of the theater. Fifteen artists are represented with a variety of works. Besides the noted Vilna artists Rachel Sutzkever (oils and watercolors), Jacob Sher (part of the album, *Vilna Ghetto*), Uma Olkenicka (graphics), and Yudel Moot (sculptures and an album of papier-mâché), a number of young artists participated. N. Drezin exhibited twelve satires and caricatures of well-known ghetto figures; four members of the Plastic Plan of Vilna showed carved medallions and miniatures of the Great Synagogue, cathedral, etc. Engineering Architect F. Rom made miniatures of her own designs for office furniture; G. Sedlis exhibited three paintings (watercolors and pencil). Of special note are the works of three children in the exhibit. S. Wolmark and Z. Weiner sketched ghetto themes (gates of the ghetto, etc.). Nine-year-old S. Bock is considered by the jury to be extraordinarily gifted, and the jury selected thirty of his drawings to show.

Award-winning works in the art contest (see February report) are also shown. The exhibit is extremely successful and is visited by hundreds daily. Children of the ghetto schools visited the exhibit together with their teachers. The exhibit will remain open until 4 April. The Ghetto Chief intends to purchase several of the exhibited works, which have ghetto themes.

(6) Support for Writers and Artists

During the month the Literary Association continued to submit works of its members, in order to obtain honoraria from the Ghetto Chief via the Culture Department. Dr. Gordon completed the first chapter of a philosophical work (*Apriorist Foundations of History*) and received another advance on his honorarium; Jacob Sher submitted to a jury his album, *Vilna Ghetto,* from which the jury selected ten sketches. Leib Turbowicz completed the first four chapters of a large work on the history of the Jews in Vilna, receiving a substantial honorarium (500 marks). The board of the Literary Association has strict standards for submissions and at its last meeting rejected various works of six authors. In the April budget the sum of 1,000 marks is expected to be assigned to support of writers and artists.

(7) Workers' Assemblies

The workers' assemblies, organized by the Brigadiers Council in cooperation with the Culture Department, are attracting ever larger audiences. In March they covered these topics: (1) Award winning writers (outside and inside the ghetto), (2) the ghetto court, (3) Itzik Manger.[9] After every lecture there is entertainment (recitations, singing, etc.). Last Sunday no assembly was held because the premises were taken over for sports. From 4 April, the assemblies will be resumed on Sunday mornings in the ghetto theater.

Vilna Ghetto: 2 April 1943
[Signed] G. Jaszunski
Director

Selections from *Surviving the Holocaust:*
The Kovno Ghetto Diary

AVRAHAM TORY

On 23 June 1941, the German army took over the city of Kovno, Lithuania. Lithuanian officials decreed on 10 July 1941 that a ghetto would be established across the river from Kovno in the suburb, Slobodka (known as Vilijampolé). Six thousand of Kovno's 35,000 Jews lived there. By the end of July 1941, an Elder Jew was assigned to manage the ghetto. Jewish Police and a Jewish Council were also established.

There were often "actions" in which Jews were taken to the nearby Ninth Fort and executed. Ten thousand Jews were executed in the "Great Action" of 28 October 1941. Deportations of Jews to Kovno from Western Europe began in January 1942. On 26 October 1943, the ghetto was transformed into a concentration camp, specifically a labor camp. Many Jews escaped, as did Avraham Tory in March 1944. Soviet forces took over the camp in August 1944.

Avraham Tory (born Avraham Golub in 1909) studied law at the university in Kovno, graduating in 1933. His active membership in Zionist committees almost got him deported once the Soviet Union began to construct military bases in Lithuania. He fled to Vilna until the Germans attacked the Soviet Union, whereupon he returned to Kovno. Tory became deputy secretary of the newly established Jewish Council. From this vantage point, he recorded events and kept copies of decrees. He eventually hid five crates of documents, buried deep beneath a cellar. Three of the five crates were recovered in August 1944.

28 June 1942

Festivities for the schoolchildren took place in the yeshiva on Yeshiva Street. An orchestra composed of well-known Kovno musicians played. The organizers asked the audience: "No applause, please." Placards with quotations in the

Originally published by Harvard University Press (Cambridge, Mass., 1990), 100, 432–33.

hall read: "God consoles in the straits of pity"; "I led you out of your grave, my people." From this very same hall of the yeshiva, 534 academics had been taken out in the first "action" in the ghetto.

24 July 1943

We devoted a great deal of thought to the subject of how the twentieth and twenty-first of Tammuz should be commemorated.[1] At first the idea was to hold a gathering of many participants, with speeches on topical subjects, but we decided not to do this, for reasons of security in the ghetto. In the end we decided to hold a concert: Hebrew music, Hebrew songs, the recitation of Hebrew poems. Our police orchestra got down to work at once; they began rehearsals of melodies such as the song eulogizing Theodor Herzl, and other songs of the Land of Israel.

The concert took place today. The police hall was packed with notables and with the most active members of the Zionist movement left in the ghetto. The public and the seating arrangements were different from any previous occasion. The first row of seats, always reserved for the officials of the labor office and others who have connections, was now occupied by the members of Matzok, and by veteran Zionists — the leaders and spokesmen of the Zionist public in prewar Lithuania. Behind them were seated several hundred Zionist comrades.

The atmosphere in the hall was festive. For the first time in three years our comrades saw one another at a mass meeting. Instead of pictures of Herzl and Bialik on the walls, a neatly designed evening program was handed to each of the participants. Our own Fritz Gadiel, director of the graphics workshop in the ghetto, designed the program: It depicted a blue-white flag lowered three-quarters way down the mast, fluttering in the wind, with black clouds above it. It was adorned by the insignia of the Committee of the Jewish community in the ghetto, and on it was written in artistically designed letters: "Herzl-Bialik, 20th–21st of Tammuz, 1943, the Vilijampolé Ghetto."

At this point it would have been only proper for one of the leaders to rise to deliver a speech to those present; words we have been waiting for and long-ing for for years, words which would warm everyone's heart, which would lift them from the depths of dejection and fly them to distant, happier worlds with no barbed wire fence, not even a reminder of it.

First, the conductor and violinist S. Hofmekler gave a signal. Then the sounds of Perlmutter's "For Thou Art Dust" and Idelsohn's "For Herzl's Soul" filled the hall. Inspired by a sense of the significance of a great moment, those gathered listened to the sounds of the orchestra. Next, a Bialik poem, "The

Word," was recited. Each phrase was absorbed by the audience as never before, its appreciation shown by the stormy applause. Then the orchestra played "Song of the Valley," followed by a selection of songs from the Land of Israel. The singer Mrs. Ratchko then sang with considerable talent "Two Letters" by Avigdor Hameiri and "Let Me In" by Bialik. Kupritz then recited the chapter "At the End of Days"; Zaks sang "The Harbor Song," and the violinist Stupel played—with great emotion—a Hebrew melody by Akhron. A string of Zionist dancing songs was then played, amid cries of joy from the enthusiastic audience. The concert was not over yet. But one such gathering had been enough for our people to come together in one mass, united and guided by one idea—the idea of the Kingdom of Israel.

At the end, the whole audience rose to its feet as one man and sang the "Hatikvah" to the accompaniment of the orchestra. The mighty sounds of the Zionist anthem went out great distances, to the mountains of Judea, to the valleys of Sharon, to the Mediterranean, to the banks of the Jordan, to Mount Scopus, and to the cities and villages, farms and kibbutzim of the Jezreel Valley and the Galilee. The sounds of the anthem conveyed greetings from here, and returned from that distant land with tidings of redemption drawing near.

Our hearts were filled with joy; tears kept flowing from our eyes. Hope and courage issued from the depths of our souls, crying aloud: "Our hope is not yet lost!" The thick pillars of the yeshiva building, where the concert took place, were soon covered with drops of moisture. A mood of enthusiasm reigned in the hall. It was a festive occasion, pervaded by splendor.

Comrades shook hands and exchanged meaningful glances. It was a magnificent moment.

"Invitation"

LEO STRAUSS

Leo Strauss, a Viennese-born cabaret writer, was deported to Terezín in the fall of 1942, where he wrote for a German-language cabaret. He was deported to Auschwitz, where he perished, in the fall of 1944. See Part III for more on Strauss and his work.

Friends and loved ones, do you suffer
From a life of want and fear
Things at home becoming tougher?
Pack your bags and join me here

Do you live in trepidation?
Is your life a vale of tears?
I'm off'ring you some consolation
Pack your bags and join me here

Are you owing lots of money?
Sunk in debt from ear to ear?
Such a state is far from funny
Pack your bags and join me here

Is it hard to find some work, sir
In the current atmosphere?
Enough to make you go berserk, sir?
Pack your bags and join me here

Had enough of constant moving?
Different houses every year?
Need a home that's calm and soothing?
Pack your bags and join me here

The original cabaret song, "Einladung," is housed at Yad Vashem, Israel, and has been anthologized in Ulrike Migdal, ed., *Und die Musik spielt dazu: Chansons und Satiren aus dem KZ Theresienstadt* (Munich: Piper, 1986), 61–63. Translated by Roy Kift.

Are your vases all in pieces?
Got a broken chandelier?
Tablecloths all stained and greasy?
Pack your bags and join me here

Got a woeful constitution?
Too much nicotine and beer?
There's clearly only one solution
Pack your bags and join me here

When neighbors see the star you're wearing
Do they start to hiss and jeer?
Had enough of hostile staring?
Pack your bags and join me here

Are your stock and shares still sinking?
Servants' wages in arrears?
Nurse has gone and nappy's stinking?
Pack your bags and join me here

Are you sick of penny-pinching?
Shops and markets far too dear?
Tormented by eternal scrimping?
Pack your bags and join me here

Do you dream of ease and pleasure?
Tea and coffee, wine and beer?
Concerts, theater, endless leisure?
Pack your bags and join me here

Here's a wacky world of show biz
Full of laughter, fun and games
The only thing I'd like to know is
How we all get out again

Drama behind Barbed Wire

DAVID WOLFF

Rudolph Carl von Ripper, interviewed by David Wolff, describes an antifascist the-
atrical performance given in the main barrack's hall of the early German concentra-
tion camp, Oranienburg, in the mid-1930s.

TWO OF THE PRISONERS in the Oranienburg concentration camp had
been actors in antifascist theater groups. They had rehearsed the principal
roles: an American and a clerk at a travel bureau. The prisoners, along with
the Storm Troop which served as guards, were marched into the main barrack's
hall, at one end of which was a platform of planks set on four barrels, a curtain
made of regulation blankets, and footlights fashioned out of lanterns. Outside,
they could hear the evening change of guards at the barbed wire gates. Heil
Hitler! and the men coming off duty ran down toward the barracks to see the
show the prisoners were putting on.

A play in a concentration camp! The idea itself has the simple and unfore-
seeable turn of irony that only life dares to present.

Baron Rudolph von Ripper, son of a wealthy Austrian Catholic family, had
been imprisoned for persistent antifascist work in Germany, and he helped to
write and stage this extraordinary play. The prisoners had obtained permission
to present a show once a month, amateur night, loud, sentimental, and up-
roarious. This time they proposed something just as loud and funny, but with a
wry and subtle undertone which the Storm Troopers would be too slow-witted
to censor.

Von Ripper drew an enormous map of Germany, marking the location of
each concentration camp with an elaborate symbol of a castle. It happens that
the German word "burg" means castle, and it happens also that nearly half

Originally published in *Theatre Arts Committee Magazine* 1, no. 8 (March 1939): 15–16.

the concentration camps had names ending in "burg": Oranienburg, Branden-burg, Papenburg, etc. It was on this cheap and bitter pun that the whole play was based.

Against von Ripper's drawings as a backdrop, the play begins. An American tourist, wearing the conventional comic-strip cap that all Americans affect, enters a travel bureau, loudly demanding assistance in planning a trip through Germany.

The clerk proposes that a highly gratifying tour would be one which took in all the famous "castles." No sooner does the American agree, than two uni-formed men leap on the platform and seize him by the shoulders. (All pris-oners wore discarded dark-blue uniforms of the Prussian police, so they had merely to button them up to the chin to present a highly official appearance.) The American objects violently, but the clerk explains that in the new Germany "one travels only under supervision." (Both prisoners and Storm Troopers roared at that one—perhaps for the same reason.)

So the American is conveyed from concentration camp to concentration camp. He is given to understand "before Germany awoke," these castles were used for criminals, but now they exist "for educational purposes only." One double-edged joke is inserted among nine innocent wisecracks. They arrive at a new castle; the name is pompously announced. "Papenburg!" A backstage prisoner, formerly a musician, blows forth a burlesque fanfare. Papenburg, the American is told, is not particularly renowned for its antiquity, but it is a very beautiful "sea-castle," entirely surrounded by water. (The Papenburg concen-tration camp is located in an enormous swamp, and here the prisoners work, thigh-deep in water all day long.) Here in Papenburg, the American is in-formed, he may enjoy "water sports."

What to the guards seemed only a rather amusing attempt by the prisoners to make fun of themselves, became to the prisoners a heart-warming anti-Nazi drama. As artist von Ripper explained, each acid jest, each shading of hatred, was seized upon by the prisoners and served to hearten them for weeks there-after. Every nuance of meaning was weighted with terrific emphasis, for most of these prisoners had survived months of nightmare before they had been shipped to Oranienburg; and they were even yet engaged in a struggle of will and personal integrity against the systematic torture that the Nazis had in-vented for them.

Von Ripper himself is such a man—a man who survived a prolonged rou-tine of horror. He begged the writer not to make this account a personal history of himself, but that is unavoidable. The reader must multiply in his own imagi-nation the thousands of men and women with similar courage.

Baron von Ripper had been engaged in secret antifascist work; distributing, for example, the famous Brown Book, bound behind the covers of Goethe's *Hermann and Dorothea*. He was betrayed by an acquaintance who had searched his room in his absence.

Arrested and taken to Columbia House, to be grilled by Hitler's Elite Guards, he refused to give information, denied everything. Then from a semi-circle of five SS men behind him, one stepped forward with a length of lead pipe and fractured his skull. They revived him with pails of water, cracked several ribs with their heavy boots as he lay on the floor, and inflicted terrible internal injuries. Iodine was doused on his wounds, and he was thrown on the stone floor of a cell, where he lay for three days. When finally a doctor visited him, he was ordered to the prison hospital. Von Ripper, riding in a truck with the guards, taunted and insulted them on the way, hoping for a shot that would end the intolerable pain, but they only knocked him unconscious.

After weeks in the hospital, he began to recover. The physicians regarded him as an interesting miracle, put him in special casts, and gave him cigarettes. When the casts were removed he found himself suffering from an uncontrollable palsy.

He was returned to a cell in Columbia House. This prison, unused from 1919 to 1933, was in disrepair: The cell doors had wide cracks near the jamb, and although it was impossible to escape, it was possible to hear the screams of the prisoners undergoing examination and the dull report of the bullets of the execution squad in the cellars. In this vast torture-chamber of cement and iron there took place the individual struggle of each prisoner against the Nazis, of human will against an assault calculated to smash it.

Smoking was forbidden; sleep was impossible. The guard at night would turn on the lights of your cell, slide open the window; and, while he inspected the premises, you had to stand rigidly at attention. You waited fifteen minutes, lying tense on your sack of straw, hearing his heavy boots strike along the stone corridor, while he completed the round of cells on the circular floor, and then turned on your lights again.

Yet von Ripper survived. He even managed to get a cigarette, which he smoked in the latrine. Once he was discovered and sent back to his cell. Some time later, two SS men entered and closed the door. The first officer gave his companion a cigarette, politely offered one to von Ripper. The latter did not move; he was standing rigidly at attention.

"So our friend likes to smoke?" said the officer. "Open your mouth!"

Von Ripper obeyed. The SS man cut a cigarette into thirds, lit each portion from his own cigarette and crammed it into von Ripper's throat.

"Is our friend's throat burning?" he inquired, and he took a cup which von Ripper used for meals, and—but it is impossible to go on with this hideous incident. It is enough to write that von Ripper resisted, remained alive even when they took him to the blood-stained courtyard, made him sign a last letter to his family, and fired actual bullets into the wall beside his head.

He survived. To make way for new arrivals, he was sent to the comparative paradise of the Oranienburg concentration camp. Here he became a member of a group of prisoners who had undertaken the responsibility of keeping up the morale of their fellows. The antifascist play that they staged at the camp was only one of their methods.

On one occasion everyone, guards and prisoners (excepting the Jews, who were forced to miss this pleasure), were assembled to hear Hitler's broadcast. After the speech the band at the Sports-Palast played a Nazi song, the tune stolen from a familiar workers' song. Five prisoners, von Ripper included, spontaneously sang the real antifascist words. The men were driven back to the cells, then hauled out for roll call. No one would say who had sung. The commander stood before them and screamed, "We are the masters in Germany now!" A low voice in the ranks asked, "How long?" As punishment, the prisoners, in a fantastic gymnastic drill, were driven by rifle butts through a maze of obstacles and pits built by the Storm Troopers to exercise themselves.

On another occasion, von Ripper volunteered to read aloud on the monthly "reading night." After reading monotonously the lives of Corneille, of Delacroix, he came to Jaurès, the famous labor leader, and began to read his life with interpolations suitable to the times. For this daring idea he was sent to the "standing cell," a niche in a wall. The door closes on your face, it is impossible even to kneel, and after a few hours you slump down a little with your knees against the door and your back to the wall. Four and a half days later, when the door was opened, he fell flat forward, his limbs swollen and incapable of movement. Yet no one of the prisoners doubted that the defiance was worth the punishment.

When von Ripper obtained his release through pressure by the former Austrian government, his body was broken and his nerves shattered. Several years were needed to recover his health. Even yet, as von Ripper talks to you, he must stop occasionally, to put his shaking hands over his eyes and forehead, to shut away the experience, too terrifying to be recalled.

He asks always that the spirit of the political prisoners in concentration camps be emphasized, their group courage and determination to resist. Any incident of defiance kindled weeks of joy and pride in the prisoners.

Returning home through the town at nightfall, the prisoners would sing the famous *Moorsoldaten,* while the streets were lined with men coming from the factories. And the final verse:

> Sometime we'll be able to say:
> Homeland, you are mine again!
> Then the swamp soldiers will march
> No more with spades into the swamp.

"Nicht mehr! mit dem Spaten, ins moor." And they would shout "Nicht mehr!" while the workmen looked on, crowded in the street, silent, watching—because, as Baron von Ripper explained, it is possible to say more inside a concentration camp than outside one.

That is what Germany is like today, under the rule of fascism, a vast concentration camp, governed by methodical insanity, in which one may live if he doesn't want to think; and if he does, there are the little islands of Columbia House and Oranienburg and all the other "castles," quite isolated, where one can act more freely—at the price of pain, physical humiliation, and death.

And this is the Germany that Dr. Carl-Ludwig Diego von Bergen, Germany envoy to the Vatican, offered to the Cardinals in Rome:

"We are assisting," he brazenly averred, "at the elaboration of a new world, which wants to raise itself upon the ruins of a past that in many things has no longer any reason to exist."

The "ruins" that Dr. Bergen mentioned are the bodies, living and dead, of the antifascists, many of them Catholic, who are today imprisoned behind the barbed wire of Germany's concentration camps.

"The Freest Theater in the Reich"

In the German Concentration Camps

CURT DANIEL

As a focus for attention this season (and as a contrast to last year's focus on retrospect over twenty-five years in the American theater), *Theatre Arts* is offering a series of articles on "A Free Theater for a Free People," all of them by distinguished men and women of other lands — mostly, but not altogether, lands in which neither the theater nor the people are free today. *Theatre Arts* bought the first of the series, on the freest theater in the Reich, over a year ago, with an unusual provision. We could keep it unpublished as long as it seemed possible that publication might suggest some new cruelty to the Nazis, some further deprivation of rights among prisoners in concentration camps. Also, permission was given to omit or change names where it seemed advisable. Today no further cruelties than those already inflicted seem possible.

— *Theatre Arts* Editors' Notes [1941]

THERE ARE so many contradictions in the organization of the Third Reich that it is only surprising at first thought to learn that theaters, both permitted and illicit, exist in the great German concentration camps. The nature and extent of this theater varies in direct relation to the conditions prevailing in a particular camp. Thus in Dachau, with its prison population of almost 10,000, where orderliness is the quintessence and *Gründlichkeit* [attention to detail] is king, any licensed theatricals are out of the question. Here the discipline is so Spartan that it would reduce a military camp to kindergarten proportions. On

Originally published in *Theatre Arts Monthly* 25 (November 1941): 801–7.

the other hand, the larger camp of Buchenwald, with 25,000 prisoners, is quite different, or was, at least, during the writer's period of "protective custody" when it contained both licensed and illicit theatrical activity.

The difference in the main was due to two factors. First, Dachau was in the nature of a show camp, often visited by distinguished foreigners. It was not intended by the Nazi "humanitarians" that these guests should leave with the impression that "dangerous" prisoners were being pampered with entertainment. Second, the atmosphere of the concentration camps always reflected the personality of the SS officer in command. Dachau always had a disciplinarian who would make the generally conceived version of a Prussian officer look like a weak sister. Buchenwald was the reverse. There was plenty of discipline but it flew around in loose, uncoordinated pieces. There was a succession of drunken and eccentric SS camp commanders. In the writer's time anything could and did happen. Thus an illicit theater thrived continuously, and, for a short time, at the order of a drunken camp commander, the prisoners were obliged to produce a show that ran from two to four performances a day. About this, more later.

Performances in Dachau were, in the nature of things, extremely undercover, being carried out by the prisoners at great personal risk. There were no specific camp orders forbidding this form of entertainment but its discovery would have so infuriated the SS camp guards that torture and death would have followed automatically.

The only day in the week when there could be anything in the way of entertainment was Sunday. On this day there was none of the hard work characteristic of weekdays, although the morning was spent in cleaning up the camp huts and in roll call. In the afternoon and evening the prisoners were left to themselves. On alternate Sundays the prisoners were permitted to write brief letters home or to read the newspapers (in Dachau, unlike the other camps, it was permitted to read any newspaper printed in Germany). As far as the SS guards were concerned, the dead hour for the camp was around 4 P.M. Under ordinary circumstances there would be no SS men nearer than the watch-towers surrounding the camp. The prisoners took this opportunity to create their own organized entertainment.

In Dachau there were two main types of entertainment, singing and dramatic. These again were divided according to whether the performers were political or nonpolitical (in addition to the political prisoners, there were five other categories). In the huts mainly occupied by politicals the chief divertissement was the singing of *Volkslieder* and the songs common to the international revolutionary movement. In addition many new songs were composed, generally around the themes of the camp and liberty. The SS men (who were invariably short of cash and who would take a bribe as easily as they would shoot a man down) permitted the prisoners to have a violin, guitar, accordion, and harmonica. Another form of entertainment favored by the politicals was the small satirical cabaret so common in pre-Hitler Europe. This was characterized by the recital of poems criticizing the regime and making fun of the camp personnel, humorous political monologues lashing the Nazis, and antifascist patter for one, two, or three actors.

There was a big change in the camp entertainment, both political and nonpolitical, on the arrival in May 1938 at Dachau of some thousands of Viennese, first victims of the Anschluß. Especially was there an increase in the number and quality of cabaret entertainments. There was quite an influx of talented and well-known actors of cabaret, stage, and screen. One of the best known was Paul Morgan, famous throughout Central Europe as actor and playwright, whose musical comedy *Axel vor der Himmels Tor* [*Axel before Heaven's Gate*] rocketed the Scandinavian Sarah Leander into prominence. The reason given by the Gestapo for Morgan's arrest was that a letter from Stresemann was found among his possessions, a simple letter of thanks for a charity performance given years before.[1] Morgan was later transferred to Buchenwald, where he died from inflammation of the lungs contracted during one of the coldest winters in Europe.

The nonpolitical entertainment at Dachau was performed mostly by the professional actors among the prisoners. With the exception of some of the cabaret acts the material was "foreign" to the camp. It was the Vienna or Berlin stage, transferred in miniature to the ill-lit huts of Dachau. Among the writer's fellow prisoners were many well-known in the world of the European theater, actors, singers, composers, and artists—the drawing cards of Vienna's leading cabarets.

The performances generally took place inside a hut, with some hundreds of prisoners grouped in a circle around the artists. Sentries were posted at the ends of the huts to make certain that there were no SS men in the locality. At times there might be three shows running simultaneously in three huts. The "Stars" ran from one hut to another for their turns.

Sometimes the excellence of a performance brought forth a spontaneous burst of applause. If the SS men on the watch-towers came down to investigate, the scene would be reminiscent of a raid on a Brooklyn speakeasy during Prohibition days, with prisoners jumping out of doors and windows in every direction.

One of the best songs composed in the camp, the Dachau song, was specially composed for the illicit theater. The circumstances relating to its creation are grim but interesting. During 1937, the *London News Chronicle* and the *Manchester Guardian* published some exposures of conditions in the Nazi concentration camps. As a Gestapo reprisal, action was taken against all Jewish prisoners in Dachau camp. For two months they were locked in their darkened huts in complete isolation from the rest of the camp. The political prisoners among them took the initiative to organize some form of entertainment that would keep up the spirit and morale of the other prisoners. During those terrible sixty days the Dachau song was born. The words were so bitter and yet at the same time expressed such hope for the future that the SS guards made it a *verboten* [forbidden] song. This, however, did not prevent the prisoners from singing it.

In Buchenwald the whole atmosphere was different. Everything was as disordered as the mind of the drunken SS camp commander. Whims came from his befuddled head like demons from a Bosch "Last Judgment." One day it would be extra rations and the next, a lashing for every fifth man. And so it came about that at *Silvester* [New Year] he commanded a week of humor from the prisoners.

A prisoner was found who had been *Compère* [an emcee] in a large Berlin music hall. He was made responsible for finding talent among the prisoners and producing it on a given date. After making a survey of the camp talent (of which there was plenty both professional and amateur) he selected about fifteen turns. Other prisoners were made responsible for constructing a theater. The partitions of a long hut were pulled down and a stage with proscenium constructed along the middle of one of the hut's long sides. Overhead lights were set up and a few crudely painted pieces of scenery representing a sylvan glade were built.

At the performance, which ran for a week before, through, and after *Silvester,* the audience, generally amounting to five hundred, were grouped in a flat crescent, some sitting and the majority standing. While the performances were extremely good in the vaudeville class, the atmosphere was always strained by the presence of a number of SS men. The succession of jugglers, acrobats, dancers, conjurers, monologists, songsters, and instrumentalists was held together by the extremely daring *Compère*. With all the *Schmalz* of the experienced cabareteer he introduced the show as follows:

My friends, you are lucky to be here this afternoon. Here, in Buchenwald, we have the best art and the best artists in the whole of Germany. Here you can actually laugh out loud at our jokes. Here is the freest theater in the Reich. In the theaters outside, the actors and the audience are frightened because they fear that they may end up in a concentration camp. That's something we don't have to worry about.

His comments and continuous patter, in the presence of heavily armed SS men who valued human life at less than a cigarette, kept the prisoner-audience breathless. This is a typical example: "You know, times don't really change. I remember that when we had the Kaiser, we always had swine pushing us around. Later when we had the Republic, was it any different? No, we still had swine pushing us around. And what of today?" He waited for an answer. The air was electric as the prisoners watched the SS men out of the corners of their eyes. No answer. He answered the question himself. "Why, today is Monday."

No one really enjoyed the official Buchenwald theater. The presence of so many SS men threw a damper over everything. But it gave the prisoners an idea and from that time until the writer left the camp there was a flourishing underground theater, both political and nonpolitical. The nonpolitical shows were after the style of those held in Dachau—small cabarets with the performances mostly by professional actors.

The political cabarets were the most interesting for, although the performers were generally nonprofessional, their acts were original. There were several groups of about five men each, who made the rounds of the political huts between 6 P.M. and "lights out" on weekdays. The audience was invariably of a high intellectual level, consisting of former members of the *Reichstag*, leaders of the pre–Third Reich political parties, writers, artists, publicists, etc.

In the five-man cabaret in which the writer played, the performance was in the manner of the Viennese *Kleinkunstbühne*, the audience being grouped in a small circle round the performers. Jura Soyfer, the young Austrian poet and dramatist whose tragedy it was to die of typhoid fever in the camp the day after word came of his release, wrote the greater part of the show. The actual creation of the show was an intellectual feat. For obvious reasons nothing could be written down, so that the script—lasting one hour—had to be transmitted to the actors by word of mouth. The program of this small group was repeated on many occasions in the various huts inhabited by the political prisoners. The players took the precaution of tearing off the identification numbers sewn on the right thigh of each prisoner's pants, in case some SS stool pigeon should want to make trouble.

The details of the program were simple. The first item was always the singing of the Buchenwald song by the group. This is an excellent song of the *Volkslied* type, in no way inferior to the better known and already recorded *Moorsoldaten*. Next came a humorous monologue of an imaginary conversation between the drunken camp leader and the equally drunken leader of the German Labor Front, Dr. Robert Ley. This was performed by a famous Central European comedian whose name cannot be mentioned because he is unfortunately still in a concentration camp, though no longer in Buchenwald. This would be followed by more political songs. The most important item would be a short play for three players, lasting for some twenty minutes, a mixture of comedy and satire attacking the administration of the camp and the blood-soaked system that maintained it.

The whole underlying idea of the theatrical activity of the concentration camps was obviously temporary release from the terrible reality of that life. In the case of the political prisoners, whose influence was great, there was the added factor of maintaining morale. The healthiest release was in the form of satire, making fun of certain parts of camp life. The amazing abundance of humor, however, must not be misunderstood. There was, and is, nothing funny about life when death can sneak up in a score of painful ways that seem to have no connection with the laws that govern the outside world.

When at some future but unknowable date not too far distant, the ghastly system of Hitler and his several hundred thousand hangmen has been destroyed by the German people, the great art of the concentration camps will come out into full daylight and be recorded as one of man's great achievements in adversity.

The Yiddish Theater of Belsen

SAMY FEDER

I REMEMBER IT WELL... It was 15 April 1945, seven minutes past three in the afternoon. The British entered Bergen-Belsen and we heard over the loud-speaker the sonorous voice of Captain Sington: "Prisoners of all nations, the British Army has occupied your camp. You are free. . . ."

We could not speak. Tears choked us. There we were, completely stunned with the news of freedom. Those of us who could stand on their feet walked up to the jeep of Lt. Sington and saw another British soldier on it. He spoke in Yiddish: "Jews? Are you Jews? Who of you is Jewish? . . ." Some of us owned up, and the soldier pronounced the blessing of *Shehecheyanu*. He could not get over it — the first Jews from the other side, still alive. . . . He started to cry, un-ashamedly.

Most of us were dangerously ill, and the rest were emaciated from starva-tion and years of suffering inside a concentration camp. We had no strength to express our joy.

We felt, however, that we might have to stay in Belsen for some time yet, until we should be able to emigrate. One of the first things we did by way of organizing our temporary existence in Belsen was to create a cultural unit with various branches. I was charged with the organization of a theater.

Conditions were still pretty chaotic, but this was no novelty to us. We had produced shows even in the concentration camps. We used to improvise a stage right in the middle of a foul barracks, make an old blanket into a curtain and put on a show, with myself as the producer, for Hanukkah, Purim, or whenever we felt that we had a "good" guard who would not be too harsh.

Sometimes we paid for it with casualties, but we never gave it up.

Originally published in *Belsen* (Tel Aviv: Irgun Sheerit Hopleita Me' Haezor Habriti, 1957), 135–39.

Well, there was no danger in putting on shows in Belsen after liberation, but our difficulties were immense.

Our first move was to publish an announcement that a theater troupe was being formed in the camp. Some of my old friends, who appeared in my shows in the concentration camps, turned up and applied to be included in the troupe. There were even one or two who worked with me on the Jewish stage in prewar Poland. It was a great reunion.

Alas, not all of them were well enough to start rehearsals.

I was deeply moved when several Jewish girls came to see me and begged me with tears in their eyes to let them join the troupe. They could speak no Yiddish at all, but they were stagestruck. When I told them that we were going to produce our plays in Yiddish, they promised to learn Yiddish in a very short time. . . .

How could I send them back?

So we started by teaching the girls Yiddish while rehearsing at the same time. These were no ordinary rehearsals. We had no book, no piano, no musical scores. But we could not wait for supplies from outside. There was a need to play, and an eager public. . . . Somebody remembered parts of a play; somebody remembered a song which we could write down—text and music. . . . This way we collected enough songs for a small volume that was published in the camp in January 1946. We improvised scenery, too.

After several months of hard work we could start preparations for our first show after liberation. Our troupe had thirty members, and I must single out, Sonia Baczkowska and Dolly Kotz-Friedler, who were among the first and keenest.

Our first show took place three months after liberation. Despite all the difficulties and improvisations, it was all right on the night, as it always is with good actors.

Just before the curtain was to go up there was an urgent summons for the producer. I came out and was faced with a score of Russian officers, who had come to the show and could not get in. I tried to explain to them that there was simply no room, but they would have none of it. One of them suddenly spoke to me in plain Yiddish: "Look here, comrade, we drove two hundred miles to see your show, are you going to turn us away?"

I took them behind the stage and they watched the show from the wings. In the very last minute there arrived Chaplain Major Isaac Levy [now Jewish Chief Chaplain to H.M. Forces] and Joe Wallhandler of the Joint [The American Joint Distribution Committee] who brought us from somewhere real makeup.

I have never played to such a grateful audience. They clapped and laughed and cried. When we gave, as our last item, the famous song "Think Not You Travel to Despair Again," the thousand people in the hall rose to their feet and sang with us. Then "Hatikvah." [1] Never was "Hatikvah" rendered with such verve as on that first night.

The Kazet-Theater of Belsen was established. We did not, however, rest on our laurels. Soon there were preparations to produce *The Bewitched Tailor,* an ambitious play by any standards and in any place. I worked on the book in hospital, having been run over by a military lorry after our first night.

Meanwhile an ORT School was established in the camp, and they made our scenery and wardrobe. Apart from the Kazet-Theater there was also in Belsen the Workers' Theater of the Left Poale Zion under the management of A. Zandman, which produced several successful plays.

Our first show was given free—those who came first took their seats. . . . But we had to charge for tickets to our second show, and the proceeds astonished us—8,255 marks. We donated the money to the Keren Kayemeth and to a relief fund. I still treasure a receipt for this amount, signed by Dr. Hadassa Bimko.

Soon we were on the road, like all good Yiddish theaters. We played in hospitals, to other camps, and in France and Belgium. The international press began to take note of our theater, and each of our new shows was an artistic event. *Two Hundred Thousand* was a real theatrical achievement. But it is the beginning which remains ingrained in my memory—the first show after liberation.

"Voices"

What follows is a selection of already published excerpts from survivors of various
concentration camps and diarists who mention cultural activities in their writing.
This is not an attempt to catalog all camps or to register as many references to
theater as possible. Rather, the array of "voices" suggests how inmates apparently
found some comfort in storytelling, music, and poetry. At the same time, diarists
like Etty Hillesum and the Dutch journalist Philip Mechanicus note with conflicted
emotion the actual practice of organized "leisure" activities in camps. Both diarists
were expendable. Both were transported from Westerbork to Auschwitz, where they
died. Other writers survived to tell their tales, after the fact, like Primo Levi, Arthur
Koestler, and Denise Dufournier. See also Part III for two accounts from surviving
participants of Terezín's cultural programs.

Selections from *Letters from Westerbork*, Etty Hillesum

Etty Hillesum (1914–43) began her diary in the spring of 1941 in Amsterdam. Several
months later, she was offered a position on the Dutch Jewish Council, exempting her
from deportation to Westerbork. But Hillesum volunteered to go to Westerbork as
a "social worker." She died in Auschwitz in November 1943. Her diaries have been
published under An Interrupted Life: The Diaries of Etty Hillesum, 1941–1943, *trans. Arno Pomerans (Jonathan Cape Ltd., 1983).*

8 July 1943

It is a complete madhouse here; we shall have to feel ashamed of it for three
hundred years. The *Dienstleiters* themselves now have to draw up the transport lists.[1] Meetings, panics—it's all horrible. In the middle of this game with

From Etty Hillesum's *Letters from Westerbork*, trans. Arno Pomerans (New York: Pantheon,
1986), 89, 133; Philip Mechanicus, *Year of Fear: A Prisoner Waits for Auschwitz*, trans. Irene Gibbons (New York: Hawthorn Books, 1964), 144–45, 158–59; Arthur Koestler, *The Scum of the Earth*
(New York: Macmillan, 1941), 134–37; Primo Levi, *If This Is a Man*, trans. Stuart Woolf (London:
Orion, 1960), 62; Denise Dufournier, *Ravensbrück: The Women's Death Camp*, trans. F. W. McPherson (London: George Allen & Unwin, 1948), 29.

human lives, an order suddenly from the commandant: The *Dienstleiters* must present themselves that evening at the first night of a cabaret which is being put on here. They stared open-mouthed, but they had to go home and dress in their best clothes. And then in the evening they sit in the registration hall, where Max Ehrlich, Chaya Goldstein, Willy Rosen, and others give a performance.[2] In the first row, the commandant with his guests. Behind him, Professor Cohen.[3] The rest of the hall full. People laughing until they cried—oh yes, cried. On days when the people from Amsterdam pour into the camp, we put up a kind of wooden barrier in the big reception hall to hold them back if the crush becomes too great. During the cabaret this same barrier served as a piece of decor on the stage; Max Ehrlich leaned over it to sing his little songs. I wasn't there myself, but Kormann just told me about it, adding, "This whole business is slowly driving me to the edge of despair."

24 August 1943

Men from the "Flying Column" in brown overalls are bringing the luggage up on wheelbarrows. Among them I spot two of the commandant's court jesters: The first is a comedian and a songwriter.[4] Some time ago his name was down, irrevocably, for transport, but for several nights in a row he sang his lungs out for a delighted audience, including the commandant and his retinue. He sang "Ich kann es nicht verstehen, daß die Rosen blühen" ["I Know Not Why the Roses Bloom"] and other topical songs. The commandant, a great lover of art, thought it all quite splendid. The singer got his exemption. He was even allocated a house, where he now lives behind red checked curtains with his peroxide-blonde wife, who spends all her days at a mangle in the boiling-hot laundry. Now here he is, dressed in khaki overalls, pushing a wheelbarrow piled high with the luggage of his fellow Jews. He looks like death warmed over. And over there is another court jester: the commandant's favorite pianist. Legend has it that he is so accomplished that he can play Beethoven's Ninth as a jazz number, which is certainly saying something. . . .

Selections from *Year of Fear*, Philip Mechanicus

Philip Mechanicus (1889–1944) was a journalist who wrote for the overseas division of the Algemeen Handelsblad. *He became known for his 1930s travel articles on the Soviet Union and Palestine. After the Germans occupied Holland, he was dismissed from his post although he continued to write articles under a pseudonym. He was arrested in September 1942, tortured at Amersfoort, and spent eight months in*

Westerbork theater: Camilla Spira and Max Ehrlich in *Humor und Melody,* 1943.
Courtesy Akademie der Künste, Berlin

the Westerbork hospital (where he wrote much of his diary). Despite having been a "protected" Jew, he could not retract his name from a transport list. He was deported to Bergen-Belsen in 1944 and later shot to death at Auschwitz.

[Westerbork 1943]

Tuesday, 31 August: Birthday of Queen Wilhelmina

There is something loathsome going on in the background when every transport leaves. This time, while the transport was being got ready and was moving off, people were dancing. Actually dancing. Rehearsals have been going on for some time for a revue. As if Westerbork itself was not rather like a theatrical show. By order of the *Obersturmführer* two thousand guilders have been made available from the camp funds for costumes. The costume-makers had to work all through the night before the transport and on the morning of the transport the dancers had to rehearse for the ballet at an early hour to make sure the premiere of the revue was not a flop. The fun starts next Saturday evening. When the commandant undertakes anything, he does it thoroughly and energetically and nothing and nobody can stand in his way. . . .

Westerbork theater reprise, 1943: the popular scene between student and teacher from Willy Rosen's Kulturbund revue, *Kunterbunt.* Courtesy Akademie der Künste, Berlin

Thursday, 16 September

Went to see the revue once again yesterday evening. Packed out. The ensemble have really got into the spirit of it and the revue is going like clockwork. The response of the audience is mixed. There is great admiration for the work of the cast and people laugh at the jokes and enjoy the words and music of the songs about the camp and the comments of the entertainer, Ehrlich. But the majority of the audience are not at all willing to let themselves go — they seem inhibited. The invitation of Camilla Spira to join in and sing the catchy choruses altogether gets a response only from some of the young people. The older generation keep quiet and cannot relax after all the suffering they have gone through and are still going through daily. Also in the matter of applause the older generation are restrained, but the younger generation are openhearted and burst out from time to time into rhythmical handclapping. Many adults who go to the revue excuse themselves by explaining that they would rather not have gone, but that later on they will be glad to chat about everything that went on at Westerbork. Of course there is a lot of self-deception in this — they do not want to miss the revue, their evening out. At Westerbork they have nothing.

Many German and Dutch Jews refuse to go to the revue, the former because they find there is a painful contrast between the "fun" and the tragedy of the transports, the latter because they cannot enjoy themselves while their relatives, their wives, their husbands, or their children are suffering an unknown fate, joyless, dreary, deprived of everything. But the young people fall over themselves to get tickets for it. They cost only ten cents each. People have never seen a good show so cheaply before, and they will perhaps never see anything as good and as cheap again.

Selection from *The Scum of the Earth,* Arthur Koestler

Arthur Koestler (1905–1983) was a Hungarian-born writer who resided in France primarily as a "resident alien"; he eventually emigrated to Great Britain. He went to Spain during the Spanish Civil War and wrote about his experiences in a Spanish jail cell. After World War II began, he was considered a "left-wing" journalist, arrested, and sent as a political prisoner to the French labor camp, Le Vernet, about thirty miles from the Spanish border.

Christmas came, and all the pitiful fuss to prepare for the traditional prisoners' ersatz rejoicings. The barracks were decorated with green branches over the door, and with the inscription 1940! VIVE LA FRANCE! LIBERTÉ, EGALITÉ, FRATERNITÉ. When all was over the branches were used as latrine brushes and the Liberté, Egalité, and Fraternité scratched out. The camp commandant, whom we saw on this occasion for the first and last time, delivered a speech and gave us permission to make a collection in the barrack for the purchase of a barrel of red wine, half a pint per head. Thus the authorities proved themselves both generous and economical. The food was not improved during the holidays; chick-pea soup and nothing was the menu on Christmas Eve, chick-pea soup and nothing on New Year's Eve.

The festivities consisted of an amateur variety show given by Section C, held in an empty barrack. It was on this occasion that the commandant's speech was delivered. I do not remember what the speech was about and I did not know even while he was speaking; but it was in the best French oratorical tradition, very melodious and elevating, reminding me of a time, when, as a student in Baden-bei-Wein, I used to earn some pocket money as an extra in the *Städtisches Schauspielhaus,* and learned that whenever the text indicated a "murmuring of the people" I should just keep on repeating the words: "Rhabarbara, rhabarbara, rhabarbara" — rhubarb, rhubarb, rhubarb.

After the commandant's speech Albert also said a few melodious "rhabarbaras" on behalf of the prisoners, and the program began; there was a Russian choir which sang Russian folk songs and a Hungarian choir which sang Hungarian folk songs; an acrobat from Barrack 32, a Jugoslav choir which sang Jugoslav folk songs, a Czech choir which sang Czech folk songs, and then we all sang the *Marseillaise* and were marched back to our barracks, to the accompaniment to our escorts' no less rhythmical *un-deux, un-deux.*

The next day a feud broke out between Storfer and Albert; both were barrack chiefs, but Pernod had appointed Albert *régisseur* of the performance which was to be repeated on New Year's Eve, and Albert wanted to cut out Storfer's clowning act, which was indeed even more sickening than the rest; on the other hand, Storfer thought that on the strength of his past as an artist and tiger-tamer, the honor of being *régisseur* should fall to him. The result was that Storfer denounced Albert for having said derisive things of the French Army while queuing up at the canteen; but Albert proved that he had never been to the canteen, as he received all the foodstuffs he wanted from his wife, and remained *régisseur.*

Section A and Section B also had their performances, and we learned that B, the "politicals," had put up an excellent satirical review about the conditions in the camp, culminating in the scene where a man, after escaping from the camp, preaches to a tribe of South Sea anthropophages the blessings of real primitive life in Le Vernet. "We have no fire to warm us and no light to see at night, and that is real happiness," he explains to them until they get angry and kill him and stuff him and put him in their museum with the label HOMO VERNIENSUS (EUROPE, 1940).

It was not that the men in B had individually more guts or wits than we had; it was the difference between the collective atmosphere of political prisoners and that of our mixed crowd. It goes to the credit of Pernod and his staff that they watched the performance of B to the end, holding their bellies with laughter and slapping their legs with delight, without any idea of interfering. Their attitude was a perfect illustration of the traditional French respect for *l'esprit*—and of the futility to which this tradition had degenerated: for naturally the conditions of life of *Homo Verniensis* remained the same as before. I suppose Pernod enjoyed the biting satire on his own regime much in the same way as Lord Beaverbrook might enjoy in his own paper Blimp's "Gad, sir, Lord Beaverbrook is right."

Selection from *If This Is a Man*, Primo Levi

Primo Levi (1919–87) was born in Turin, Italy, and trained as a chemist. He was arrested for being part of the antifascist Resistance and deported to Auschwitz in 1944. After his incarceration, he devoted himself full-time to writing about his experiences. He has authored such classic memoirs as Survival in Auschwitz *(1947),* The Reawakening *(1963), and* The Drowned and the Saved *(1988). He committed suicide in 1987.*

[1944]

From the outside door, secretly and looking around cautiously, the storyteller comes in. He is seated on *Wachsmann*'s bunk and at once gathers around him a small, attentive, silent crowd. He chants an interminable Yiddish rhapsody, always the same one, in rhymed quatrains, of a resigned and penetrating melancholy (but perhaps I only remember it so because of the time and the place that I heard it?); from the few words that I understand, it must be a song that he composed himself, in which he has enclosed all the life of the *Lager* in minute detail. Some are generous and give the storyteller a pinch of tobacco or a needleful of thread; others listen intently but give nothing.

Selection from *Ravensbrück: The Women's Death Camp,* Denise Dufournier

Denise Dufournier was a member of the French Resistance who rescued English and American airmen, guiding them across France to the Spanish border. She was arrested in June 1943. After four months in solitary confinement at the French prison, Fresnes, she was transported to Ravensbrück. She wrote her book in the months after the camp's liberation.

In Quarantine at Block 22
[1944]

I was asked to organize our "spare time." Although all intellectual activities were strictly prohibited, under pain of the most severe penalties, the *Stubova* who liked neither noise nor disorder gave us her tacit consent to organize a whole series of lectures. There were among us journalists, professors, students, doctors, peasants, working class, and business women. We even had a tamer of wild animals. Travel talks, philosophical dissertations, discourses on our folklore alternated with the précis of one of Shakespeare's plays, a talk on child delinquency, a visit to the capitals of the world, the study of Chinese civilization from the early centuries as well as the rearing of rabbits or the taming of lions. Some of the lectures were most interesting, others terribly boring. The response which they evoked was lacking neither in spontaneity nor enthusiasm. Sometimes the audience became so out-of-hand that the speaker, embarrassed, had to retire. But what did it matter? It was all part of the risks incurred; it was absolutely essential that we should try to go on living. A revue of great originality was staged in twenty-four hours. Choruses were trained to sing classical music in perfect harmony. Poets were invited to read their verses, and artists yet unknown to reveal their talents. But above all there was the delight of intimate intercourse, which enabled us to express those innermost thoughts upon which we had dwelt during our long solitude in the cell. Kindred spirits drew together, friendships were formed, and a real solidarity came into being which, for my part, I can never forget.

III

"The Model Ghetto"

Theatrical Performance at Terezín

Theresienstadt

REBECCA ROVIT

AFTER THEY HAD EVACUATED inhabitants from the Czech town of Terezín in the summer of 1942, the Nazis touted the new "Theresienstadt" as a "model resettlement center" for West and Central Europe's unwanted Jews. Referred to interchangeably by inmates and historians alike as a "concentration camp" and a "ghetto," Terezín still embodies paradox, perhaps more than any of the other Nazi "containment" centers. This is especially true regarding Terezín's well-known cultural program and its legacy. The first inmates to arrive were the two privileged *Aufbaukommandos* (AK I and AK II) whose job was to build barracks in the camp and ready Terezín for its first inmates. The men in these "construction details" — administrators, artisans, and engineers — were practically, but not entirely immune to deportations. Mirko Tuma (see memoir in this section) came with the second "building crew," late in 1941. Among these privileged prisoners (some of whom volunteered) were the members of the Council of Elders, the ghetto's Jewish self-administrators — a concept the SS had already established and exploited in Eastern Europe ghettos.

Also among Terezín's first arrivals were elderly Jews from Germany and Austria, led to believe that they would be provided for in their old age at Bad Theresien (or Spa Terezín). Then came many young and old Jews from Bohemia and Moravia (the nineteen-year-old Zdenka Fantlová, for example, in January 1942). Finally, prominent Jews from Holland and Denmark joined the Terezín compound as late as 1943 (note Kurt Singer's fairly late May departure from Amsterdam for the ghetto). Many of these Jews, Singer included, believed that they would continue to prove their artistic worth within the camp's organized cultural activities or *Freizeitgestaltung* (literally, the "shaping" or "structuring of leisure time"). Except for the particularly renowned musicians and artists who were imprisoned at Terezín, however, leisure time to "create" came only after eight-hour days and various work duties.

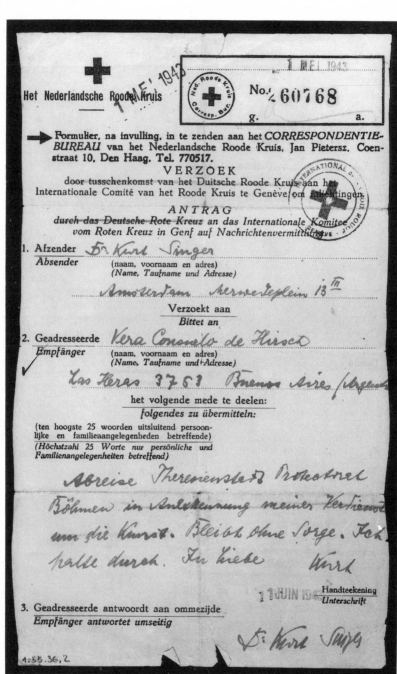

Het Nederlandsche Roode Kruis

1 MEI 1943

1 MEI 1943

No. 260768

g.   a.

➤ Formulier, na invulling, in te zenden aan het *CORRESPONDENTIE-BUREAU* van het Nederlandsche Roode Kruis, Jan Pietersz. Coenstraat 10. Den Haag. Tel. 770517.

VERZOEK
door tusschenkomst van het Duitsche Roode Kruis aan het Internationale Comité van het Roode Kruis te Genève om inlichtingen

ANTRAG
durch das Deutsche Rote Kreuz an das Internationale Komitee vom Roten Kreuz in Genf auf Nachrichtenvermittlung

1. Afzender *Dr. Kurt Singer*

Absender
(naam, voornaam en adres)
(Name, Taufname und Adresse)

Amsterdam Merwedeplein 13ᵐ

Verzoekt aan
Bittet an

2. Geadresseerde *Vera Consuelo de Hirsch*

Empfänger
(naam, voornaam en adres)
(Name, Taufname und Adresse)

Las Heras 3753 Buenos Aires (Argent...)

het volgende mede te deelen:
folgendes zu übermitteln:

(ten hoogste 25 woorden uitsluitend persoonlijke en familieaangelegenheden betreffende)
(Höchstzahl 25 Worte nur persönliche und Familienangelegenheiten betreffend)

Abreise Theresienstadt Protektorat Böhmen in Anerkennung meiner Verdienste um die Kunst. Bleibt ohne Sorge. Ich halte durch. In Liebe   Kurt

11 JUIN 194.

Handteekening
Unterschrift

3. Geadresseerde antwoordt aan ommezijde
Empfänger antwortet umseitig

Dr. Kurt Singer

1-55.36,2

Although Terezín was not a death center, living conditions, including malnutrition, overcrowding, rampant disease, as well as frequent transports eastbound (to Auschwitz, we now know) could not have made it easy for artists to create art or do much of anything, save survive imminent transport; nonetheless, everyday life included an array of community activities as the ex-inmate painter and architect Norbert Troller has made clear: "There was work and leisure, concerns with sanitation, housing, health care, child care, record keeping, construction, theater, concerts, lectures, all functioning as well as possible under the circumstances. Life pulsated with incredible optimism, fatalism, with life-affirming self-deception, with never-ending hope so inherent in Jewish people. It seemed at times almost normal, carefree, without much thought."[1]

In the ghetto's early years, the move toward legalizing concerts and plays, and engaging inmates to lecture and perform appear to have been well-meaning attempts on the part of the ghetto's Jewish administrators to provide emotional and intellectual respite for inmates. The Jewish leadership coordinated activities under the auspices of the buildings' administration, a neutral group headed by one of the Council Elders, the Czech, Fredy Hirsch. To "camouflage" its purpose from the Nazis, the administration appointed a young rabbi, German-born Erich Weiner, to direct cultural activities. Weiner was responsible for prayers and leisure activities. But as is evident in Weiner's report from Terezín (included in the following section), the Jews were more experienced in artistic fields than in Jewish religious matters; this was apparently typical of the Czech Protectorate Jews who made up the majority of the ghetto. The director of the Youth Welfare Department at Terezín, Gonda Redlich, attests to this in his diary. On 2 January 1943, he writes, "again a paradox possible only in the ghetto of Terezín. A hall. Up front, on stage, a revival of [Jiri] Wolker's *Hospital*. In the back, Jews are praying." Then on 26 March 1943, Redlich rejoins, "Jews pray in the *Freizeitgestaltung* hall. In the back of the hall are dancers, actors, a stage. There aren't any orthodox among us, for the real orthodox would not pray in a hall such as this."[2]

The ghetto's administration and its various departments were peopled with both Czech Jews and German-born Jews. But in reality, the ghetto's Czech and German or Austrian-born inhabitants were strictly separated, as were the

FACING PAGE: Postcard document 1.55.36, 2. 1 May 1943 (Amsterdam), Kurt Singer to Vera Consuelo Hirsch, Buenos Aires, Argentina. Vera Hirsch was a young singer whom Dr. Singer taught in Amsterdam before her family emigrated to South America. "Departure Theresienstadt Protectorate Bohemia in recognition for my contributions to art. Remain without worry. I'll pull through. With love, Kurt"

ghetto's other nationalities. They lodged in separate quarters and their cultural activities were separate. In the realm of theatrical activity, it was the young Czechs who initiated a vibrant theater, while the Germans excelled with their lecture series, eventually directed by Philipp Manes. The Nazi overseers eventually authorized performances. They also promoted Theresienstadt's special status as a ghetto for the cultural elite. But as is clear in Rabbi Weiner's report, not even the Germans were privy to the extent of the *Freizeitgestaltung* within the ghetto's first year. Musical instruments were originally banned, and clandestine performances took place before official approval had been granted. The Nazis' toleration of cultural activity eventually led to exploitation. As the war progressed and the international community became increasingly aware of existing concentration camps, a Red Cross delegation visited Theresienstadt. This visit on 23 June 1944 epitomized the phase in which the Nazis perverted Theresienstadt's initial commitment to cultural activity. The Nazis gradually transformed their "Paradise Ghetto" for Jews, stage-managing the illusion of a village for Jews—replete with playgrounds and flowers, real street names, stores, and of course, culture. The *Verschönerung* (beautification), including a bogus film made by the Jewish cabaret director and inmate Kurt Gerron— ordered by the Nazis (August 1944)—was the ultimate step the Nazis took to distort the promising reality of the *Freizeitgestaltung* culture of Theresienstadt.

As in the Vilna, Warsaw, and Kovno ghettos, Theresienstadt ghetto inmates portrayed daily life, often analyzing concerts and even performances in their diaries, drawings, or memoirs years later (see Weiner's report, Ehrlich-Fantlová and Tuma's memoirs which follow). So too do historians and writers today look with hindsight to those times with horror at the thought that transports and theatrical performances took place on the same days. The ultimate paradox of the situation resounds in an anecdote about news received during a performance of Gogol's *The Matchmaker:* Another transport was to leave and the actors and audience members did not know whether a transport order would await them when they returned to their quarters. The actors wanted to stop the play, but the audience would not allow it.[3]

The essays and documents within this section may be compared to those of the previous section generally. But Terezín was different from the other camps. "It wasn't a concentration camp," says actress Ehrlich-Fantlová, who performed in six plays during her two and a half years at Terezín before being deported east to Auschwitz in October 1944 and eventually west to Bergen-Belsen in 1945. In Terezín, on her home "territory," Czechoslovakia, Ehrlich-Fantlová has said that the large number of creative people, living close together, provided a "seeding element," in which "people fed hope and togetherness."

For her, the cultural program of *Freizeitgestaltung* was not merely fun and entertainment; rather, "it had a completely different mission. It rose so high that it can't be compared to any entertainment in normal life" (see following memoir selection and 1998 interview). It is vital to remind oneself while reading the following selections that the inmates did not know what was going to happen the next day or the next week. The threat of the next transport east was apparently dreadful to Terezín prisoners (the Czech inmates especially, had only been deported once within their own Protectorate), but the destination of the transports remained nebulous to most of the Jews. We on the outside, however, cannot "un-know" where those transports led and what inevitably happened to many ghetto inmates. On the "inside," however, the Terezín artists held out hope for their predicament, creating and performing as long as they could. Leo Strauss's cabaret sketches and *Chansons,* the Czech satires on ghetto life, Peter Kien's *Emperor of Atlantis* libretto, and Hans Krása's opera exhibit a playful, but mordantly serious attempt to provide an atmosphere of hope and enlightenment to audiences who might recognize in these performances their own Terezín experiences.

References to the ghetto's "living quarters" recur in the following reports and memoirs. It is useful to keep in mind the basic shape and street construction of Terezín: The town was arranged on a geometric street grid, about two-thirds of a mile long and across. Two hundred two-storied houses and fourteen large stone barracks were set within the walls with moats surrounding the town like an eight-pointed star. The River Ohre (German *Eger*) separated the town from the "Little Fortress," where the Gestapo kept Russian prisoners of war, Czech noncollaborationists, and such unlucky Jews as the Terezín Painters, incarcerated in 1944 for their "horror Propaganda" against the Reich.[4]

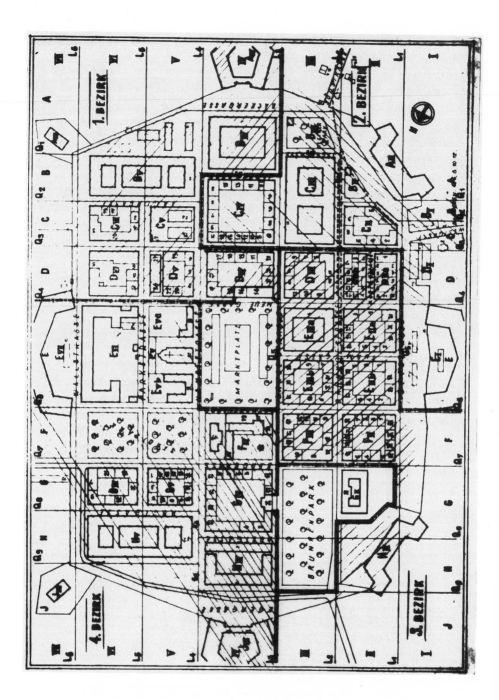

Map of Terezín, numbered with barracks and streets. Photo by Wiener Library, London. Permission from Terezín Patmánk [Memorial] and the Jewish Museum, Prague

Key to selected barracks and blocks [compiled by Rebecca Rovit]

B V — Magdeburg, administration, central headquarters of Jewish administration. Large performance hall in barracks. This is where the FZG "office" was located.

B IV — Hannover, men's barracks; an attic stage "A" was created here in late 1942.

C III — Hamburg, Zdenka Ehrlich-Fantlová originally lived here. This barracks housed a theater space.

H IV — Bodenbacher, eventually evacuated in 1943 and used as Berlin Reich Security Archives.

H V — Dresden, women and children's barracks, also contained a theater space. Attic performances also took place here.

E I — Sudeten, housed Halls 5 and 7 and a potato peeling room used for performances, including Švenk's cabaret premiere. Johann [Hans] Krása became director in the fall of 1942. The building was evacuated in July 1943 to house security archives from Berlin.

E VI — Vrchlabí, central hospital, also known as the Hohenelber barracks.

E VII — Kavalier, housed old people's home and section for mentally ill, "Cvokárna." Artists from the Hamburg barracks toured here in 1942.

Building C I — Became a cultural hall under the "beautification" phase.

Block C II, L 203 — Attic stage created here in late 1942 for block performances.

Block C IV, L 304 — Used for cultural activities. A library was here in November 1942.

Block D III — Kurt Singer lived in Q 410. The attic of house Q 307 became an experimental theater space used for plays, lectures, and play readings.

Block D IV — Coffeehouse at Q 418, December 1942.

Block E III — A Sapper barracks, known as the "Genie" barracks, housed the elderly and ill. Cultural activities and performances took place here.

Block E III b — Seat of the ghetto watch; performances were given in L 315.

Complex F IV — Adjacent buildings include an attic in L 318 used for performances and the youth home, L 417, where *Brundibár* was performed. Q 619 was the former town hall, used for performances and the post office.

Block G VI — Mothers and infants were housed here. A hall in L 514 was used for theater performances and concerts.

ESSAYS

Creation in a Death Camp

AARON KRAMER

Professor Kramer suggested that the following essay accompany his libretto translation. This essay was published after his death as "Creative Defiance in a Death Camp."

"THOSE WHO WERE NOT THERE cannot possibly understand." Again and again, witnesses at the trials of death camp officials say this. But the records—riskily scrawled, miraculously preserved—are now published, and the images of that horror-world have grown familiar. Each survivor of that hell is a wonder; that an opera should have been created, rehearsed, come close to performance is almost beyond belief. But Terezín, or Theresienstadt—as its German masters called it, was unlike other camps.

On 28 September 1941, Reinhard Heydrich came to power in Prague. Twelve days later, at a meeting attended by SS-Sturmbannführer Eichmann and other high officials, the fate of Czechoslovakia's Jews was decided. To help "evacuate the Jews from the Protectorate," Heydrich proposed using Terezín as a ghetto. Two to three trains containing a thousand Jews each could be sent every day. Straw would be allocated to the empty flats in the ghetto: "Beds would take up too much room. Let the Jews build flats under the earth."

A week later, at a second top-level meeting, Heydrich expanded his plan. "All armed forces will be completely evacuated from Theresienstadt. The Czechs will move elsewhere. Fifty to sixty thousand Jews may be comfortably accommodated. From there they will go east. After the complete evacuation of the Jews, the town will be settled by Germans and become a center of German

This chapter is based on Kramer's BBC script "Death Takes a Holiday." Two versions of this essay have been posthumously reprinted in the *Journal of Humanistic Psychology* (1998) and in Kramer's *The Last Lullabye: Poems of the Holocaust* (Syracuse University Press, 1998).

life, in keeping with the ideas of the Reichs Commissar for the Propagation of German Culture. Under no account must any details of these plans become public."

The Jews of Prague suspected none of this. They eagerly believed the SS promises of a model Jewish city to be planned, built, and administered by a Council of Jewish Elders; a team of experts and workers would be sent there, and the families of these volunteers would not be transported to the east.

When Heydrich addressed the infamous Final Solution Conference at Wannsee on 20 January 1942, several death camps were already operating, and others were about to begin the extermination process Göring had called for the previous July. By then it had become clear, even to the most optimistic, that Terezín would be no final stop, no permanent refuge, for them. On 9 and 15 January, the first two transports left Terezín for Riga. A thousand people were in each. They were driven—with numbers tied round their necks and carrying their packs—to the train and stuffed into the goods cars, seventy to ninety in a car.

But Terezín was to have a new and truly distinctive function: Here would come Germany's oldest Jews and those seriously wounded in World War I, distinguished for war service. Interned here as well would be prominent German Jews with international connections, whose whereabouts might be questioned abroad. The Potemkin village would soon be ready to show Red Cross inspectors how benignly Germany treated its Jews. This device counteracted the ever-increasing rumors of atrocities at such places as Auschwitz and Buchenwald.

How could visitors guess that behind the Hollywood set was in fact nothing more than a detention center, a way station, a staging post through which the cream of Germany's Jewish intellectuals and artists were funneled into the gas chambers of Auschwitz? How could they imagine that, behind the scenes, Terezín's inhabitants lived in the most hideous filth and disease—many in huge, cold, airless attics where they perished by the thousands—33,430, to be precise, almost one-fourth of the 139,606 who came here. No gas chambers were needed. Exhaustion, starvation, disease, and the whip did the job quite well. And overcrowding: a population density about fifty times as great as Berlin's before the war.

But this the Red Cross did not see. The population density was solved before each of their visits. And those whose faces told of misery were first to vanish. What the Red Cross saw was a diabolic public relations diorama: make-believe shops, a bank that printed funny money, a coffeehouse, and a great deal of cultural activity. Thanks to Hitler's lootings, there was an impressive library— all but two of whose nineteen staff members were shipped east after the Red

Cross visitors were gone. Like the rest of Terezín's cosmetic props, the library was shown in a film directed under protest by the Dutch Jew, Kurt Gerron, formerly a well-known director and actor. For this public relations monstrosity, called *The Führer Presents the Jews with a City,* many pleasant activities were staged, including a symphony concert conducted by the once famous Karel Ančerl, who now worked in the Terezín kitchen. The first act of *Tales of Hoffmann* was also performed.

In fact the SS did encourage artistic productions of an amazing variety— from cabaret entertainment to puppet shows to classical theater, including plays by Shakespeare, Shaw, and Molnár. Music they particularly supported, and opera flourished. On 28 November 1942 [Bedřich] Smetana's *The Bartered Bride* was performed; a half-demolished piano without feet substituted for an orchestra. The auditorium was the physical culture room in a home for boys. Still, it made an unforgettable impression. When the first bars, "Why should we not rejoice . . . ," sounded, there was not a dry eye in the house. That opera was done about thirty-five times. Its success was followed by Mozart's *Magic Flute* and *Marriage of Figaro.*

The Nazis preferred "safe" works. *Tosca, Aida, Carmen, La Bohème,* and *Die Fledermaus* were presented—some with simple piano accompaniment, some with orchestra and full staging. During 1943 and 1944 this activity was stepped up for the benefit of the Red Cross and other international agencies. In these *Stadtverschönerung,* or "window dressing" shows, the inspection teams found a remarkably high level of artistry. This is not surprising, since many of Europe's finest composers, vocalists, instrumentalists, and conductors were incarcerated there. Among them was the young Bohemian-born basso, Karel Berman, who amazingly survived.

"How often," he later reminisced, "did we sing out resistance and give the people strength to endure! We were indeed risking our necks when we sang: 'The hour has struck—the gates are opening' from Smetana's *Brandenburg in Bohemia,* or, in Czech, the opera, *In the Well,* though it was officially forbidden to speak Czech in public." On Czechoslovakia's national holiday Berman offered a concert in the barracks, beginning with "O wicked time, the present time," from *In the Well,* continuing with such numbers as the aria from *Dalibor,* "You already know how this lovely kingdom has become the victim of wild passions."

Before 1939, at the Prague Conservatory, Raphael [Rafael] Schächter could find no better work than as assistant conductor. It was at Terezín that his true genius was recognized. From the time of his *Bartered Bride* production he was acclaimed as the camp's foremost musician; artists competed to be in his ranks.

He was allotted a little cellar room for rehearsals. There he revealed his great dream, to do Verdi's *Requiem,* realizing what the *confutatis maledictis,* and the *dies irae,* and the *libera me* would become, roared from Jewish throats in the pit of Hell itself.

For eighteen months this seemingly doomed effort gathered momentum, with the Terezín police themselves involved in smuggling score and music paper to the obsessed young conductor. Instrumentalists were also acquired somehow, and eventually an immense choir was being rehearsed—in segments, due to lack of room. Often the rows were decimated as performers were removed to Auschwitz. Many felt the work would never have its premiere. They were astounded when Schächter announced that the commandant had pledged the company would henceforth remain intact.

That pledge turned out to be more diabolic in its subtlety than an outright act of violence. The musicians were spared, but not their families. Despite Schächter's pleading, many in the choir and orchestra, as well as three of his four superb soloists, elected to join their loved ones in the death-transport. Those who remained had no heart for singing. But Schächter was more obsessed than ever. Once again he began the task of rebuilding. His rehearsals helped keep them alive from day to day. Other conductors pitched in; they lent him singers from their own projects: the brilliant Gideon Klein, working on *Rigoletto* [Verdi], *Tosca,* and *Carmen* [Bizet]; [Karl] Fisher, preparing the oratorios *Elijah* and *The Creation.*

News from the outside seeped into Terezín: Hitler's military dream was disintegrating; his own cities smoked in ruin. For this reason, the genocide project was rushed toward completion. In June, the Lwów ghetto was liquidated. Through the summer the Jews from Upper Silesia and elsewhere in Poland were transported to Auschwitz, and the Bialystok ghetto was wiped out. In September, Minsk and Vilna followed suit; by year's end the Riga and remaining White Russian ghettos were empty. At this time the Danish Jews, along with those from southern France, northern Italy, and Rome, were deported. In the spring the Jews of Athens and Hungary were shipped—most of them to Auschwitz, which now had a capacity of ten thousand human bodies per twenty-four hours, and some to Terezín: artists, intellectuals, others of international reputation among them.

The Verdi *Requiem* was finally done in early summer, a festive premiere in the committee room of the former town hall. On the platform stood the 150-member mixed choir, before them the soloists: Marion Podolier, Heda Aronson-Lindt, David Grunfelt, and Karel Berman, and in front on a little box stood Raphael Schächter, who knew the difficult score by heart. It was a revolutionary and militant feat that had no equal. An inspired performance, many said. The crowd, after a long silence, leaped to their feet with an ovation that couldn't seem to end. But Schächter was not satisfied. The conclusion struck him as too resigned. He wanted a *libera me* that would make the hair stand on end.

He revised Verdi's musical phrase, giving to those final words the Beethoven victory code: three short notes, one long. . . . This new version was thundered from the stage at Eichmann and other dignitaries from Prague and Berlin later that summer. They had come, by Himmler's order, to bemedal the camp commandant of Terezín, which had played its special role so splendidly in achieving the Final Solution of the Jewish problem. It was told later that Eichmann applauded this "unique" interpretation of the *Requiem.*

But soon the summer ended. In September, the deportations from Slovakia were renewed and the last transport of French Jews left for Auschwitz. True to its pledge, the Terezín command did not separate Schächter's huge company. Together, on 28 September [1944], they climbed into the first wagons of the first transport, along with thousands of fellow-inmates, including many Czech scientists and artists. They had known their fate the night before, when they gave the final performance of the *Requiem.*

The extraordinary cultural flowering at Terezín is hard to understand, but we must remember that the SS were, first of all, confident nothing heard here would ever reach the outside world; then too, they could not fathom the undermeanings of what was created and performed, such as Schächter's reworking of the *Requiem,* or a piano interpretation of Moussorgsky's *Pictures at an Exhibition.* When the bells began to boom in "The Great Gate of Kiev," only the audience sensed the approach of the liberating Red Army [June 1944].

What matters is the ferocious energy with which the inmates seized every opportunity to create original work. The most stunning example at Terezín — and perhaps in all history — of cultural defiance, is offered by Peter Kien and Viktor Ullmann, who created *The Emperor of Atlantis,* a one-act opera they described as "a legend in four scenes," with the subtitle *Death Abdicates.*

Of the librettist, a promising graduate student, we know little. He was born in 1919 in Varnsdorf [Germany], where his father owned a small textile factory. After Munich [Hitler's putsch], the Kien family fled to the interior, but was deported from there to Terezín in late 1941. Even as a child he had shown extraordinary versatility as a musician, poet, and especially as a graphic painter with a strong bent for caricature. He was an architect as well. A few hundred of Kien's drawings from his pre-Terezín years have been preserved. Several poems have also survived; these have been praised for a lyrical power as noteworthy as his graphic art. His photo reveals a handsome, wavy-haired young man with a wistful half-smile and bright, probing eyes behind glasses.

Of Ullmann, on the other hand, a good deal is known, thanks to the data in music encyclopedias. Born in Teschen on 1 January 1898, he studied with [Arnold] Schoenberg in Vienna in the early 1920s, became a theater conductor at Aussig, and was active as conductor and teacher in Prague before its fall to the Nazis. He was a founding member of the *Verein für Musikalisches Privataufführungen* [Society for Musical Performances]. His *Variations and Double Fugue on a Theme by Schoenberg* for orchestra was performed in 1929 at the Festival of the International Society for Contemporary Music in Geneva, one of his two string quartets was given at the 1938 London Festival, and other chamber works were heard at concerts of modern music in Europe and America. He wrote two operas — *Peer Gynt* and *The Fall of Anti-Christ* — as well as a wind octet, a piano concerto, and several song cycles. His style was atonal, but he adhered to the classical pattern in formal design.

At the death camp Kien was one of a gifted group called "The Terezín Painters," who did their assigned poster work by day while secretly using their off-hours to record the hell around them. At least one formal exhibition of paintings by Kien and two colleagues was mounted. The other two, [Fritz Taussig, alias Bedřich] Bedřich Fritta and [Otto] Ungar, were arrested and fatally tortured when their clandestine work was discovered to have reached the outside world. As for Ullmann, probably encouraged by the presence of many superb performers and a sophisticated, music-hungry audience, he composed prolifically: seven piano sonatas, a string quartet, songs and choruses, and a melodrama based on [Rainer Maria] Rilke's *The Lay of the Love and Death of Cornet Christoph Rilke.*

In terms of age and achievement, composer and poet seemed a strange pairing. But at Terezín age and temperament meant little. Survival was as much a requirement of the spirit as the body. Survival! That was the common denominator for all who rejected resignation, who refused to surrender the pulse of selfhood and turn into *Muselmänner,* walking corpses.

For Ullmann as composer, Terezín had been a transforming experience. From his opera it would be difficult to tell that he had been Schoenberg's pupil in Vienna. *The Emperor of Atlantis* gives a much stronger impression than his earlier work would lead one to expect. Here is a composer of depth and imagination, whose powerful musical and dramatic technique never masks his humanity. Humanity, yes, but no condescension, no oversimplification. The roles and the instrumental parts are extremely demanding; only an exceptional group of professionals could have coped with them; and the rich subtleties in the score could nourish the bestrained musical ear. But Terezín, where humanity fought hour by hour against the most heartless, technically brilliant onslaught ever known, was no place for the atonality he had acquired from Schoenberg. He arranged a group of Yiddish folk songs for the chorus. The tenderness and purity of those arrangements showed very clearly how his musical sympathies had shifted. Well, Heydrich had declared him a Jewish rather than a Sudeten German composer. He knew now that he was both.

Having united their gifts for the creation of an opera, librettist and composer moved forward realistically. Singers and instrumentalists disappeared with each transport—so did large segments of their potential audience—so might they. It was necessary to shape a modest work: Six singers could suffice, with the doubling of certain parts, plus two female dancers for the intermezzi and an orchestra of thirteen. Modest in length as well (less than an hour in performance time), it would follow a close-knit pattern of recitative and aria, molded at certain strategic points into vocal ensembles and punctuated twice by dance interludes. With utmost modesty, it would declare itself a legend rather than an opera. Legends, parables, can be rich with underlying significance yet on the surface be simple enough for a child to grasp and harmless enough to allay any suspicions of the camp guards:

Ruled by the Emperor Überall, Atlantis has become a land of horror. Declaring universal war, the Emperor patronizingly appoints his "old ally" Death to serve as standard-bearer. Death retaliates by breaking his sword: Henceforth no one will be able to die. Two enemy soldiers, a boy and a girl, are commanded to fight to the death, but fall in love. As the forces of life advance against him, the Emperor begins to see that he has turned into a self-isolated monster. He begs Death to end his holiday, but Death insists that Überall be the first to die. As Death leads him away, the moral of the tale is given: Let us learn to respect the joy and pain of life, and not take the mighty name of Death in vain.

The elements of Kien's story were not unfamiliar. *Death Takes a Holiday* had recently been an international cinema hit, and through the centuries Death had been personified in parables and folk ballads of many cultures. Clearly, to us at least, the text is a thinly disguised satire on Hitler's despotic, psychotic, unprecedentedly arrogant and murderous career, which—as in the opera—was already collapsing by 1944. But it had to be more than a satire, more than a critique of absolute power. Probably their final say, it had to be large in scope and feeling, if not in cast and performance time. Not the Emperor, but Death, is the principal character—dignified, almost fatherly, as in Schubert's "Death and the Maiden." The Emperor insolently conceives of Death as his servant, an instrument for genocide. But Kien, at the very threshold of Death himself, redefines its ancient and only proper function — as humanity's release from intolerable pain. Without Death, life is impossible, and with him he brings hope.

Ullmann's music translates whatever is in the text, whether elusive or sardonic. Clearly the master of many styles, he uses them — in the presence of a knowing audience — parodistically, to underscore a point or characterize a moment. The Emperor sounds Wagnerian. Death's aria about his glorious battles of the past is sung to a blues-like, saucy fox-trot step. For Pierrot's horror lullaby the composer borrows a grim children's tune from old Germany, "Maybug Fly." When the Drummer rolls out the Emperor's most pompous titles, such as Arch-Pope and King of Jerusalem, we hear an ironic paraphrase of "Deutschland Über Alles."

This tune had been used before to make a political statement. Carlo Taube had presented, in the prayer room of the Magdeburg barracks, a private premiere of his *Terezín Symphony.* The third movement had a shattering effect. His wife Erika recited, in a moving way, with a *pianissimo obbligato* from the orchestra, a lullaby of a Jewish mother, which she had written. There followed a turbulent finale in which the first four bars of "Deutschland Über Alles" were repeated over and over again, ringing out in more and more wrathful spasms, until the last outcry "Deutschland, Deutschland" did not continue to "Über Alles," but died out in a terrible dissonance. Everyone had understood and a storm of applause expressed thanks to Carlo and Erika Taube and all the musicians.

Such an audience, if not their jailers, would have savored the subtle irony of the Drummer's *passacaglia,* from the French *passo caille,* meaning goose-step. Just as the libretto starts out tantalizingly obscure and ends up deeply moving, so does the music, in the concluding hymn, paraphrase Bach's setting of [Martin] Luther's "A Mighty Fortress Is Our God." But perhaps the most brilliant stroke by Ullmann and Kien is their use of the harmonium. This strange instrument was discovered in the old, abandoned church of Terezín, and the Nazis allowed it to be borrowed. Its metallic sound came as a kind of radio signal whenever the Emperor wanted to speak. What a comment on a mentality that glorified man's inhumanity to man!

The obtuseness of the camp officials had been demonstrated before. A Czech inmate, Hans Krása, had revised and thoroughly reorchestrated for a Terezín production by orphan singers his hitherto unheard children's opera, *Brundibár.* It tells how a wicked organ grinder is finally defeated by the children of the town. A new ending was provided: "Whoever loves justice / and will defend it / and is not afraid / is our friend / and may play with us." *Brundibár* was a great success; it was done fifty-five times, including a command performance for the

Red Cross visitors [June 1944]. Kien and Ullmann may very well have been inspired by its example.

Allegory and allusiveness have always been used as weapons of resistance by writers in times of repression. Malcolm Cowley reminds us that during World War II, nineteen issues of the militant journal *Poesie* somehow achieved legal publication in France: "This was possible because the collaborationist and German censors either did not scan its pages too closely, or were singularly thick-skulled and could not understand all its pointed barbs." If this could happen openly before the whole French population, one can hardly expect the commandant of Terezín to care much about the goings-on in a closely guarded camp from which no one was expected to escape alive. Besides, the Nazis at first saw nothing more than an innocuous tale.

The project may seem suicidal, but Kien and Ullmann worked with extreme prudence. They made two distinct versions of the libretto. The first, handwritten, has all the references to genocide and the power of the ruler. It is sharper and stronger than the second, the typewritten version submitted to the camp officials, which was probably typed for Kien by an SS officer, who used the backs of Terezín admission forms no longer of value since the inmates whose biographical data appeared on their pages had already been shipped to Auschwitz.

Karel Berman, the sole surviving participant, recalls the rehearsals "on the stage of the Sokol gymnasium. . . . Its tendency was so strongly anti-war that it was prohibited before it was ever performed. Specifically, the end of Hitler was the theme." Even on its most simplified nonallegorical and noncontroversial level, the plot should have been held suspect. But as allegory, the moral taught by Death defies the very core of Hitler's creed and career.

When Pierrot, the symbol of suffering humanity, asks Death to kill him since he can no longer make people laugh and life has become unbearable, Death declares: "No power on earth can kill you." How could the performers, and at last the censors, not translate this line to read: "The Nazis—any totalitarianism—have no ultimate power over mankind." When Death says: "The laughter that mocks itself is immortal," he obviously means: "The ability to laugh at yourselves in the face of your greatest agonies will help you survive."

The joyless, bloody world of Atlantis itself, no matter with how much universality Kien and Ullmann present it, bears too close a resemblance to Hitler's Europe. Most unacceptable of all is the Emperor's final recognition of Death's—and therefore Life's—supremacy over him. It would not do to show two enemy soldiers choosing love over war, singing: "Are there words on earth free of spite and hatred?" and defying the Emperor's exhortations by declaring:

"No. Death is dead. Humanity need fight no more!" There was nothing innocuous about a parable ending with these lines: "Make us prize all human worth; /
to other lives awaken!" sung to a melody that definitively judges the Third
Reich in terms of Germany's greatest spiritual voices — Luther and Bach. . . .

It is unclear whether the work was well under way or rehearsals had just
begun when the authorities forbade it to go on. As for its creators, they may indeed have been shipped to Auschwitz because of *Atlantis* and almost as soon as
the production of the opera was halted. But Terezín's musicians often participated in more than one project simultaneously. Mid-1944 saw the transportation of many to Auschwitz, including a large portion of Raphael Schächter's
choir and orchestra, along with most of his soloists. Ullmann may have been
among the thousands sent to the extermination center the morning after the
27 September performance of the *Requiem*. Certainly his singers were, and
probably his instrumentalists as well. The circumstances of Peter Kien's death
contradict the theory that Auschwitz was his punishment for having written the
libretto. We know that he elected at the last minute to jump on the train carrying his parents to the gas chambers, and at twenty-five, joined them in death.

It was long believed that the opera had been lost; but, along with other Ullmann pieces, it survived, smuggled out of the camp by a friend of the composer
after Ullmann and Kien were dead. Apparently, the struggle for survival in the
death camps involved not only the inmates but the written records of their cap-
tivity. We are not surprised to learn that in the ghetto of Lódz the superb poet
Miriam Ulinover wrote prolifically but none of her work survived the journey
to Auschwitz's crematoria. What continues to amaze us is that when Vilna was
liberated, partisans found a bloody bundle of Leib Apeskin's songs beside his
body; that after the war several of partisan Jack Gordon's haunting poems were
unearthed in the Bialystok ghetto; that the manuscript of Isaac Katzenelson's
epic "Song of the Slaughtered Jewish People," along with other of his Yiddish
poems in manuscript, was discovered in three hermetically sealed bottles in
the hollow of an old tree in the Vittel camp from which he had been deported
to Auschwitz. We read of the unbelievable care taken, at extreme risk and with
breathtaking ingenuity, by the partisan-poets Avrom Sutzkever and Shmerke
Kaczerginsky to preserve not only themselves and their writings, but every
piece of ghetto and death camp poetry they could get their hands on, as well as
a priceless treasury of Jewish culture in Vilna, sought by Hitler, which they hid
in a bunker until the end of the war.

The English-language version of *Atlantis*, in my translation, finally received
its premiere at the San Francisco Opera in April 1977. On opening night many
in the audience stood in tears after an extraordinary number of curtain calls.

The central issue of this work's intrinsic merit aside from the circumstances of its creation cannot be ignored. As one critic has written, "A knowledge of the conditions which produced the opera adds an extra emotional resonance, but it would stand as a powerful theater piece even if it were possible to detach it from its tragic background." In *Time Magazine*, reporting the Amsterdam premiere, Lawrence Malkin asked: "Confronted by a vision of hell, does one stand in silent reverence for the suffering or praise the spirit that surmounted it? Last week a Dutch audience faced this dilemma. At the end, after a few seconds' pause, the listeners burst into applause for a work that stands on its own as a music drama of great power." Perhaps Hubert Saal of *Newsweek* put it best: "It is incredible that in the hell where they were confined, Ullmann and Kien retained the will to create. They speak to us like dying men whose last words cannot be denied. Amazingly, they were able to convert their own agony into a universal, hypnotically theatrical drama."

Obviously, objective judgment is not easy, and it may take a long time before *The Emperor of Atlantis* can be accurately gauged as art; but there is no question of its uniqueness as an affirming of the human spirit in the teeth of physical obliteration. Perhaps it was by the very act of creation that both men survived almost until the end of the Holocaust. The same can be said of the audience for whom it was created. Karel Berman, the sole survivor of the cast, recalls: "If the historians one day succeed in writing the cultural history of the ghetto of Terezín, mankind will be amazed. Grown-ups and children, in constant expectation of death, lived a full, noble life, between outcries of pain and anxiety, among the *Müselmen*—those more dead than alive—; in hunger and misery, among the hundreds of corpses of those that died daily, among hearses taking the corpses out of town and bringing back bread, under constant great physical exertion, they lived a life that was a miracle under the given conditions."

After the collapse of France a few years earlier, the supreme Resistance poet Louis Aragon had written: "It takes a great deal of courage to write without knowing what will happen to one's work." Yes—but what joy it must have given this composer and his young librettist to have found a vehicle worthy of their awesome theme, and to have achieved its completion with sustained artistic integrity. On 25 May 1941, under the Nazi heel, a strangely exhilarated Aragon wrote of his reawakened purpose: "With the greatest freedom of expression we said nothing—magnificently. And now we have found what we had to say, more than we had ever dreamed. Can we say it well enough?" Surely this was the challenge and the glory experienced by Viktor Ullmann and Peter Kien as their opera took shape.

Operatic Performances in Terezín

Krása's *Brundibár*

JOŽA KARAS

Brundibár defeated, we caught him finally,
Beat your drums, we've won the war!
We won, because we were not afraid and stood fast . . .
He who loves right and adheres to it
And who is not afraid,
Is our friend and he can play with us.

P O W E R F U L, courageous words, especially when one considers by whom and under what conditions they were uttered!

The scene was Terezín, the Jewish concentration camp in Nazi-occupied Czechoslovakia, some forty miles northwest from Prague. The singers were Jewish children between the ages of five and fifteen years, who were imprisoned there for their "crime" of being born to Jewish parents. The occasion was the final chorus of one of the fifty-five performances of Hans Krása's children's opera, *Brundibár.*

In the history of the cultural activities in the Terezín (Theresienstadt) concentration camp, music played the most prominent role, encompassing simple performances of folk songs without accompaniment, formal recitals of soloists and chamber music ensembles, jazz music, orchestras, and even operas and oratorios. While most of the programs had usually relatively few performances,

The author has written this essay specifically for this book, based on material from his *Music in Terezín 1941–1945* (New York: Pendragon Press/Beaufort Books, 1985). A revised edition will appear in 1999.

Verdi's *Requiem* was presented about twelve repeat performances and the most popular Czech opera, *The Bartered Bride* by Bedřich Smetana, was enjoyed by the ever-enthusiastic Terezín audience thirty-six times. However, none of these could compare with the success of the little gem by Krása.

The history of *Brundibár* predates the outbreak of the Second World War. Hans Krása, who was born in Prague on 30 November 1899, was a German-speaking and educated Czechoslovak citizen, who, already in 1935, met the Czech playwright, Adolf Hoffmeister, in a newly formed Club of Czech-German Theatrical Workers. This meeting led to the immediate collaboration when Krása composed music for Hoffmeister's comedy *Mládí ve hře* (*Youth in Play*). Later, in 1938, they embarked on a second joint venture, *Brundibár*, a children's opera written for a competition of the Ministry of Education and Culture, scheduled for the same year.

The original score of the opera had been lost and only the piano reduction was available during the Nazi occupation. However, in 1972, a calligraphic copy of the original score was found and is now deposited in the archives of the Terezín Museum. From this score, one may presume that Krása entered the competition anonymously, perhaps encouraged by his previous success in 1933, when he received the Czechoslovak State Prize for Composition for his German opera, *Verlobung in Traum* [*Betrothal in Dream*]. Due to the worsening political situation, however, the competition never took place and it is questionable whether Krása could repeat his previous success. Hoffmeister's libretto has quite a bit to be desired from the poetic point of view and Krása's only partial knowledge of the Czech language certainly did not help. Still, the music itself is very buoyant, melodic, and charming and that compensates for all the inadequacies in the text.

Almost immediately after the Nazi invasion into Czechoslovakia [March 1939], the Jews were eliminated from public life, thus deterred from attending concerts, theatrical performances, sport events, and even from taking strolls in a park. To top it off, they had to give to the authorities their radio receivers, which, in those days, had to be registered. So, instead, Jews arranged clandestine meetings in private homes and institutions to attend lectures and recitals, or to plan projects which often combined educational activities for children. One such place was the Jewish orphanage for boys in Prague, on Belgická ulice (Belgium Street), in the city district called Vinohrady. The orphanage director, Moritz Freudenfeld, was a music lover and amateur singer, who fostered the musical training of his wards, particularly after formal education of Jewish children was banned. Musical programs performed at the orphanage varied from arrangements of well-known tunes, sung by the director, to the staging of

Drawing of Hans Krása sketched
in the Terezín ghetto by inmate
painter, Otto Ungar: Photo
courtesy Joža Karas

children's operas by the German composer Paul Hindemith and by the Czech, Jaroslav Křička.

In July 1941, Director Freudenfeld celebrated his fiftieth birthday. Among the host of well-wishers were the composer Hans Krása, pianist Gideon Klein, poet Emil A. Saudek, architect František Zelenka, former stage director from the National Theater in Prague and conductor Rafael Schächter, who informed his colleagues about Krása's children's opera *Brundibár*. Three years after its completion, it still awaited its premiere. The decision was reached then and there to bring the opera to life. Schächter, ably assisted by the director's son, Rudolf Freudenfeld, commenced weekly rehearsals almost immediately. The preparations progressed smoothly, but before the opera could be put on stage, Schächter was sent with the first transport to Terezín, on 24 November 1941. When the situation calmed down, young Freudenfeld took over the musical preparations and *Brundibár* was finally presented for the first time in the orphanage in the winter of 1942–43. Zelenka designed an ingenious set with pictures of three animals on the fence with holes instead of heads. At proper times the singers would stick their faces through the holes and sing the roles of the dog, the cat, and the little sparrow. As a joke, Zelenka added a poster on the fence with the inscription *Volte 62541* (*Vote for 62541*), which was the telephone number of the Jewish Community in Prague. Instead of the orchestra, three instrumentalists, the pianist Löffelholz, violinist Berkovič, and drummer Kaufman played from the one and only piano score, used also by the conductor.[1] According to a member of the cast, Leopold Löwy, all roles were sung by boys, and Aninka's portrayer, Josef Mautner, had to endure quite a bit of good-natured teasing.

The story of the opera tells about two children, Pepíček and Aninka (Little Joe and Annette), who have a sick mother. They do not have money for milk, which was prescribed for her by the doctor. After they see an organ-grinder, whose name is Brundibár, playing his hurdy-gurdy on the street corner and obtaining money from the passersby, they try to sing. Yet they are only chased away by Brundibár and a policeman. However, the next day, with the help of three animals and a group of schoolchildren, they manage to sing a touching lullaby and receive donations. The mean organ-grinder steals their money, but in the end all the children and the animals catch him and then sing the song of victory.

The premiere of *Brundibár* in the Prague orphanage was seen only by some 150 people. Still, it was a tremendous success and the opera had at least one repeat performance. On 10 April 1942, Krása was deported to Terezín. Then the boys had to join the transports heading for Terezín and in July 1943, the final contingent, including the director of the orphanage and his son, reached the same destination. By that time the musical activities in Terezín were in full swing and Rafael Schächter honored Freudenfeld with the concert performance of Smetana's *The Bartered Bride*. In return, Freudenfeld gave Schächter the vocal score of *Brundibár*.

In Terezín, Schächter entrusted Rudolf Freudenfeld with a new presentation of *Brundibár*. He had received an enthusiastic review of the premiere in the orphanage and now was willing to advise his protégé once again. The rehearsals were held in the attic of Block L 417, and this time the ensemble, accompanied by an old harmonium, comprised of boys and girls as well. Schächter recommended for the title roles Pintă Mühlstein (Pepíček) and twelve-year-old Greta Hofmeister (Aninka). Zdeněk Ornstein,[2] who played Pepíček in the orphanage, became the "dog." Ella Stein played the "cat," and Maria Mühlstein alternated between the roles of Aninka and the "sparrow." Whenever necessary, the six-year-old son of the pianist Alice Herz-Sommer, Rafael, substituted in the latter role. The ungrateful part of the evil organ-grinder fell to Honza Treichlinger, an orphan from Plzeň (Pilsen), who actually requested it from the conductor, when he met him by chance in the washroom. Honza's portrayal made him into a Terezín "celebrity." In his article about *Brundibár,* Rudolf Freudenfeld described him with the following words:

Brundibár is a negative hero. He is a wicked old man, an organ-grinder who does not want to let the children sing for money in the district which he considers his beat. In the end, he steals their purse with the collected money. It is a character full of mental conflict for children who always have sympathy for beggars and poor people; but this one was wicked, ugly. Honza, quite instinctively, made the character of Brundibár so human that, although he played a wicked character, he became the darling of the audience. He learned to twitch the whiskers which stuck under his nose. He twitched them so well, and at just the right time, that tension relaxed in the auditorium, and often we could hear the children releasing their bated breath.

From the moment in which he "made" the character, he played all performances without understudy. Anybody else would have failed.

What might he have become? An actor or engineer? How he could have humanized his own life as he had his role! That he was rather short was fateful to him.[3] He was fourteen years old. He went to Auschwitz with the old and the small children and directly into the gas chamber.[4]

Rafael Schächter, affectionately called Rafík by the children, often rehearsed the chorus and the soloists and tutored the young Freudenfeld in orchestral conducting. During one rehearsal, he conducted the entire opera himself and then asked Freudenfeld to do it all over again under his watchful supervision.

The Terezín premiere of *Brundibár* took place on 23 September 1943 in the Magdeburg barracks. Once more, the architect, Zelenka, designed the set similar to the one in the orphanage, but this time the "animals" wore costumes, so that they could sing either through the holes in the fence or move freely on the stage. For this production Schächter also had a very talented assistant director, the choreographer Kamila Rosenbaum.

There are conflicting stories about the accompaniment to the children's opera. While some survivors insist that a harmonium was used, others, including Rudolf Freudenfeld, remember an entire orchestra. It stands to reason that the early performances, which began about two months after the arrival of Freudenfeld and the last of the children in Terezín, had only the harmonium accompaniment at first. Krása later wrote a new orchestral score for a true virtuoso ensemble, available to him in the concentration camp: the violinist Karel Fröhlich, cellist Fredy Mark, pianist Gideon Klein, clarinetist Fritz Weiss, the Kohn brothers, and others. The score called for a flute, a clarinet, a trumpet, a guitar, an accordion, a piano, percussion, four violins, a cello, and a bass.

Dr. Kurt Singer (born 11 October 1885 in Breent, Silesia), a musicologist from Berlin, gave the following testimony about the merits of the opera, shortly before his death in Terezín, in January 1944:

Brundibár shows how a short opera of today should look and sound, how it can unite the highest in artistic taste with originality of concept, and modern character with viable tunes. We have here a theme which has appeal for children and grown-ups alike, a moral plot motif recalling the old fairy tales, popular singing kept simple in choral sections but occasionally becoming quite complex in duets and trios, and a sensitive balance of dynamics maintained between a dozen instruments and three dozen singers. We have also a Czech national coloration, music-making without recourse to modern experimentation (at which Krása is a master), a clever balance of scenic effects between the orchestra pit and the stage, an orchestra used with taste and economy and a singing line which is never obscured or smothered by the instruments. . . . In the little opera, born of a serious mind and yet so pleasant to the ear, idea and form, thought and preparation, concept and execution are joined in fruitful marriage of mutual collaboration: Whether it be cast in a large or small form, whether it be song or symphony, chorus or opera, there can be no higher praise for a work of art.[5]

The young participants of *Brundibár* took a less sophisticated point of view of the production of the opera. A fifteen-year-old member of the chorus, Rudolf Laub, described in a humorous fashion not only the circumstances surrounding the preparations and performances of the opera, but also the impressions and effects which *Brundibár* had on the minds and life of his peers for years to come. Laub lived in the same block where the rehearsals were being held, in Room No. 1, together with ninety-seven other boys born in 1928 and 1929. Their supervisor, Professor Walter Eislinger, encouraged them to publish a clandestine handwritten weekly newspaper, *Vedem* (*We Lead*), which lasted from 1942 until August 1944. The entire collection was saved by another inhabitant of the room, Zdeněk Taussig, and published in 1995, under the title *We Are Children Just the Same.*[6] One of Laub's friends and fellow-performers, Leopold Löwy, gave me a copy of Laub's own words concerning *Brundibár*:

Organ-grinder Brundibár — children's opera which is now being presented to the Terezín public in an unending number of repeat performances, deserved for sure the success which it had received. I do not want to argue about the quality of the libretto or music or about its correct or incorrect stage direction. After all, that is up to the critics and altogether people who look at *Brundibár* from the auditorium. However, I can say that . . . it was not easy to master the drilling of a ten-piece orchestra, a forty-piece children's choir, and ten soloists, also children, in a relatively short time of one and a half months. . . . I have to pay my tribute to Rudi Freudenfeld, because during the entire practice he lost his temper only a few times and he calmed down each time immediately. . . . The first rehearsals were mostly boring. We came to an attic covered with dust, where a creaky harmonium stood and where it was choking hot. The chorus sang a couple times "This is Little Joe . . . ," learned another verse and recapped "Brundibár defeated . . . ," and with joy ran out from the dusty space to breathe some fresh air. In the meantime, the candidates for the solo roles stood with trembling voices in front of sweating Rudi and sang after him "lalallala." We were in suspense to find out who will sing which role and who will say on the stage a few more words. There was enough competition, spite, and intrigues on a diminished scale, but finally even the roles were assigned and the rehearsing began slowly but in the earnest, first just the singing. The rehearsals were sleepy, although some people liked it and often it seemed that the whole affair will go to the dogs. However, some kind of mysterious fluid held us together, a presage of that "when it will all be over, it will be fine." We made more and more progress, we got a better rehearsal room, and so the interest grew, everyone enjoyed coming to the rehearsals and with certain pride to their friends that "we are practicing a children's opera." Finally, the day arrived when we were able to sing it almost all. Architect Zelenka came and the staging began.

. . . the premiere . . . succeeded perfectly. We arrived one and a half hour before curtain time, and after we got used to our makeup, which seemed to us hideous looking, we started roughhousing, so that Rudi had to curb us. The moment, the first people have been admitted into the hall, the stage fright began to take a hold of all the little souls, slowly but surely. The three "seasoned" ones were pacing the floor in the back of the stage, saying "I don't have stage fright, nothing can unnerve me," etc., but their ears were purple from fear, how it will go. However, the moment the first measures of music sounded, we all forgot about our fear and acted. Brundibár — Sára (*sic*) Teichlinger, with the tradesmen, took care of the fun on the stage, while Pepíček, Aninka, and the animals contributed to the musical side of the affair. And the choral lullaby, "Mommy is rocking a cradle . . . ," won over the entire audience. . . . And when we were finished and a long lasting ovation thundered through the hall, we were happy and content, since man is a glory seeking creature. . . .

Now we sing the repeat performances routinely and our greatest concern is to have a lot of fun. Of course, we don't take into account unexpected incidents; such as, when in the midst of a performance one can hear the bloodcurdling howl from twenty girl throats, and after anxious questions . . . one finds, out that the bench with the delicate load of twenty singers toppled over. . . . *Brundibár* will soon disappear from the minds of those who saw it in Terezín, but for us, participants, it will remain one of the few beautiful memories which we will have from Terezín.[7]

There is a Czech maxim, "In children the nation is eternal." The audiences were well aware of it when the children sang the final song of victory over the mean Brundibár, who in their minds, represented Hitler himself. As a matter of fact, Honza Treichlinger even resembled him with his dark hair parted on the side and a black mustache. The political connotation was accentuated even

Brundibár performance for the International Red Cross visit to Terezín, summer 1944.
Photo by the Jewish Museum, Prague

more when the poet Emil A. Saudek, another involuntary resident of Terezín, changed the last couple of lines from "He, who loves so much his mother and father and his native land, is our friend and he can play with us," to a more poignant version, "He, who loves right and abides by it, and who is not afraid, is our friend and can play with us." The hope for survival and the perpetuation of Czech Jewry depended on the survival of these courageous youngsters. No wonder that the opera had to be repeated over and over and the same people tried to obtain tickets for still another performance. There is a story about an older man, who approached the young conductor and exclaimed: "Das ist nicht möglich! Von hinten sind Sie der ganze Toscanini!" ("That's not possible! From the rear you are Toscanini all over"). It is not known, however, whether the flattery resulted in another hoped-for ticket.

Perhaps the only people who did not recognize the hidden significance and implication of *Brundibár* were the obtuse Nazis. And so, when the Committee of the International Red Cross announced a visit to the "Paradise ghetto," its commander, *SS Hauptsturmführer* Karl Rahm, decided that the performance of the children's opera would be a fitting example of the "leisurely" life in Terezín. For that reason the production had to be moved from the small auditorium in the Magdeburg barracks to the Sokolovna, a large gymnasium outside the Terezín ramparts, which was equipped with a modern stage, an orchestra pit, and makeup rooms. When Rahm noticed the rather somber and dark scenery, he ordered the stage director (Zelenka) to build a new set overnight with bright and cheerful colors; Rahm even provided him with all necessary material and helpers, just to make sure that the visitors would be duped into giving a complimentary report.

There is a common opinion, based on writings and statements of survivors, that the cast of *Brundibár* was constantly changed, due to the frequent transports from Terezín to Auschwitz, and that only one or two young participants lived to witness the liberation. However, the facts are quite different. Actors for the three main roles, Brundibár, Pepíček, and the "cat," did not have understudies and therefore had to sing all the performances. Only a relatively few children were sent to Auschwitz, while *Brundibár* casts cheered up and encouraged their audiences. The situation changed drastically in the fall of 1944, when Hans Krása, František Zelenka, Rafael Schächter, and a number of musicians and children, including Honza Treichlinger and the Mühlstein siblings, perished in the Auschwitz gas chambers. A fair estimate puts the number of surviving children between fifteen and twenty. Of course, that does not diminish the Nazi culpability for inflicting such atrocities on the millions of their victims, and the loss of even one innocent life calls for wrath from the Heavens.

MY INVOLVEMENT with *Brundibár* started on a very inauspicious note. In the summer of 1970, I made my first research trip to Prague. Through some of my former colleagues and friends I contacted the basso from the National Theater in Prague, Karel Berman, a former Terezín prisoner. The Czech Music Information Center office was the first stop in my quest for information about musical activities in the Terezín concentration camp. There on 3 August 1970, I met Professor Eliška Kleinová, herself a survivor of Terezín, who gave me an hour-long, extremely revealing lecture on the musical life in the ghetto. She handed me six original manuscripts, composed in Terezín by her late brother, Gideon Klein. Then, to my utmost surprise, she gave me another five scores by Hans Krása, and among them the piano reduction as well as the complete orchestral version of *Brundibár,* written in Terezín. Without asking for any receipt, she allowed me to take all this music and make photocopies to be used in any manner I would find suitable.

At that moment, I realized with horror that the librettist, Adolf Hoffmeister, was the man who had indirectly caused the death of my father. As a result of the communist takeover in Czechoslovakia in 1948, my father temporarily lost his position as a high official in the Ministry of Information. Half a year later the newly established work council at the Ministry was deciding whether my father should be dismissed for his democratic orientation or promoted to head one of the departments. During the ensuing vote, his superior, Hoffmeister, broke the tie by voting against him. Subsequently, my father was imprisoned and killed slowly through medical interference. I now faced the dilemma: Should I exert my energy to bring to life an unknown and neglected part of history and the Holocaust in particular, while promoting the work of a man who so drastically altered the life of our entire family, depriving it of a father and bread winner, the possibility of a higher education for my siblings, and spurring my eventual exile? Or should I pack my suitcases and take the first plane out of Prague and forget the entire project? For a couple of days I wrestled with various aspects of the problem, trying to imagine what my father would have decided in a similar situation. A humanitarian, who always worked for the common good, he would stand tall above the paltriness of narrow-minded people. And there was my answer.

Shortly after my return from Prague, my friend, Ivor Hugh, contacted CBS and offered them a special program featuring the compositions written in the Terezín concentration camp. In September 1971, music of Terezín was performed for the first time on American television.[8] The program devoted a ten-minute segment to the melodies from *Brundibár*, sung in Czech by a children's chorus I had coached from the Hartt School of Music in Hartford, Connecticut. It became obvious that the opera had to be translated into English to make it more attractive and usable. My wife, Milada Javora, and I began the task. We were about halfway through, when it occurred to me that the libretto might be copyrighted. My concerns were substantiated by the State Literary Agency, DILIA, in Prague. It took almost a year before the permission was granted to me, one of eight petitioners (no doubt because of my knowledge of both languages and music). Unfortunately, in the meantime, my wife died in 1974.

I finally was able to resume work on the translation. Strangely enough, I did most of it in the car on my frequent trips to New York. By that time, I knew the Czech text and the tunes by heart, so I would concentrate on a few lines, first translating them into English word by word and then shuffling them back and forth and making little changes. When I was satisfied with a section, I would stop the car and write the final version on a piece of paper. On 8 April 1975, I conducted the American premiere of *Brundibár* in the original Czech version in West Hartford, Connecticut, and the English premiere in Ottawa, Canada, on 14 November 1977, thanks to the tireless efforts of the late Dr. Hugo Fischer and his wife, Gretl.

Since then, the opera has become very popular and had hundreds of performances in various languages and forms. It has also been recorded in Czech, English, and German, and was produced several times on television. My own recording for the Dutch company, Channel Classics of Amsterdam, was made in Prague with the Disman Radio Children's Ensemble and it is the only one adhering to Krása's Terezín version. A few years ago the *Publishing House Tempo* in Prague issued a trilingual vocal score, thus facilitating new productions around the world.

Looking back, I feel the satisfaction of making the right decision in Prague at the onset of my Terezín research. I also believe that every new presentation of *Brundibár* is a monument to the memory of the wretched youngsters who were spreading a little joy and hope in the midst of the most tragic era in the history of mankind.[9]

DOCUMENTS AND MEMOIRS

Theresienstadt Questions

LEO STRAUSS

Most of the inmates of Theresienstadt were simply rounded up, packed onto trains, and sent there by the Nazis. But many older and wealthy prisoners were tricked by the Nazis into giving up their homes and savings in exchange for the guarantee of a pleasant life in the "spa town" of Terezín, Czechoslovakia. Here, so they were told, they would receive good-quality housing overlooking parks or a lake and be able to enjoy their old age among their own people. On arrival, however, they were brutally stripped of their belongings and "sluiced" through the gates of the garrison town into appallingly overcrowded and filthy barracks. The shock resulting from this brutal deception caused many of them to fall into chronic states of apathy or even insanity. The worst cases were confined in a psychiatric ward in the Kavalier barracks. This place was known to the inmates by the derogatory term of cvokárna *(derived from the Czech word for "eccentric"), which might roughly be translated into English as "loony bin."*

The musical sketch Theresienstadt Questions, *written by Leo Strauss, is a sharp satire on the naiveté of many new arrivals in the garrison camp. The sketch strips away the typical illusions of newcomers to Terezín in a manner which is, on the surface, light-hearted but has an underlying bitterness about it. This is made immediately clear in the second verse of the song, which reveals the antisemitic attitudes of many Western European Jews, who had lost all sense of their ethnic origins in their desire to be assimilated. Thus the very last people with whom they wanted to be associated were the poor tinkers and street-traders of Poland and other regions of Eastern Europe, typified in the sketch by the region of Tarnopol, whose population was approximately 50 percent Jewish. The irony of the song is that there seem to have been little or no* Ostjuden *permanently imprisoned in Terezín for the camp was designated by the Nazis as a showplace, and "reserved" for VIPs, academics, artists, actors, musicians and composers, veteran officers from the First World War,*

The original *Theresienstädter Fragen* is housed at Yad Vashem, Israel, and has been anthologized in Ulrike Migdal, ed., *Und die Musik spielt dazu: Chansons und Satiren aus dem KZ Theresienstadt* (Munich: Piper, 1986), 71–74. Translated, with an introduction, by Roy Kift.

and prominent Jewish politicians from Austria, Germany, Czechoslovakia, Denmark, and Holland. Any Jews arriving here from the east would have been mostly in transit to the death camps. Nonetheless, the fear of contact with Eastern Jews seems to be a source of major concern to the new arrival and sheds a sad light on Jewish antisemitism, which has been confirmed by many other sources. Indeed, there seems to have been a hierarchy of antisemitism in the camp, whereby Czech Jews hated their German counterparts because they associated them en bloc with the Nazis; the Germans looked down on the Austrians; and the Austrians looked down on the Ostjuden, with the result that many inmates stayed among their own kind in order to avoid conflict.

Leo Strauss, who wrote the sketch, was the son of the opera composer, Oscar Strauss. He was born in Vienna in 1897. In October 1942 he was deported to Theresienstadt with his wife, Myra. Here he quickly made a name for himself as one of the leading cabaret artists alongside Hans Hofer and the Czech, Karel Švenk. Apart from his own literary cabaret he also wrote for Kurt Gerron's "Karussell" cabaret. On 12 October 1944 he was deported to Auschwitz, where he was murdered in the gas chambers.

The original German text is written throughout in rhyming couplets (aa, bb). Apart from one verse, I have followed this scheme in my translation. The form of the sketch is based on a series of four-line questions from the newcomer, each of which is followed by an equivalent reply from the cleaning lady. Both then sing the refrain together. Toward the end of the sketch there is an eight-line block that contains a German pun, which has defeated all my efforts at translation. Nonetheless, I have retained the block in a literal translation, so that readers will know what was in the full German original. As for the rest, I have tried to remain as true as possible to the content of the original within the constrictions imposed by rhyme and rhythm.

(Lady number one enters in traveling clothes with a Tartan woolen shawl and a bird cage. Lady number two is wearing cleaning-brigade overalls. She is casually sweeping the streets.)

LADY I've just arrived from the countryside
And here I've no friends far or wide
I'm looking for the best location
To get some useful information
CLEANER Lady, use me at your leisure
At your service! What a pleasure!
I came from Vienna long ago
And know the place from top to toe

B O T H Theresienstadt, hooray, hooray!
  The most up-to-date ghetto in the world today
L A D Y Yesterday I had no star
  And now I find it most bizarre
  To hear some quite disturbing news
  I'm in the midst of Polish Jews
C L E A N E R Lots of people rub their nose
  Put on airs, adopt a pose
  Might it not be also true
  That you're a Tarnopolack too?
B O T H Theresienstadt, hooray, hooray!
  The most antisemitic ghetto in the world today
L A D Y Has the town a healthy climate?
  Or do lice and bugs begrime it?
  Does one eat well at midday?
  Can you keep disease at bay?
C L E A N E R Food is short for hearty eaters
  Those who eat best are the cheaters
  If you want to stay top-fit
  Get among the long-term sick
B O T H Theresienstadt, hooray, hooray!
  The most humane ghetto in the world today
L A D Y It's really true, there's nought to eat!?
  No fresh veg and no fresh meat
  Will I end my life in bed
  Craving for a crust of bread?
C L E A N E R Stop it! Silence! Please! For shame!
  I've never heard such infamy!
  Here hunger has a finer name
  Vitamin deficiency
B O T H Theresienstadt, hooray, hooray!
  The most elegant ghetto in the world today
L A D Y And what about a place to live?
  Simple but not primitive
  Kitchen, lounge and w.c.
  A bedroom-suite and balcony
C L E A N E R With a little fantasy
  A house will be your just reward

Your dreams become reality
Sleeping on your wooden board
B O T H Theresienstadt, hooray, hooray!
The dreamiest ghetto in the world today
L A D Y And what's the code for evening dress?
I'd really hate to look a mess
Do the men wear tie and tails
When sipping at their cock-a-tails?
C L E A N E R There's one or two as put on airs
But most folks opt for casual wear
To be quite honest, what the heck!
My husband dresses like a wreck
B O T H Theresienstadt, hooray, hooray!
The most fashionable ghetto in the world today
L A D Y Traveling here, I must confess
Has been something of a stress
A nice hot bath would be a treat
To soothe my bones and aching feet
C L E A N E R Get on home and find a bed
Close your eyes and sleep instead
Baths are in such short supply
You'll have to wait till next July
B O T H Theresienstadt, hooray, hooray!
The most hygienic ghetto in the world today
L A D Y And while we're at it, may I say
My portmanteau has gone astray
Half my luggage misdirected
I'll need a porter to collect it
C L E A N E R Forget your bags, not worth the bother
You'll only get into a pother
Never mind, in any case
Where you'll be sleeping there's no space
B O T H Theresienstadt, hooray, hooray!
The most accommodating ghetto in the world today!
L A D Y (*literal translation*) By the way tomorrow I'd like to
Get a hold of some bird-food
Oh, my bird needs a diet
It will only eat the best quality

CLEANER We don't import that stuff here
    Give the bird away quickly
    Anyone here *with a bird (in German this means: a bit crazy)*
    Is a candidate for the Cvokárna *(loony-bin)*
BOTH Theresienstadt, hooray, hooray!
    The wackiest ghetto in the world today
LADY One last question, please don't groan
    I'd like to write a letter home
    And put my family in the clear
    How long will we be staying here?
CLEANER Now that request I can't refuse
    Ain't you 'eard the latest news?
    According to reliable rumors————
(The band drowns out her words in a cacophony of noise)
BOTH Theresienstadt, hooray, hooray!
    The most up-to-date ghetto in the world today!

Letter from Theresienstadt

KURT SINGER

Dr. Kurt Singer wrote the following card from Theresienstadt shortly after his arrival. He wrote to a former colleague from the Jewish Advisory Board in Amsterdam [Beirat des Joodsche Raad Amsterdam].[1] This board served a similar function to the German Reichsvertretung der Juden in Deutschland—the primary group (based in Berlin) representing the Jewish communities within the Reich and overseen by the Nazi authorities. The card was sent via the Reichsvereinigung der Juden [Reich Union of Jews] to Amsterdam. It is vital to note that all outgoing mail from Theresienstadt was censored.

* * *

Dr. Kurt Singer to Dr. Fritz Silten

7 May 1943

My Dear Silten! I am writing today to inform you that we arrived safely. I am quite well. I live at Q410.[2] Soon I will participate musically in the *Freizeitgestaltung* [leisure time activity].[3] The mood is as positive as at the last Sunday speeches in Amsterdam. This goes for all of the advisers and ladies, as well as for Mandl, Lissauer, Lindberg.[4] Men from Berlin helpful.[5] Letters and packages arrive safely here at the reception; the mail functions excellently. Unfortunately, there is still no word from all of you. Smoker's catarrh disappeared in good climate. The travel companions— Heidesheimer, Lilienfeldt, Rosenblatt—are well and send their best to all acquaintances.[6]

From my heart, I wish you only the best. And with much yearning, I am

Your old Kurt Singer

From the Kurt-Singer Archives, Akademie der Künste, Berlin.

Freizeitgestaltung in Theresienstadt

RABBI ERICH WEINER

Weiner led the Freizeitgestaltung *(FZG—"organized leisure time") in Theresienstadt. I have tried to preserve Weiner's formal, bureaucratic reporting style, which in German, relies on the passive voice. The department responsible for leisure time (or recreational) activity is referred to in German as a single mass noun. I use that as well, except when referring to "those" in the plural and "their" activity in the department. I have altered Weiner's sentence and paragraph form to facilitate reading the report. R.R.*

The Time Before the Official Leisure Time Activity (FZG), November 1941 to February 1942

The first leisure time activity was actually a fellowship evening that was organized in the former Sudeten-Barracks, Room 69 on 5 December 1941.[1] The large transport of workers, AK 2, arrived the day before.[2] The evening was improvised as a reunion celebration. It was not very difficult because the J-Transport [Transport of Jews] brought a number of good musicians who had their instruments with them. Of course this improvised evening was extraordinarily well received, so that in a short while, two further events took place in the same room. Thus, a few enthusiasts came together who decided to organize evenings of entertainment on a larger scale. These people were namely Messrs. Salus, Anton Rosenbaum, Mirko Tuma, Dr. Béhal, and Otto Ružička.

Soon a new program was arranged; and the first large fellowship evening took place in front of nine hundred to a thousand persons, for whom four more programs followed soon after. The program consisted mainly of recitations and light music. A jazz orchestra played whose participants were Messrs.

The original document is housed at Yad Vashem, Israel, and has been anthologized in Ulrike Migdal, ed., *Und die Musik spielt dazu: Chansons und Satiren aus dem KZ Theresienstadt* (Munich: Piper, 1986), 131–50.

Fritz Weiss, Honza Seelig, Franz Goldschmidt, Freddy Mautner, Wolfgang Lederer, and Paul Kuhn. Teddy Berger improvised a drum on a wash basin and
harmonica cases; Kurt Maier and Wolfgang Lederer played a harmonica duet;
Kurt Maier presented rhymed couplets and songs; Viktor Kohn played the
flute; and Herbert Lewin revealed his talents as a magician. Mirko Tuma and
Miška recited Czech poems; Dr. Béhal presented German poems for listeners.

It turned out that both a cello and a drum were lacking; some art enthusiasts made a sacrifice and procured these instruments.

This blossoming activity suffered its deathblow in December 1941, when the
possession of musical instruments was forbidden. The energetic organizers,
however, did not allow themselves to be frightened away and arranged lectures
almost every day in the office of the Buildings-Elder.[3] For example, Prof. Teller
spoke on Palestine; Prof. Blum presented his well-known lectures: "5 Years of
French Prison" and about humor; Dr. Baumel from his own law practice.

Even in those days, the organizers struggled with great difficulties. The lecturers were reluctantly released from their duty stations; the offices were not
vacated. If finally, the lecturer was given time off from his work station, there
was no suitable lecture space. If there was space, often the lecturer was busy
again. In this way, the organizers were so weary that they gave up their activity
at the end of February 1942.

At this time, the leisure time activity (FZG)[4] was by coincidence officially
called to life.

The Formation and Beginnings of the Leisure Time
Activity, February 1942 to February 1943

One lovely day in February 1942, I was sent for by the administrative director
of the Bodenbach barracks at that time. He gave me a letter from Fredy Hirsch
in a more or less celebratory fashion, informing me that I had been designated
by Hirsch's division to organize the FZG.

Fredy Hirsch was the director of the Central Administration at that time.
According to this letter, I was to be the official in charge of the leisure time activity. As I later discovered, this letter followed an earlier letter in which Herr
Zucker, Engineer, made Fredy Hirsch aware that he thought me qualified to
participate in the recreational activity, to stimulate interest, and to take control
of programs, etc.

He would suggest first testing me and giving me a job in Fredy Hirsch's
office; in addition, I would have to attend to religious instruction.

More than a half of a year later, I found the following notice on the leisure time activity in the monthly report of the directorship for buildings, February 1942: "In the month of this report, Rabb. Weiner was entrusted to organize the recreational activity, arrange religious services, etc."

My task to organize religious services and to provide religious training was concealed from me. Today I can no longer establish whether this was just co-incidental or deliberate. I saw only the one official task before me: the organization of recreational activity. Thus I saw my work in the rabbinate as more or less voluntary. Indeed I was a member of the "official" unofficial three-member rabbinate. But this duty could not satisfy my effort, nor fill my time. The rabbinical office was only silently tolerated by the administration; its work was highly inhibited and so my own work became limited to burials and betrothals, of which each one had to be approved by the "Jew-Elder," Edelstein.[5]

I never actually got to religious instruction because the youth welfare [department] organized this according to its own terms. When I had to decide sometime around August 1943 to work either as a rabbi or within the extraordinary developing recreational activity, I remained a member of the rabbinate, but left my sphere of preparing marriage petitions. I only operated as a rabbi for special occasions or by special request.

The leisure time activity and its tasks drew me completely under its spell. I saw progressive spiritual deterioration; I saw the brutalization of the ghetto inmates. This was especially palpable during the time that they all lived locked in their barracks. [This is prior to July 1942, before all the non-Jewish townspeople of Terezín were evacuated.]

In the beginning of March, then, I moved into the office of the buildings' management, where I first struggled together with the meal preparation staff—consisting of Hans Korner—for use of a work table with an armchair. A folder and a pencil were generously provided me by the buildings' management and it now meant: Organize leisure time activity.

Fredy Hirsch wanted to take me to the barracks, to show me around there, and to introduce to me qualified people whom he believed would direct the recreational activity within the barracks under my guidance.

So he introduced me to the director of the work mission in the Hamburg barracks at that time, Frau Ellinor Braun, who was to stimulate leisure time activity within the barracks. Frau Braun promised support, but explained right away that she could not contribute to this work alone. She delegated the work to one of her co-workers, the singer Hedda Grab-Kernmayer. Fredy Hirsch led me farther to the Dresden barracks, where he acquainted me with the youth director there, Dr. Renée Bittner. This lady also promised her most extensive support.

Fredy Hirsch's selection of co-workers was in one respect very unhappy. Fredy Hirsch had forgotten that the task of leisure time activity in Theresienstadt was also a Jewish task, and that the leisure time activity would have to be geared toward this in its work. The co-workers at that time did not have the foggiest notion of Judaism, even though they were as efficient as those in the Hamburg barracks.[6]

To be fair, though, we must admit that the Hamburg barracks began its work very energetically.

Still in March — indeed, on the 21st — they announced an artistic afternoon in Room 105; this was repeated twice on 28 March. In this way, Frau Grab-Kernmayer demonstrated her artistic work. Further, on 17 March, registration began for elementary and advanced foreign language classes in Czech, English, French, and Spanish. In addition, vocal tests and choir auditions began under the leadership of Fräulein Ella Pollak; and on 19 March there was singing instruction as well as voice training.

The eager co-workers also wanted to try a theater right away. Frau Dr. Marieluise Adler was instructed to write a play. She dramatized a Jewish legend from Prague, 1760, entitled *Schwarze Spitzen* [*Black Lace*]. The play was completed still in March and rehearsals were supposed to begin in early April.

The Magdeburg barracks had only two lectures on the program at the beginning. Herr Hans Hirsch, Engineer, spoke on the transmission of sound films and television; Otto Brod on Voltaire and the Huguenots. Herr Leopold Sonnenschein directed this work at first on behalf of the buildings' management.

The Sudeten barracks began its work with two lectures. Moreover, they prepared an evening variety show contributed to by a group of soloists who proudly called themselves "The Dolfi Reich Soloist Group."

Dolfi Reich was talented, but even more, they were ambitious and rehearsed diligently. The result was a colorful, jumbled program of recitation, song, and accordion music.

This evening took place in Hall VII and had the advantage of providing about four hundred inmates of the Sudeten barracks with three hours of distraction.

Less active was the Dresden barracks. Fräulein Renée Bittner was too much burdened with the social welfare of youth. She elected a few older women as co-workers whose only good quality was to run eagerly from room to room to sign up those interested in language classes. The classes never took place. One cannot speak of creative work here. The Dresden barracks [leadership] was badly selected. In the long term, this produced unfavorable results.

In the preceding section, I described the work in separate barracks; now I must proceed to describe the almost insurmountable difficulties that generally interfered with our work.

Already the plural, "our work," is exaggerated because the only civil servant was I. All the other co-workers—as much as one could speak of colleagues in this beginning phase—worked voluntarily and part-time. Out of necessity, this led to special consideration for these workers.

It could hardly be the case here that my desires and aims for the program were executed precisely. A further reason for hindrance was an absolute lack of literary and musical materials. One had to be satisfied with original creations or what individual participants knew by heart from their earlier profession.

But the really great difficulty lay in the rather unclear attitude of the leisure time activity [department]. The abstract for the leisure time activity was indeed created within the parameters of the buildings' management and entrusted to me, but the business of the recreational activity was practically only tolerated as a necessary evil. The administration did not want this activity to be openly exercised. One did not know how the commandant's office would react to it. The events of the leisure time activity were viewed as an internal matter of the ghetto-inhabitants and not communicated to the commandant's office. In this way, a certain secretiveness was established. Often, an evening had to be interrupted because a German visit was announced. Applause was often forbidden so as to avoid unnecessary attention.

One of the halfway plausible reasons for this secrecy was the musical instruments. Indeed, the Council Elders were permitted to possess musical instruments, so one could say that the instruments had been borrowed from the councilors; it remained questionable, however, whether one was allowed to publicly use the instruments. Sometimes an especially courageous musician brought an instrument; but mostly one dispensed with music altogether and even the singers sang their opera arias without accompaniment.

A further reason was the audience. It was strictly forbidden for men to visit women's barracks or women to visit men's barracks. For the participating men [in the FZG] we were able with effort and urgency to procure passage-permits to women's barracks. We could never bring participating women into the men's barracks. Now there were always some happy owners of passage-permits in the audience, however, who understood how to swindle their way into performances. The hunger for entertainment, music, and the company of women could not be stayed. These quasi-illegal visitors to the barrack performances created a certain danger for the leisure time activity and even for the whole ghetto, so that we always attended these events with fear.

In spite of all of these difficulties, we organized four fellowship evenings in March with about nine hundred listeners and four lectures with 240 listeners. In the monthly report for the buildings' management, March 1942, we still found no mention.

April 1942: The work this month caused a few sensations. When we say sensations, then we must consider that time, of course, where from a cultural viewpoint, nothing existed. The first of these thrills was the Taube concert in the Magdeburg barracks. The barracks presented the first performance of the *Theresienstadt Suite* by Karl [Carlo] Taube as well as the performance of Dvořák's *American Quartet*. The *Theresienstadt Rhapsody* by Ledeč could no longer be performed because of the lack of time. The technical preparations stretched out too long. One had no podium and had to wait until those at work in Room 118 left for the day, in order then to quickly push tables together. On top of these [tables] the orchestra members took their place. The Hamburg barracks presented a new afternoon of culture whose program we cite:

Trude Adler	Recitations
Grete Asser	*Kaddish* and Convocation[7]
Rosa Chitz	Two Arias (*Gilda* and *The Bartered Bride*)[8]
Franz Weissenstein	Neopolitan Songs
Trude-Lisa Adler	Stuart Parody
Hedda Kernmayer	Slovakian Folk Songs
Margot Weiss	Silent Pantomimes
Lisa Brandt	Tango (Solo Dance)

The Sudeten barracks registered a repeat of the Dolfi Reich evening in Halls 5 and 7 as well as a grand fellowship evening in the potato peeling room.

The artistic ensemble of the Hamburg barracks gave guest appearances and toured for the first time to the Bodenbach barracks. With this began the work in the Bodenbach barracks. Nevertheless, the work of the Bodenbach barracks was quite weak, as was that of the Dresden barracks.

More important was that the Kavalier barracks began its work this month. We succeeded here in finding an energetic, clever collaborator, Prof. Drachmann, who was above all, Jewish-minded. Prof. Drachmann approached his work with real eagerness and awareness of purpose. Already in his first report of 22 April, he stated that he had founded a work committee and established Hebrew, English, Czech, and Spanish language courses.

French language classes were also earmarked, but there was no qualified teacher in the Kavalier barracks. A teacher from another barracks was supposed to be appointed. The appointment could not be made at first, because there was no passage-permit for the teacher. Herr Prof. Drachmann further reported that a chess circle was in preparation. Lecturing also began in the Kavalier barracks. His report is so characteristic that I quote him: "In preparing for music offerings, we encounter the difficulty that no musical instruments may be found in the barracks so that neither instrumental music in the most modest form may be offered, nor may singing be accompanied. We lack a violin and a guitar, resp. an accordion in order to have the necessary means at our disposal." He also reports that evenings of recitation are being prepared. Further, the procurement of books causes difficulties, so that it is absolutely necessary to ferret out books from the barracks. In a last point of his report, he announces a touring performance of the female group of artists from the Hamburg barracks.

From this report we see once more the great difficulties that exist: Some of the barracks, for example, the Kavalier barracks as well as the Bodenbacher barracks, could scarcely contribute a halfway good program by themselves. One had to progress to an exchange of programs whereby again the difficulty of procuring passage-permits and the danger of a visit always existed. But even simple evenings of recitation or evenings with Jewish content encountered troubles, because there were no books there; the few that existed in the ghetto had to be laboriously gathered together.

Prof. Drachmann set a precedent by having organized the first Jewish evening, [a practice] that was then taken over by other barracks. With this, however, the difficulties of the work were not exhausted. The Messrs. Barracks-Elders had, in part, very little understanding for our work. And when a speaker organized an evening, there awaited him — as certain as death — the task of scrounging benches, hauling them by himself, finding a platform, and eventually building everything himself. And when the guests came, then he could also stand at the door to regulate the immense crowd.

Even when we used admission tickets later on, there were always people who tried to force their way into our performances.

When a concert was supposed to be arranged in another barracks, for example, in the Sudeten barracks, the instruments had to be brought over very carefully. One often even made use of the transport delivery vans in order to avoid the very curious looks of the [ghetto] police.

Time and again one had to admire the enormous work zeal with which our voluntary artistic collaborators put themselves at our disposal; and fully gratis, [they] made it their business to lift the spirits of the barracks' inmates, offering them something from the artistic sphere.

The Dresden barracks presented an evening variety show this month several times, contributed to mostly by mother and daughter Klinke. However, they presented mainly synagogal songs.

The work in April was badly inconvenienced by the departing Pürglitz-Transport, as well as by an East-Transport at month's end.[9] In spite of all of the difficulties, however, we succeeded in organizing 16 evenings of camaraderie with approx. 3,300 spectators and 16 lectures with approx. 1,040 listeners.

The leisure time activity also saw it as its duty to be medically enlightening and already began this month to organize lectures on medicine which gave the ghetto inmates rules of conduct for their life in Theresienstadt.

The Sudeten barracks gained Herr Dr. Otto Hönig as the new barracks' director. He applied himself to his work eagerly, but always had to combat difficulties that inhibited his work greatly.

May: This month again yielded a very large gain in co-workers for us. Rabb. Schön took over the direction of the Magdeburg barracks from Herr Sonnenschein. Now the recreational activity here too could fulfill Jewish tasks. We still always had to pay attention not to hurt the feelings of the inmates from different groups and barracks.

In May several important events were registered. In the Kavalier barracks, the Taube Orchestra gave a concert; and the Dresden barracks provided a fellowship evening. In the potato peeling room of the Sudeten barracks, a concert by the quartet of the Magdeburg barracks took place to great acclaim.

On the occasion of the Shavuot[10] festival, Shavuot celebrations were organized in all of the barracks; credit for the realization of these festivities went mainly to Messrs. Rabb. Schön and Prof. Drachmann.

On 24 May a celebration of the first half year of the AK I took place in the potato peeling room of the Sudeten barracks; this was the premiere of the later well-known Švenk-cabaret. We will speak again about the Švenk-cabaret.

This event—which was also attended by closed units of AK people from the Magdeburg barracks—was extraordinarily successful. Nevertheless, one had to overlook much, because—like the later Švenk-events—this evening was greatly improvised. The stage and the lighting, assembled with great difficulty, were not fully completed when the guests entered; the program was ill-prepared and too long; the guests, not permitted to transgress the curfew, became rather impatient; and the event had to be ended prematurely. Nonetheless, it was a great success. The beginning of the Švenk-cabaret, despite all of the deprivations, was a major event. The young organizers brought forth courage, cheerfulness, and variety into the life of the ghetto. This month, the Kavalier barracks initiated a cycle of lectures on Jewish history; this was taken over by the Magdeburg barracks. Herr Rabb. Schön presented the lectures.

The language courses proceeded likewise in all of the barracks.

We cite here the program of the Magdeburg barracks on occasion of the Shavuot celebration:

1. Beethoven	*Die Himmel rühmen . . . [The Heavens praise . . .]* (Hebr. text)
Ki hasamajim mesaprim Shavuot	choir, under direction of Karl Fischer
2. *Shavuot* Address	Eugen Weisz
3. Prologue to *Young David* by Richard B.[eer] Hoffmann[11]	Dr. Otto Guth
4. *Wehogen* by Levandowsky	sung by choir, under direction of Karl Fischer

While the other barracks struggled against space limitations, the Magdeburg barracks, of course, had an advantage over them. For in the Magdeburg barracks one could use the room occupied by the production [staff], Hall 118 (later numbered 241).

During the last week of the month, the work of leisure time activity suffered an interruption that lasted until 28 June. In spite of this, we organized 16 fellowship evenings with 2,900 spectators and 36 lectures with 2,460 listeners.

June: Once the organized activity was permitted again at the end of June, an afternoon variety show took place in the Dresden barracks with three repeat performances for approx. 500 spectators.

The Rapid Rise of the Leisure Time Activity

July [1942]: Our events met with such praise that not enough of them could be offered. New programs and new groups were established; one competed with the others for the number of events. [Theodore] Herzl celebrations took place in all of the barracks; and in the Kavalier barracks there was also a celebration for Bialik. Further, a *Tischa b'av* [ninth day of the month, commemoration of destruction of first and second temples] prayer hour was arranged for the whole ghetto in the Magdeburg barracks. Walter Freund rehearsed a group in a series of episodes from Stefan Zweig's *Jeremiah;* this met with great approval and was performed in almost every barracks. The Jewish work flourished. A noteworthy ensemble formed under the direction of Trude Popper. They were for the most part young girls who returned from Pürglitz and put together a cabaret mostly based on Pürglitz motifs. Popper's cabaret met with the most approval: It was full of ideas and comic in its makeup. Popper's group presented guest performances in all of the barracks. The artist ensemble Grab-Kernmayer tried for the first time to organize a concert in the yard of the Hamburg barracks. It became clear on this occasion that choral concerts without musical accompaniment did not resound sufficiently enough, so that we did not use this courtyard for future events.

The question of space naturally presented the biggest difficulty for all of the barracks. This was one of the obstacles against which we had to fight in the end. The Sudeten barracks had after all no room; the potato peeling room was rarely at our disposal. I do not want to judge whether this was because of little cooperation on the part of the administrators or really due to frequent use.

In the beginning, the Hamburg barracks made Hall 105 available to us. However, the room was soon occupied. So the events had to be moved to one of the garrets. Because of the rapid increase of ghetto inmates, this attic was also taken from us again. Sometimes the Bodenbacher barracks made the carpenter's shop available to us. It was certainly not an ideal space—but at least it was something. The space in the Kavalier barracks was relatively good; we could hold our performances in a sleeping room. The Magdeburg barracks was, however, the best equipped. As already mentioned, Hall 118 (where the production staff officiated) was available to us. But we could only occupy its premises after [work] hours and then only together with the rabbinate.

Once again we lacked a platform and stage lighting [equipment]. Later we succeeded in erecting a podium. If I am not very much mistaken—this was made possible through the self-sacrificing work of the Švenk group, whose very energetic manager, Ládă Neuschul, took care of everything one could think of.

This first makeshift platform was exchanged for a permanent one after the recreational activity was officially recognized. Ládă Neuschul helped us voluntarily and procured materials for us over several months. This month, the leisure time activity arranged 34 fellowship evenings with 8,020 spectators and 13 lectures with 760 listeners.

In July, nevertheless, interest in serious lectures waned considerably; this remained true throughout the summer. Only in the fall and winter months could the lecture activity be revitalized—the Interior Administration and the Central Administration knew nothing to report on our activity.

August: An upward swing set in this month. The rise is not only marked by the number of performances; it is also due to the formation—and activity—of new artistic groups which, naturally, limited themselves to cabaret and short one-acts because of lack of materials. The Thorn and Hofer cabaret began its activity this month.

Rafael Schächter publicly presented a vocal concert of Czech and Hebrew songs.

So too was the first play performed; and in fact, it was Jean Cocteau's melodrama, *The Human Voice,* starring Vlasda Schön. Frau Klinke emerged with a series of Jewish composers. Several Czech artists presented an evening of recitation in Czech, reading Mácha, Dyk, Březina, Neruda, Goethe, Musset, Jehuda Halevy, Heine, and still others. Vlasda and Marie Schön, and Herr Miška participated.

After the hall in the Magdeburg barracks had a permanent stage, and because the other barracks had no theater space, we allowed all the events for other barracks to take place in the Magdeburg barracks. The large throng, incited by the extraordinary interest of ghetto inmates, led to the introduction of admission tickets. This did not lessen the crowd, but it helped us to assess who had the right to attend a performance and who did not. The security police had to be enlisted. The fire brigade also exercised its established service in the space. And already at this time, we heard the first complaints that the number of admission tickets is far too low for the great need of the ghetto.[12] We were unsuccessful in solving these difficulties in spite of our greatest efforts, because even later when we found new rooms, that quantity was still too small, given the constantly rising number of inhabitants in Theresienstadt.

A noteworthy innovation was the development of the so-called BLOCKVER-ANSTALTUNG ("block" performances)[13] about which we will speak separately.

With our construction of the ghetto, what led us to introduce the block performances were the poor accommodation possibilities for the constant influx of ghetto inmates from all corners and ends of the German Reich. The mood of these people left much to be desired, since they had all imagined something quite different; perhaps they were also promised something other than what they found here.

In order to improve this mood and to make them forget the poor accommodation possibilities and much else, we immediately proceeded to organize afternoon variety shows and lectures in the blocks. The warm summer was advantageous for our efforts. We could use the yards. So in August we arranged 37 fellowship evenings with approx. 10,900 spectators, 24 lectures with 1,380 listeners, and 13 major events in the blocks with approx. 8,050 spectators. This brought the number of listeners this month to an impressive high of 20,330. I contributed to all of this with 4 colleagues and a permanently hired musician, in addition to the voluntary collaborating artists.

In the month of August, our group of co-workers was strengthened by the arrival of Johann Krása, the national prize recipient for music of the former Czech Republic.[14]

His task was mainly to oversee the programs. In addition, he took over the directorship of the Sudeten barracks after the departure of Herr Dr. Hönig.

September: Two important events gave our work direction this month: (1) The High Holy Days and (2) the major departing transports of the elderly.[15] This limited our operation to practically only serious presentations and lectures. There were times of meditation for the holidays whose programs we cite. Of the lectures, particularly the first one by Prof. Utitz is noteworthy: "Psychological Impressions in Theresienstadt." Prof. Utitz identified different symptoms in the ghetto through psychological analyses. The theater operation was almost completely brought to a standstill. There was only one premiere: *Heitere Einakter* [*Cheerful One-Acts*], directed by Hans Hofer.

The elderly people who came to the ghetto in such great numbers last month were unhappy in Theresienstadt because they had imagined everything differently from what we could offer them here. They accused whomever they could of being guilty of these abuses.

The leisure time activity established the task of bringing the life of the ghetto closer to the newcomers and to inform them especially of the construction in the ghetto and the work accomplished here. So in honoring the three-quarters of a year anniversary of the ghetto's existence, several lectures were presented by us on life in the ghetto and its construction. Karl Schließer spoke in the Magdeburg barracks; Ing.[16] Otto Zucker at the Sudeten; Ing. Freiberger in L 315; Otto Brod in the Hamburg barracks; and Ing. Koralek in L 233, etc. To some extent, they spoke at large in the yards.

These events could easily have been disastrous for us. But the way it was — and is — in Theresienstadt; on the contrary, they brought us a great advantage. One could have almost spoken of a comedy. In the Sudeten, the "Barracks-Elder" allowed posters to announce Ing. Zucker's speech. The newly appointed head of E I, Johann Krása, lacked the necessary experience and so the posters were also hung at the barracks' entrance. The O.D. man[17] was commanded immediately to tear down the posters if a visitor should appear. The visit came in the person of Oberleutnant Janeček. The poster was senselessly torn down again and naturally noticed by Janeček. Now there was suspicion, of course, of some kind of underground propaganda. A great uproar in the ghetto, and especially in the recreational activity division — there was great fear about the following day. But something quite different occurred. Jakob Edelstein explained to the camp commandant at that time, Dr. Seidl, that the lecture should have been announced. But because Dr. Seidl could no longer be reached, the lecture was supposed to be postponed, and the poster was to be torn down. The commandant took note of this and the planned lecture took place two days later in the 2nd courtyard. Since this time, the leisure time activity [department] has to submit a program notice to the commandant's office. This is how the work of the leisure time activity became legalized for the first time after many long months. From a semi-tolerated, rather concealed operation, the recreational activity became a totally official undertaking.

The expansion of the city [Theresienstadt] also necessitated a reorganization of the FZG. The districts had to be managed as well as the barracks. Prof. Drachmann, who had been active in the Kavalier barracks, took over Districts IV and also I. For District III we had gained an energetic, goal-oriented man who applied great control to his work, Prof. Emil Utitz. District III was clearly the most important [district] because it was the most densely populated of all districts. It was also in this district that most of the block performances had to be held. Our colleagues in District III were responsible for erecting a small stage in the attic of Q 307. This stage was to serve, above all, the inhabitants of District III. But Prof. Utitz also found a room in E III a, the "Genie" barracks,[18] where he could allow lectures to be held regularly. All of this was not enough for me however. I saw that hundreds of old people in hospitals lay abandoned—both invalids and the incurably ill. And I wanted to offer them some amusement. Thus I created the institution of the reader. These were mostly very old people who approached their task with dedication and eagerness: to regularly visit hospitals to provide the elderly with an hour of distraction through reading aloud, lectures, or storytelling.

In this month an unusual occurrence in the cultural life of Theresienstadt also began. This was a lecture series by the emergency service [*Hilfesdienst*] of the ghetto-watch, managed by Herr Manes. Philipp Manes respected culture. He knew how to attract a circle of literary and culturally minded people around him. Then he organized lectures and play readings for them, also borrowing artistic ensembles from us. Briefly, he developed a lively cultural operation.[19] Help came now also to me personally in Zdeněk Jelinek. Up until then, I was in charge of all administrative work. I had to oversee everything, supervise the programs, hold meetings with the artists, submit programs for inspection— briefly, everything was in my sole power. And then Zdeněk Jelinek came— a talented and adept poet who also understood theatrical affairs. He was to stimulate Czech theater and to help me administratively in the office, especially to keep files on the artists. Now we both sat at one table; office help and a typewriter were still a dream.

In order to oblige the avid reading needs of the ghetto inmates, Frau Hanna Weil organized a private book exchange in the Hamburg barracks. We took her under our wing, giving her the chance to occupy herself exclusively in the library and to develop the library from the broadest base.

Despite the aforementioned difficult situation, we organized 8 fellowship evenings with approx. 2,000 spectators, 10 Block performances with approx. 1,700 spectators, and 23 lectures with approx. 1,500 listeners. It should be noted that the lectures also already entailed performance; and a part of these already took place in the blocks. Also, the label "fellowship evening" is somewhat misleading. These were cabarets (Švenk, Hofer, Thorn) which for simplicity's sake, we called semi-fellowship evenings. We rarely had a really private "fellowship" evening. The participating artists were volunteers who worked unselfishly. But they could not be expected to pursue their work in the ghetto and outside of their working hours produce art for ghetto inmates. Because except for Wolfgang Lederer and Frau Hedda Kernmayer, there were no practicing artists within the FZG ranks at this time. After difficult negotiations, however, we accomplished the following: Overtime hours devoted to the FZG would be recognized, so that now at least the artists received remuneration for their overtime in the form of increased rations of margarine and sugar.

The Interior Administration reported in September 1942 the following about our activity:

"The FZG is on an upward swing because they can develop their operation in an uninhibited manner. There are also more workers available to them. It has now been agreed upon by the Central Department of Labor that the overtime devoted to the FZG is to be valued. Because the FZG is in active expansion, numerical overviews are currently irrelevant. It can be said, nonetheless, that several lectures and similar events of the most diverse kind are taking place in each district every day."

October: Despite the losses suffered (departures of ghetto inmates) and in spite of the setback in September, the FZG begins its work in October with a new impetus. Above all, two new attic stages have been created, one in B IV; the second in L 203. The one in B IV was in all respects quite primitive; it did not ever even have a curtain. The demands were not very high though. The stage fulfilled its purpose of providing house inmates with distraction and entertainment almost daily through performances which took place there. The theater housed approx. 200 spectators of which the majority had to stand, because no one was there (except our presenter) who might have collected benches and carried them upstairs; not to mention that the chancelleries only very reluctantly made seating available.

The second attic stage in L 203 was much better constructed thanks to the eager work of the house inmates themselves. It was above all meant for the house inmates and was later made available one to two times a day as a permanent stage for theater and block cabarets. Almost all of the old programs were performed: the Švenk cabaret; Trude Popper cabaret; Jean Cocteau, *The Human Voice;* the Hofer cabaret; Thorn presented an original cabaret that was mostly self-written one-acts that he called *Dreimal Humor* [*Thrice Humor*]. The Bobby John group began new work with true zeal as it supported our efforts to bring entertainment and humor to the blocks.

Due to bad weather, we had to move our performances inside the buildings among the ghetto inmates in their living quarters. The living situation was worst in the large unheated attics of, for example, the Hannover and Dresden barracks. I remember with pleasure the first major performance in the Dresden barracks attic on 10.21.42 with Herr Dr. Neuhaus as my guest. The John-Group organized a cabaret right there in the attic on the gangway among the inmates.

Otherwise, except for the usual evenings of song and such events, the only other event to note this month is a serious Sukkot celebration.[20] This month we already had 70 artists working voluntarily for us, but our readers also visited old-age homes and hospitals. Our 12 permanently placed readers read 240 hours this month at 66 places for 1,300 listeners.

We proceeded to move the reading operation to the blocks as well. But the ban on the FZG on 25 October hindered us from doing so. Despite the early end to the month's activities, we organized 30 fellowship evenings with approx. 7,500 spectators, 16 block performances with approx. 3,200 spectators, and 46 lectures for approx. 2,860 listeners. I must note that many smaller lectures with presentations in the blocks (recitations and such) are included in this number.

The Administrative Interior writes about the FZG in its monthly report:

"Despite the tragic events in regard to the departing transports, the FZG could, nonetheless, register a larger circle of interested people. Countless lectures, evenings of entertainment, and variety hours are being organized in houses and blocks. And these performances were organized, for the most part, by persons who after their full day's work, summoned the desire to offer thousands of ghetto inmates several hours of entertainment and instruction."

The Independent Subdivision

Once the leisure time activity had recorded these kinds of successes and become so popular, it was decided that the FZG be moved from the area of buildings' administration and made an independent subdivision of the Interior

Administration. As director of the department I now only acknowledged the authority of Herr Dr. Egon Popper — director of the Internal Administration. Frankly, I must admit that Dr. Popper accorded to our work the broadest field of influence and allowed us to work without restrictions.

That did not mean, however, that we got an office for ourselves. On the contrary, the clerks, whom I finally got to help me, squeezed in with me at two tables; they had to plead with and beg other departments just to borrow a typewriter. But work was done and that was the important thing.

November: The month of November brought [with it] diverse events of great importance. The thrill was the premiere on 28 November of *The Bartered Bride* [*Verkauften Braut*].

It is now time for me to also speak about a big secret in Theresienstadt: about our first piano. A piano torso was found somewhere after the city was evacuated by the Aryans [summer of 1942]. Through his skill, Mg. Pick properly reassembled it and art enthusiasts brought the piano secretly to the attic of the youth home, L 417. We were not allowed to own instruments. Although one could not refer to a piano torso as an instrument, one did not want to come forward with it publicly. And so there were small concerts in those days by Kaff, Gideon Klein, etc. Schächter used this piano for exercises and after laborious month-long work, produced the concert performance of *The Bartered Bride*. That was a great art event that has not been surpassed to this day, nor can it hardly be surpassed again; at best, perhaps, only by Schächter's *Requiem* by Verdi.

The month of November was, on the whole, marked by premieres as the first anniversary of the Theresienstadt ghetto approached. Our artists also wanted to demonstrate, of course, what they were capable of achieving. Besides the already mentioned premiere of *The Bartered Bride*, Zdeněk Jelinek's *Falle* [Trap] premiered on 22 November. The premiere took place in the utmost primitively equipped attic A of the Hannover barracks. A small theater space had been created here in the interim. This name is terribly exaggerated indeed. There was a raised platform on the sides of which hung paper on wires to darken the sides and to separate the stage from the audience area and from the so-called dressing room. The house electrician installed there four to five lamps onto two circuits as spotlights, presenting the great luxury of stage lighting. Benches were scarcely available; the audience mostly had to stand. For the especially prominent, one to two rows of benches were carried up by our lecturers or colleagues. Otherwise, anyone could sit who brought a little stool. But the theater space suited the play excellently. The participants were true amateurs; however, Jelinek's beautifully recited and pure verse demonstrated the enthusiasm that the young artists dedicated to their task, allowing the author and director to lead them.

The play was cast as follows:

Columbina .... Eva Korálek
Pierrot .... Otto Spektor
Pantalone .... Jonny Miška
Kapitán .... Frante Bergmann
Rarach .... Ota Witz

The premiere itself took place under special circumstances. Herr Poljak[21] came to it. We nearly thought that this meant the end to our performances, if not worse than that. But Herr Poljak watched the play with great interest and left silently when it was over. The play itself—written and directed in the manner of *commedia dell'arte*—found great favor with the audience.

On 18 November, we produced our first costumed play. It was two one-acts by Chekhov—indeed, *Mědvěd* [*The Bear*] and *Námluvy* [*Courtship*].[22] *Mědvěd* starred Sonya Soníková and Jonny Miška; Zdeněk Ekstein, Marie Schön, and Ota Kohn acted in *Námluvy*. The performance was produced in B V; the costumes were procured and made over by the clothes distribution area.[23] The difficulties can hardly be described. We organized a special premiere for an invited audience and I did not miss the opportunity to introduce the performance. I indicated what kind of work the recreational activity branch and its participants accomplished; I indicated that already one-quarter of a million listeners had attended our performances; I pointed out that the FZG was presenting a costumed theater performance for the first time; but I also drew attention to the circumstances under which we had to work. If we needed a typewriter we could always have one—after working hours. If we needed work tables and space, we could have everything—when the other departments were no longer working. If we needed helpers, we could also have this as long as they worked with us voluntarily. And so I told the men about our work in a few concise sentences. This introduction brought me a friendly rebuke from the General Secretary at that time, Leo Jannowitz, but it helped. We got the first typewriter; and we got two tables, several chairs, and an empty cabinet. Given our circumstances at that time, this was a luxury even though our whole operation was crowded together into a corner of the Internal Administration.

The Czech cabaret also produced a premiere on 23 November. It was the *Lustige Ghetto-Revue* [*Comic Ghetto-Revue*], which met with an overall favorable response.

A few young people who were enthusiastic about art joined forces in complete silence and tried to produce a montage of poems under the title *The Mother*. The premiere took place on 19 November in L 203. This group tried to do too much and therefore this presentation only had two repeat performances.

The German theater emerged with a play for the first time. It was *Thor und Tod* [*Death and the Fool*] by Hofmannsthal. This took place on a stage as primitively equipped as B IV, in Q 307. The light muse [cabaret] brought forth a novelty as well and indeed under Hofer's direction. The premiere on 17 November took place in the Magdeburg barracks. It was an arrangement of separate arias from operettas by Jewish composers — from Offenbach to Abraham in a nonstop sequence. Dr. Österreicher introduced and commented on the presentations. There was enormous praise for this novelty.

Jewish art was represented in one evening of East European art; this met with great favor indeed, but nevertheless, left a lot to be desired.

Played from the old repertory were Švenk's cabaret, Thorn's *Thrice Humor*, Cocteau's *The Human Voice*. The serious art produced further Walter Freund's episodic *Jeremiah* and Schächter's old vocal concert.

Hence, this month we had ten theater programs with thirty-two repeat performances; two concerts with three repeat performances — quite a respectable program, I believe.

The Health Department also introduced a novelty in that medical lectures were held regularly. The first medical lecture took place on 7 November in the Magdeburg barracks, Room 241. Dr. Klapp spoke on typhus. These lectures were then expanded. A scientific community evolved at the Health Department, giving itself a task to deepen the knowledge of the doctors, especially in regard to Theresienstadt, and to provide nurses with more thorough training.

Especially noteworthy lectures this month were the lectures by Jakob Edelstein on Jewish self-administration [self-rule] in Theresienstadt and the lecture, "One Year Theresienstadt," on 11.24 in the Sudeten barracks, Room 7. Prof. Emil Utitz's lecture, "Mental Hygiene in Theresienstadt," marked the prelude to the foundation of a scientific community in Theresienstadt. Another important event this month was the opening of the ghetto library. The first inventory was approx. three thousand books. Of course, this by far was not enough to allay the hunger for books. Thus one proceeded from the idea of a public library to sending boxes of books to barracks and blocks and then after a certain period of time, exchanging them. At the beginning twenty-five of these book boxes were sent.

Performances in the courtyards of the block houses finally had to stop this month because of weather conditions. We proceeded to allow performances in the separate rooms of the block houses. The following excerpt from a report by Myra Strauß on the block performances shows what kinds of difficulties we encountered:

In the late fall 1942, the block performances began—that is performances within separate block houses and in sick rooms. At first, we lacked all provisions. Instruments were not allowed; artists were not included; musical notes and texts were unavailable; we lacked all supervision of the playing spaces. (It was natural that we with our primitive office equipment could not have calculated what would be required. We had to struggle for everything ourselves even though we convinced those in authority within the ghetto daily of our successes.) But because, on the other hand, the purpose of these performances—namely, to distract the old and sick people from their worries—would not tolerate a delay, we began helter-skelter using the most primitive means. A singer or a recitator stood in one of small rooms among the inmates, presenting from memory what we came upon as repertory. (It must be said on behalf of the artists that they willingly devoted themselves to this work; did not expect remuneration; rather, they did everything to cheer up the old and sick people.) The first months were used, above all, to meet quantitatively the immense need. All the artists were enlisted; notes and texts were sought and new ones written feverishly.

Here I must devote some words to the colleague we gained and whose report I just cited: Myra Strauß.

It was my wish that the married couple, Herr Dr. Leo and Myra Strauß,[24] should work for us, but the Internal Administration did not approve of this, since they did not want too large a personnel in the FZG. So Myra Strauß came to us as our permanent colleague, while Herr Strauß voluntarily made himself available to us. Frau Strauß was appointed the official in charge of block performances for Prof. Utitz who, as I mentioned, was in charge of District III. District III was the most important district and Frau Strauß went right to work. She visited all of the houses of her block; she put together a filing system in which each house was registered; and noted what kind of interests existed within the separate houses. Briefly, she applied enormous energy to the deed.

The department for Internal Administration attached to its monthly report a special report on the leisure time activity, because, meanwhile, we had been promoted to an independent subdivision of the internal administration. The internal administration writes in this report:

The leisure time activity made progress this month not only in the number of lectures, evening and other performances, but mainly in the quality of these performances.

This month for the first time, plays, as well as an opera were produced. It may be said that the enthusiasm of the organizers and participants enabled the execution and the high quality of these performances.

This month a library was also opened, making three thousand books available. This library will be organized as a kind of mobile library; and in the next days, the first boxes of books will be sent to the barracks. It is already noticeable that this new institution rouses great interest; a colossal throng of inmates prevails during the established hours for social intercourse.

The numerical success of this month was as follows:

10 plays with 32 repeat performances
2 concerts with 3 repeat performances
1 opera with 3 repeat performances
22 fellowship evenings
with 18,500 spectators altogether; 38 lectures with 4,000 listeners; 170 block performances with 10,000 listeners. In addition, 11 readers were busy for 150 hours.

It must be stressed that for all of that, nevertheless, our theater performances and concerts suffered from the absolute lack of theater scripts and musical works.

I also have a change to record in the lecture organization that, to be sure, had already developed over many months. Once the operation became so large, I had no time to control the lecture organization. And to my regret, I had to neglect the Jewish lectures. Then Ing. Lolo Drucker came to my assistance. With his circle of associates,[25] he organized a Jewish program and Jewish lectures which I then took over for the mass public as part of the recreational activity. Usually, these took place on a Sunday evening. I also had to make a change in the program. Through the activity of especially Lolo Drucker, a small lecture operation developed which was not geared for the public for reasons of space.

So I had to organize a double program. All program events were cited in the so-called program proposal, as well as in the remarks from the commandant's office. For the reasons cited above, neither the program proposal nor the commandant's notice was meant for the public.

Therefore, after the program was assembled, I had to condense the program proposal and from this abridged program, we received twenty to thirty copies, from the Supervisors, specifically for the public.

The major development of the leisure time activity was that we proceeded to use a ticket office. It was Dr. Popper's intention to enable everyone access to the performances. And so tickets were distributed during the afternoon hours in our office 107. This led to the formation of long fronts[26] in the corridor in front of the office often reaching to the central headquarters [*Evidenz*].

But I can say with satisfaction that those waiting could almost always be gratified, since they certainly received tickets to one of the performances. At that time, several hundred tickets were distributed daily.

December: December was an unmistakable work month. There were but few premieres. The Fröhlich string quartet produced its new program; in addition, there was an evening of chamber music. The Czech artists produced a recitation series entitled *A Winter's Fairy-Tale,* directed by Zdeněk Jelinek. This evening, however, did not bring the desired success. We introduced a change on Friday evening within the lecture series. Every Friday evening a lecture was supposed to take place in B V on a Jewish topic in the areas of science and art. This introduction proved such a success that it has been continued the whole time until today.

We must record an event this month; the "coffeehouse" was opened—an insignificant matter in itself. More important is that musical instruments arrived for the coffeehouse. In this way, we were also able to use musical instruments for our performances. We got scores from time to time. And what is even more gratifying is that several parlor organs came with the various furniture transports. Indeed, these instruments were in desolate condition, but they were, nonetheless, capable of repair by our artist Herr Mg. Pick who could reassemble them.

In numbers, our work in December looks as follows:

9 theater programs with 46 performances,
1 evening of recitation,
2 concerts,
1 opera with 5 repeat performances, and
92 fellowship evenings, cabarets, and not to forget things like that, various
    Hanukkah festivities attended all together by 36,500 guests; 50 lectures
    with 6,000 listeners; and 350 block performances with approx. 16,700
    spectators. In addition, 12 readers read aloud for 1,000 hours in 660
    rooms. Further, one might mention yet another 6,500 guests in the
    coffeehouse.

With this, the recreational activities reached the height of their capacity this month.

January 1943: The monthly report of the subdivision of the internal administration, FZG, begins with the following paragraphs:

The performances of the FZG this month suffered greatly under different circumstances. First, several stages had to be shut down because the attics—where they were—could not be heated. Second, anxiety was caused by the departing transports and, in part, also by the departure of various employees.

In spite of this, the performances of the recreational activities were executed with the greatest effort.

The effort also applies especially to the colleagues of the "Zentrale," because the thirteen to fifteen workers have approx. six seats available to them.

The space is then absolutely unsuitable.

At the end of December or the beginning of January, a new quartet was added to the Ledeč Quartet which existed since the beginning of the ghetto. The quartet consisted of four young people: Karl Fröhlich, Heini Taussig, Romouald Süssmann, Fredy Mark.

At the beginning they worked with Herr Prof. Luzian Horwitz and dedicated themselves to their task with the greatest eagerness. Moreover, Herr Karl Fischer came into prominence; he produced his first synagogal concert with a chorus of approx. fifty participants.

Otherwise, this month was an unmistakable work month. There were no new performances; rather, the old programs were played through. Besides the Fröhlich quartet, the Grab-Kernmayer evening of song took place, as well as chamber music performances by the Ledeč quartet, evenings of arias, and moreover, *The Bartered Bride*. The theater did not change its repertory either. In January then, we had 5 concert programs with 20 performances, 7 theater programs with 40 performances, and an opera with 4 performances. In addition, approx. 20 different fellowship evenings with about 15,600 guests; 24 lectures with approx. 2,000 listeners, and approx. 20 block performances with 18,100 spectators.

Furthermore, the first floor of the "coffeehouse" was opened this month. An orchestra had to be established under the direction of Ledeč, as well as a small jazz ensemble for the programs in the "coffeehouse." The Coffeehouse Orchestra (with all that belonged to it) was entrusted to Herr Kapellmeister Dr. Josef Stross. He had to ensure that the concerts attained high standards. The library worked worse this month, because it suddenly had to make a large number of books available to the *Kamaradschaftsheim*.[27] From the beginning, it became noticeable that our library lacked Czech books and *Belles-lettres* [light fiction], a deficiency that could not be rectified with the later shipments.[28]

The Czech Theater in Terezín

ZDENKA EHRLICH-FANTLOVÁ

Ehrlich-Fantlová was deported as a nineteen-year-old to Terezín in January 1942 and transported to Auschwitz in October 1944. She was transported in early 1945 to Kurzbach, Gross-Rosen, and Mauthausen before reaching Bergen-Belsen in March 1945. She was liberated in April 1945. After the war, she eventually emigrated to Melbourne, Australia, where she was an actress for twenty years. She now resides in London.

I CAN SEE NOW that the testimonies of us—survivors—will possibly be of some value, if at least to clarify some of the gaps and misconceptions in understanding the real significance that the arts played in the process of survival in Terezín. Terezín was not a concentration camp. It was a regular Czech town, which was built by the son of the empress Maria Teresa, Joseph the Second, in 1780 as a fortress against the Prussians. As it happened, by nobody's prediction, it was built in the shape of a Jewish star. A shape of things to come. We, the inmates, lived in the town, walked freely in the streets, wore our normal clothes and behaved normally, but under abnormal conditions.

Apart from running the town under our own management under the government of Jewish Elders, we had the time and inclinations to create the arts. Not so much as entertainment but rather a support for the fighting spirit. A kind of food for the soul which in time for the struggle for survival is more important than bread (letter to Rebecca Rovit, London, 5 February 1998).

The following chapters (29–32, 35–37) are from Ehrlich-Fantlová's memoirs, *"Klíd je Síla" rek' tatínek* (*"Calmness Is Strength"—said Father*), published in Czech (Prague: Primus, 1996) and in German translation by Weidle Verlag, Bonn (1999). This unpublished English translation is by Deryk Viney.

Chapter 29. "Can You Cry, Miss?"

Back in Terezín, I immediately resumed my place in the kitchen and was soon reaccustomed to the old routine and discipline.[1] During my absence several of our group had been sent east. New people had taken their places among the kitchen staff, dishing out food and punching meal slips.

Among these was a pale, young man in a belted raincoat and blue beret. He had big, sad eyes and looked like Pierrot. I had no idea then of his name or what he had been doing before he came to Terezín. One day there were hundreds of people in the soup queue, impatient to be served. I was on duty, standing with my ladle at the ready and waiting for the *parták* [supervisor] to give the word. This pale, young man stood there too with his punch for clipping the meal tickets.

Suddenly he turned to me and said, "Excuse me, miss. Can you cry?"

I wondered why I should be asked such an unusual question, but without much hesitation answered: "Mmm, yes, I can."

"Right then. Come along to the Magdeburg barracks this evening to our play rehearsal. We're trying something new, our own cabaret, *Prince Confined-to-Bed*. Something I wrote with a friend. My name's Josef Lustig."

I soon found out that Josef Lustig was an established actor and playwright, best known, despite his appearance, for comedy and satirical cabaret.

Such was my entrée to the stage world of Terezín.

Chapter 30. Theater in Terezín

The theater made a modest, gingerly start in Terezín, slinking in on tiptoe as it were. Among the inmates were numerous well-known Czech actors, directors, stage designers, writers, and artists, as well as professional musicians, conductors, and composers. So there was no shortage of artistic talent.

Many people had a deep yearning to express themselves artistically, both in words and music, and the rest welcomed the results with gratitude as a compensation for their confinement. Every cultural event buoyed up their hopes and morale, and reinforced their faith in human values. Culture was a spillover from prewar civilized life, but in these trying and uncertain conditions it acquired a deep new significance as well.

It all started with solo performances in the top floors of the barracks. Sometimes poetry recitals, sometimes readings from whatever literature people had brought along in their cases. Later on came dramatic fragments involving several voices.

The first efforts were cautious and faltering, as though the actors tried the ice out to see if it would bear their weight. The thought in everyone's mind was simply, "What will the Germans think?"

Surprisingly, the Germans had no objection at all to these innocent experiments. On the contrary, they gave official blessing to what they named *Kamaradenabende*, "friendly evenings." From that moment on, artistic activity in Terezín grew by leaps and bounds. Little stages were constructed in the attics with wings and curtains; then benches were set in front of them — instant theater! Some plays were imported from outside, some were written by the inmates themselves. Theatrical companies were formed, sometimes with separate groups specializing in different genres. Directors were on tap, back cloths were painted and costumes made from whatever was available — sacking, bed sheets, paper, and scraps of old clothing that had accumulated.

The same sort of thing happened with music. Instruments, sheet music, and scores appeared from nowhere. Enough talent was discovered to assemble a jazz band, then a string quartet, a choir, and even an entire orchestra.

Everyone gave of their best, whatever their abilities and for no reward at all. There were no names in neon lighting, no fame, no fortune. Only the satisfaction of a job well done and the appreciation of a grateful audience. To this end professionals and amateurs worked hand in hand, free of envy or self-importance.

Chapter 31. Dancing under the Gallows

I turned up punctually that evening at the Magdeburg barracks, feeling rather important and special now that I was moving in artistic circles.

Josef Lustig was standing on the stage, talking to his friend and collaborator, Jiři Spitz. Karel Kowanitz was with them too. He had written the lyrics of the songs that ran through the show. They had decided to base their cabaret on the style of the famous Voskovec and Werich partners, so that the Terezín Theater would be a miniature version of the radical Liberated Theater in Prague. The content would be allegorical. Between the scenes Lustig and Spitz, as clowns, would deliver a topically colored commentary in front of the curtain, punctuated with songs to the original [Jaroslav] Ježek music but with words of their own.

Their play *Prince Confined-to-Bed* was a fairy-tale allegory set in the reign of King Gumboil XII with his son, Prince Confined-to-Bed and his daughter, Princess Off-Duty. The palace scenes were done like a puppet-play with jerky movements and squeaky voices, a take-off on the "puppet government" that ran the Terezín camp. The audience cheered wildly at every satirical scene or remark. The action of the play was pretty simple.

Prince Confined-to-Bed falls ill, is declared by his doctor unfit for work and hence unfit for transport. But the wicked magician releases him from bed so that he can join the transport. At that point a young girl in the audience bursts into tears over the Prince's plight. Hearing this, the clowns invite her up on stage and assure her that the Prince is going to stay bedridden and everything will turn out all right.

I was supposed to take the part of the tearful girl. I promised to have a good try. Rehearsals proceeded and at a given cue I had, at first, to sob quietly and then to weep out loud. At the opening night they put me among the audience in the third row. No one took notice of me and the play began. Every seat in the attic auditorium was filled.

But things went all wrong. When my cue came, I began quietly sobbing and everyone round me tried to shut me up. "Sh-h-h!" "Don't interrupt!" "For Chris' sake be quiet!"

But I went on realistically howling and desperately waiting for the clowns to rescue me by saying, "Hang on! What's that young lady crying about?" and fetching me up on the stage. Whereupon the audience would sigh with relief and realize it was all part of the action.

However, nothing of this kind happened. The clowns had decided to build up the tension. But meanwhile, the fire attendant in the doorway took action. With one leap he rushed up and started dragging me out as a disruptive element. Not to spoil the play I went on crying while hissing at him between my teeth, "I'm part of the play!"

That didn't impress him at all. "Oh yes? Just come along quietly!"

At that moment a voice came from the stage, "Hang on! Why's that young lady crying?"

The fireman was impervious. His job was to keep law and order, and I was already halfway out the door. There was great commotion among the spectators, who were not sure what was going on. At the very last moment one of the clowns jumped down and hauled me back, to the audience's great relief. And mine.

It wasn't an easy role. Something different happened every night. At the second performance things went quite differently. On the given cue I started sobbing, and then crying loudly. Across the gangway an elderly man was sitting with a case on his lap. Evidently a doctor. He jumped up, opened up his instruments, and was on the point of giving me a sedative injection for my hysteria.

Just in time, the actors onstage saw what was happening and came to my rescue.

Each evening there was some new incident. But the rumor got around quickly; and after a few days, everyone in Terezín knew about this girl who cried in the audience. In the end, people started looking around long before my scene was due and laughing prematurely.

"Watch it now. The girl in the third row's going to start crying any moment, ho-ho-ho. . . ."

IF IT HADN'T BEEN for the transports to the east, taking place at irregular intervals and hanging over our heads like swords of Damocles, we could almost have fancied we were living normal lives. The Germans began actively to support our cultural efforts and, at the same time, to exploit them for propaganda purposes. Hitler had "given the Jews an independent city," they claimed.

True, we had more freedom of movement inside the fortified walls of Terezín than outside. But it was all a mirage.

They had their own definite plans for our future—and kept them strictly to themselves. They had condemned us to death, but meanwhile allowed us to play and sing. Why shouldn't we? The smiles would soon be wiped from our faces.

So we all went on dancing under the gallows. Thus from the unlikely but supremely fertile soil of overcrowded Terezín, amid the wretched hunger, fear, and constant deaths—but also amid hope and refusal to succumb to pain and humiliation—there arose an unprecedented theatrical and musical culture of the highest quality.

The Czech theater in this camp was no mere entertainment or social distraction, but a living torch showing people the way ahead and lending them spiritual strength and hope. For many, a cultural experience became more important than a ration of bread.

I really felt at home among those actors and artists. On top of their eight-hour working day, they threw themselves into acting, rehearsing, writing. Their ranks included many men and women of exceptional talent and ability who, no sooner had they arrived in Terezín, fit into its cultural life, stamped its plays and concerts with their individual genius, and raised its creative standards to extraordinary heights.

One such man was Karel Švenk—a writer, composer, choreographer, actor, and clown. Something of a Czech Chaplin. He was about twenty-five and his twinkling eyes, under their bushy black brows, radiated energy. He wrote, acted, and *compèred* his own cabaret. Unlike Lustig and Spitz with their domestic topics, Švenk's satires were markedly political. In his first revue, *Long Live Life*, complete with mime and ballet, Švenk played the part of a persecuted clown.

What achieved overnight fame, however, was the closing song, in jolly march rhythm. It echoed the suppressed longings of every inmate, and we promptly adopted it as our Terezín anthem:

> Where there's a will there's always a way
> so hand in hand we start
> whatever the trials of the day
> there's laughter in our heart
> day after day we go on our way
> from one place to another
> we're only allowed 30 words to a letter
> but hey, tomorrow life starts again
> and that's a day nearer to when we can pack
> and leave for home with a bag on our back
> where there's a will there's always a way
> so hold hands now, hold them fast
> and over the ghetto's ruins we
> shall laugh aloud at last

. . . which is how we all honestly believed things would end up.

Švenk's second production, *The Last Cyclist*, has a definite plot and a provocatively anti-Nazi message. The story was roughly this: All the madmen and psychopaths in some imaginary country rebel and escape from their asylums. After causing a public uproar, they seize the reins of government. They are led by a ruler called "The Rat." To find a scapegoat for all the misrule and shortages they have caused, they pick on one group of people who can be blamed for everything—cyclists.[2]

Cyclists, they say, are the root of all evil and responsible for everything that has gone wrong. Cyclists are, moreover, a dangerous element backed by an international conspiracy. The country must get rid of them. A list of all cyclists has to be compiled, except for those who can prove that their ancestors over the last six generations were all pedestrians. Any cyclists to be caught are loaded on board a ship and taken to the Island of Horror. Among the deportees is Borivoj Abeles.

Leaning over the railing, he loses balance and falls in the water. He starts swimming toward the nearest shore and thinks he is now safe. But the madmen see him, fish him out, and lock him in a cage in the zoo, where he is exhibited as The Last Cyclist. But the Rat-dictator has other ideas. He orders the country to rid itself of this last cyclist. He is to be put into a rocket and shot off into the stratosphere. When everything is ready for take-off, the Rat and his female companion, the Lady, come with her staff to inspect the rocket. They grant Borivoj Abeles one last wish. He asks to be allowed a cigarette.

He strikes a match but absent-mindedly, instead of lighting his cigarette, puts the match to the fuse of the rocket. The rocket hurtles off complete with the Rat, the Lady, and her staff, while Borivoj stands watching it disappear into outer space.

The Last Cyclist somehow eluded the German censorship, but its effect on the audience was like dynamite. However, its run was cut short. When the members of the Council of Elders came to see it, they were struck by the obviously provocative allegory—and banned it. Many of the inmates had already had a chance to enjoy the play, but many others were denied the pleasure. Its story became part of Terezín legend and the courageous Karel Švenk became a local hero.

Chapter 32. Ben Akiba Was No Liar—or Was He?

In the course of 1943 it seemed that transports to the east had become considerably fewer and then came to a halt. Part of the explanation was that the German government had transferred one sector of its war production to Terezín and needed all available manpower. The sector in question involved laminating mica for military purposes. Wooden cabins were quickly erected for hundreds of workers, mostly women, who sat all day splitting sheets of mica.

The continuous fear of being transported to the east suddenly abated and a period of apparent calm spread through Terezín. A rumor that began to circulate around this time was that, according to reports from abroad, the German war front was retreating and the war would be over in two months. How eager we all were to believe this! But two months went by and the war still wasn't over. Hopes were then transferred to the next two months, and the next. So time went on and somehow one could always survive two months at a time.

The time seemed appropriate for some further theatrical experiments. Lustig and Spitz assembled a sizable body of actors for a new play, *Ben Akiba Was No Liar—Or Was He?*

The play, or rather cabaret, has two clowns disputing the wisdom of the legendary Rabbi Ben Akiba in his famous pronouncement that "There is nothing new under the sun. Everything has happened before."

The first clown sets out to convince his partner that every event is merely a repetition of some earlier one, albeit in different form and circumstances, so that there is really nothing quite new under the sun. To prove the point, he transports him through time into a Roman circus where Christians are being cast before the lions. One of the victims is Mordechai Pinkas. He tries to explain to the hungry lion that it is all a mistake, since he is a Jew and not a Christian at all. The lion sniffs him and finds no difference. Mordechai starts to negotiate and addresses the lion:

"Mr. Leo, sir, Mr. Levi, sir, be reasonable, I shouldn't be here at all, I'm Jewish . . ." After a long argument, he persuades the lion there has been an organizational mix-up and is allowed to leave the arena.

"You see?" the second clown bursts in. "Now that has never happened before." So Ben Akiba was lying.

Between this scene and the next, the clowns come to the front of the stage and start delving into old Czech history with a punning dialogue in the manner of Voskovec and Werich interludes.

"Taking things from the very beginning, then, we have the ancestor of all Czechs, the Grand Ancestor Czech, standing on Rip Hill, stretching his arm out to the sun and declaring: This is the land overflowing with milk and mead — *tato zeme oplévá mlékem a strdim.*"

"Sorry to interrupt you . . . really sorry . . . but could you please tell me exactly what this 'mead' is?"

"I beg your pardon? You've never heard of mead?"

"Terribly sorry . . . but honestly . . . I never really have known what 'mead' is."

"Ought to be ashamed. Everyone knows what mead is; any child can tell you."

"Any child, yes . . . yes . . . but me, I've no idea."

"Have you never seen it written up in front of a restaurant? Like *Today's special, sour mead?*"

"Not really, no."

"For goodness' sake, man, how can I explain? 'Mead' is simply . . . well . . . mead . . . isn't it? So let's not waste any more time and get on with the next stage of Czech history. The ancient Czechs were a very advanced people who burned their dead and put their ashes *do uren umne zdobenych,* into artistically decorated urns."

Second clown (pretending he heard phonetically identical *do uren u mne zdobenych,* i.e., urns decorated in my house): "Is that so now? I never realized you did your business in urns as well as textiles!"

"No, you've got me wrong. I said *umne,* artistically like."

"Oh well, if it was done in your place I've no doubt it was very artistic."

The wordplay continued endlessly and the audience loved it. The "mead" episode was particularly successful and people were forever buttonholing each other when they met and repeating parts of the dialogue. Two venerable members of the Council of Elders were even overheard conversing in the corridor:

"I say, very amusing that bit about 'mead' in the Ben Akiba piece, eh?"
"Indeed."
"But tell me, professor, what actually is mead?"
"You don't mean to say you don't know?"

And so it went on, all around the town. No one knew what "mead" was. The next scene was set on Olympus, where the gods were holding council round a table. Arguing and failing to agree about anything. Zeus was in the chair, trying to moderate. Their quarrels were meant to echo the divisions within both the Council of Elders and the German political leadership.

I played the part of Aphrodite. Instead of just being pretty and quietly seducing all the gods, she kept on interfering, correcting the others and disrupting the proceedings.

Scene 3 was set in Heaven, where the empress Maria Theresa and her son Joseph were sitting on a cloud, looking down through a telescope. What should come swimming into their field of view but Terezín, the town they had founded as a fortress against the Prussians. They look harder and harder but the place seems so unfamiliar. What can have happened to it? They speculate.

Then suddenly two Jewish souls come floating up, straight from Terezín, and offer to give the empress and her son a detailed account of events down there. But Their Majesties reject it out of hand. From which the second clown deduces that what is happening in the fortress is truly unprecedented. So Ben Akiba was lying.

One of the theme-songs running through the cabaret was written by František Kowanitz to the tune of Jaroslav's Ježek's famous satirical song, "Civilization":

> A certain ruler issued a decree
> as we can read in any History
> fearing attack by enemies afar
> to build a fortress-city like a star.
> To make invasion really difficult
> He had a ring of mighty earthworks built
> With creeks and coves to each redoubt
> Plus soldiery within the walls
> To fire their canon-balls.
> The citizens were super-posh,
> Prime pork and *haggis* [mince meat] was their nosh,

They loved to sing pub-songs, and those
Were meant to terrify their foes.

But many years have passed since then
the world has somewhat changed is face
word came that those of a certain race
must all wear stars and live inside
by thousands, filling every shop, wall, inn,
barrack, and café, till there was no space,
no food, and anyone was glad
to eat the cold
potato-skin.
Rations were short because there was a crisis,
No booze, no cash for paying silly prices,
When suddenly the town's true role
In a new light was seen
To serve as propaganda both
In newspapers and on the screen.

In view of the last-mentioned revelation
There arose a new organization
New insights and new points of view
New parties and new leaders too
All labor was deployed by *Hundertschaften*
A *Raumwirtschaft* saw to each inmate's comfort
Verteilungsstellen issued them fine clothes
Bettenbau got them snug asleep at night
Entwesung saw to bodily hygiene and
Freizeitgestaltung put their souls aright.

All the organizations with German names mentioned in the last verse really existed and saw to it that life went on in Terezín in as orderly a way as possible.

The *Hundertschaften* was a labor unit of one hundred men.

The *Raumwirtschaft* allocated living space in the billets [living quarters].

The *Verteilungsstelle* collected clothes from those who died, sorted them, and "sold" them in shops set up for the purpose.

Bettenbau was a carpentry workshop which made bunks, as well as partitions, and "furniture" for the elite in their penthouses and cubby holes.

Entwesung was the delousing and disinfection station.

The Germans were obsessed by the danger of epidemics of any kind.

Freizeitgestaltung — "leisure structuring" — was a new department within the self-governing administration which had arisen during the great cultural upsurge and dealt with all its requirements. It authorized new sites (mainly in the attics) for plays and concerts, organized scientific and literary talks, assigned rehearsal time to pianists on the two available pianos, allocated materials for scenery, and printed theater and concert programs and tickets. It was responsible for the choice of dramatic material for performance [see report by Rabbi Weiner in this section].

Music occupied an even larger place than the theater in our cultural life. Terezín was awash with outstanding musical performers, conductors, and composers. The famous Prague conductor, Karel Ančerl, who used to stir the soup beside me in the kitchen during the working hours, organized a string quartet in his free time, and later on, a complete orchestra.

The composer, Hans Krása, already established before the war, made his name in Terezín with his unique children's opera, *Brundibár*. This was a musical fairy story played and sung by children in the camp between eight and twelve years old. It was rehearsed and performed countless times for both young and adult audiences in the Sokol Hall. The story was simple and topical:

Two little children, Pepíček (Joey) and Anna, find that their mother is ill. They would like to bring her some milk, but they have no money. So they decide to sing in the streets. . . . They sing their best and passersby throw coins into their cap. But then along comes the wicked organ-grinder, Brundibár, who tries to stop them and steals their cap and all the money. With the help of some animals . . . they overcome Brundibár and chase him off. Justice has been done and the piece ends with the children's chorus:

> *Nad Brundibárem jsme vyhrály, my jsme se nebály . . .*
> We fought old Brundibár and won, because we weren't afraid . . .

The little performers and their audiences were equally thrilled. I remember squeezing into the hall where seats and standing room were all crammed. Lovely, healthy, talented kids they were, and all of them prisoners. Their eyes shone with excitement at the fall of wicked Brundibár.

This was in September 1943. Soon afterwards came the order to resume transports. Most of the children who had so merrily performed in *Brundibár* were sent to their fate in the "east." End of fairy tale.

SEVERAL of our *Ben Akiba* cast went off too and we had to suspend the cabaret. In the end we were never able to perform it again because our treasured Josef Lustig's tuberculosis suddenly got worse. He lay in the sick-bay in the Kavalírka (Kavalier) barrack. I used to visit him as often as I could and, as a little treat, take him part of my own ration from the kitchen. There were no medicines. He knew he would never live to see his home again.

When I was sitting on his bed one day, Josef said to me, "You remember the first time I ever spoke to you, and asked you, 'Can you cry, miss?' Well, when I die, don't cry. If you survive it all, you must tell people how we kept the show going in Terezín."

Two days later he died. When I went to see him they were carrying him out of the room, wrapped in a sheet.

Our group now dissolved, having completed its mission: to use satire for projecting the truth, while trying to give the audiences some moral support and hope.

It was not long after Lustig's death that his inseparable colleague, fellow-writer and fellow-actor, Jiři Spitz, was also taken off somewhere "eastward." I sat with him until the early hours before he was loaded onto the cattle truck, helping him sort out the few things he was taking with him. We speculated about where he might be going. We had just had time to sing Švenk's "Terezín anthem" to ourselves:

> Where there's a will there's a way . . .
> So hold hands, hold them fast
> And over the ghetto's ruins we
> shall laugh aloud at last

And then he was off.

In the darkness of Terezín, our cabaret had been like a sparkler on a Christmas tree that lights up and dazzles for a brief moment, then suddenly goes out. But everyone who saw it retained in his mind's eye the memory of its short, vivid existence.

Chapter 35. The Czech Theater Carries On

The theatrical world of Terezín could never have functioned without the activity behind the scenes by the enormously experienced and ingenious František Zelenka. Architect and stage designer by training, he had made his name long before the war with his avant-garde décors for leading Prague stages, including the Liberated Theater.

As soon as he came to Terezín, he threw himself into theater work, which was enjoying its golden age at that time, 1943. He had his own workshop where backcloths were set up and painted, stage properties constructed, and costumes designed and created. He had to make bricks without straw. He used any material that came his way—paper, sawdust, rags, empty tins, old sheets—and achieved miracles with it. His skill was responsible for the brilliant décor of the children's opera, *Brundibár,* and of the stage productions that followed.

He worked closely with that most able of directors, Gustav Schorsch, who had been an assistant director of the National Theater in Prague before coming to Terezín. Schorsch was a theatrical purist, pedagogue, and theoretician of the old school and would tolerate no departure from the highest standards. Using a group of young Prague professional players and Zelenka's designs, he put on a production of Gogol's *Wedding* that would have won acclaim anywhere in the world.

In his "spare time," Gustav organized recitals of Czech poetry and held a seminar for young actors. After the great success of the *Wedding,* he started working on a play by Griboyedov but had to abandon it after a few rehearsals, when some of his cast were sent off eastward. The same fate attended his planned production of Shakespeare's *Twelfth Night* after his remaining actors were swallowed up in the new wave of transports.

After the dispersal of Lustig's cabaret group, the few of us who remained had been transferred to other projects. One of these was Stech's *Tretí Zvonení* [*Third Time Lucky*]; and soon after that, the actress Vlasta Schönová started rehearsals for František Langer's comedy, *Velbloud Uchem Jehly* [*A Camel Through the Eye of a Needle*].

It was the mere coincidence of both texts turning up in Terezín that made it possible to produce these two light-hearted plays, familiar from prewar days. They were given a great welcome and for one evening, at least, revived memories of happier times in better places.

Chapter 36. Esther

It was some time in 1943 that the director-writer, Nóra Frýd, and the composer, Karel Reiner, arrived in Terezín. Each had worked in his own field with E. F. Burian and his avant-garde *Divaldo D* [Theatre D] in Prague. Nóra Frýd brought with him in his luggage the text of the biblical folk-play, *Esther,* which had been rehearsed under Burian but never reached the stage. The Terezín theater world seemed to have been waiting for these two men, who both got down to work immediately. Frýd took on the production and Reiner composed music for it. He would sit at his little piano in front of the stage, extemporizing half-tone melodies as the play proceeded.

František Zelenka, in turn, took on the staging and costume designs. They

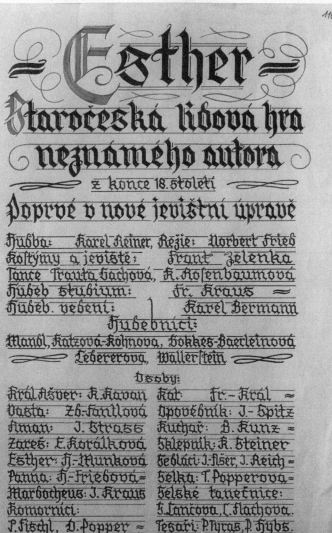

Facsimile of poster announcing *Esther* production, 1943, Terezín. Photo by Terezín [Memorial], Patmáník

made a happy trio. *Esther* was a contrast to all the other plays staged in Terezín. For a start, it was written in verse, and in near-medieval Czech at that.

The production completely dispensed with realism and was imaginatively stylized. The story itself, telling how Queen Esther saved her Jewish tribe from certain annihilation, was deeply meaningful for Terezín and its inhabitants.

The plot was simple and straightforward.

The play is set in a land ruled by the mighty Persian King Ahasuerus, whose loyal servant and palace gatekeeper is the Jew, Mordecai. One day Mordecai overhears two chamberlains plotting to kill the king. To save his master from certain death he reports the plot to him. The king orders the chamberlains executed, and promises his servant a rich reward for saving his life. Mordecai, however, declines any reward, continuing to render faithful service. The king then arranges a great banquet for his subjects to which he invites his wife, Queen Vashti. But she refuses to attend and the king, angered by her disobedience, removes her crown and has her barred from the palace.

Then summoning a parade of young virgins, he chooses the one he likes best, Esther. This Esther is also Jewish and a niece of Mordecai. Meanwhile, out of generosity and relief at escaping death, the king has appointed his counselor, Prince Haman, as minister with unlimited powers. Both Haman and his wife (Zeresh) are greedy for wealth, power, and fame. Following his promotion, Haman now orders that all the king's servants and subjects should pay homage to him. But Mordecai refuses; he will only bow before the king.

Haman is furious at this impudence and conceives a plan to hang Mordecai and wipe out his entire tribe, so purging the Persian land of all Jews. In no time, Haman has a gallows erected in the palace courtyard.

When he hears of this, Mordecai breaks into lamentation. Esther, learning of Mordecai's sadness, decides to appeal to the king to save her people. The king accepts her plea and, incensed at Haman's arrogance and unjust spite, has him hanged on the new gallows, refusing all mercy. So all ends well, his subjects rejoice and wish King Ahasuerus glory and long life.

Rehearsals went ahead at a feverish pace and the production began to take shape. Out of nothing, Zelenka produced sets that would have done credit to any theater of international standing. The whole backcloth was a semicircle of "straw" to lend pastoral color. There were three separate tents on the stage with sackcloth curtains. Sitting in each one was a leading character: the king in the middle tent, the queen on the right, and Mordecai in the left-hand tent.

The Narrator, stick in hand, walks around in front of the tents and tells the story. Then with his stick, he pulls aside the curtain of one tent, announcing: "And the King said . . ." or the Queen, or Mordecai, as the plot developed.

Zelenka dreamt up quite ravishing costumes. King Ahasuerus was put into a white sheet, cut out in the middle for his head, a row of empty tins were sewn on to the bottom hem so that they tinkled when he walked.

"When you cross the stage," Zelenka explained, "I want to hear the cans rattling against each other."

On his head the king wore a cut-out paper crown, with blobs of auburn-colored sawdust stuck on his head and forearms. He carried a whip stick in his hand, and looked very impressive.

Zelenka dressed Haman's wife, Zeresh, in loose, flowing, multicolored robes. "I want you," he said "to look like some figure flying through a window display in Asher's 'House of Silk' on Mustek in the middle of Prague." Which is just what she did look like.

I played the part of Queen Vashti. Zelenka dressed me in two sheets sewn together, the inside one white, the outer dyed black. The outer one had large peacock eyes cut out of it, so that the white under the sheet showed through. His instructions were simple: "When you walk along the stage and the clothes flap around you, I want you to look like a baroque angel over a grave."

And thus it appeared. He was full of ingenious ideas and humorous fancies.

At last the rehearsals were over. Each of us knew the words and music to perfection. The play was a great success and everything went well each night. Then, one evening I hatched a devilish plot. I'd had a heated argument before the performance with Karel Kavan, who played the king. I was sure that he was in the wrong and I was determined at any price to punish him by spoiling his act.

I didn't quite know how to achieve this when suddenly a way occurred to me of diverting the whole drift of the play. In my first scene the king's minister comes up to me and says:

> "We are sent by his Majesty
> to bid you come join him"

Whereupon the queen, who has already turned down his invitation to the banquet, answers:

> "I told you once I would not come,
> to change my mind I see no need.
> So once again I tell you, No,
> I'll not, however hard he plead."

The minister goes off to tell the king of her decision. He is furious:

> "Lo now my anger doth wax great
> so take the crown from off her head
> have her without the palace led."

The minister duly returns to the queen, removes her crown, and bans her from the court. She paces to and fro, singing dolefully:

> Alas for my great misery
> The gods have quite forsaken me.
> Where can I seek a friend
> Now that my fortune's turned?
> My crown is gone from me
> and I on petty grounds
> am stripped of royalty.
> Now must I to the woods
> My life with beasts to spend
> and make my home with them
> till life draws to its end.

Her song over, the queen leaves the palace. Curtain. End of Act 1.

But on the night in question, things went differently. The minister as usual comes to tell the queen that the king wants her at the banquet, and she should go with him now. At this point, something clicked in my mind; and instead of refusing the invitation, I answered in impeccable old Czech:

> "Na královské porucení
> uciním tak bez prodleni"

In other words,

> "If the King so desires of me
> I'll meet His wishes instantly"

Then I dutifully went over to the king's tent.

Kavan had quite a shock when he saw me coming, as he had no words appropriate to the situation. So he desperately continued with the original text, saying how I had to be punished for my disobedience. My crown was removed; I crossed the stage, sang my doleful song, and exited. Curtain.

I don't know what the audience made of it all. The king had invited her to the feast, she had accepted, and then been thrown out for her pains. (Eh?) Nóra Frýd, however, was quite clear in his mind. He rushed up to the stage from the back row, shouting, "You really screwed it up, didn't you? You silly cow!"

He was very angry, justifiably so. I was hauled in front of the *Freizeitgestal-*

tung committee, who gave me a drubbing for unprofessional behavior. I apologized profusely to Nóra and to Karel Kavan. And the show went on.

Like everything else, this little episode soon became the talk of the town.

THE *ESTHER* PRODUCTION, however well-rehearsed and well-received, finally fell victim to another series of transports. Several of the cast were taken off and the end was inevitable. With a heavy heart, Nóra told us he could not embark on fresh rehearsals with new actors. So that was the end of *Esther* in the little Magdeburg theater.

But it was certainly a vintage production and retains a lasting place in the memories of the participants and of those spectators who had the chance to see it.

Chapter 37. Georges Dandin

After the collapse of *Esther,* another director, Otakar Ružička, decided to put on the Molière comedy *Georges Dandin.* This only needed a small cast and I was assigned the part of the society lady, Mme. De Sottenville, starchly buttoned-up and with monocle permanently poised.

The rehearsals went badly and Ružička gave up. He was succeeded by Zelenka who was willing to take on directing as well as stage management. The production was transferred to the larger and better equipped stage in the "Dresden" top floor where there was room for a larger audience too. But despite these advantages, the play was a flop. Whether it was the fault of the production or the weakness of the play itself, Molière and his subject didn't fit into the Terezín of those years [this was in November 1943].

So even though none of the cast was lost to the transports this time, the play closed.

I NOW FOUND MYSELF with evenings free and was finally able to enjoy one of the concerts that Terezín was so well endowed with. I chose a piano concert by Alice Herz-Sommerová, playing all the Chopin *Études* without a break. Her virtuosity transported listeners from wretched, starving Terezín to a different world and a different epoch. Sitting on that wooden bench, I listened spellbound. It was an unforgettable evening.

Among the inmates were many professional musicians — concert leaders and soloists, composers, singers, and conductors. Karel Ančerl had his little orchestra. Conductor Rafael Schächter assembled another opera chorus and performed the *Bartered Bride* that made the audience cry. There was an outstanding young pianist and composer, Gideon Klein. Also, Viktor Ullmann, professor of musical theory, who wrote a striking, modern opera while he was in Terezín: *Císar z Atlantidy* [*The Emperor of Atlantis*].

This opera had a topical text with a political edge, written by young Peter Kien. It was bound to strike the German censors as provocative. Though rehearsals had been completed, it was banned and never saw a performance. But the plot is worth retelling:

An imaginary country is ruled by the cruel emperor, "Überall" — "Overall" — who wages war against everyone. The slaughter is pitiless. Thousands die. Death himself cannot stand the sight of it any longer and informs the tyrant that he is going to strike. People stop dying and just crawl around with as much strength as they can muster. There are hordes of them, and constantly their numbers increase.

The Emperor summons Death and begs him to resume his duties and allow people to die. Death accepts his pleading, but on one condition only — that the dictator is the first to die. End of opera. If only it might come true!

The Emperor of Atlantis [Der Kaiser von Atlantis]

Music by V I K T O R   U L L M A N N
Text by P E T E R   K I E N

In the chaos and uncertainty of late September and early October 1944, as the Nazis accelerated the mass transportation east to Auschwitz of the inmates at Terezín (Theresienstadt) ghetto, Viktor Ullmann sealed twenty-three of his scores, including a string quartet, piano sonatas, choral arrangements in Hebrew, Yiddish, French, and German, and the complete text of the opera Der Kaiser von Atlantis oder der Tod dankt ab [The Emperor of Atlantis, or Death Abdicates], *into an airtight container and placed them into the safekeeping of his friend and fellow inmate, Dr. Emil Utitz. In the desperate hope that his creative output might not be destroyed in the Holocaust, his wish was that Utitz give the container to another of Ullmann's close friends, Dr. H. G. Adler, were they to survive the war. Then on 16 October 1944, Ullmann and his wife Elizabeth were shipped to their deaths at Auschwitz. Peter Kien, Ullmann's librettist for* Der Kaiser, *preceded his partner's transportation by two days, having voluntarily joined his parents by leaping onto their cattle car as it moved east.*

Both Utitz and Adler miraculously survived, along with about twenty thousand other inmates, to be liberated by the International Red Cross on 8 May 1945. In 1947, Adler moved to London. After Adler's resettlement, Utitz and he apparently met and, following Ullmann's instructions, Utitz turned over the entire collection of manuscripts. Soon thereafter Adler explored the possibility of getting some of Ullmann's works performed, perhaps including Der Kaiser, *but the events of World War II and the Holocaust were too recent in people's minds, and he was unsuccessful. As a result, Ullmann's work remained in the care of Dr. Adler and his family for another two-and-a-half decades.*

During the fall of 1972, the Czechoslovakian government approached Dr. Adler concerning the work of Viktor Ullmann to determine if a reconstructed edition could be prepared for performance. With this purpose in mind, Dr. Adler's son, Jeremy,

Adapted from the opera by Viktor Ullmann, this adaptation of Peter Kien's libretto has been translated by Aaron Kramer. Introduction by Don Gilzinger Jr.

contacted Julie Woodward, a young American musicology student at the British Museum, to see if she would be interested in looking at Ullmann's manuscripts and preparing a working edition of them. Because she felt she could not reconstruct the scores, Julie Woodward suggested that her husband, Kerry, an aspiring conductor, might have the skills and interest to do so. In December 1972, after the Czech government subsequently dropped the project, Kerry Woodward asked the Adlers if he could attempt to make an edition of Der Kaiser von Atlantis with the goal of performing the opera. Dr. Adler agreed, and the Woodwards took home all Ullmann's manuscripts for cataloging and microfilming. Twenty-eight years after Ullmann's death, his scores were finally transferred from the backs of the Terezín ghetto inmate transportation forms on which they were written (the only paper available to Ullmann and Kien) to a safer, more permanent medium.

Aaron Kramer first learned of the opera while visiting the Woodwards in London in September 1973. Julie Woodward recalls that when Kramer saw the manuscript on their piano, he "was stunned and asked if he could make an English translation." Already an internationally renowned lyric poet and translator of German and Yiddish poets such as Heinrich Heine, Rainer Maria Rilke, and Morris Rosenfeld, Kramer seemed a natural choice to make a lyrical English translation of Peter Kien's German libretto. As Kerry Woodward reconstructed the score, Aaron Kramer began to translate the libretto.

Because Kramer's philosophy of translation was, in his own words, "to transmit as completely but also as artistically as possible all that the original has to offer by way of feeling, idea, cadence, rhyme, image, and whatever other devices make the original effective," he shunned introducing new material into Kien's libretto solely for the sake of rhyme, rhythm, or increased interest. However, neither did he aim to create an adaptation or loose translation of the opera. As a result, he and Kerry Woodward spent long hours wrestling with the libretto in an attempt to make the English work musically, with Woodward concerned with literal accuracy and Kramer demanding lyric honesty. By June 1974, Kramer, satisfied that he had achieved equivalence with Kien's intentions and had not misrepresented the original libretto, finished the translation as Woodward completed editing the score.

The world premiere of the reconstructed Der Kaiser von Atlantis oder der Tod dankt ab, using Kramer's English translation of Kien's libretto and Woodward's edition of Ullmann's score, was scheduled for 10 May 1975 at the Annenberg Theater in Philadelphia, with Kerry Woodward conducting. A musicians' strike forced the cancellation of the performances. The Netherlands Opera finally premiered Der Kaiser in English on 16 December 1975 in Amsterdam, while the American premiere by the San Francisco Opera followed in San Francisco on 21 April 1977. Murderously denied its original premiere in Terezín ghetto, Ullmann's opera now lives worldwide in regular performance.

PROLOGUE

LOUDSPEAKER: Hello, hello! This work
is called: 'Death Abdicates' — a sort of
opera in four scenes. The characters
include Emperor Overall in person, who
hasn't been seen for some years; he shut
himself away in his giant palace, totally
isolated, so that he might rule better; the
Drummer, whose appearance is not
quite real, like a radio; the Loudspeaker,
whom one hears but does not see; a
Soldier and a Girl, in the third scene;
Death, as a discharged soldier; and
Pierrot, who can laugh in spite of his
tears: that's life.
  The first scene takes place somewhere;
Death and Pierrot sit at the borderline
of a living that can no longer laugh, and
a dying that can no longer cry, in a
world that has forgotten how to enjoy
life while living and how to achieve
death when dying. Death, who has been
repelled and offended by the hustle and
bustle, the speed, and the technological
developments of modern life, breaks his
sword to teach mankind a lesson, and
decides that from now on he will allow
no one to die! Hello, hello! We're beginning!

PIERROT: The moon on stilts is skirting the rooftops of the town;
  the young are thirsting
  for love and for wine. The moon, despite their yearning,
  takes both away: there's no returning — love nor wine returning.
  So what are we to drink now?
  Blood, blood is what we'll drink now.
  And what are we to kiss now?
  The Devil's backside.
  The world's all topsy-turvy now and whirling like a carousel;

and we are forced to ride.
The moon is white
and blood is hot;
the wine is sweet
and love has gone to Paradise.
In this poor world, then, what's our share?
We'd sell our souls at the nearest fair.
Will nobody buy us? Will nobody buy us?
Since each man wants to be rid of
himself,
we must go wherever the four winds
drive us.

DEATH: No more. What song was that?

PIERROT: Oh, just a song . . .

DEATH: Well, tell me what day it is today?

PIERROT: I've stopped keeping track of
days as I used to, since I've got no shirt
to speak of, and will not take up a new
day till I've got some fresh, clean
underwear.

DEATH: Then you must be deep in
months that are long gone by.

PIERROT: Perhaps Tuesday? Wednesday?
Friday? Each is like the other.

DEATH and PIERROT:
One day, two days,
who'll buy new days?
lovely, fresh days, undiscovered;
each is like the other.
Perhaps one of them will bring luck,
good luck;
you'll be a king then!
Who'll buy new days?
Who'll buy old days? Buy one!
Old days cheaper, come try one!

PIERROT: From the day I first looked
with loathing on myself, there's been a
sickness deep inside me. I wish you

would kill me; it's your profession, after
all — and I am *so* bored, every moment's
unbearable!

DEATH: Leave me in peace; no power on
earth can kill you. The laughter that
mocks itself is immortal. You're still
yourself; there's no escaping. What you
are is Pierrot!

PIERROT: And what is that? Only a
memory, paler than all the yellowed
photographs of these wretched creatures
who can smile no longer. I get laughs
from no one . . . If I could just forget what
young wine tastes like! If once more the
long-forgotten touch of a woman could
stir my being . . .

DEATH: Ridiculous! It makes me laugh
when I hear you. You're scarcely three
hundred years old, and I, I've been part
of this theater ever since time was! Now
I am old and cannot keep up . . . If only
you'd seen me back there!
They had such wars then! The most
spectacular clothes were worn to pay me
homage! Gold and purple, glittering
coats of mail . . . They decked themselves
for me the way a bride prepares for her
consort. Colorful banners fluttering over
the cavalry . . . Foot-soldiers rolled out
their dice on the battle-drum; and when
they danced, the bones of the women
would crack — they were wet from the
sweat of their partners . . . So often I
raced beside the little horses of Attila as
they galloped! and ahead of Hannibal's
elephants, and the tigers of Djehangir —
that my old legs are so weary they can
no longer follow the motorized legions

of fighters. What can I do now but limp
in the wake of Death's new battalions of
angels, a lowly tradesman of dying?

DRUMMER: Hello, hello! Attention.
Attention, please! In the name of his
Majesty, the Emperor Overall. By the
grace of God, we, Overall the Glorious,
pride of the Fatherland, blessing to
mankind . . . ruler of both Indies, Emp'ror
of Atlantis, Imperial Duke in the land of
Ophir, High Priest of Astarte, Ban of
Hungary, Card'nal-Prince of Ravenna,
King of Jerusalem, and—to glorify our
divine descent from God—Arch-Pope,
have, in our flawless, truly perfect, all-
penetrating wisdom, decided to declare,
through all our lands, total, God-
inspired War! Each against the other! To
the finish! Every child, both male and
female; every maiden, wife and mother;
every man, deformed and able-bodied—
shall now carry weapons in this holy
crusade, which must end in victory for
our most apostolic Majesty, and the
destruction of wickedness in our
dominions. And as you hear these
words, we proclaim our campaign
triumphantly opened. Our old ally,
Death, will lead the way with his
glorious banner, in the name of our
great future and his great past. Fight
bravely! Decreed in the fifteenth year of
our prosperous reign. Signed: Emp'ror
Overall!

DEATH: Hear that? Hear how they mock
me? It's only I who can take men's souls!
My banner lead the way! My great past!
Your great future! Big Shot!

PIERROT: Ha-ha, ha-ha!

DEATH: Hi-hi! In the name of your great
future!

PIERROT: What are you doing?

DEATH: I'm making the future of
mankind great — and long . . . . . . long!!

LOUDSPEAKER: From his office, the
Emperor of Atlantis communicates with
his ministers by telephone and radio.
Following the execution of several
prisoners, he realizes that Death has
decided to stop working. People cannot
die; the old and the sick are doomed to
endure the throes of death forever. The
Emperor tries to prevent the panic this
news must bring; he tells his subjects
they will be liberated by Death's
abdication: set free from a tyranny that
till now has subjugated every living
creature.

SCENE II

EMPEROR: What time is it?

LOUDSPEAKER: Five thirty-two. Hello,
hello. Royal guard reporting, sentry commander.
The cordon 'round the palace has been tripled as ordered.

EMPEROR: Armed and ready?

LOUDSPEAKER: Armed and ready.

EMPEROR: Good.

LOUDSPEAKER: Hello, hello! Assaulting battalions,
dive-bombers, underground
torpedoes have demolished the ramparts
surrounding our third largest city. The
inhabitants are dead. Corpses have been
delivered to the recycling plant.

EMPEROR: How many?

LOUDSPEAKER: Ten thousand kilos of
phosphorus.

E M P E R O R : Fine! The Ministry!

L O U D S P E A K E R : Hello, hello. Ministry.

E M P E R O R : The execution?

L O U D S P E A K E R : Performed as commanded at
four thirteen.

E M P E R O R : Well then, are they dead?

L O U D S P E A K E R : Death's certain to come any
moment now!

E M P E R O R : What? Certain to? When was
the sentence carried out?

L O U D S P E A K E R : Four thirteen.

E M P E R O R : But it's now five thirty-five!

L O U D S P E A K E R : Death's certain to come any
moment now!

E M P E R O R : Have you lost your senses?
Has the hangman, in an hour and
twenty-two minutes, failed to kill them?!

L O U D S P E A K E R : Death's certain to come any
moment now!

E M P E R O R : Am I mad? Have I gone crazy?
Are they wrestling death away from me?
Who in the future still will fear me?
Does Death refuse his duty? Has he
smashed his ancient saber? Who now
will give allegiance to the Emperor of
Atlantis? — Hello! Fill them with
bullets!

L O U D S P E A K E R : Performed as ordered.

E M P E R O R : Well?!

L O U D S P E A K E R : Death's certain to come any
moment now.

E M P E R O R : What?! — The Doctor!

L O U D S P E A K E R : Hello, doctor speaking.

E M P E R O R : Well?

L O U D S P E A K E R : He's still alive. A very strange
sickness has broken out. People can't
die.

E M P E R O R : Is it such a bad thing that

people can't die? How many have died
since the epidemic began?

LOUDSPEAKER: None. Thousands, mortally
wounded, are grappling with life so that
they can die.

EMPEROR: Thank you. Issue commands.
Ministry! Posters on every corner.
Special announcements on the radio.
Drummers in the villages:
We, Overall the Glorious, give to all
our deserving citizens a secret formula
for life everlasting. He who possesses it
shall be safeguarded from death, and
neither sickness nor any injury can
henceforth stop him from carrying the
sword of his fatherland and his master.
Death, where is thy sting? Where's thy
victory, Hell?!

LOUDSPEAKER: A man and a girl, from
the two enemy camps, confront each
other, brandishing weapons. The news
that people are unable to die transforms
their warlike spirit into love. Instead of
killing one another, they embrace. The
Drummer tries in vain to persuade the
man to follow him.

SCENE III

SOLDIER: Who's there?

GIRL: Halt! Stop! Who's there?

SOLDIER: A man.

GIRL: Yes, but a foe!

DRUMMER: 'Give to all our deserving
citizens a secret formula for life everlasting. . .'

SOLDIER: Such lovely skin!

GIRL: Shoot! Why don't you?

DRUMMER: '. . . shall be safeguarded from death . . .'

SOLDIER: In my young days, I would
    sometimes walk with a girl and stroll
    beside the river. She had eyes that were
    bright, like yours!

GIRL: I'm not yet old enough to have such
    moments to remember . . . Hear him
    calling!

DRUMMER: '. . . Death, where is thy sting?
    Where's thy victory, Hell!'

SOLDIER: Heavy weapons, steel adornments,
    press upon your tender flesh!
    Girl, you should endure no torments;
    see, the world is bright and fresh.

GIRL: Is it true? Are there landscapes
    on earth, free of blight and parchedness?
    And say — are there words on earth
    free of spite and harshness?
    And say — are there fields on earth
    full of brightness and fragrance?
    Is it true? Are there hills on earth
    that shimmer blue in the radiance?

DRUMMER: You must not stay; come go
    with me! Go with me!

GIRL: You must not stay; come go with
    me! Come away!

DRUMMER: Both King and Duty bid you
    fight!

GIRL: We're beckoned by the distant
    light . . .

DRUMMER: You're called to death; you're
    called to war.

GIRL: No, Death is dead; Humanity need
    fight no more!

DRUMMER: The war drum, war drum
    whines and pounds;
    a man can't help but be lured
    by its sounds.
    For its skin is smooth, its feel is warm,

and rounded like a woman's form.
It speaks a language loud and full.
A man must follow at its call!

GIRL and SOLDIER:

We see what makes fair even
Death's grim face:
the flower of love that inspires us all
to embrace.

SOLDIER and GIRL:

See, the sullen clouds that hovered
have been lifted from our sight,
and the landscape, grayly covered,
suddenly is bathed in light.
Deepest shadows turn to fire
at the rising of the sun.
Death takes up the poet's lyre
now that he and Love are one.

LOUDSPEAKER: Because of Death's
refusal to let the people die, the
Emperor witnesses a total collapse of
society. The sick are terrified at being
robbed of deliverance from their pain,
and a chaotic madness has set in. The
Emperor, too, is seized by the universal
excitement; long-forgotten impressions
from his childhood emerge, embodied
by Pierrot. However, the Drummer tries
to inspire him to hold firm. In conflict
with himself, the Emperor has a vision.
Death steps out of the mirror; he regrets
the suffering his abdication has caused,
and is ready to return to mankind; but
the Emperor must agree to be the first to suffer
the new death. The Emperor of
Atlantis agrees, and humanity, redeemed,
greets the return of Death.

SCENE IV

LOUDSPEAKER: Hello, hello, Supreme
   General here: Hospital 34 for the Living
   Dead was captured by the rebels at three
   o'clock. Doctors and instructors surrendered
   en masse. The insurgents carry
   black flags and display a bloody plough
   on their coat of arms. They fight without
   a battle-cry, silent and bitter. The
   General Staff of the 12th Army has not
   yet submitted its report.

EMPEROR: What else?

LOUDSPEAKER: That is all!

EMPEROR: Good! Hello, Ministry! Which
   headquarters have fallen into the hands
   of the rebels?

LOUDSPEAKER: 57–3-Roman VIII,
   120-Roman XXXII/1/10/11B.

EMPEROR: Is the proclamation printed?

LOUDSPEAKER: Printed and dispatched.

EMPEROR: Yes.

LOUDSPEAKER: An awesome surgeon has
   removed the cataract from our eyes and
   healed us of our blindness; great as the
   madness of our sins is the punishment,
   frightful the anguish, we must endure.
   Let us bear it with humility, and never
   rest till we've rooted out of our hearts
   the last rank weed of hate and
   disharmony. With bare hands we shall
   tear down the tyrant's steel ramparts . . .

EMPEROR: Has no one else died? No sick, old, wounded?

LOUDSPEAKER: No one.

EMPEROR: I can hardly believe it. I'm
   getting all mixed up. Once we were
   children . . .

PIERROT:
   We skipped to the candy store for

choc'late and for peppermint;
we dreamed that one day we'd be stars
of the circus tent.
We often used to ride the hobby-horse
together!
We sledded on our schoolbags in
snowy weather.
Before the gaze of little girls we quaked
and quivered.
We shattered injustice with pure
thoughts — and the world was delivered!

DRUMMER: 'We Overall, we Overall,
the world is full of all our doing.
Go if you dare, no matter where, we'll
meet you there, and be your ruin.
Sense is but nonsense, wisdom but a
fool —
We Overall.'

PIERROT: Bye, lullaby,
an epitaph am I.
Your father perished in the war,
your mother's red mouth finished her,
bye, lullaby.
Sleep, baby, sleep;
the Man in the Moon doth reap.
He reaps our joy, he cuts the crop,
and in the sun it all dries up.
You'll put your little red dress on then,
and start the same old song again.
Bye, lullaby . . .

EMPEROR: Five, six, seven, eight, nine,
ten, hundred thousand bombs, and how
many million cannon . . .

DRUMMER and PIERROT: Don't you
worry, don't you worry.

EMPEROR: I hid behind my formidable
walls without windows. This item also
was in my calculations! . . . But what are
men like?

DRUMMER: For years he kept the mirror
  concealed!

EMPEROR: Can I be called a man, or just
  the adding machine of God?

DRUMMER and PIERROT: Am I a man?

DRUMMER and PIERROT: A living dead
  man. Ha-ha-ha . . .

DEATH: There's nothing you can do to
  me. I've been dead since the beginning
  of time.

EMPEROR: Who are you?

DEATH:

  I'm known as Death, the Gardener Death;
  I sow the seeds of sleep in pain-cut
  furrows.
  I'm known as Death, the Gardener Death;
  I pull pale weeds exhausted after many
  morrows.
  Men call me Death, the Gardener Death;
  and in the fields I reap the ripened corn
  of sorrows.
  I'm not the Plague that brings you pain;
  I bring relief. I'm not the one who tortures men,
  but he who soothes their grief.
  I am the comfortable, warm nest
  to which an anguished life at last can fly.
  I'm freedom's festival, the last and best.
  I am the final lullaby.
  Hushed is my house and glad to greet
  each guest . . .
  Come, take your rest.

EMPEROR: Then you'll come back to us?
  Without you we people could not live.

DEATH: I'll come back if you agree to be
  the first to die.

EMPEROR: I have the courage to make
  this sacrifice. But the people don't
  deserve it . . .

DEATH: In that case I can't return to you.

EMPEROR: Should I refuse what all who
    suffer beg of you? . . . . I'll do it.
DEATH: Give me your hand. The war is
    over.
EMPEROR: The war is over?
EMPEROR: The war is over. So you say
    with pride. No other war has stopped,
    no war but this. The last one? White
    banners fluttering, from every tower the
    bells sound forth their festive tidings;
    and the fools will all come dancing,
    singing, leaping. Ah, but how long will
    there be peace? The flame is merely
    weakened, not put out. It soon will blaze
    anew. Once more shall murder rage, and
    I yearned to share the grave's repose! O
    were my task accomplished! Freed from
    these fetters forged by man, the land
    would stretch in golden realms of
    unploughed meadows. Ah, were we
    turned to dust! The wilds which we have
    maimed would bloom forever! None
    would tame the roaring of a mighty
    river. Death would come as hunger, love
    and life come: sometimes slowly or swift
    as lightning — but never to slay! Into
    your hand we place our life; lead me
    away, take it, take it away.
GIRL DRUMMER, PIERROT and
LOUDSPEAKER:
    Come, Death, our worthy, honored guest,
    into our hearts descending. Lift all life's burdens from our breast;
    lead us to rest,
    our sorrows ending.
    Make us prize all human worth;
    to other lives awaken.
    Let this commandment be our truth:
    The great and sovereign name of Death
    must not be lightly taken!

Memories of Theresienstadt

MIRKO TUMA

Mirko Tuma was born in Prague in 1921. Tuma spent three and a half years during World War II in the Czech ghetto, Terezín (Theresienstadt), where he wrote numerous poems, translated, and adapted plays. In 1951, he emigrated to the United States and resided in New Jersey, where he was a drama and music critic and frequent lecturer. Since this essay was published, new studies and testimonies have been written; some of the details differ from one another in several of these accounts.

THERESIENSTADT—Terezín in Czech—is a hexagonal fortress town in northern Bohemia that used to be known as Sudetenland. Built in the latter part of the eighteenth century, it was named after Empress Maria Theresa, a woman of passion, culture, and taste, who was genuinely fond of the *Wunderkind* Mozart. In the old Austrian Hungarian Empire Terezín was a typical garrison town.

In 1918, when the Apostolic Monarchy crumbled, Sudetenland became part of Czechoslovakia—the enlightened model democracy endowed by its founder, Professor Thomas Garrigue Masaryk, with Platonic virtues and a progressive social order unequalled in Europe since then. In 1933, when Hitler became Chancellor and later *Führer* of the defeated, frustrated Germany, the Sudetenland, inhabited by Germans, most of whom had never made peace with the Czech reality and with Masaryk's humanism, became a ready target of Nazi propaganda.

Under the presidency of Masaryk's pupil and heir designate, Dr. Eduard Benes, a historian, sociologist, and diplomat prone to pedantry and a far lesser intellectual than Masaryk, the tiny island of democracy, Czechoslovakia, hated by Hitler and misunderstood and ultimately betrayed by its principal ally,

From *Performing Arts Journal* 1 (1976): 12–18.

France, and treated with cynical indifference by England and with cunning and pious platitudes by Stalin's Russia, ultimately fell—in two stages—to the Nazis.

In 1938, the infamous Munich Pact allowed Germany to swallow the Sudetenland (including Terezín) and, in March of 1939, totally to occupy Czechoslovakia. Bohemia and Moravia were turned into the Protectorate Böhmen und Mähren. Slovakia, ruled by the pro-Nazi regime, gained a very fictitious independence.

During the Masaryk and Benes regimes the Jewish population was treated equally, and hard antisemitism which existed primarily in the Sudetenland and the latent quasi-religious antisemitism elsewhere were unable to manifest themselves openly to any significant degree. Masaryk had become a prophet for the Jews and, particularly in Bohemia and Moravia, a great part of the Jewish population, led by the younger generation of intellectuals, retained Judaism as a religion, yet assimilated itself into the social fabric of Masaryk's "promised land." There was a minority—mainly the very wealthy element of Jews—who with regard to culture maintained their German ties. These were cosmopolitan or were at least considered to be.

The Yiddish and the Zionist element that came primarily from the eastern part of the country (neighboring Poland), was closer to the German Jews than to the assimilated Czechs who, while having sympathy with the ideals of Herzl, never really joined the Zionist movement. When the Germans after occupation created the Office for the Handling of the Jewish Question (Kanzlei für die Regelung der Judenfrage), their dealings were predominantly with the German and Zionist elements rather than with the naive Czech Jews who, like my own family, "could never believe it could happen to them." Many of the German Jews and Zionists were somehow capable of emigrating, when emigration was still possible, until the early 1940s.

The Czechs, on the other hand, with totally quixotic idealism and disregard of reality, decided to share the destiny of their "Fatherland," come what may, without quite realizing that in Nazi eyes, a Jew was a Jew. I would be remiss not to mention that while a number of non-Jewish Czechs were heroic in assisting the Jews, some of the latent antisemitism suddenly emerged. There were many Czechs who, while hating the Germans, were quite happy to get rid of the Jews.

In the fall of 1941, prodded by the Nazi leadership of the Protectorate on the one hand and Eichmann from Berlin on the other, the government decided to enforce "the final settling of the Judenfrage"—liquidation. Over two thousand Jews were hustled to the Lódz ghetto in occupied Poland.

Meanwhile, the Nazi hierarchy, still faced with pressures from the outside world, came up with a plan to establish a model camp in Bohemia that would serve two purposes: First, it would be a detention center where Jews—mainly those with important international connections—could be interned, and within such internment supposedly build their own life and "govern themselves" (under German supervision, of course): second, such a camp would serve as a selection or "sift" station from where—without too much public display—those who wouldn't fit the requirements of living in a "model camp" would be shipped to the extermination camps in Eastern Europe. A total of approximately sixty thousand Jews went through this "model ghetto" to either labor camps or death camps. Terezín was indeed ideal for such a project. The thousand "Aryan" inhabitants were relocated to the neighboring hamlet called Bohušovic and the "ghetto Theresienstadt" was created in November of 1941.

A group of 342 able-bodied men, including some 25 or 30 top officials of the Jewish Community Center in Prague—municipal engineers and planners, scientists, sewage experts, builders, administrators, and physicians—were dispatched to the Ghost Fortress as a building commando (*Aufbaukommando I*) to be followed on 1 December by another 1,000 young men—the muscle power (*Aufbaukommando II*). I was one of them.

The transports came in droves, including old people, women, and children: A few families were reunited only to be split later; a few died in Terezín itself but the great majority were transported to Poland. By some rule of thumb, members of the two *Aufbaukommandos*—not all, mind you—were allowed to remain in Terezín and have, at least physically, a far more comfortable life than those in other concentration camps.

Mentally and spiritually, of course, Terezín was the worst hell of the German hells because delusions and hope and macabre pretensions were nourished there. In other camps the Nazis wanted the prisoners to manifest their Dantean suffering by screaming in infernal pain and terror, while in Theresienstadt the prisoners were required to smile as if they were in a photographer's studio.

Especially in the monstrous period of the 1943 and 1944 window-dressing attempts called *Stadtverschönerung*—when the town was getting ready for the inspections by the International Red Cross and other groups of humanitarian agencies from neutral countries—the "paradise island created for the enemies of the state," and existing in the midst of war-torn Europe, was supposed to show the world that the powers of the Third Reich were "compassionate," and that all the talk of hunger, torture, and death in concentration camps was nothing but allied *Gruelpropaganda* [horror-propaganda].

There was a lot of "culture" in Terezín during the *Stadtverschönerung* days, followed by the vicious killing of five thousand Jews in ensuing transports, but it wasn't then that the life of the spirit really began. That started early in 1942 with public hangings. The Germans were fond of "exemplary punishments"—another misapplication of Nietzsche whom they violated to a point of grotesqueness: *Entweder-Oder* [Either-Or].

Nine young men from *Aufbaukommando II* were caught either smoking or trying to smuggle out letters to their families by bribing a Czech gendarme or one of the journeymen in the electric works who came daily from Bohušovic. When the news came that the young men were thrown into an improvised death row, a group of us found ourselves in a forlorn stable. Sitting on straw and half-insane with pain and fear, helplessness and hate, we started to mumble poems we knew from memory. There was nothing else in that poorly lit stable but art, that is, the Pascalian key to immortality. We agreed that on the night of the hangings we would recite Heine in the brilliant Czech translation of Otakar Fischer, a great Czech Jewish poet who died before the onslaught. A young man who later became the *spiritus agens* of most of the cultural activities in the camp, Karl Švenk, brought with him an anthology that included Fischer's version of Heine.

The day of the hangings came. We stood—eyes closed—near the gallows constructed under German supervision by concentrationaires. The hangman was an inmate, a butcher by profession, and later the first suicide in the camp. That night in one of the barracks, without uttering a word about the horror scene we scarcely witnessed, we recited a verse about the "hated German Majesty driving through the ravished lands toward its execution."

The ghetto, since its beginning, was filled with people who were professional artists or dabbled in the arts as dilettantes—all of them *knowing* that the only means to survive, if at all, was for the spirit to transcend the pain of the body. Although it sounds much more romantic that most of the artistic events, ranging from poetry readings to cabaret, legitimate theater, opera, and concerts, were clandestine, the fact remains that in Terezín the only clandestine expression was in allegory: Cultural and artistic life in Terezín was, in the creative sense, similar to the cultural life in occupied France, where Sartre was mounting his allegoric *No Exit*. It has become a vogue, unfortunately, to place heroism in the wrong perspective.

Heroism wasn't in the clandestineness but in the will to create, to paint, to write, to perform, and to compose in hell.

The Germans permitted the rich Jewish library to be moved from the Jewish Community Center in Prague to Terezín and, even before the *Stadtverschönerung*, allowed musical instruments, art supplies, and even some stage materials—costumes, primitive lights, and flats—to be shipped to Terezín.

We mustn't forget that the first commandant of the camp, Dr. Friedrich

Seidel, was *sui generis* an intellectual experimenting like a sophisticated Satan with the alleged *mysteries* of the Jewish psyche. Indeed, Dr. Seidel hated the Jews much more fervently than the later butcher-commanders, but in addition to hate (a little bit like Eichmann) his curiosity about the *Untermenschen* was similar to the entomologist's curiosity about insects — ants, in particular.

It was typical for Dr. Seidel to allow the Jews to play Jewish music and perform Jewish works (which were, of course, forbidden in the rest of Germany), as long as they were not aimed directly against the Nazi regime. It is here where the camouflage of allegory came fully into play. Although theater in Terezín showed enormous effort, the key to cultural survival was music.

Three great Czech Jewish musicians were concentrationaires: conductor Rafael Schächter, [Gideon] Klein who later died in Auschwitz, and Karel Ančerl who survived and passed away only a few years ago in Canada where he was music director of the Toronto Symphony and a frequent guest conductor of the New York Philharmonic. (After the liberation in 1945 Ančerl became music director of the Czech Philharmonic. He lived in the West after the Dubček regime was crushed by the Soviets.)

The first *total event* in the performing arts was Schächter's "concert version" of Smetana's national opera, *The Bartered Bride*. At the time — I think it was 1942 — there was only one piano available, an old legless Bechstein found in some attic and smuggled into the recreation hall in the Magdeburg barracks where the Council of Elders (*Ältestenrat*) had their offices. Around this piano, which couldn't have been tuned to perfection, Schächter assembled singers ranging from top professionals such as Karel Berman, the noted basso of the National Theater in Prague, to dilettantes with nice voices but unable to read music, and mounted a most extraordinary performance of a work that starts with the famous chorus, "Why shouldn't we be merry as long as God grants us health?"

With transports from other parts of Europe — Denmark and Holland, in particular, brought to Theresienstadt other singers of repute — Schächter produced in concert form a brilliant version of Mozart's *The Marriage of Figaro* (in German) and *The Magic Flute*. A group of musicians around him later staged excerpts from *Tosca* and *Die Fledermaus*. The most symbolic performance in the history of Terezín was, of course, Verdi's *Requiem*, conducted by Schächter in September 1944, after the Red Cross inspection of the camps. The *Requiem* was first performed for the visiting guests as part of the "Potemkin villages" sham. The last performance, however, was mounted when the German order of the ensuing transports was already known. To balance the temporary feeling of "relief," the Germans ordered five thousand Jews within a span of a month to be shipped to Auschwitz, where most of them died in gas chambers, including Schächter, Klein, and Švenk.

There is no adequate description of a moment in music when the "Dies Irae" and "Sanctus" were sung by a chorus, three-quarters of which *knew* they'd be shipped in cattle wagons to Auschwitz the following day. This concert of the *Requiem* I feel — more than all the artificial games of heroism that were more fictitious than true — was the ultimate outcry and triumph of the human spirit and the final defiance of Nazism: a metaphysical defiance.

It was with music that the camp celebrated under Ančerl's baton the liberation with a hastily organized chamber concert doing the works of Smetana, Janacek, Dvořák, and Mozart. The theater grew from improvised literary cabarets which included simple variety numbers as well as poignant and courageous sketches like Švenk's *The Last Cyclist* [mentioned in the accompanying memoir]. Švenk staged excerpts from *Cyrano de Bergerac* and two major productions: Molière's *Georges Dandin* and, significantly, Gogol's *The Marriage*.[1] These performances were no makeshift events, but subtle professional productions, designed by František Zelenka, the Jo Mielziner of Czechoslovakia, who in the 1930s designed most of the major productions at the National Theater in Prague. Švenk was deeply influenced by K. B. Hilar, the greatest stage director of post–World War I Czechoslovakia, himself a pupil of both Reinhardt and Piscator. (It is hard to believe, but the costumes, particularly for *The Marriage,* were rich and authentic and the lighting design a work of art in itself.)

Švenk directed the old Czech folk story "Esther" in an experimental style which he learned not only from Hilar whose experiments retained the romantic or expressionistic flair, but from the avant-garde Czech director E. F. Burian (himself a concentrationaire in a different camp) who, after creating a powerful avant-garde, anti-establishment theater in Prague in the 1930s, became very much more establishment (Socialist Realism) when he returned to Prague after the liberation. Burian's influence — prewar Burian, that is — was particularly traceable in Švenk's cabaret work.[2]

The much-heralded production of the children's opera, *Brundibár,* with music by Hans Krása and text by Adolf Hoffmeister, the Czech version of Jules Feiffer [see Karas chapter], was mounted during the second *Stadtverschönerung* in the set by Zelenka who, if I recall correctly, also directed it. Again, it was a very elaborate production of a clever and sophisticated work. Its allegoric impact, however, was superimposed only by the circumstances under which it was revived.

There was also a feverish playwriting activity in the camp. A young German painter, Peter Kien, wrote a *commedia dell 'arte* — a total escape from camp reality which was not produced in the original German but rather in a brilliant Czech translation by the poet Zdeněk Lederer who, incidentally, wrote the most definitive and intensive study of Terezín after the war in London. I translated Shakespeare's *Measure for Measure* and adapted Calderon's *The Judge of Zalamea,* published in Prague in 1947, and dedicated to the memory of Švenk who had worked with me on the new structural concept of this great antimilitaristic play.

The theatrical activities of groups other than the Czechs were on a much smaller scale and played to fewer audiences. The cultural division in the camp, which I mentioned in my lengthy introduction, prevailed in the arts. There is no doubt that some 90 percent of the creative effort was in the hands of the Czechs.

Indeed, I believe that the equation between artistic activities in Terezín (particularly in theater and music) and rebellion or rather calculated rebellion, has been in most instances a *myth.* The theater and music were quintessentially *l'art pour l'art,* with *l'art,* however transcending itself and acquiring a dimension of sheer survival. What reason would there be for mounting plays as removed from political reality as Cocteau's *The Human Voice* (played by Czech actress Vava Schön, who after the war became a renowned Israeli star)? As a matter of fact, most of the plays — and operas — dealt with totally personal romantic themes or, as in the instance of Mozart's *The Magic Flute* and Verdi's *Manzoni* and *Requiem,* with metaphysical matters.

Audience tastes were as diversified as in society outside the camp. There were the sentimentalists escaping to old-fashioned trash, and there were the more discriminating intellectuals who sought the same type of work they would have looked for anywhere in the world.

I repeat, the claim to clandestineness and heroism is a well-sounding myth. One could read clandestinely Heine or revolutionary poets within the confines of a few bunks in the barracks, and one could indeed stress allegories as in *Brundibár.* But one couldn't clandestinely mount a full season.

The Nazis, particularly in Theresienstadt, which was designed as the ultimate *Potemkin Village* in order to detract attention from cruelties committed elsewhere and in the unseen parts of Terezín, tolerated artistic expression and often attended the performances — particularly the musical ones. Whether in the atmosphere of hangings, transports, dying, hunger, or in the make-believe of the *Stadtverschönerung,* the Jews — all and without exception — were considered by the Nazis to be *morituri:* those who are about to die. If anything, the

From Philipp Manes's Papers: Drawing from Ghetto: Faust evenings — June 1944 by inmate Etta Veit Simon. "Souvenir of lovely Faust evenings at Theresienstadt, June 1944. . . ." Permission by Ms. Manes. Photo by Wiener Library, London

Germans showed indifference toward what the Jews did in their free time be-cause, in the mind of the Eichmanns, it was a matter of time before the "Final Solution" would be administered anyway.

Only the graphic artists and poets captured in their works the true horror of Theresienstadt—not only the dying, but the shame as well.

To understand Terezín and the grotesqueness of the experiment of a "model ghetto" one has to understand both Schopenhauer and Wagner. The Nazis, somewhere in the back of their minds, had a constant vision of the *Götter-dämmerung*. Terezín, despite the cynicism with which it had been conceived, was an escape passage from the burning Valhalla: Wotan's guilt was ever-present and the Jewish artists knew it. With both phenomenal insight and imagination they used the reality of the German guilt as a means—and here comes the miracle—not only to survive and keep some semblance of sanity, but to grow toward universality.

Only in that sense was art in Terezín an act of revolution.

Epilogue

Lost, Stolen, and Strayed: The Archival Heritage of Modern German-Jewish History

SYBIL H. MILTON

CURRENT ARCHIVAL PRACTICES are determined largely by historical methodology, but the task of selecting and preserving those records that
characterize and document an ethnic or religious group within a host country
is inherently subjective. Certain problems are common to all types of contemporary records from the Enlightenment to the Holocaust; others are unique
to German Judaica. Until recently, the standards of historical significance have
been frankly elitist, concerned with the careers of prominent personalities,
with the role of political, economic, and cultural elites and organizations, and,
for German Judaica, with the history of autonomous Jewish communities in
Germany. The newer perspectives of social, quantitative, and women's history,
as well as the study of the Holocaust, have placed increasing demands on the
surviving fragmentary archival record.

The most striking characteristic of modern records is that they are fractured
or fragmented, despite their initial creation by a single organization, common
agency, or person (called "provenance"). Thus the personal literary estates of
most major twentieth-century figures reflect the migratory patterns of careers
split among government service, university employment, and private business. This has resulted in the scattering of official and personal papers of one
individual among several archival depositories, assuming that the records do

"Lost, Stolen, Strayed: The Archival Heritage of Modern German-Jewish History." From Jehuda Reinharz and Walter Schatzberg, eds., *The Jewish Response to German Culture* (Hanover,
N.H.: University Press of New England, 1985), 317–35. The author has written a postscript specifically for this anthology, "The Remnants of Culture under Duress."

not altogether disappear with the emigration or demise of their creators. The several archival agencies holding different fragments of one figure seldom correlate bibliographic data about their common subject holdings in joint finding aids or even exchange data on more than an informal and sporadic basis. This neglect has contributed to the recent international discussion about subject retrieval and problems of scholarly access to records and manuscripts.[1]

Access is also determined by other variables, and conditions range from virtually open door with minimal restrictions (usually about copyright and privacy) in Western Europe and North America to restrictive legislation and arbitrary access in Eastern Europe and the Third World.[2] For German Judaica, Jewish separateness in Christian-German society has resulted in the administrative division of extant Jewish records between two parallel types of agencies: state repositories with jurisdiction over files about Jews within their geographic boundaries and private institutions under Jewish auspices. The first central depository for the records of German-Jewish communities and organizations, the Gesamtarchiv der deutschen Juden, was established in 1905 in Berlin. In the mid-1930s its archival holdings were seized by the Reichsstelle für Sippenforschung (State Office for Ancestral Research), and, despite losses, many Jewish communal birth, marriage, and death registers were saved from destruction as an ironic by-product of the Nazi pseudoscientific obsession with racial biology. In 1945 the U.S. Army recovered many of these files and subsequently transported them from the Offenbach archival depot for captured documents to Jewish successor institutions in the United States and Israel. Noncaptured remnants of the Gesamtarchiv still remain in both East and West Germany.[3] The Gesamtarchiv was never as comprehensive as the name implied, and Jewish records often remained in situ in the offices, seminaries, and synagogues that created them. The complex pattern of migration of records and manuscripts alienated from their geographical or administrative points of origin has been further complicated by the existence of private Judaica archives, bibliophiles, and collectors. In 1924, for example, the librarian of the Jewish Theological Seminary in New York, Alexander Marx, purchased 39.6 pounds of documents for $293 from the Berlin bookdealer Louis Lamm. The materials included communal records from fifty-nine German-Jewish and Polish-Jewish communities in the province of Posen.[4] In the late 1930s, Jewish emigrants fleeing Nazi Germany often carried family papers and other archival files to localities scattered throughout the world. One emigrant carried the memorial book of late-nineteenth-century Zerkow, Upper Silesia, to her new home in Montevideo; after her death, the volume was inherited by distant American relatives who donated it to the Leo Baeck Institute in 1983.[5] This illustration is not atypical.

The idiosyncrasies of German geography and political history are also re-flected in surviving German-Jewish records. The amalgam of more than three hundred sovereign entities that existed prior to the unification of Germany further increased the fragmentation and decentralization of German and Jew-ish records alike. Thus the papers of Jewish communities on the west bank of the Rhine were already split between France and Germany at the time of the French Revolution and Napoleon. Similarly, the files of the Jewish consistories in Alsace and Lorraine have been repeatedly transferred between France and Germany throughout the last hundred years: from France to Germany in 1871, back to France in 1919, reconquered by Germany in 1940, and only partly re-trieved by France in 1945. In fact, some of the materials recovered by the U.S. Army in 1945 were eventually shipped to several American-Jewish depositories (the YIVO Institute for Jewish Research, the Leo Baeck Institute, and the Jew-ish Theological Seminary) and to Israel (Central Archives for the History of the Jewish People).[6] Analogous shifts in the citizenship of both German and Jew-ish archival holdings also occurred in Breslau (today Wroclaw in Poland) and Königsberg (Kaliningrad in the *former* Soviet Union).[7] Non-German records captured by German soldiers during the invasion of Russia were eventually captured in turn by the U.S. Army, as for example, the Communist Party ar-chives of the Smolensk region.[8] The result of these repeated changes of sover-eignty is a gigantic jigsaw puzzle with numerous torn and missing pieces.

Neglect and the ravages of time have also influenced the quantity and quality of the surviving historical record. Thus most records of the Sephardic commu-nity of Berlin had been lost before the 1930s.[9] It is clear that Jewish communal records, kept intermittently since the seventeenth century, became more sys-tematic as the administrative organization of the modern German state evolved during the nineteenth century. But Jewish records prior to the nineteenth cen-tury were not always complete, accurate, or even systematic, especially during periods of tension and persecution. Occasionally the absence of some records was deliberate, a stratagem to evade harassment, military conscription, resi-dence restrictions, or discriminatory taxation in the preemancipation period. Often problems resulted from the nature of the record itself. *Mohelbücher* (cir-cumcision registers) were not records of all male children born in a specific town or region but the private record of the individual circumciser. Circumci-sion registers did not, of course, contain data about Jewish female children.[10]

World War II and the Holocaust intensified the dispersion and destruc-tion of Jewish documentation and artifacts. Although the Security Police Chief Reinhard Heydrich stipulated in his directives during the pogrom of 9 November 1938 that "the archives of Jewish communities are to be confiscated by the police, so that they will not be destroyed," there was nevertheless widespread Nazi looting and records stored in synagogues were often destroyed.[11] The pattern established inside Nazi Germany soon spread to all of occupied Europe from the Pyrenees to the Urals. Often German military and police units saved rare Judaica volumes and manuscripts as curiosities for their own collections, for use in potential antisemitic exhibitions organized by German museums, for deposit in the Institut zur Erforschung der Judenfrage in Frankfurt, and for resale in foreign auctions to obtain hard currency. In April 1943, Cecil Roth stated that he had received offers to buy rare Judaica from Nazi individuals and organizations transmitted via Switzerland.[12] For the most part, conditions that threatened human life also endangered the preservation of documents. Nazi lootings and confiscations were compounded by the firestorms and resultant damage during Allied bombing raids, the vulnerability of most storage places, the deliberate burning of incriminating records by retreating German soldiers and the SS to hide their complicity in mass murder, and the taking of souvenirs by both Allied liberators and civilian noncombatants. Whether records were destroyed or not was often only a matter of chance.

One anecdote, possibly apocryphal, about the disarray of Joseph Goebbels's diary in liberated Berlin, is typical for the fate of all records at the time. In a publisher's note to Louis P. Lochner's edition of Goebbels's diary, Hugh Gibson wrote:

When the Russians occupied Berlin in 1945, they went through the German official archives with more vigor than discrimination; shipped some materials to Russia, destroyed some, and left the rest scattered underfoot. They often followed a system that is difficult to understand—emptying papers on the floor and shipping to Russia the filing cabinets that contained them.

Considerable fragments of Goebbels's diaries . . . were found in the courtyard of his ministry, where they had evidently narrowly escaped burning, many of the pages being singed and all smelling of smoke. Apparently they were originally bound in the German type of office folder. Thin metal strips in the salmoncolored binders were run through holes punched in the paper, bent over, and locked into place.

At that time all Berlin was one great junk yard, with desperate people laying hands on anything tangible and movable that could be used for barter. The unburned papers were taken away by one of these amateur junk dealers, who carefully salvaged the binders and discarded the contents—leaving more than 7,000 sheets of loose paper. A few binders had not been removed but most of the pages were tied up in bundles as wastepaper. It later proved a considerable task to put them together again in the right sequence, as they were not numbered.[13]

Several characteristics are common to all German Judaica records, irrespective of date: the multiplicity of languages (German, Judeo-German, Hebrew, and occasionally also Ladino or Aramaic) and extensive damage through neglect or deliberate destruction. The fragmentation of textual and visual records in widely scattered government and private archives has unfortunately limited the systematic reappraisal of criteria for archival retention of documents, artifacts, and audiovisual materials. Although there were mandatory religious and secular legal requirements for certain types of genealogical records before the twentieth century, the pervasive pattern of destruction and dispersal has led to the practice that everything that survived is considered intrinsically valuable. This has, in effect, limited the archivist's role as "prophet" in deciding what new records might give us a better understanding of the past and be usable in planning for the future. Potential duplication and overlap of collections for pre–World War II records are not viewed as serious problems, despite the increasingly prohibitive costs of scholarly travel. But the practice of allowing duplication and overlap is far more debatable for textual and audiovisual records created after 1945. The paper and film heritage of the Nazi period, the Second World War, and the Holocaust (1933–45) have several distinctive problems that must be discussed separately.

Many early Judaica records were saved virtually intact, as for example, the records of the Jewish community of Worms shipped to the Jewish Historical General Archives in Jerusalem in 1939 and subsequently incorporated into the holdings consolidated in the Central Archives for the History of the Jewish People.[14] Other documents about the Jews of Worms remained in the Worms Municipal Archives, and substantial numbers of original and transcribed records were carried by immigrants to the United States. During the 1960s and 1970s the literary estates of three refugees who died in the United States—Berthold Rosenthal, Isidor Kiefer, and Fritz Nathan, all containing significant fragments of documentation about Worms—were deposited in the Leo Baeck Institute in New York.[15] Alongside his research notes about the Jews of Baden and Mannheim, Berthold Rosenthal packed in his luggage a complete transcript of the Green Book of Worms, 1560–1812. Isidor Kiefer, former president of the Worms Jewish community, who emigrated to the United States via Belgium in 1934, took eighteenth- and nineteenth-century administrative and correspondence files from the Worms Jewish communal offices; a copy of the Worms *Judenregister*, 1739–1814; an inventory of the Worms Jewish Museum, whose contents were later impounded and partly vandalized during the pogrom of November 1938; and photographs of the Rashi synagogue and ritual objects. The architect Fritz Nathan brought to the United States forty-two rare glass positive slides with detailed structural images of the Rashi synagogue prior to renovations completed at the beginning of the twentieth century.[16] These slides and photographs provided essential data for the reconstruction of the Worms synagogue and museum during the 1970s.[17]

The records of the demise of the Worms Jewish community under Nazi persecutions were located in depositories other than those holding earlier archival material. Deportation lists for Jews residing within the city and district of Worms were found in the municipal and police archives of Worms, the Hessen State Archives, the International Tracing Service at Arolsen, Yad Vashem in Jerusalem, and the Leo Baeck Institute in New York.[18] Furthermore, the YIVO Institute in New York acquired several hundred identity cards for Worms Jewish inhabitants as part of the record group of captured German documents containing the files of the Institut zur Erforschung der Judenfrage.[19] The records of Worms from the Nazi period were thus fragmented among more than six institutions in three countries on three continents.

The first contact between unassimilated *Ostjuden* and the Prussian bureaucracy occurred during the Napoleonic era, when the regions of Bialystok and Plock were annexed to New East Prussia with the Third Partition of Poland in 1795 until the creation of the Napoleonic duchy of Warsaw in 1807. The newly annexed territories were administered from Königsberg by Gustav Schrötter and became the testing ground for many of the later Stein–Hardenberg reforms that led to the emancipation of Prussian Jews. Initially, all historical records from this period were deposited in the Prussian State Archives in Königsberg. After the Second World War, the files of the Kriegs- und Domanenkammer of Bialystok and the Generaldirektion Neuostpreussen were separated; the former were returned to Poland in 1947 and the latter dispersed between the East German State Archives in both Potsdam and Merseburg and the temporary storage depot for Prussian cultural property in Göttingen in West Germany. The records center in Göttingen was dissolved in 1978, and all East Prussian records subsequently transferred to the State Archives in West Berlin.[20] Independently, a partial parallel and duplicate record existed; during the 1920s, Jacob Jacobson visited the State Archives in Königsberg and took copious extracts and research copies from Schrötter's reports. These notes survived with the remnants of the Gesamtarchiv and were eventually deposited along with Jacobson's literary estate at the Leo Baeck Institute.[21]

Often artifacts from the past have been rediscovered by chance. In 1978 the Jagellonian Library in Cracow renovated an almost forgotten sub-basement and accidentally unearthed the original correspondence of Rahel Varnhagen, scores by Wolfgang Amadeus Mozart and Franz Schubert, and several manuscripts about ichthyology from the early nineteenth century.[22] Such spectacular finds are admittedly rare.

Nonliterary evidence and older printed literature often make possible the reconstruction of a past otherwise lost. Thus the history of the Danzig Jewish community was written because its ritual objects are extant, having been shipped intact in 1939 to the Jewish Theological Seminary in New York.[23] Similarly the history of eighteenth-century Jewish communities in Mecklenburg can be found in late-nineteenth-century publications available in major Judaica libraries.[24] The use of art, artifacts, and older secondary literature makes scholarship about the early period of German-Jewish history possible.

Nazi and Jewish records about the Holocaust, however, present distinctive problems that rarely occur in the archival heritage of earlier epochs. First is the problem of the colossal size of even the incomplete record. More than sixteen hundred tons of paper (many millions of pages, often torn out of context) were captured by the Western Allies in 1945 and shipped to the United States and England for microfilming.[25] Known today as captured German documents, they contain a great variety of material: the records of German government agencies; the records of Nazi Party organizations; the records of private business enterprises (e.g., I. G. Farben); the papers, art, and artifacts of other nations and Jewish individuals looted by the German army; and many personal German and non-German literary estates.[26] These records were barely intact even in 1945. Documents from an intact common provenance were often dispersed at the end of the war. American, French, British, and Russian troops seized those papers left behind by the Germans for tactical and intelligence information, the needs of occupation government, the preparation of war crimes trials, historical study, and as souvenirs.

By 1960, many of the original records had been returned from the Captured Records Section of the Federal Records Center at Alexandria, Virginia, to successor institutions in West Germany, and from the Soviet Union to depositories in East Germany.[27] In addition to the more than thirty thousand microfilms at the National Archives in Washington, D.C., many original records in a multiplicity of languages (French, German, Italian, Polish, Russian, Hungarian, and Yiddish) were dispersed to specialized subject research centers like the Library of Congress, the Hoover Institution, the YIVO Institute, and the Leo Baeck Institute.[28] Similar records were also deposited in analogous foreign research centers, as, for example, the Centre Documentation Juive Contemporaine in Paris, the Netherlands State Institute for War Documentation in Amsterdam, the Wiener Library in London, the Institut für Zeitgeschichte in Munich, and Yad Vashem in Jerusalem.[29] Other German government, corporate, and personal papers were pulled from filing cabinets and torn out of context for use in the International Military Tribunal in Nuremberg and other subsequent U.S. Army trials. The surviving files were not historical archives arranged for scholarly use; they were usually current office files from the Weimar and Nazi years captured *in situ*. The Nuremberg documentation alone amounted to thousands of pages in twenty-five series. Often the newly created record series were purely arbitrary; the famous PS designation, for example, stood for Paris-Storey, or the documents collected by Col. Robert G. Storey in Paris.[30] It is important to remember, moreover, that traditional distinctions between private and public records did *not* apply to documents created under totalitarian rule. Thus, the Gestapo (a government agency) and the Sicherheitsdienst (a Party agency) functioned in reality as a single unit. It is also important to remember that denunciation and reprisals meant that some types of documentation remained unwritten and unrecorded in order to evade state censorship and police control. Fortunately, the German bureaucracy used duplicating and mimeograph machines with abandon, and even if the original of a letter or report was lost, one of the many copies often survived—as, for example, did a copy of the Wannsee protocol.

In the world of official Nazi documents and captured German records, the filmed copy rather than the original document is the norm. This has led to certain problems of bibliographical control for both the scholar and the archivist. Despite the relatively large number of guides and published inventories to American, German, and Israeli depositories, there is colossal confusion about the location and nature of the records.[31] In the United States, the National Archives used RG (record group) numbers, T numbers, and microfilm roll and frame numbers; in Britain, the Foreign Office used multiple-digit serial numbers with letter tags like EAP, although naval records filmed in England have PG or TA labels. "At times," Henry Friedlander has observed, "this profusion of letters and symbols resembles the secret designations of the ancient cabala."[32] This complexity and confusion is repeated in the footnotes and citations of published scholarship. The same document can be, and often is, cited in different books as a Nuremberg document, a National Archives microfilm, and an item from the Bundesarchiv. Because there are few, if any, concordances, the citation depends on when and where the research was done. Compounding the confusion, many depositories have subsequently acquired original captured document collections and then imposed their own classification systems without reference to identical documents in parallel microfilm collections. Thus the Berlin Collection at YIVO lists one document as Occ E-284, in fact identical with Nuremberg document PS 1472, a report dated 16 December 1942, about the shipment of forty-five thousand Jews from Bialystok, Theresienstadt, the Netherlands, and Berlin to Auschwitz.[33] All of the institutions have also purchased microfilms from the National Archives, the Berlin Document Center (BDC) [now part of the German Bundesarchiv], or the Bundesarchiv in Koblenz.

The liberalization of reprography rules has led to an increase in the number of microforms and photocopies purchased by American scholars in foreign archives and subsequently deposited as part of their literary papers in American repositories.[34] Although there are no common standards for cataloging archival microfilms, three distinctive patterns can be identified. The first practice is to classify foreign microfilms containing archival records as if they were books, assigning them Library of Congress classification numbers. The Hoover Institution on War, Revolution, and Peace, in Stanford, California, has adopted this practice, and its card catalog integrates microfilms of captured German documents from the British Public Record Office and the Berlin Document Center with published literature.[35] The second practice is to use the archive accession or record group number of the depository, meanwhile retaining the original inventory or collection identification of the primary depository. This is the practice of the Institut für Zeitgeschichte in Munich and the Leo Baeck Institute in New York.[36] The third usage is to give archival microforms new numbers without out connection or reference to the originals, a practice similar to laundering out the identity of the primary depository; this is occasionally followed by Yad Vashem.[37] All three patterns coexist in the United States, Europe, and Israel, creating additional bibliographical confusions. Consequently identical materials available on film and as originals are given different citations if located in two repositories. Furthermore, this freedom to cite the same material in a multiplicity of ways makes it virtually impossible for scholars to identify duplicative and unique materials; it also hampers any possibility of correlating or linking segments of a fractured record group between repositories.

The residual archival papers of Julius Streicher form an archival maze through the different cataloging styles of four American and two West German depositories. The surviving fragmentary records consist of Streicher's correspondence and manuscripts about the early history of the Nazi Party in Franconia and the Nuremberg police files about his journalistic and party activities, 1920–40. These records were transferred from the former BDC to the Bundesarchiv in Koblenz and also duplicated as a segment of the microfilmed NSDAP Hauptarchiv at the Hoover Institution.[38] A second part of the Streicher papers is the partial editorial files of *Der Stürmer,* which include Streicher's correspondence with contributors, illustrators, photographers, and readers. The letters to the editors between 1933 and 1945 come from all of occupied Europe and often contain illustrations or photographs submitted for potential use in the paper. These fragments are located at both the Leo Baeck Institute and the YIVO Institute in New York. They originate, however, from different sources: The files at the Leo Baeck were "liberated" from the larger *Stürmer* archive and library in Nuremberg; the YIVO records came via the U.S. Army and the Offenbach records depot in the immediate aftermath of the war. These two fragments are the missing files of the larger editorial archives of *Der Stürmer* that are today deposited in the Nuremberg Municipal Archives (Stadtarchiv Nürnberg). An additional splinter of seventy-seven microfilm frames of *Der Stürmer* correspondence with authors and illustrators is found on captured German documents films deposited in the National Archives in Washington, D.C.[39] The fifth and last set of Streicher files includes his interrogation, trial, and sentencing by the International Military Tribunal in Nuremberg. These official records resulting from the American presence in postwar Germany are American administrative records and deposited at the National Archives.[40] Currently available institutional guides and national catalogs do not unravel this maze of duplicative and unique Streicher materials, nor can these dispersed records stemming from a common or similar provenance be currently linked by subject retrieval. The result is surely not cost-effective, nor does it prevent the blind passages of research, since scholars must visit or contact at least four institutions.

The German looting of rare Judaica artifacts, manuscripts, and books occasionally—unwittingly—led to their survival. Alfred Rosenberg created the half-million-volume Judaica library at the Institut zur Erforschung der Judenfrage in Frankfurt am Main, which incorporated more than seven hundred crates from the holdings of the International Institute for Social History (Amsterdam), the Rosenthaliana Library (Amsterdam), the YIVO Institute (Vilna), and other private collections (such as the Warburg Library in Hamburg, the Rothschild archives in Paris and Vienna, and the holdings of the rabbinical seminary in Berlin).[41] Eight Jewish scholars were employed as library catalogers in this bizarre Nazi enterprise, and the Reichsvereinigung der Juden in Deutschland eventually acceded to the requests of the Reich Security Office and appointed an additional twenty-five Jewish librarians, professors, and scholars to administer this collection. These books and papers eventually were transferred to Theresienstadt, where they formed the core of the Ghetto Central Library. Even the 1944 propaganda film *Der Führer schenkt den Juden eine Stadt* included one scene in the ghetto library.[42] Although many of the original libraries were destroyed initially by Nazi vandalism and later by Allied bombings of German cities, the U.S. Army captured many items in 1945 and restored them to either the original owners or designated successor institutions around the world via the Offenbach depot.[43]

It is important to remember that there is also a Jewish record of the Holocaust created at the time or in the immediate postwar period. The secret archives of the Warsaw ghetto, *Oneg Shabbat,* were buried in milk cans under the supervision of Emanuel Ringelblum and recovered from the rubble in 1946 for deposit in the Jewish Historical Institute of Warsaw.[44] Similar ghetto archives and historical projects recording the fate of the Jews of Nazi-occupied Europe existed in Kovno, Bialystok, and Lódz; memoirs, chronicles, diaries, and artworks were buried by their creators in windowsills, in the ground, in walls, and in attics, and only partly relocated and retrieved after the war.[45] In the DP camps and centers, Jewish historical commissions sought to record the experiences of the survivors.[46] These well-defined postwar projects have had few successors in more recent oral history ventures.

Many German-Jewish refugees sought to reconstruct the history of their former communities. Rudolph Apt, for example, residing in London, corresponded with fellow emigrants and survivors from Dresden in order to compile a card and manuscript file about the fate of Dresden Jews between 1933 and 1947.[47] Morris Vierfelder took his chronicle of family and Jewish life in Buchau, a village in southern Wurttemberg, with him to the United States. His daughter was subsequently stationed as an army nurse near Buchau shortly after the war. She was able to retrieve a rare series of lantern slides showing the unique village synagogue with steeple and bell. The building had been destroyed during the pogrom of November 1938.[48]

Historical records were often saved by accident. Two instances drawn from the experience of the Leo Baeck Institute are probably typical. The case files of the Gildemeester rescue effort to aid the emigration of Austrian Jews after 1938 were found together with the papers of the group's secretary, Hermann Fuernberg, by an attentive neighbor in Fuernberg's New York apartment house. After Fuernberg's death, his landlord had stored his papers and possessions in the trash room, where they were found virtually intact though filthy, as they had been dumped near a coal furnace.[49] A similar incident occurred when a Long Island garbage hauler retrieved rare Berlin Jewish communal photo albums inscribed with dedications to Heinrich Stahl, chairman of the Berlin Jewish community from 1938 to 1942. The albums contained several hundred illustrations showing the concerts and other cultural programs of the Jüdischer Kulturbund, the offices and activities of the Jewish *Winterhilfe* campaign, life in a suburban old age home of the Berlin Jewish community, and other Berlin Jewish organizations at work between 1936 and 1940.[50] Most lost records went unrecorded and consequently unknown. Only in the rarest instances could the written record be reconstructed through the use of oral history. The papers of the *Verein der Ostjuden* and the *Reichsverband polnischer Juden in Deutschland* from 1933 to 1939 have vanished, and two slender postwar oral histories amounting to about sixty pages are insufficient to tell us much about these self-defense organizations before the expulsion of Polish Jews from Germany in late October 1938 and their relationship with other German-Jewish organizations.[51]

The uses of oral history to recover lost fragments of the German Jewish experience have several troubling features when applied to the period of the Holocaust. Although the value of oral history to fill historical lacunae is clear, it is important to remember that oral testimony is subjective for both the interviewer and interviewee. The usual criteria for selecting interview subjects are either topical or biographical and may focus on either prominent figures or the average person.[52] The constraints of time and money in audio- or video-taping and transcribing interviews require selectivity in project design, so that those subjects for which aggregate data are needed or unclear events (where, perhaps, only a handful of survivors are available) receive priority. Instead, American oral history projects about the Holocaust have had little focus and often elicit vague, repetitive, emotional, and often factually erroneous testimony from all survivors residing in any given community who volunteer to be taped, simply because funding was available for these interviews. The resulting mishmash trivializes the events and exploits the individual survivor, who must recall emotionally charged events at a distance of forty years and whose evidence may be useless for future historical scholarship. Few recent programs have aided scholarship, although they do produce impressive results for classroom use in the public schools.

One of the best-designed postwar interview series was completed by the Wiener Library with participants in the women's demonstration in Berlin during March 1943, the so-called *Fabrikaktion,* protesting the roundups of Jewish relatives living in protected mixed marriages.[53] This demonstration was a unique instance of mass popular resistance that did not bring Gestapo reprisals upon the demonstrators; it certainly requires further analysis and study. A second project that would have value for scholarship is the collection of aggregate data about Jews who survived by passing or in hiding between 1941 and 1945. Since altruism was not normative behavior during the Third Reich, this type of oral history project would allow systematic analysis of the profiles and motivations of individuals and groups who aided Jews in hiding without profit or reward.[54] Oral testimonies could also be used to elicit data about Jewish folklore and popular culture under Nazi terror, the role of religion, humor, family life, and the gender-specific experiences of women.[55] Such subjects would add to our historical knowledge and understanding of this tragic epoch, whereas random interviews of survivors are probably useless for historians and social scientists.

Film and photographic records are important historical artifacts; the absence of formal academic training in the interpretation of visual communication, however, has led to abuses tantamount to visual illiteracy.[56] Historical use and interpretation of visual images, whether art or photography, depend on the quality of supplementary written data. Dating or assigning authorship to unlabeled photographs is difficult in any epoch; even dated photographs present difficult interpretive problems. The huge number of photos (approximately one million images) available as part of the captured German documents from the Second World War present some the same problems as parallel written and textual records. Multiple copies of the same photograph often are located in several repositories, frequently with completely different descriptive labels.[57] Systematic and comprehensive information rarely accompanies the original negative or file reproductions. The record includes battle scenes and aerial photography; photos showing the persecution of German Jews and liberation from the camps; social, industrial, or architectural photos; and portraits of family groups and individuals. Archival control of these images must be improved so that the historical record is not further damaged or lost by inaction and indifference.

There will never be a perfect archive, but our existing resources can be more skillfully managed if scholars and repositories find cooperative solutions to the problems of intellectual and bibliographical control of our archival heritage. It would be utopian to assume that computer-assisted indexing alone could overcome some of the problems caused by the absence of common descriptive standards for dispersed historical materials. The veritable maze of splintered and fractured collections in German Judaica and the wild array of possible scholarly citations are neither cost-effective nor good scholarship. The liberalization of conditions of access and use, the growing number of theme-specialized Judaica archives and Holocaust repositories with overlapping and often duplicative collecting areas, and the international expansion of archival clientele since the Second World War have created both new problems and new opportunities for cooperative solutions. The ravages of time, the destruction caused by wars and natural catastrophes, and the almost inevitable fragmentation of materials have certainly damaged the surviving historical record. But it is just as certain that our own attitudes and actions as archivists and historians can make an important difference in the quality and availability of the historical record documenting the modern German-Jewish experience.

Postscript: The Remnants of Culture under Duress

Although it was published fifteen years ago, the contents of my article, "Lost Stolen, and Strayed," still apply to a large degree. The basic issues of fragmentary and fragmented state and private archival collections that document the cultural heritage of the Holocaust have remained unchanged.

First, we must establish some definitions. The *cultural heritage of the Holocaust* consists of art, music, theater, cabaret, and dance created and sometimes performed *in situ* by professional artists and talented amateurs in Nazi Germany and occupied Europe, 1933–45. *In situ* means that these works were produced by the victim artists incarcerated in ghettos, transit camps, prisons, concentration camps, and hiding places. The precariousness of art and culture in the face of virulent and destructive events is clear from the comparatively large number of unsigned works; many of these works are identifiable only because diaries, memoirs, records, and other testimonies of the artists survived. Obviously, conditions that threatened human life also endangered the preservation of art, musical scores, and theater pieces. Many works fell prey to confiscations, Allied bombings, vulnerable hiding places, the artists' deaths, repeated deportations, and the inherent fragility of the materials the artists were able to acquire. We do not even know the current locations of all works that do survive; those that did not remain in the possession of the artists were, like Holocaust survivors, scattered all over the world. They have been found throughout Europe, North America, Israel, and even South America and Australia. Works were often traded for food and clothing; occasionally, they were smuggled out of the camps by fellow prisoners or members of the Resistance. Some works were extorted from the victim artists by corrupt camp guards; others were voluntarily given as gifts to relief workers and fellow prisoners. Artists also destroyed their own works because of SS surveillance and fear of discovery. It is thus impossible to reconstruct the full range of art and culture produced during the Holocaust.

Most broadly, the Holocaust can be identified as the crimes committed by Nazi Germany between 1933 and 1945. At the Nuremberg Trials after World War II, those crimes were enumerated as the crime against peace, war crimes, and crimes against humanity. The list covered people victimized because of their national origin or political affiliation or activities—the series of unprovoked attacks on Germany's neighbors; the deportation of large numbers of foreign nationals, particularly from Eastern Europe, for slave labor in German industry; and the construction of concentration camps for the confinement of political opponents at home and members of the Resistance abroad. Popular culture has, however, focused on only one aspect of the Holocaust, on the Nazi genocide of the European Jews: that is, the systematic killing of an entire group of human beings because of their heredity by means of modern, industrial, assembly-line methods for mass murder. The latest historical research does not support the conventional argument that the Jews were the only victims of Nazi genocide. True, the murder of Jews by the Nazis differed from the killing of political and foreign opponents because it was based on the genetic origins of the victims, not on their behavior. But the Jews were not the only victims selected for death on the basis of their heredity. Moreover, the art and culture of the victims came from all prisoner groups, not only from Jewish victims. I am thus defining the Holocaust as the collective designation for the mass murder of human beings because they belonged to certain biologically defined groups (Jews, Gypsies, Afro-Germans, and the handicapped) and for the related persecution of groups for their political affiliations (Communists, Socialists, Soviet prisoners of war), their national origins (Poles, Ukrainians, Czechs), their behavior (homosexuals), or their activities (members of the political resistance, Spanish republicans, Jehovah's Witnesses).

Throughout the twelve years of the Third Reich, an indomitable group of artists risked their lives to record the crimes of the regime and the agony of its victims. They have left us a body of material that, with careful study, can reveal much about the era in which it was created and about the role of culture in an epoch dominated by atrocity and destruction. Despite the availability of a substantial but fragmentary record since 1945, this culture has been dismissed by many scholars because of the mistaken belief that aesthetic considerations automatically distorted the factual accuracy of its contents, whereas most museums and cultural forums have ignored and dismissed these works as aesthetically marginal and of transient significance. Religious groups, and on occasion educators, have used these works of art and theater as appropriate decorative background for lachrymose commemorations and popular education. Few scholars have used the work of the Holocaust art and culture in their research. There are limited and incomplete biographical dictionaries that cover the enormous geographical range of Europe during World War II, and no handbooks for the elusive political and sociological details of concentration camps, ghettos, and other localities of Nazi persecution. This compounds the difficulties of charting the multiple locations and products of artistic activity.

The surviving works of art are primarily located in five institutional settings: (1) research centers on the Holocaust; (2) memorial museums located in former concentration camps; (3) museums on resistance movements and World War II; (4) Jewish successor institutions in Europe, the United States, and Israel, which include the Holocaust among their collection areas; and (5) private collections, including those held by the artists themselves.

The first category includes four central institutions: the *Centre de Documentation Juive Contemporaine* (CDJC) in Paris, the *United States Holocaust Memorial Museum* in Washington, D.C., *Yad Vashem* in Jerusalem, and the *Kibbutz Lohamei HaGhettaot* in the Galilee. These institutions hold German documents in original and on microfilm as well as survivor and liberator records, including arts works by Jewish and non-Jewish artists from the French transit camps, the ghettos of Theresienstadt, Kovno, Lódz, and Warsaw, and many concentration camps.

The second category includes collections at museums and memorials on the sites of former concentration camps in Eastern and Western Europe. These museums have research collections that include art, music, memoirs, and documents. In Poland, this includes the memorial museums at Auschwitz, Majdanek, Gross-Rosen, and Stutthof; in Germany, the memorial museums at Bergen-Belsen, Dachau, Buchenwald, Flossenbürg, Neuengamme, Papenburg (the Emsland camps), Ravensbrück, and Sachsenhausen as well as more than fifty other state and municipal memorials; in the Czech Republic, the State Jewish Museum in Prague and the Theresienstadt Memorial; and in Austria, the Mauthausen Memorial. Since the artists were repeatedly deported to multiple concentration camps, each memorial museum often holds works of art from several concentration camps. There is no centralized collection or memorial for the Vichy and northern French internment camps (including the North African transit and labor camps) and thus documentation of the active cultural life there is unusually fragmented among archives, welfare organizations, and private collections in many countries (the United States, France, Germany, Spain, Mexico, Austria). Almost all the French internment camps had a wide variety of cultural, educational, and sports programs, usually developed by the prisoners (Spanish and German refugees, members of the International Brigades, and some Roma Gypsies). There was, for example, an orchestra, a chorus, a camp library, and prisoner art exhibitions in Gurs. The reconstruction of the surviving artistic and cultural record from these camps is handicapped by the absence of any central collection about the fate of republican Spaniards and the absence of a memorial and research center for the French internment camps. The proliferation of national and local memorials and their decentralized research collections offer a multifaceted perspective on the complex subject of culture during the Holocaust, but the logistics of linking these collections is formidable.

The third category, national and regional museums and repositories specializing in the history of resistance movements during World War II, is a veritable jigsaw puzzle. Since individual resistance fighters were incarcerated in many different prisons and concentration camps, the larger institutional collections have a broad geographic spread. Thus, the Documentation Archives of the Austrian Resistance Movement in Vienna contains an extensive cultural collection of works from Gurs, Mauthausen, Flossenbürg, and Theresienstadt. The Museum of the Order of Liberation in Paris includes works from Dachau, Theresienstadt, Buchenwald, and Ravensbrück, and the regional resistance museum at Besançon that focuses on resistance in the Franche-Comté focuses on the artworks of their local resisters, including Léon Delarbre (whose art ranges from Auschwitz to Dora and Bergen-Belsen). Similar collections in Ljubljana at the Slovenian Resistance Museum emphasize work by Yugoslavs interned in German and Italian jails and concentration camps.

Museums specializing in the military history of World War II frequently include art and music from the Holocaust. Thus, the collection of the *Musée des deux Guerres Mondiales* in Paris includes numerous drawings and manuscripts by French artists in concentration camps and ghettos. Similarly, the Dutch *Instituut voor Oorlogsdocumentatie* (the Netherlands State Institute for War Documentation) in Amsterdam includes material from theater at Westerbork to works of art and theater performances from Theresienstadt.

The fourth category includes Jewish successor institutions holding Holocaust cultural works among their collections. These repositories are located in Europe, Israel, the United States, and Australia. In Europe, they include such research libraries and archives as the Wiener Library in London and the Jewish Historical Institute in Warsaw. In the United States, the YIVO Institute for Jewish Research and the Leo Baeck Institute in New York contain significant collections of Holocaust art and literature. In Israel, Moreshet and the Kibbutz Beit Theresienstadt have relevant collections.

The fifth category includes private collections, many held by survivors and their organizations. There are also individual artistic and literary estates deposited in many academies of fine arts, national libraries, and archives throughout Europe. The absence of serious scholarly interest has diminished the pressure of coherent linked data bases between these multiple depositories and museums. The newly available sources in the [former] Soviet Union have been relatively disappointing in writing the history of Nazi Germany and the Holocaust; we do not know anything about the Holocaust cultural holdings from the camps and ghettos liberated by Soviet troops in 1944–45.

Despite the plethora of available sources, there are still serious gaps about documenting the culture produced under duress in Nazi Europe. It would be impossible today to do a complete study of clandestine cabarets that existed in such diverse settings as Gurs, Buchenwald, Auschwitz, and Theresienstadt. The artistic heritage of the Holocaust is an area disturbed by neglect, the ravages of time, and the destructive effects of war. Holocaust culture is simultaneously a record of subjective reactions and one of objective observations. In extreme conditions, art and music provided a form of self-conscious discipline that occasionally ensured the survival of the individual artist or writer. It also created a bond to other prisoners, a bond reinforced by the ordeal of deportation and common experiences in the camps and ghettos. The need to articulate and document the Holocaust provides a complex legacy that is still not fully understood. Art and culture served as a psychological escape from confinement, enabling the victims to regain some control of their personal space and time. Until recently, the significance of this art has largely been ignored and dismissed as transient. Most of what we know about the survival of the human spirit in the camps and ghettos comes to us from the pictures, drawings, sculptures, music, theater, and the memories of the survivors. This heritage is at serious risk of becoming a legacy of absence, without an international research and scholarly infrastructure that focuses on the history of culture under duress in Nazi Germany and occupied Europe.

NOTES

Introduction

1. I have excerpted verse from the following poems: Emily Dickinson, "Glass was the street —," from *The Complete Poems of Emily Dickinson*, ed. Thomas H. Johnson (Boston: Little, Brown, 1960), 630; Paul Celan, "Death Fugue," trans. Michael Hamburger 1972, as reprinted in *Art from Ashes*, ed. Lawrence L. Langer (New York: Oxford University Press, 1995), 601.

2. Professor David Bloch is producer of an evolving series, The Terezín Music Anthology, sponsored by the Terezín Memorial Project. Compact discs in this series include Viktor Ullmann's *Emperor of Atlantis*, as well as songs and orchestral works by Hans Krása, including *Brundibár*. Joshua Jacobson of the Zamir Chorale of Boston has also produced (and conducted) a compact disc, *Hear Our Voices: Songs of the Ghettos and the Camps*, HaZamir HZ-909. Director Ilona Ziok's new documentary film about the cabaret master Kurt Gerron, *Kurt Gerrons Karussell* (Berlin: TV Ventures, 1999), has been issued with a music CD of cabaret songs from Theresienstadt (Warner).

3. See Hildegard Brenner, *Die Kunstpolitik des Nationalsozialismus* (Reinbeck: Rowohlt, 1963); Boguslav Drewniak, *Das Theater im NS-Staat: Szenarium deutscher Zeitgeschichte, 1933–1945* (Düsseldorf: Droste, 1983).

4. See Joseph Wulf, *Theater und Film im Dritten Reich: Eine Dokumentation* (Gütersloh: Sigbert Mohn, 1964).

5. The spate of articles in English includes Bruce H. Zortman, "Theater in Isolation: The *Jüdischer Kulturbund* in Nazi Germany," *Educational Theatre Journal* 24 (1972): 159–68; Glen W. Gadberry, "Nazi Germany's Jewish Theatre," *Theatre Survey* 21 (1980): 15–32; Alvin Goldfarb, "Theatre in Concentration Camps," *Performing Arts Journal* 1 (fall 1976): 3–11; Rebecca Rovit, "Collaboration or Survival, 1933–1938: Reassessing the Role of the *Jüdischer Kulturbund*," in *Theatre in the Third Reich, The Prewar Years: Essays on Theatre in Nazi Germany*, ed. Glen W. Gadberry (Westport, Conn.: Greenwood, 1995), 141–56; Roy Kift, "Comedy in the Holocaust: The Theresienstadt Cabaret," *New Theatre Quarterly* 12 (November 1996): 299–308; Michael Brenner, postscript to *The Renaissance of Jewish Culture in Weimar Germany* (New Haven, Conn.: Yale University Press, 1995). Finally, there is Barbara Müller-Wesemann's recent German-language study of the Hamburg Kulturbund: *Theater als geistiger Widerstand: Der Jüdischer Kulturbund in Hamburg 1934–1941* (Stuttgart: M & P Verlag, 1996).

6. See Robert Skloot, *The Theatre of the Holocaust: Four Plays* (Madison: University of Wisconsin Press, 1988). Skloot also has a new edited anthology, *The Theatre of the Holocaust*, Vol. 2: *Six Plays* (Madison: University of Wisconsin Press, 1999). See also Edward R. Isser, *Stages of Annihilation: Theatrical Representations of the Holocaust* (Cranbury, N.J.: Associated University Presses, 1997); Vivian Patraka's book, *Spectacular Suffering: Theatre, Fascism, and the Holocaust* (Bloomington: Indiana University Press, 1999); and Claude Schumacher's edited *Staging the Holocaust: The Shoah in Drama and Performance* (Cambridge: Cambridge University Press, 1998).

7. Philip Mechanicus, *Year of Fear: A Prisoner Waits for Death*, trans. Irene Gibbons (New York: Hawthorn Books, 1964), 159.

8. Zdenka Ehrlich-Fantlová, interview by Rebecca Rovit, tape-recording, 20 March 1998, London.

9. An ethnologist, Germaine Tillion, published her definitive book on the camp, *Ravensbrück* (Paris: Éditions du Seuil, 1973, 1988) in 1946. It has been reissued with new documentation twice since. She refers briefly to the operetta on pages 161–62. The term *Verfügbar* refers to those workers who were available for any kind of work at the camp.

10. Anise Postel-Vinay, interview by Rebecca Rovit, tape-recording, 28 March 1998, Paris.

11. See Dawidowicz's introduction in her edited *A Holocaust Reader* (New York: Behrman House, 1976), 9–13.

12. 1 July 1943 in Etty Hillesum, *Letters from Westerbork*, trans. Arnold J. Pomerans (New York: Pantheon, 1986), 72.

13. Dawidowicz, *A Holocaust Reader*, 10.

14. Michael Berenbaum, ed., *Witness to the Holocaust* (New York: HarperCollins, 1997).

15. Bettelheim committed suicide in 1990 at age eighty-seven.

16. See *The Terezín Diary of Gonda Redlich*, ed. Saul S. Friedman, trans. Laurence Kutler (Lexington: University Press of Kentucky, 1992), 20.

17. Ibid., 12 May 1943, 117.

18. Letter, 24 June 1907, to wife from Rainer Maria Rilke, in *Letters on Cézanne*, trans. Joel Agee (New York: Fromm International, 1985), 4.

19. Postel-Vinay, interview.

20. Lawrence L. Langer, "Cultural Resistance to Genocide," in *Admitting the Holocaust: Collected Essays* (New York: Oxford University Press, 1995), 55–63, especially 61.

21. Postel-Vinay, interview.

Hans Hinkel and German Jewry, 1933–1941 | Alan E. Steinweis

1. PG 287 [PG = Party comrade #287], in *Allgemeine Wochenzeitung der Juden in Deutschland*, 26 February 1960. This obituary will be referred to hereafter as PG 287.

2. Although after the refounding of the Nazi Party in 1925 Hinkel received a much

higher membership number, he remained quite proud of the original number 287, boasting of it whenever he could. See, e.g., the entry for Hinkel in *Das Deutsche Führerlexikon 1934/1935* (Berlin, 1934), 197.

3. See especially Volker Dahm, "Kulturelles und geistiges Leben," in *Die Juden in Deutschland 1933–1945. Leben unter nationalsozialistischer Herrschaft*, ed. Wolfgang Benz (Munich: Beck, 1989), 75–267; and Akademie der Künste, Berlin, *Geschlossene Vorstellung. Der Jüdische Kulturbund in Deutschland 1933–1941* (Berlin: Hentrich, 1992). Also see Rebecca Rovit, "Collaboration or Survival."

4. Hans Hinkel, *Einer unter Hunderttausend* (Munich, 1938), 11–12. This memoir does not specify the nature of the Hinkel family business in Worms. According to a report of his postwar interrogation by American officials, his father owned a "butcher shop and a vineyard." Washington, National Archives and Records Administration (hereafter NARA), Record Group 238, Collection of War Crimes Records, Report No SAIC/28, Seventh Army Interrogation Center, "Hans Heinrich Hinkel," 28 May 1945.

5. Hinkel, *Einer unter Hunderttausend*, 13–16.

6. Herbert Freeden, *Jüdisches Theater in Nazideutschland* (Tübingen: J. C. B. Mohr, 1964), 40–41. Reprint, Frankfurt am/Main: Ullstein, 1985.

7. Hinkel, *Einer unter Hunderttausend*, 33.

8. Ibid.

9. Willi Boelcke, ed., *Kriegspropaganda 1939–1941. Geheime Ministerkonferenzen im Reichspropagandaministerium* (Stuttgart, 1966), 86.

10. Berlin Document Center, Reichskulturkammer Collection, File of Gustav Havemann, "Auszug aus dem Tatsachenbericht," no date, attached to Seidel to Göring, 6 May 1933. The Berlin Document Center, once overseen by the American military, has now been incorporated into the German Federal Archives, Abteilung III, Zehlendorf-Berlin.

11. For example, when the Deutsche Grammophon-Gesellschaft decided to declare its loyalty to the new regime it did so in the form of a letter to Hinkel. Bundesarchiv Koblenz, R561 (Reichskulturkammer-Zentrale), file 66: Wuensch to Hinkel, 27 April 1933.

12. Comité des Delegations Juives, *Die Lage der Juden in Deutschland 1933. Das Schwarzbuch—Tatsachen und Dokumente* (Paris, 1934; repr. Frankfurt/am Main, 1983), 412–15.

13. Dahm, "Kulturelles und geistiges Leben," 108; Uwe Dietrich Adam, *Judenpolitik im Dritten Reich* (Düsseldorf, 1972), 106.

14. See Alan E. Steinweis, *The Reich Chamber of Culture and the Regulation of the Culture: Professions in Nazi Germany* (Chapel Hill: University of North Carolina Press, 1993), chap. 4.

15. *Die Tagebücher von Joseph Goebbels. Sämtliche Fragmente. Teil 1: Aufzeichnungen 1924–1941*, ed. Elke Fröhlich, 4 vols. (Munich, 1987 (hereafter referred to as *Goebbels-Tagebücher*), entry for 8 September 1935.

16. Ibid., entry for 19 September 1935.

17. Ibid., entries for 4 September 1935; 5 October 1935; 2 July 1936; 11 December 1936;

3 February 1937; 5 May 1937; 5 June 1937; 21 September 1937; 9 October 1937; 4 November 1937; 24 November 1937; 15 and 17 December 1937; 13 January 1938; 9 February 1938; 18 May 1938; 27 July 1938; and 26 January 1939.

18. Dahm, "Kulturelles und geistiges Leben," 112.

19. Ibid., 111.

20. Institut für Zeitgeschichte, Munich, *Zeugenschrift* Collection, ZS 1878, "Hans Hinkel Zeugenschrift," February 1960. It is important to consider the complexity of the Kulturbund for those involved. Without question, Hinkel's initial commitment to Singer and the Kulturbund enabled the performers substantial protection. See Michaelis interview in this section, for example. As with all collaborative endeavors, Singer and Hinkel together created the Kulturbund as it evolved. It is, however, a matter of hindsight to suggest that the Kulturbund "lulled" German Jews into a false sense of security. See the related Kulturbund materials in this section.

21. Freeden, *Jüdisches Theater in Nazideutschland,* 40. Freeden's recollection of Hinkel's polite, respectful demeanor toward Jewish officials is borne out by the surviving minutes of the *Reichsverband*'s founding meeting of April 1935. Leo Baeck Institute Archives, New York, Estate Alfred Hirschberg, Jüdischer Kulturbund AR 166: "Protokoll der Tagung der jüdischen Kulturbünde Deutschlands," 27–28 April 1935.

22. PG 287.

23. Dahm attributes the change of mind not to foreign policy considerations, but rather to Goebbels's fear that the SS-SD would seize upon the shutdown of the Reichsverband as an opportunity to expand its power over Jewish policy. Dahm's case for this interpretation, however, is circumstantial, providing no supporting documentation: Dahm, "Kulturelles und geistiges Leben," 224.

24. Hans Hinkel, ed., *Judenviertel Europas. Die Juden zwischen Ostsee und Schwarzem Meer* (Berlin, 1939).

25. Ibid., 16.

26. See the documentation in Bundesarchiv Koblenz, R58 (*Reichssicherheitshauptamt*), file 984. On the power rivalry, see Dahm, "Kulturelles und geistiges Leben," 224–25.

27. Adam, *Judenpolitik im Dritten Reich,* 258–63.

28. See the correspondence in NARA, Microfilm Publication T-175, *German Records Filmed at Alexandria, Virginia. Records of the Reich Leader of the SS and Chief of the German Police* (hereafter T-175), T-175, roll 42, frames 2553576–610.

29. T-175, roll 42, frame 2553564, Hinkel to Himmler, 16 September 1940.

30. See note 17 above.

31. Boelcke, *Kriegspropaganda 1939–1941,* 431.

32. Ibid., 492.

33. Adam, *Judenpolitik im Dritten Reich,* 256–57.

34. Lale Andersen, *Der Himmel hat viele Farben. Leben mit einem Lied* (Stuttgart, 1972), 251.

35. PG 287.

An Artistic Mission in Nazi Berlin: The Jewish Kulturbund Theater as Sanctuary | Rebecca Rovit

1. Kortner in Walter Firner's edited *Wir und das Theater: Ein Schauspielerbildbuch* (Munich: Bruckmann Verlag, 1932), 94. Both this translation and all subsequent ones from German are my own unless otherwise noted.

2. Ibid. In his preface, Firner declares: "At a time when the need for theater is sharply contested and when the future of the stage is referred to with hasty and unproductive pessimism, it seems fair to allow the actors themselves—as theater representatives—to express their personal points of view" (n.p.). Besides Kortner, such actors as Emil Jannings, Gustaf Gründgens, Conrad Veidt, Elisabeth Bergner, and Käthe Dorsch provided testimony (and self-portraits) to attest to their artistic achievements.

3. See the unpublished memoirs of Kurt Katsch, *Zurück ins Ghetto* (n.d), 191. Katsch (born Isser Katz) describes his life as an actor in Germany both before and after 1933. Leo Baeck Institute, New York, doc. ME 419.

4. See Firner, *Wir und das Theater,* 33, for Bergner's response, and 112–13 for Mosheim's words.

5. By 1938, the network of regional cultural leagues extended throughout the German Reich (including Vienna). After the *Kulturbünde* were disbanded on 11 September 1941, the enterprise continued in occupied Holland as the *Joodsche Kulturbund* at the *Schouwburg*. On 12 July 1942, the Amsterdam theater was converted to a deportation center.

6. See my "Collaboration or Survival."

7. Katsch, *Zurück ins Ghetto,* 196–97.

8. *Jüdische Rundschau,* August 1933, 405. I will refer to Berlin's Zionist newspaper hereafter as *JR.*

9. This was featured in a 1992 exhibition at Berlin's Akademie der Künste and has been reproduced in Ingrid Schmidt and Helmut Ruppel, "Eine Schwere Prüfung ist Über Sich," in *Geschlossene Vorstellung: Der Jüdische Kulturbund 1933–1941,* ed. Akademie der Künste (Berlin: Ed. Hentrich, 1992), 44–45. The catalog will be referred to hereafter as *Geschlossene Vorstellung.*

10. Bab's entry in the accompaniment to the first issue of the Kulturbund's *Monatsblätter,* 1 October 1933, part of the archives at the Akademie der Künste, is reproduced in *Geschlossene Vorstellung,* 239–40.

11. Hinkel's article, "Judenreine Theaterpolitik," appeared in the *Göttinger Tageblatt,* 18 September 1936. This is also in the Fritz Wisten Archives (FWA) 74/86/Kb 21/73.

12. Ibid. Hinkel boasts that his superiors used "clever foresight and a great sense of responsibility" in agreeing to *his* suggestion that a Jewish cultural organization be founded. This is interesting in light of Hinkel's collaborative relationship both with the theater's directors and with Nazi officials. Further research on Hinkel's role in Jewish theater affairs may highlight the complexity of his motives—whether in self-interest or in the interest of the German state—for supporting a Jewish theater. Much

of Hinkel's correspondence is accessible to researchers at the German Federal Archives, Außenstelle III, Zehlendorf-Berlin as well as at the Wiener Library, London, and the Wiener Library, Tel Aviv.

13. Ibid. As I intimated in the preceding note, the Nazis' motives for supporting the Jewish theater were not clear-cut. While the main objective in 1933 was to simply segregate the races and their cultures within Germany, by the time of the 1936 Olympics and later after the *Kristallnacht*, Nazi Germany could use the Jewish theater to show other countries how magnanimous they really were to Jews.

14. The recollection by co-founder Kurt Baumann (1977) is in Monika Richarz, ed., *Jewish Life in Germany: Memoirs from Three Centuries*, trans. S. Rosenfeld (Bloomington: Indiana University Press, 1991), 379.

15. *JR*, 25 July 1933, 365.

16. Katsch, *Zurück ins Ghetto*, 195. The actor also admits to identifying with Othello, whom he played in a 1934 Kulturbund production (198).

17. For background reading related to the German-Jewish sense of self and race theory, see Hannah Arendt, *The Origins of Totalitarianism* (New York: Harcourt, Brace, and World, 1973), Part I; Walter Zwi Bacharach, "Jews in Confrontation with Racist Antisemitism, 1879–1933," *Leo Baeck Institute Yearbook* 25 (1980): 197–219; Yehoyakim Cochavi, "Kultur und Bildungsarbeit der deutschen Juden 1933–1941: Antwort auf die Verfolgung durch das NS Regime," *Neue Sammlung* 26, no. 3 (1986): 396–407.

18. Referring to German Jews who felt more German than Jewish, Bacharach, "Jews in Confrontation with Racist Antisemitism, 1879–1933," 210, points out the "tragical element in the determination of Jews to remain impervious to the fact that *völkisch* thought and racism were . . . poised for total war against the Jew, who, in the eyes of the *völkisch* nationalists personified the anti-German."

19. Michael A. Meyer, *The German Jews: Some Perspectives on Their History*, The B. G. Rudolph Lectures in Judaic Studies (New York: Syracuse University Press, 1991), 53.

20. Fritz Stern, *Dreams and Delusions: The Drama of German History* (New York: Alfred A. Knopf, 1987), 111–12.

21. *JR*, 25 July 1933, 365. The editors were understandably cautious about a premiere performance that might provoke the German authorities.

22. Eike Geisel in his and H. M. Broder's edited *Premiere und Pogrom: Der Jüdische Kulturbund 1933–1941, Texte und Bilder* (Berlin: Siedler Verlag, 1992), 14. Accompanied by several introductory essays by the editors, this anthology features memories of surviving theater performers and members from the Kulturbund. These memories stem from filmed interviews, *Es Waren Wirlich Sternstunden*, 1988. The book will be referred to as *Premiere und Pogrom*.

23. Review of *Nathan the Wise, JR*, 4 October 1933, 624.

24. Jörg W. Gronius, "Klarheit, Leichtigkeit, und Melodie: Theater im jüdischen Kulturbund Berlin," in *Geschlossene Vorstellung*, 69, cites the disapproval of the *Israelitisches Familienblatt* (11 October 1933); the newspaper would have preferred to see the play staged as Lessing meant it to be played, with "all around embraces."

25. Kurt Singer's daughter, Margot Wachsmann-Singer, in *Premiere und Pogrom*, 196: "My father loved German culture. . . . The German Jews of the Weimar Republic were more German than Jewish. They were Germans first and thereby so connected to German culture that nothing in the world could separate them from that culture—not even the Nazis." And Leni Steinberg remembers how she recited Goethe when she was alone (*Premiere und Pogrom*, 236).

26. 5 September 1936, No. 452/53 (doc. 47/2594, Leo Baeck Institute, New York).

27. The conference took place from 5–7 September in Berlin where the speakers represented the major national branches of the centralized Kulturbund theaters. Some of their speeches are documented in the Fritz Wisten Archives, Stiftung der Akademie der Künste. To facilitate easy referral, the documents, also in *Geschlossene Vorstellung*, 266–97, are numbered from 36 to 45. For more on the conference aims, see my essay, "Collaboration or Survival," 147–48.

28. *Geschlossene Vorstellung*, doc. 38, 273–79. Rabbi Joachim Prinz labels the actor as cultural representative in his speech, "Die kulturelle situation der Juden in Deutschland und das jüdische Theater," FWA 74/86/5032. See *Das Israelitisches Familienblatt*, 10 September 1936, No. 41.

29. In *Premiere und Pogrom*, 125, Martin Brandt recalls how he was replaced by another actor for a religious role. Wisten's production of *The Golem* (1937) was reportedly beguiling in terms of its production values. Arthur Eloesser attributes to the audience an "enthusiastic acknowledgment" of the play's mysticism. See *JR*, 12 October 1937, 3.

Not everyone in the Jewish community belonged to the Kulturbund, of course. Some Jews did not like the subscription system; others preferred to frequent non-Jewish theaters (while they could). There were 17,000 members of the Kulturbund, Berlin, during 1936–37, the year Geisel reports on the Shakespearean success (*Premiere und Pogrom*, 27).

30. Freeden, in *Premiere und Pogrom*, 262.

31. Ibid., 262. My essay addresses the relationship among the Kulturbund repertory, censorship, and the political climate within Germany: "Permission Granted: The Jewish Kulturbund Theatre Repertory and Censorship," chapter in John London, ed., *Theater under the Nazis* (Manchester: Manchester University Press, 2000).

32. Ibid., 266. After the Kristallnacht pogrom, it was clear to many Jews that their situation was precarious. It is interesting to note that the Gestapo had special orders not to burn the Kulturbund theater; in fact, Hinkel ordered the theater to reopen less than two weeks after the mass action against Jewish institutions.

33. Alice Levie, in *Premiere und Pogrom*, 158.

34. Interview with the journalist, Henryk M. Broder, "Selbstbehauptung in der Sackgasse," *Die Berliner Zeitung* 27 (January 1992): 25.

35. Geisel couches his introductory statements to *Premiere und Pogrom* in critical terms, 15.

36. The first historian to document the events of the Jewish cultural association the-

ater was one of its dramaturgs and eyewitnesses, Herbert Freeden. See his *Jüdisches Theater in Nazideutschland*. Volker Dahm provides an in-depth account of the Kulturbund activities in his lengthy chapter, "Kulturelles und geistiges Leben," 75–267. In English, Glen W. Gadberry surveys "Nazi Germany's Jewish Theatre," *Theatre Survey* 21 (1980): 15–22, as does Bruce H. Zortman in "Theater in Isolation: The *Jüdische Kulturbund* of Nazi Germany," *Educational Theatre Journal* 24 (1972): 159–68. Cochavi, "Kultur und Bildungsarbeit," explores the relationship between identity and resistance, while Freeden refers to it in "Vom geistigen Widerstand der deutschen Juden: Ein Kapitel jüdischer Selbstbehauptung in den Jahren 1933 bis 1938," in *Widerstand und Exil 1933–1945*, ed. Otto R. Romberg et al. (Bonn: Bundeszentrale für politische Bildung, 1986), 47–59. Freeden reiterates his notion of a spiritual resistance among Jews vis-à-vis art in 1992: "Jüdischer Kulturbund ohne 'Jüdische' Kultur," in *Geschlossene Vorstellung*, 55–66.

37. Gronius, in *Geschlossene Vorstellung*, 94, forcefully sums up this view that journalists like Henryk Broder have also expressed.

38. The two instigators of the exhibition, Henryk M. Broder and Eike Geisel, tracked down a small group of surviving members of the Kulturbund whom they interviewed on film (*Sternstunden*, 1988). As a result of this exhibition, the Akademie der Künste now houses several archival collections pertinent to the study of the Kulturbund, including the recently acquired (postunification) personal collections of Kulturbund members.

39. See Dahm, "Kulturelles und geistiges Leben."

40. Cochavi, "Kultur und Bildungsarbeit," 400.

41. Ibid., 397. Cochavi, who emigrated from Germany to Israel, but was never directly associated with the Kulturbund, uses the parenthetical "German-Jewish" to refer to the theater.

42. Actor Martin Brandt and dramaturg Herbert Freeden, for example, in *Premiere und Pogrom*, 125 and 261, respectively.

43. Paula Lindberg-Salomon, in *Premiere und Pogrom*, 177.

44. In *Premiere und Pogrom*, 82.

45. As quoted in Miriam Niroumand, "Freiheitshauch und tödliche Illusion," *Die Berliner Zeitung*, 4–5 April 1992, 66.

46. Susanne Stein, in *Premiere und Pogrom*, 109. Stein emigrated to the United States in 1938.

47. Besides Susanne Stein, those performers interviewed in *Premiere und Pogrom* who express this view are Steffi Ronau, 150; Lena Steinberg, 236; Shabtai Petrushka, 193. This was quoted by Niroumand, "Freiheitshauch und tödliche Illusion," 66.

48. Shabtai Petrushka emigrated to Palestine in 1938 and refers to the Kulturbund as a necessary institution that engaged hundreds of Jews, allowing them to keep their "heads above water," in a financial sense. *Premiere und Pogrom*, 193.

49. Freeden, in *Premiere und Pogrom*, 266

50. Brandt, in *Premiere und Pogrom*, 126. Brandt played Saladin opposite Katsch in *Nathan the Wise* and emigrated to the United States by early 1940. He returned to Berlin in 1965, where he worked in the theater until his death in 1989.

51. *Premiere und Pogrom,* 266.

52. Freeden promotes this view throughout his writing, most recently in *Geschlossene Vorstellung,* 65–66, and *Premiere und Pogrom,* 266. The ex-performers' testimonies also corroborate Freeden's view.

53. This stems from the accompanying translation of Mahler's words to the fourth movement, "Primeval Light" [*Urlicht*] of Gustav Mahler's Symphony No. 2 in C Minor, "Resurrection." Leonard Slatkin and the Saint Louis Symphony Orchestra, Telarc CD-80082, Part Two, 1983.

"We've Enough Tsoris": Laughter at the Edge of the Abyss | Volker Kühn

Note: Kühn's references are to unpublished interviews with Camilla Spira and to documents from the Fritz-Wisten and Elow archive collections of the Akademie der Künste, Berlin. Notes compiled by translator.

Tsoris is Yiddish for "troubles, pain, concerns."

1. Friedrich Hollaender and Rudolf Nelson were part of the Berlin cabaret tradition. The name of Hollaender's club, Tingel-Tangel, means "variety theater." Kühn produced an exhibition for the Akademie der Künste, Berlin, in October 1997, "Bei uns um die Gedächtniskirche rum . . . Berlin Cabaret, Friedrich Hollaender und das Kabarett der Zwanziger Jahre."

2. Kurt Tucholsky and Erich Kästner were well-known German satirists and writers. Tucholsky, a Jew, emigrated immediately after Hitler's takeover. Kästner's work was immediately blacklisted by the Nazi government.

3. The author's reference here distinguishes between simple rhymes and the more sophisticated verse geared for cabaretgoers of a higher economic class.

4. The Herrnfeld Theater (named after two brothers) was the first Berlin theater to offer comic skits in Yiddish during the late 1890s. The touring companies from Vilnius and the Habima theater performed at this theater during the 1920s. The Kulturbund theater eventually moved into the Herrnfeld Theater on Kommandantenstraße.

5. The Berlin "N" and "W" refer to different districts of the city. Kühn uses them to suggest different populations and different kinds of humor. Residents of the city's north, for example, were typically working-class and preferred coarse humor incorporating social-criticism to the high-brow fare that appealed to intellectuals of West Berlin during the 1920s.

6. "Obwohl sich schon die Balken biegen, nehmt meine Verse gnädig hin."

7. The German play on words by Curt Bry refers to family trees and ancestry: "im Stolze manch grosser Stammbaum . . . aus gleichem Holze wie ein kleiner Baumstamm."

8. "Was nutzt, wenn man traurig ist und nicht mehr froh, denn pleite sind mer sowieso!"

9. See "Protocol" from 5 January 1940 in Part I, documents.

10. The Yiddish words *Eizes* and *Nebbich,* respectively, mean "good advice" and "so what." The German original text is as follows:

Haben Sie gehört? Ja? Wissen Sie schon?
Der Dings, der, na von dem Dings der Sohn,
Der Sänger hat kein Engagement mehr. Wie?
Was er nun macht? Ja, wissen Sie,
Der Junge ist direkt ein Genie.
Was? Er soll zum Kulturbund gehn?
Sie, danke! Mit Eizes bin ich versehn.
Versetzen Sie sich doch in seine Lage.
Da hört man: Nebbich!

11. *Gemauschel* is a German expression that Singer used to refer to the text. The word comes from an expression used in medieval Germany to refer to how Jews spoke, mumbling over their words.

12. This was Hitler's manifesto.

13. These plays are by Noel Coward and Bruno Frank.

14. Mascha Kaléko was a successful East European lyric poet living in Berlin during this time. See interview with Benya-Matz.

15. The German text is as follows:

Wir sausen mit tausend PS dahin,
Wir können es nicht mehr lassen.
Wir sitzen im Turm vom Babel drin
Und können uns nur noch hassen.
Wir haben das Licht elektrisch gemacht
Und können uns trotzdem nicht sehen.
Wir haben ein Esperanto erdacht
Und werden uns niemals verstehen.
Die Welt ist weit geworden
So furchtbar weit geworden
Und alle Hoffnungen sind Trämerein.
Du bist gescheit geworden und bist bereit geworden
Auf dieser Welt nur Spreu zu sein. . . .

16. *Ehrlich* is the German word for "honest"; the newspaper reviewer puns using a German proverb on honesty.

17. "Immer langsam, immer langsam, immer mit Gemütlichkeit / es ist noch nicht soweit, wir haben noch lange Zeit. . . ."

18. "Kalau" is a make-believe place which in this context refers to a stale joke that makes you groan, "an old chestnut," or "Kalauer."

19. Julius Bab was a writer and drama critic who became the Kulturbund's first dramaturg. He eventually emigrated to the United States. See his letters to Fritz Wisten in Part I, documents.

20. The reference in German uses a hunting term, "zum Halili blasen," which is when hunters blow their horns to signal that an animal is dead.

21. "Wenn man kein Glück hat, dann hat das Leben keinen Sinn; wenn man kein

Glück hat, dann rutscht man aus und fällt man hin / drum bitt ich dich, Fortuna, bleib mir treu. . . ."

22. *Pojaz* is the sad clown. The German text reads as follows:

> Überall gibt's immer einen, über den man lacht,
> Überall gibt's immer einen, der die Witze macht.
> Einer ist dazu bestimmt, den Narren abzugeben,
> Das fängt in der Schule an, und bleibt das ganze Leben.
> Einer muß als ewiger Clown durch das Dasein wandern,
> Ach, die Menschen lachen gern — auf Kosten eines andern:
> Überall gibt's immer einen, über den man lacht,
> Überall gibt's immer einen, der für euch — den Pojaz macht.

Interview with Mascha Benya-Matz | Rebecca Rovit

1. From *Musar* [ethics]. This movement emphasized piety and stressed the goodness in people and in human relationships.

2. This was Berlin's Zionist newspaper, edited by Robert Weltsch.

3. Kaléko was a well known lyric poet of the times, whose husband had compiled a Hebrew grammar. Mascha Kaléko left her husband for Chaim Vinaver, with whom she emigrated to New York. Their emigration was sponsored by the Warburg family.

4. Landau's lectures were particularly popular with Kulturbund audiences, in part because she used singers and instrumentalists like Benya-Matz to accompany her many lectures. During the 1937–38 season, 40 percent of all lecture evenings in Berlin alone were given by Landau. Each of her lectures on music was repeated up to four times. And often three thousand listeners attended her lectures. See Matthias Harder, "Messianische Erziehung?", in *Geschlossene Vorstellung*, 132.

5. *Ostjude* is an East European Jew. The German Jews distinguished between themselves and the East European immigrants who settled in Germany.

6. The production of Donizetti's opera took place in May 1937; the Adam production was in February 1938.

7. Benjamino Gigli.

8. This was in March 1936, after the Germans remilitarized the left bank of the Rhine River, which bordered France at the time.

9. These unorganized controls of Hitler supporters on German city streets preceded government-organized roundups of citizens by SA and SS men.

10. The former Kulturbund actor Bert Bernd originally said this in a joint interview with Madam Benya-Matz by Eike Geisel for a film, *Es Waren wirklich Sternstunden* (Berlin SFB, 1988). Geisel and H. Broder edited the film transcripts, which were published in *Premiere und Pogrom*.

11. This is Yiddish for "temple."

12. A side dish that is a sweet mixture of vegetables and fruit; noodle pudding.

Interview with Kurt Michaelis | Rebecca Rovit

1. This reference is to the Nazi law that forced all Jews in Germany to adopt the middle names "Israel" and "Sara" after 1 January 1939.

"Protocols," Nazi Propaganda Ministry

1. This play, *The Pastry Chef's Wife,* was written by the Hungarian Jew, Ferenc Molnár. The light comedy, set in Budapest, features a pastry chef who believes his wife is having an affair with a customer. The play's characters represent typical people who are not ostensibly Jewish and could be in Vienna or Berlin. The play had already been cast before word came that it was to be banned. See FWA 74/86/5080, 1, for original cast list.

2. This play was never performed. It is a farce set in the Middle East in a sultan's palace. The playscript is part of the Fritz Wisten Archives.

3. The implication is that the Jewish communities in these cities must oversee the production costs.

4. *Winterhilfe* refers to special performances held to generate extra funds for the winter months' "Winter Relief."

5. Leo Kreindler was in charge of the Kulturbund's publishing department.

6. The comedy was written by Molière.

7. Cläre Arnstein was a cabaret songstress. See Kühn's essay in this section.

8. Pollack is to be hired for the Cologne branch of the Kulturbund [Rhein-Ruhr]. At the time of this meeting with Kochanowski, all Kulturbund business was bureaucratically managed in Berlin.

9. Martin Brasch was an assistant judge and an important member of the Kulturbund board of managers.

10. This modern Italian comedy by Aldo de Benedetti was performed in March 1941.

11. This Spanish comedy by Jacinto Benavente was featured during November and December 1940.

12. Oscar Wilde was Irish. And Ireland was neutral during World War II.

13. The Reich's national organization of Jews in Germany had central headquarters in Berlin.

Letter from Actor Kurt Suessmann to Martin Brandt

1. Martin Brandt emigrated with his mother to the United States.

2. The Europeia appears to be a shipping agency.

3. Sea passage via southern Europe would be impossible if the waterways were closed.

4. "Over there" refers to the United States.

5. This reference is to Goeteborg, Sweden.

6. The "HV" refers to the Jewish help organization, the *Hilfsverein,* which helped

secure ship passage for those whose quota number came up, had money, had an overseas sponsor, and had papers that were in order.

7. The play in repertory was Aldo de Benedetti's *Thirty Seconds of Love.*

Letter from Fritz Wisten to Max Ehrlich

1. Dr. L. refers to Dr. Werner Levie, who had been a managing director at the Berlin Kulturbund before his departure for Holland (his birthplace). The references to Levie's "ambiguous" character suggest his collaboration with Nazi authorities, particularly in Holland. In the summer of 1941, Levie sought to interest the Amsterdam authorities in creating a cultural organization like Berlin's Kulturbund. While this may have seemed like a magnanimous move, evidence suggests that Levie's self-interest motivated him more than his desire to create a new artistic endeavor in a new country. Ehrlich and Levie were co-administrators of the new organization; there was apparently a great deal of tension between them.

In spite of his collaboration with the Nazis, Werner Levie was dispensable: His deportations ended at the Bergen-Belsen concentration camp. He died of typhus shortly after the camp was liberated.

2. This is the abbreviated term used for the Kulturbund.

3. This refers to the Jewish New Year, which takes place each autumn.

4. These long-standing performers of the Kulturbund perished before the war's end. They were Hans Lipschitz, Emil Berisch, and Ernst Raden.

5. This was a very well known and popular book written by a Berliner Jew, Georg Hermann, about an assimilated German-Jewish family in Berlin during the 1840s. It was adapted for the Kulturbund stage and performed to great acclaim in July 1935. The play centers on the girl, Jettchen, her love for a Christian, and her eventual suicide because of her love.

Theatrical Activities in the Polish Ghettos during the Years 1939–1942 | Moshe Fass

Abbreviations

Note: Various authors use slightly different transliterations from Yiddish. We do not change the authors' original writing.

AG   *Azoy iz es Geveyn* [*That Is How It Was*], by Yonas Turkow [also transliterated as Turkov] (Buenos Aires, 1962).

FS   *Farloshene Shtern* [*Extinguished Stars*], by Yonas Turkow (Buenos Aires, 1953), vol. 1.

GG   *Geshtaltn un Gesheenishn* [*Personalities and Happenings*], by Yeshaya Trunk (Buenos Aires, 1962).

GZ   *Gazeta-Zydowska*

KG   *Ksovim fun Ghetto* [*Writings from within the Ghetto—A Diary from the Warsaw Ghetto*], by Emanuel Ringelblum (Warsaw, 1961–63), vol. 1.

TG   *Yidish Teater in Poilen* [*Yiddish Theater in Poland*] by Tschak Turkow-Grudberg (Warsaw, 1951).

1. The order was announced in *Verordungsblatt des General-Gouveneurs für die Besetzten Polnischen Gebiete* (Cracow), 9 (28 November 1939), 72.

2. KG, 47; TG, 111, about Warsaw. About Lódz, see ibid., 123. Also see FS, 23. For the testimony of the actress Dara Rubina about Vilna, see *Yad-Vashem Archives*, 11/M-134; AG, 195–96; for Lódz, cf. TG, 123, 125, and FS, 57.

3. David Flormann, "Warsaw's House Committees" (Hebrew), *Yediot Beit Lohamei ha-Getaot* 16–17 (1956): 32; Peretz Apatshinsky, "The Tragedy of a House Committee" (Yiddish), *Bleter far Geshikhte* 14 (1961): 173.

4. AG, 198. For a parallel illustration from the Lódz ghetto, see Mosheh [also Moische] Pulaver, *Geveyn iz a Ghetto* [*Once There Was a Ghetto*] (Tel-Aviv, 1963), 60.

5. AG, 200–201.

6. Ibid., 61–62. Also see Michael Weichert, *Yidishe Alaynhilf* [*Jewish Self-Help*, 1939–1945] (Tel-Aviv, 1962); AG, 232; GZ, 40 (6 December 1940); Yaakov Kurtz, *Sefer Edut* [*Testimony Book*] (Tel-Aviv, 1944), 129–30.

7. AG, 130. He points out that there were more than thirty nightclubs on Leszno Street alone (ibid., 198). It should also be noted that the names of the nightclubs lend some insight into their nature; see KG, 215.

8. Ibid., 200. See also Miriam Berg, *Ghetto Varsha* [*Ghetto Warsaw*] (Tel-Aviv, 1946), 31; GG, 194 for Lódz.

9. *GZ*, 50 (24 June 1941), 2.

10. Yaakov Tselemensky, *Mitn Farshnitenem Folk* [*With the Slaughtered People*] (New York, 1963), 73–74.

11. KG, 327. By the end of the ghetto period there were already hundreds of such clubs in existence (ibid., 332).

12. Menahem Linder, "The Situation in Warsaw Ghetto" (Hebrew), *Dror* 13–14, published in *Yediot Beit Lohamei ha-Getaot* 18–19 (1957), 9. For a literary description, see Yitshak Katzenelson, *Ketavim Aharonim* (*Last Writings*) (Merhavia, 1956), the poem, "Ha-Mishteteh" ("The Banquet"), 26.

13. Herman Kruk, *Togbukh fun Vilner Ghetto* [*A Diary from the Vilna Ghetto*] (New York, 1961), 221. A forthcoming English translation will be published by Yale University Press.

14. *Radom-Sefer Zikaron* [*Radom-Memorial Book*], ed. Irgunei Yotsei Radom be-Yisrael (Tel-Aviv, 1961), 234.

15. *Dertsiungs Entsiklopedie* [*Educational Encyclopedia*] (New York, 1957), s.v. "Oysrotung un Bashitsung fun Yidishe Kinder" ["Rescue and Protection of Jewish Chil-

dren"], 83; Noach Gross, *Kinder Martirologie* [*Children's Martyrology*] (Buenos Aires, 1947), 34. ["Joint" refers to the American Joint Distribution Committee, a private relief organization.]

16. "The Murdered Teachers of CIZO Schools in Poland" (Yiddish), *Lerer Yizkor Bukh* [*Teachers' Memorial Book*], ed. C. S. Kasdan (New York, 1952), 561.

17. *GZ,* 38 (29 November 1940), 2, writes of the agreement of the German authorities to the opening of an unnamed theater and, in 42 (13 December 1940), 11, we see an advertisement for a new theater, the Eldorado. Also see Leib Speizman, *Di Yidn in Nazi-Poilen* [*The Jews in Nazi-Poland*] (New York, 1942), 339; TG, 126; AG, 206–7; FS, 25; Bernard Goldstein, *Finf Yor Varshever Ghetto* [*Five Years in Warsaw Ghetto*] (New York, 1947), 112; Abraham Ayzenbach, "Scientific Research in Warsaw Ghetto" (Yiddish), *Bleter far Geshikhte* 1, no. 1 (1949): 108. Ringelblum, in his diary for 12 December 1940, mentions his visit to this theater, KG, 196. According to *GZ,* 36 (10 May 1941), 6, the Nowy Azazel was opened on 6 May 1941. Also see FS, 285–87, 59, 24; Berg, *Ghetto Varsha,* 49; Speizman, *Di Yidn in Nazi-Poilen,* 339. According to *GZ,* 37 (14 May 1941) 8, the Na-Piaterku opened on 9 May 1941. Also see Speizman, *Di Yidn in Nazi-Poilen,* 340. According to *GZ,* 50 (24 June 1941) 2, rehearsals were held on 24 June and the premiere was on 17 July 1941; cf. *GZ,* 59 (16 July 1941), 3. Also see Berg, *Ghetto Varsha,* 49; Emanuel Ringelblum, "The Murder of the Stage Actors" (Yiddish), *Bleter far Geshikhte* 12 (1959): 27; Speizman, *Di Yidn in Nazi-Poilen,* 339. According to *GZ,* 59, the Femina opened on 4 July 1941 with nine hundred seats, the largest in Warsaw ghetto. Also see Berg, *Ghetto Varsha,* 49–50.

18. Zvi Shner, "Cultural Activities in the Lódz Ghetto during the Years 1940–1941" (Hebrew), *Beit Lohamei ha-Gataot-Dapim le-Heker ha-Shoah ve-ha-Meved* 1 (1957): 93, mentions 24 October. See GG, 232; FS, II, 46; Wolf A. Yasni, *Di Geshikhte fun Yidn in Lódz* [*The History of the Jews in Lódz*] (Tel-Aviv, 1960), 347–48; Pulaver, *Geveyn iz a Ghetto,* 42–43; Yeshaya Trunk, "Study of the History of the Jews in Warteland" (Hebrew), *Bleter far Geshikhte,* 2 (1949): 127. The premiere took place 16 January 1942. See Kruk, *Togbukh fun Viler Ghetto,* 136; Dworzhetsky, [The original Fass essay does not include the title of the book.], 231; TG, 129; GG, 207; Avraham Sutskever, *Ghetto Vilna* [*Vilna Ghetto*] (Tel-Aviv, 1947), 88; Israel Segal, "The First Concert in Vilna Ghetto" (Yiddish), *Fun Letsten Hurban* 1 (1946): 13; Kruk, *Togbukh fun Vilner Ghetto,* 570–71; Dworzhetsky, 234.

19. *Radom-Sefer Zikaron,* 235. The theater was established in May 1941; see *Dos Yidish Radom in Hurves, Andek Bukh* [*Jewish Radom in Ruins, A Memorial Book*] (Stuttgart, 1948), 207–8. A third performance was held; see ibid. and TG, 128; Brener [There is no source in the original.], 52–56; Binyamin Orenstein, *Der Umkum un Vidershtand fun a Yidisher Shtot* [*The Destruction and Resistance of a Jewish City*] (Montreal, 1949), 12; Tselemensky, *Mitn Farshnitenem Folk,* 101; Binyamin Orenstein, *Hurbn Otwock, Palenits, Karshev* [*The Destruction of Otwock, Palenits, Karshev*] (American District, Germany, 1948), 17; FS, 293. In *Dos Yidish Radom in Hurves,* 208, it is mentioned that the texts of the show were sent from Radom to Krakow, but nothing else is said about it. See Trunk, "Study of the History of the Jews in Warteland," 127.

20. Weichert, *Yidishe Alaynhilf,* 322; Tselemensky, *Mitn Farshnitenem Folk,* 101; Leyb Gerfunkel, *Kovna ha-Yehudit be-Hurbanah* [*Jewish Kovno in Destruction*] (Jerusalem, 1959), 259.

21. The date of the establishment of the shows in the orphanage is unknown; see TG, 127; GZ, 43 (30 May 1941), 3; GG, 196–97; Speizman, *Di Yidn in Nazi-Poilen,* 340. The Warsaw puppet theater was already mentioned in May 1941. The name of the Polish theater was Boritino. CENTOS even organized a special course for the teachers at the "food corners" on how to stage puppet shows (see Gross, *Kinder Martirologie,* 43), but the date of the establishment of their theaters remains unknown; see GG, 196–97. The first performance of the Vilna puppet theater was in April 1942; see Kruk, *Togbukh fun Vilner Ghetto,* 246. The first performance of the Had-Gadya troupe was in December 1940 according to an advertisement preserved in the Yad Vashem archives, J. M. 1163. Also see GG, 236, who, in another place, gives a date of 1941, with a question mark. See Yeshaya Trunk, *Lodzer-Ghetto* [*Lódz Ghetto*] (New York, 1962), 398; Liber Brenner, *Vidershtand un Umkum in Czestochover Ghetto* [*Rebellion and Destruction of Czestochowa Ghetto*] (Warsaw, 1951), 57.

22. "For a theater in the Polish language you can receive any concession you would like, but for the Yiddish theater you can't. Only Miss Yehudit holds a concession for the Yiddish theater and she will allow no competition" (AG, 208).

23. Published in *GZ,* 19 (7 March 1941), 2.

24. KG, 141.

25. Ringelblum writes, "The reason for giving performances in Polish is the large number of converts and assimilated elements. Secondly, there are converted actors from the Polish stage" (KG, 283, August 1941). Also see FS, 53; AG, 212–13.

26. AG, 213. The differences between the Polish and Yiddish theaters were great, and Ringelblum, in an outline he prepared on the theater, differentiated between them; KG, 299–300.

27. The Eldorado presented the "Song of Songs" and afterwards, the "Village of Youth" which became a major cultural event in the Warsaw ghetto; FS, 88; AG, 214; TG, 127. The Nowy Azazel also showed an improvement in its last two performances. *Susati* [*My Horse*] by Mendele Mocher Sforim, and *Shmattes* by Leivick, as well as the *Dybbuk* by Anski.

28. The change in atmosphere can be seen in the following two examples: In August 1941, Ringelblum writes in his diary, "A famous Polish actress wrote a letter to a Jewish friend about the fact that the Polish language is not tolerated in the Yiddish theater; generally, Polish is looked down upon in the ghetto" (KG, 291). Nine months later, in May 1942, Ringelblum notes in connection with Turkow's leaving the Yiddish theater, "It shows the great assimilative power of the ghetto. The public speaks fine Polish. Yiddish is very seldom heard in the streets" (ibid., 371). The movement toward "Polonization" produced heated debate among the people of the ghetto; see Yosef Kermish, *Yediot Yad Vashem* 10–11 (1956): 9.

29. There were plans to form a theater to perform selected plays, AG, 213; FS, 30, 60. A drama studio in Hebrew and Yiddish was founded by the youth movements and by the Hebrew cultural organization, Tekumah; see Speizman, *Di Yidn in Nazi-Poilen*, 340; Blatberg [There is no source in the original.], 421; Nathan Eck, "The Last Days of Warsaw" (Hebrew), *Mishmar*, 2 November 1945, 6. The dramatic group of "Dror" was famous for its biblical shows; *Sefer Dror* [*The Book of Dror*] (Tel-Aviv, 1947), 463. Also see "Within the Walls of Warsaw" (Hebrew), *Mi-Yomanei Halutsim ba Mahteret* [*Diaries of the Pioneers in the Underground*] (En-Harod, 1944), 25; Nathan Eck, *Ha-To'im be-Darkhei Mavet* [*Wanderers in the Pathways of Death*] (Jerusalem, 1960), 201; Rachel Urbach, *Be-Hutsot Varshah* [*In the Streets of Warsaw*] (Tel-Aviv, 1954), 145. To this period we may also assign the directors' attempts to perform such plays by famous non-Jewish authors as Molière's *L'avare*. By changing the name of the author or the title of the play the Jews could deceive the Germans and circumvent the law that prohibited them from performing plays by Aryan authors; AG, 213–14; TG, 127.

30. *GZ*, 50 (24 June 1941), 3. The theater was founded in order to perform serious works by Jewish authors in Polish. An announcement of the performance appears in *GZ*, 59 (16 July 1941). Also see AG, 210; Goldstein, *Finf Yor Varshever Ghetto*, 113. Ringelbum writes about this as follows, "Of the four theaters it is worthwhile to mention Mark Orenstein's production of *Mirele Efros* in Polish" (KG, 283).

31. There were altogether 3,500 to 4,000 seats in the ghetto theaters. Thus, at the rate of one performance (at 5:30 P.M.) six days a week and two on Sunday, some 30,000 people out of half a million could attend the theater weekly.

32. FS, 25.

33. In Lódz, where programs had to pass the stiff censorship of Rumkowski, only revues were allowed; see Pulaver, *Geveyn iz a Ghetto*, 60. Because of the special conditions in the Lódz ghetto and the character of the theater organizers (all of whom were veteran actors and directors), the theater soon came to odds with Rumkowski. His attitude made it impossible for entire plays to be performed; instead, only sketches and poems by Jewish poets were put on; see Yasni, *Di Geshikhte fun Yidn in Lódz*, 347. According to Yasni, Rumkowski tried to prevail upon the theater to add complimentary comments in his favor but the actors refused to comply, even at the risk of seeing the theater closed. On the other hand, the actors tried to refrain from all political criticism in order to avoid giving Rumkowski an excuse to close the theater; ibid., 351; Pulaver, *Geveyn iz a Ghetto*, 45–48. Even this could not prevent the theater from having clashes with Rumkowski. When the sketch *Patsifisten* [*Pacifists*] was performed with the actors mounting the stage with red lights upon them and hammers in their hands, Rumkowski sprang to his feet and began to yell in a fury, "Where have you brought me, Revolutionaries? Stop!" (Yasni, *Di Geshikhte fun Yidn in Lódz*, 350). In a similar incident, when "Ghetto Vig Lied" ["Ghetto Lullaby"], which described the suffering in the ghetto, was sung, Rumkowski wanted to prevent the theater group from performing together; ibid., 351; Shner, "Cultural Activities," 97. There is one case when the Germans closed down

a revue called *Svert Zayn Besser* [*Things Will Be Better*]; TG, 124. The theater also performed excerpts from the repertory of the Ararat theater group (a prewar theater), one of whose directors had been Pulaver; Yasni, *Di Geshikhte fun Yidn in Lódz*, 348; GG, 235. After Rumkowski assumed full control of all performances, he demanded that the accent be placed on Jewish tradition and folklore, on Jewish music and cantorial pieces; Shner, "Cultural Activities," 97. Shner also cites a letter by Halperin, the first head of the *Kultur Hoys*, complaining that he was fired from his job on the excuse that he was turning his back on the Jewish heritage; ibid. In Vilna, too, shows at first included classical Jewish pieces because the audience could not bring itself to enjoy light entertainment right after the German roundups. For that reason the early performances often had the character of memorial meetings. Only later did the Vilna theater groups turn to satires of life in the ghetto; see Appendix 2. The picture of the nature and contents of performances in the other ghettos is not clear. In Czestochowa it is known that the "classics" and bits of "local color" were performed; TG, 128: Brener [There is no source in the original.], 54. In Radom we know of a play, *Abi Vayter* [*Onwards, Above All*]. From its title we can tell that it was comprised of current happenings in the ghetto; *Radom—Sefer Zikaron*, 234; *Dos Yiddish Radom in Hurves*, 207–8.

34. The collection of laws enacted against the Jews by the Germans can be found in Bruno Blau, *Das Ausnahmerecht für die Juden in Deutschland 1933–1945* [*Laws Banning Jews in Germany 1933–1945*] (New York, 1952). The law connected with the establishment of the "Government Cultural Office" served as a basis for removing Jews from literary, musical, artistic, and theatrical activities by making their licenses depend on the General Occupations Offices which the Jews could not use until the Kulturbund was organized; ibid., 32, 24. "Anordnung des Präsidenten der Reichskulturkammer über den Reichsverband des Jüdischen Kultur Bundes (*sic*) ["Order by the President of the RKK on the Reich Association of the Jewish Cultural League"]: (von 6.8.35, *Völkischer Beobachter* von 7.8.35)." The order established a national organization of Jewish cultural organizations that was to supervise all non-Aryans who were engaged in intellectual and cultural activities within the country. "Für die Überwachung der im deutschen Reichsgebiet geistig und kulturell tätigen Nichtarier" ['The Supervision of Non-Aryans Active in the Cultural Field in the Territories of the Third Reich']; ibid., 72, 29. "Anordnung des Präsidenten der Reichskulturkammer über die Teilnahme von Juden an öffentlichen Veranstaltungen" ['The Regulations of the Office for Cultural Affairs of the Third Reich on the Participation of the Jews in Official Bodies']; ibid., 189. Actually, the laws were not published all at once but gradually, and came out as supplements to previous German laws. For example, the Nuremberg Laws (published 9 September 1935) were included in a special order published in the *Reichgesetzblatt*, I, 297, for the area annexed to the Reich. Another example is the law of citizenship of the Reich, "Elfte Verordnung zum Reichbürgergesetz von 25.11.41": "Die Verordnung gibt auch im Protektorat Böhmen und Mähren und in den eingegliederten Ostgebieten" ["The Regulation is also in effect in the Bohemian and Moravian Protectorates and the Integrated Eastern Territories"]. A list of these laws can be found in Trunk, "Study of the History of the Jews in Warteland," 71–75.

35. The law was published in *Verordnungsblatt,* No. 21 (8.3.40). *GZ,* 15 (9 September 1940), 6, stated that the general law also applied to the Jews. The same held true for scientific activities and language instruction by correspondence. Permission for those activities had to be obtained from the Propaganda-Amt [Department of Propaganda]. The publication of the law's applicability to the Jews was in *GZ,* 38 (16 May 1941). The only national law in which specific mention was made of the Jews is the one pertaining to gambling establishments and amusement areas of the General Gouvernement: "Juden ist das Betreten der Spielbanken des General Governments untersagt" ["Jews are forbidden to enter gambling establishments"]. In orders connected with cultural activities published by the General Gouvernement in *Verordnungsblatt des G.G.* (23 September 1940), 471, i.e., the censorship of publications, newspapers, and book distribution, there is no specific paragraph referring to Jews.

36. It was published twice in *GZ,* 43 (12 December 1940) and 46 (27 December 1940), 2.

37. The license for the establishment of the theater in Vilna was granted by Maurer, the German ruler of the ghetto.

38. Trugovov, "A Theatrical School in the Vilna Ghetto" (Hebrew), *Ha-Galgal* 5, no. 1 (1947): 8; Dworzhetsky, *Bein ha-Betarim* [*Between the Corpses*] (Jerusalem, 1956), 65; Mosheh Gelblum, *Geza Karut* [*A Severed Trunk*] (Tel-Aviv, 1946–47), 43.

39. Kruk, *Togbukh fun Vilner Ghetto,* 487, entry of March 1943, written a year after the establishment of the ghetto.

40. KG, 196.

41. The order was published originally in the *Verordnungsblatt* (8 March 1940) and *GZ* (10 September 1940) as a statewide order dealing with the Polish theater. An amendment was published to the effect that the order also applied to the Jews. Turkow tells how the Jews managed to circumvent German censorship by performing Aryan plays under changed names; AG, 213. It was previously mentioned that cultural activities in the ghetto were controlled by local orders of Nazi rulers of the areas and not by a statewide directive.

42. Only in August 1940 did Hans Frank, the Polish governor, publish an order applying to the Jewish educational institutions and this is, as far as we know, the only countrywide order issued about Jewish cultural activities; *Verordnungsblatt* (31 August 1940).

43. AG, 237–38. Turkow notes that Czerniakow, the head of the Judenrat in Warsaw, claimed "that he will not agree to a state within a state and that it is not possible that there should be two parallel institutions in the ghetto." But he himself was ready to accept members of ZAK as members of the Judenrat.

44. Trunk, *Lodzer Ghetto,* 395; Shner, "Cultural Activities," 90–96; GG, 233; Yasni, *Di Geshikhte fun Yidn in Lódz,* 353.

45. Brener [There is no source in the original.], 56.

46. Segal, "The First Concert," 12; *Yad Vashem,* JM/1199, Document 342, list of institutions belonging to the Judenrat.

47. The first mention of its activities is found in Ringelblum's diary for 5 January

1941, KG, 211: "Ganzweich, people said, is forming a cultural organization with Stupnitsky and Katznelson." He later mentions that Ganzweich organized the Hanukkah ceremonies (322). Also see Mark Ber, *Di Umgekumene Schrayber in Ghettos un Lagerin* [*The Murdered Writers of the Ghettos and Concentration Camps and Their Writings*] (Warsaw, 1954), 42–43; Avraham Rozenberg, "The Thirteen" (Yiddish), *Bleter far Geshikhte* 5, no. 3 (1952): 118; AG, 208, 358; Kurtz, *Sefer Edut*, 158, Abraham Levin, "From a Ghetto Diary" (Yiddish), *Bleter far Geshikhte* 5, no. 4 (1952): 46. It is probable that Ganzweich's fondness for culture stems from the fact that he was a journalist in Lódz and, before that, a literary editor in Vilna according to information from the underground preserved in the JGI archives; see *Bleter far Geshikhte* 5, no. 3 (1952): 143. When Ganzweich's father died, obituary notices were posted by the literary and artistic circles of Warsaw; GZ, 25 (29 March 1941). Another fact that Ringelblum felt worth mentioning is that Ganzweich's partner was Shubert, the head of the Propaganda-Amt and the man responsible for cultural activities in Warsaw; KG, 222.

48. Rozenberg, "The Thirteen," 211, 215; AG, 208; KG, 294.

49. Berg, *Ghetto Varsha*, 99.

50. Ibid.

51. Because of the many missing details in *GZ*, the exact dates of performances are not known, but the titles of the plays were collected from the bibliography of this article.

52. A notorious underworld figure of that time.

53. AG, 210; TG, 126.

54. Ibid.; Berg, *Ghetto Varsha*, 49–50.

55. Ibid. This source also references *Rags, Mary Duggen*, and *A Kiss before the Mirror*.

56. Mark Dworzhetsky, *Yerushalayim de-Litah be-Meri u-va-Shoa* [The Jerusalem of Lithuania during the Revolt and the Holocaust], [Full publication information not in original.], 231; Avraham Sutskever, *Ghetto Vilna*, 88.

57. Ibid.; TG, 129.

58. Ibid.; *Yad Vashem*, 1 M 1199, Doc. No. 408.

59. Kruk, *Togbukh fun Vilner Ghetto*, 770.

Theatrical Activities in the Nazi Concentration Camps | Alvin Goldfarb

1. Yonas Turkov, "Teater un Konsertn in di Getos un Kontsentratsye Lagern" ['Theater and Concerts in the Ghettos and Concentration Camps'], in *Yidisher Teater in Yirope . . . Poylen* [also transliterated as *Poilen*] [*Yiddish Theater in Europe . . . Poland*] (New York: Knight, 1968), 500–501. All translations from the Yiddish are my own. Transliterations have been prepared in accordance with the table found in Uriel Weinreich's *Modern English-Yiddish, Yiddish-English Dictionary* (New York: McGraw-Hill, 1968).

2. Nico Rost, *Goethe in Dachau: Literatur und Wirklichkeit* (Germany: Verlag und Welt, 1948), 57–58, 71, 79, 180–81.

3. Turkov, "Teater un Konsertn," 501.

4. "Canada" was a desirable work detail responsible for sorting prisoners' personal effects. Turkov, "Teater un Konsertn," 502.

5. Ibid., 502–3.

6. Kitty Hart, *I Am Alive* (London: Abelard Schuman, 1961), 72.

7. Mark Dvorzhetski, *Jewish Camps in Estonia: 1942–1944* (Jerusalem, 1970), see the chapter entitled "Cultural Life." In Hebrew with an English abstract.

8. Turkov, "Teater un Konsertn," 511.

9. Ibid., 505–6.

10. Denise Dufournier, *Ravensbrück: The Women's Death Camp*, trans. F. W. McPherson (London: George Allen & Unwin, 1948), 29.

11. Corrie ten Boom, *A Prisoner and Yet . . .* (Toronto: Evangelical Publishers, 1947), 66.

12. Micheline Maurel, *An Ordinary Camp*, trans. Margaret S. Summers (New York: Simon and Schuster, 1958), 75–76. [Fanny Marette wrote her own memoir, *I Was Number 47177*, trans. Robert Laffont (Geneva: Ferni, 1970).]

13. "Belsen," in *Belsen* (Tel Aviv: Irgun Sheerit Hapleita Me'Haezor Habriti, 1957), 135–36.

14. Judith S. Newman, *In the Hell of Auschwitz* (New York: Exposition, 1963), 57–58; and R. J. Minney, *I Shall Fear No Evil: The Story of Dr. Alina Breuda* (London: William Kimber, 1966), 93–94. [Fania Fénelon writes about her extra privileges as a singer in the SS-supported Birkenau orchestra. See her memoir, *Playing for Time*, trans. Judith Landry (New York: Atheneum, 1977; repr. New York: Syracuse University Press, 1997).]

15. Gisella Perl, *I Was a Doctor in Auschwitz* (New York: International University Press, 1948), 102.

16. Curt Daniel, " 'The Freest Theater in the Reich': In the German Concentration Camps," *Theatre Arts* 25 (November 1941): 804–5.

17. David Wolff, "Drama behind Barbed Wire," *Theatre Arts Committee Magazine* 1 (March 1939): 15.

18. Arthur Koestler, *The Scum of the Earth* (New York: Macmillan, 1941), 134–37.

19. Horst Jarka, ed. and trans., *The Legacy of Jura Soyfer, 1912–1939* (Montreal: Engendra, 1977), 346–50. Soyfer also authored the lyrics to the well-known Dachau *lied.* The lyrics and music to this camp song can be found in ibid., 351–54.

20. Bruno Heilig, *Men Crucified* (London: Eyre and Spottinwoode, 1941), 121.

21. Victor Frankl, *Man's Search for Meaning: An Introduction to Logotherapy* (Boston: Beacon, 1963), 40.

22. Bruce H. Zortman, "Theater in Isolation: The Jüdischer Kulturbund of Nazi Germany," *Educational Theatre Journal* 24 (1972): 159. [Zortman's footnote refers to Adler, *Theresienstadt 1941–1945. Das Antlitz einer Zwangsgemeinschaft* (Tübingen: J. C. B. Mohr, 1960), 590, but Adler refers to Spanier's Molnár staging, among other cultural events, on pages 596–97. See Kühn, Part I, and Hillesum, Part II, for more on Ehrlich and Rosen.] A 1975 Israeli documentary, *The 81st Blow*, which uses captured

German footage to illustrate Jewish oppression under the Third Reich, contains a few filmed moments of cabaret performances in Westerbork.

23. Turkov, "Teater un Konsertn," 510–11.

24. Ibid., 514.

25. Ibid., 508.

26. For a detailed synopsis of *The Two Kuni Lemels*, see Nahma Sandrow, *Vagabond Stars: A World History of Yiddish Theatre* (New York: Harper and Row, 1977), 48–49. [Syracuse University Press reissued the book in 1996.]

27. Turkov, "Teater un Konsertn," 507–9.

28. David S. Lifson, *The Yiddish Theatre in America* (New York: Thomas Yoseloff, 1965), 37–39.

29. Sergei Mikhailovich Tretyakov, *Roar China: An Episode in Nine Scenes*, trans. F. Polianovska and Barbara Nixon (London: M. Lawrence, 1931).

30. Paul Moscanyi, "Foreword," *Art in a Conce·ration Camp* (New York: New School, 1968), 6.

31. Jorge Semprun, *The Long Voyage*, trans. Richard Seaver (New York: Grove, 1964), 60.

Singing in the Face of Death: A Study of Jewish Cabaret and Opera during the Holocaust | Samuel M. Edelman

1. Yad Vashem, *Jewish Resistance During the Holocaust* (Jerusalem: Yad Vashem, 1971), 35–59.

2. Lloyd Bitzer, "The Rhetorical Situation," *Philosophy and Rhetoric* 1, no. 1 (1968): 3–4.

3. Ibid., 6.

4. Rosen, 1943: unpublished transcript. See references to Willy Rosen in Kühn essay, Part I, and in Etty Hillesum, Part II, documents.

5. Garcia, 1983: unpublished transcript of symposium statement. Also useful was Max Rodriguez, *As Long As I Remain Alive* (Tuscaloosa, Ala.: Portals, 1979).

6. Ibid.

7. Lewin, 1984: unpublished transcript of interview. For more on *Brundibár*, see Karas, Part III.

8. Hans Krása, 1944: unpublished manuscript of opera, *Brundibár*.

Cultural Activities in the Vilna Ghetto, March 1942

1. The ghettos in the smaller Lithuanian towns were being liquidated. Some skilled workers who were spared were transferred to the larger ghettos. Several hundred Jews arrived in Vilna from Oszmiana, Święciany, and Michaliszki at the end of March 1943.

2. Lit. "Haman's pockets," a tricornered Purim pastry filled with poppy seeds.

3. Pen name of Solomon Bloomgarden, Yiddish poet and Bible translator (1870–1927).

4. Abraham Sutzkever, a Yiddish poet of the Young Vilna literary circle. He emigrated to Israel, where he edited *Di goldene keyt,* a Yiddish literary journal.

5. David Pinski (1872–1959) was a major Yiddish dramatist.

6. Káilis was a factory located outside the Vilna ghetto, employing Jewish labor in fur production for the German army.

7. The Communal Relief Committee was organized by the underground political parties in the Vilna ghetto and supported by voluntary contributions. The Winter Relief Committee devoted itself mainly to the distribution of clothing.

8. The Vilna ghetto sports field was made by clearing a small area of bombed buildings. Kalmanovich noted in his diary on 21 August 1942 that the place was filled with young people, especially on Sundays, when games were played: "My pious friend laments: 'So many woes, so many deaths, and here merriment and celebrations! That's how life is. But live we must as long as God gives life. He knows best! Jewish children give themselves up to sports; may God give them strength.'"

9. Yiddish poet (1901–69).

Selections from Surviving the Holocaust: The Kovno Ghetto Diary | *Avraham Tory*

Note: Footnote by Dinah Portman.

1. On the Jewish calendar the twentieth of the month of Tammuz was the birthday of Theodor Herzl, the founder of political Zionism. The twenty-first of Tammuz was the birthday of the Hebrew national poet Chaim Nahman Bialik. In Zionist circles, the two days were combined as a joint celebration and memorial.

The Freest Theater in the Reich" | *Curt Daniel*

1. Gustav Stresemann (1878–1929) founded the conservative German People's Party (1918), was chancellor in 1929, and foreign minister from 1923 to 1929.

The Yiddish Theater of Belsen | *Samy Feder*

1. "Hatikvah" ("Hope") is the national anthem of Israel.

"Voices"

Selections from *Letters from Westerbork* Etty Hillesum

1. Hillesum refers to "section leaders" who were all Jewish.

2. Ehrlich, Goldstein, and Rosen were all prewar cabaret entertainers. See Part I for Ehrlich's letter. Also see Kühn's essay for more on Ehrlich and Rosen as a cabaret team.

3. Professor David Cohen presided over the Jewish Council with Abraham Asscher.

4. Hillesum refers to Willy Rosen here.

Theresienstadt | Rebecca Rovit

1. Norbert Troller, *Theresienstadt: Hitler's Gift to the Jews*, trans. Susan E. Cernyak-Spatz, ed. Joel Shatzky (Chapel Hill: University of North Carolina Press, 1991), 35.

2. *The Terezín Diary of Gonda Redlich*, trans. Laurence Kutler, ed. Saul S. Friedman (Lexington: University Press of Kentucky, 1992), 94, 117. For more references to cultural events, see entries of 24–25 March 1943, 109, on operetta by members of the Jewish police to improve their image and performed by families, *Das Ghettomädel*.

3. Ruth Bondy, *"Elder of the Jews": Jakob Edelstein of Theresienstadt*, trans. Evelyn Abel (New York: Grove, 1989), 292–93.

4. See Troller, *Theresienstadt*. For more on Theresienstadt in general and on specifics of daily life there, see Zdeněk Lederer's *Ghetto Theresienstadt* (New York: Howard Fertig, 1983). Lederer, like H. G. Adler, was incarcerated at Terezín. Also see Adler, *Die verheimlichte Wahrheit: Theresienstädter Dokumente* (Tübingen: J. C. B. Mohr, 1958), for German documents from the ghetto.

Operatic Performances in Terezín: Krása's Brundibár | Joža Karas

1. The first names of the musicians are not known.

2. After the war Ohrstein changed his name to Zdeněk Ornest.

3. Reference to the selection of children in Auschwitz: Those who could not reach string stretched above their heads had to go to the gas chambers.

4. Reprinted with permission from *Terezín* (memorial volume), ed. Fratišek Ehrmann, Otto Heitlinger, and Rudolf Iltis (Prague: Council of Jewish Religious Communities, 1965).

5. Reprinted with permission from the book, *The Jews in Czechoslovakia* (New York: Jewish Publication Society of America, Philadelphia, and the Society for the History of Czechoslovak Jews, vol. 1, 1968; vol. 2, 1971). [See especially Part I of this book for more related to Kurt Singer, the first managing director of Germany's Jewish Kulturbund.]

6. *We are Children Just the Same. Vedem, The Secret Magazine by the Boys of Terezín*, selected and edited by Marie Rút Křižková, Kurt Jiří Kotouč, and Zdeněk Ornest; trans. R. Elizabeth Novak (Philadelphia and Jerusalem: Jewish Publication Society, 1995).

7. Used with permission of Leopold Löwy (translated by Joža Karas). [Leopold Löwy, who performed in *Brundibár* and survived, gave Karas Laub's statement in Czech long before the 1995 publication of excerpts from *Vedem*. This is Karas's translation. The same reminiscence by Laub was translated in the 1995 publication, pp. 154–56, albeit by a different translator.]

8. The TV special, "There Shall Be Heard Again . . . ," was aired on 26 September 1971, during the Jewish High Holidays.

9. The children's opera piano reduction and vocal score has been published in one volume in English, German, and Czech by Tempo, Prague, 1993. This is the only available score to the opera and its libretto. In Germany, a countrywide organization of youth ensembles, the *Jeunesses Musicales Deutschland,* has committed itself to staging numerous productions of *Brundibár.* For 1998, over seven hundred people and institutions will have realized 130 productions of *Brundibár* across Germany. The Website for this organization is http.//www.jeunessesmusicales.de.

Letter from Theresienstadt | Kurt Singer

1. The Jewish Advisory Board, Amsterdam. The one-sided card was written in old German script and has been reproduced in Paula Salomon-Lindberg, *"Mein C'est La Vie-Leben,"* ed. Christine Fischer-Defoy (Berlin: Im Verlag Das Arsenal, 1992), 129. Silten himself was eventually transported to Theresienstadt from Westerbork in January 1944. He was a pharmacist and survived the war. See H. G. Adler, *Theresienstadt,* 811.

2. The streets in Theresienstadt were lettered Q (*Querstrasse*) for cross-streets and L (*Langstrasse*) for length-wise streets. The 410 stands for house number 10 at the 4th cross-street. The so-called house was in the block houses, separate units (not barracks) arranged in a square. The squares were arranged according to the capital letters A through I to which were often attached Roman numerals I–VII, with an occasional a or b to connote building complexes. Singer likely lived with other prominent inmates in Block D III. Hugo Friedmann describes the one-story rococo style house 410 in "An Art Tour through Theresienstadt" ("Eine Kunstreise durch Theresienstadt"), doc. 169, p. 244, in H. G. Adler, ed., *Die verheimlichte Wahrheit: Theresienstädter Dokumente.*

3. The *Freizeitgestaltung* (FZG) or leisuretime activity began clandestinely in 1941 and was later tolerated by Nazi camp commanders. See the report by Rabbi Erich Weiner, the first director of the FZG. It is unlikely that Singer fully understood the meaning and context of life at Theresienstadt when he wrote this letter. The correspondence permitted inmates was strictly regulated and censored. There was a set pattern to writing cards and letters. Thirty words was the usual word limit (excluding the date, "Dear so and so," and signature). Certain topics were encouraged such as the weather or that one might receive packages. It was forbidden to mention more than just a few names of fellow-inmates. Jewish Elders, prominent individuals, and, later, the Danish inmates, could write more and longer letters. Singer's letter is nearly ninety words. For more on mail, see Adler, *Theresienstadt,* 574–78.

4. These people are in Amsterdam. Paula Salomon-Lindberg is an opera singer and Singer's friend who sang at the Kulturbund, Berlin.

5. This veiled reference suggests Singer's Nazi contacts like Hinkel in Berlin.

6. As mentioned, one was not permitted to list more than a few of one's fellow inmates. These men would have been known in Amsterdam.

Freizeitgestaltung *in Theresienstadt* | *Rabbi Erich Weiner*

1. The barracks at Theresienstadt were named for regions within the German Reich as well as for German cities. Sudetenland was the area in former Bohemia in between the present Czech and German borders. The headquarters of the Jewish administration (as well as the site of a theater space) in the Magdeburg barracks was also known as B V.

2. There were two *Aufbaukommando* transports of workers (AK1 and AK2) that came from Prague to build and to "socially" improve the ghetto. These workers belonged to the ghetto's elite. AK2 brought a thousand men to the camp. In "Memories of Theresienstadt," in this section, Mirko Tuma refers to having been part of the AK2 transport which he claims arrived in Theresienstadt on 1 December 1941. Weiner's account states 4 December 1941. It is understandable to find discrepancies within the recollections of eyewitnesses. The AK transports should not be confused with the J-Transports (Jews).

3. Director of the Buildings' central management.

4. Weiner abbreviates *Freizeitgestaltung* as FZG.

5. The *Judenältester* was the administrative leader of the self-run Jewish administration in the ghetto. The Elder was always subordinate to the SS camp leaders, however. At the time of this report, Jacob Edelstein was Theresienstadt's first *Judenältester* (December 1941–November 1943). The Elder organized work, provided housing for new inmates and oversaw hygiene, care of the old, cultural life, and the maintenance of order in the ghetto. The Elder also assembled the deportation lists for transports to extermination camps. See Ruth Bondy, *"Elder of the Jews": Jakob Edelstein of Theresienstadt,* 292.

6. The German and the Czech Jews at Theresienstadt were assimilated Jews and therefore not well versed in Judaism. See Adler, *Theresienstadt.*

7. *Kaddish* is the prayer for the dead.

8. This is an opera by Bedřich Smetana.

9. Of these transports, one included a thousand women who were sent to neighboring Pürglitz, Czechoslovakia, to work in the woods there. The Ost-[East] Transport refers to the deportation of inmates farther east to Auschwitz.

10. *Shavuot* in Hebrew means "weeks." Originally an ancient agricultural festival, the holiday—during May or June—marks the giving of the Torah at Mount Sinai.

11. Richard Beer-Hoffmann was a Jewish-born Austrian playwright.

12. See Zdeněk Lederer, *Ghetto Theresienstadt,* 130. Tickets cost 5 crowns each and were generally available. Performances began at 6 P.M.

13. The *Blockveranstaltungen* refer to outdoor performances, which took place in the inner courtyards, around which the block houses stood. In warm weather the lectures often took place in the courtyards.

14. For more on Krása and *Brundibár,* see especially the essays by Kramer and Karas. Also see Ehrlich-Fantlová and Tuma's memoirs.

15. This refers to Rosh Hashanah (the Jewish New Year) and Yom Kippur (The Day

of Atonement) occurring annually during the month of September or October. The *Alterstransport,* or transport of the elderly, was reserved for people over sixty-five.

16. "Ing." is the German abbreviation for *Ingenieur,* or Engineer.

17. *Ordnungsdienst,* or Jewish police, served as security guards within the locked barracks until the summer of 1942.

18. The "Genie" barracks was named after the *Genietruppen,* an Austrian term to connote engineer troops. The police lived here until the summer of 1942, when they moved to the officers' casino.

19. Philipp Manes directed the lecture series within Theresienstadt's German-speaking cultural programs. He directed play readings of classics, among which were the *Urfaust* and Goethe's *Faust.* His diaries have been bequeathed to the Wiener Library, London. Among the one thousand pages of these "Manes Papers" are sketches, poems, and commentary written by members of the German-speaking camp contingent in his own journals (so-called *Poesie-Bücher*). These papers remain unpublished. Klaus Leist offers the first look into these papers in his summary article, "Philipp Manes: A Theresienstadt Chronicle," *Journal of Holocaust Education* 6, no. 2 (1997): 36–70. The publication was delayed until 1998. See Adler, *Theresienstadt,* 602–3, on Manes.

20. *Sukkot* is a harvest festival, normally held in the autumn.

21. Poljak was a camp official, notorious for his brutality. His random acts of cruelty include running over a woman with a tractor before she could cross the street. See Adler, *Theresienstadt,* 579.

22. These one-acts were performed in Czech.

23. After September 1942, civilian stores were established for inmates. The *Verteil-ungstelle,* for example, was the "shop" that sold clothes once belonging to the inmates; these clothes had been stolen or "sluiced" upon arrival at the ghetto.

24. Leo Strauss was the son of opera composer Oscar Strauss. See Roy Kift's introduction to the cabaret sketch we include in this section.

25. Weiner uses the Hebrew word *chug,* meaning "circle."

26. "Fronts" is used here in the military sense.

27. The *Kamaradschaftsheim* was the SS headquarters that was set up in Terezín's old hotel "Victoria," and remained off limits to Jews. See Adler, *Theresienstadt,* 103.

28. The report ends here abruptly. Rabbi Weiner probably wrote this sometime after February 1943.

The FZG continued after 1943. Cultural events were performed as late as the summer of 1944, when the Red Cross delegation visited the camp. In fact, the FZG continued right up to the mass transports of October 1944 to Auschwitz which took many of the artists away. Gonda Redlich's diary offers glimpses of the Theresienstadt stage over the course of 1943 as one of "The oddities of the ghetto" (26 March 1943). On 11 May 1943, he reports, "They are permitting FZG again." Redlich's final reference to cultural events came on 12 September 1943: "A coffeehouse, with empty tables. Each man lingers two hours. Melodies—but one can only order tea or coffee. In the houses nearest the street where the Germans walk home, it is forbidden to open windows." Redlich wrote this several days after mass transports to Auschwitz. Zdenka Ehrlich-Fantlová reports her experiences with the Czech theater prior to her own deportation to Auschwitz in the fall of 1944.

The Czech Theater in Terezín | Zdenka Ehrlich-Fantlová

1. Ehrlich-Fantlová had been sent with a small group outside the ghetto walls to plant trees.

2. The premise that cyclists could be scapegoats for all evil was a popular joke among liberals in West Central Europe after World War I, according to Hannah Arendt. In the joke, an antisemite claimed that the Jews had caused the war. The reply: "Yes, the Jews and the bicyclists. Why the bicyclists? Asks the one. Why the Jews? Asks the other." Švenk was undoubtedly familiar with this joke. See Arendt, Part One, Antisemitism, of *The Origins of Totalitarianism*, 5.

Memories of Theresienstadt | Mirko Tuma

1. Tuma has mistaken the directors of these productions. As is evident from Ehrlich-Fantlová's participation in the Czech theater at Terezín—and her accounts of her performances—we know that Otakar Ružička began the direction of *Georges Dandin,* but was replaced by Zelenka. Gustav Schorsch directed the Gogol play. Lederer corroborates this in *Ghetto Theresienstadt,* 128.

2. Nóra Frýd directed *Esther,* not Švenk. Zelenka directed *Brundibár,* which is what Tuma remembers.

Epilogue | Sybil H. Milton

1. Richard H. Lytle, "Intellectual Access to Archives: Provenance and Content Indexing Methods of Subject Retrieval," *American Archivist* 43 (1980): 64–75, 191–207.

2. Michel Duchein, *Obstacles to the Access, Use and Transfer of Information from Archives* (Paris, 1983). This seventy-nine-page study was prepared as "A RAMP study of UNESCO," PGI-83/WS/20.

3. Information provided by Elisabeth Kinder of the Bundesarchiv in Koblenz, March 1981, and Dr. Hermann Simon of the East Berlin Jewish Community, June 1983. See also the inventory to the Jacob Jacobson Papers, Archives of the Leo Baeck Institute, New York (hereafter LBI, NY), AR 7002. The statement of purpose of the Gesamtarchiv is published in Eugen Täubler, "Zur Einführung," *Mitteilungen des Gesamtarchivs des deutschen Juden* 1, no. 1 (1908): 1–8.

4. List of communal records, Rare Books and Manuscript Division, Library of the Jewish Theological Seminary, New York, No. 8683. See also Michael Moses Zarchin, *Jews*

in The Province of Posen: Studies in Communal Records of the Eighteenth and Nineteenth Centuries (Philadelphia, 1939).

5. LBI, NY, AR 5165, includes the records of the Hevrah Kadisha of Zerkow, 1865-1914.

6. For a discussion of French Judaica, see Bernhard Blumenkranz, ed., *Documents modernes sur les Juifs XVIe-XXe siècles réunis par l'Équipe de recherche 208 "Nouvelle Gallia Judaica"* (Toulouse, 1979); and Phyllis Cohen Albert, *The Modernization of French Jewry* (Hanover, N.H., 1977), 387-402.

7. The records of the Breslau Jewish Theological Seminary and the Breslau Jewish community are today located at the Zidovske Institute in Warsaw and the Wroclaw University Archives. The records of the Jewish community of Königsberg are dispersed among the Prussian State Archives in Berlin, the German State Archives in Potsdam and Merseburg, and Polish Archives.

8. Smolensk Archives, records of the All-Union Communist Party, T 87, 64 rolls (inventory located on T 87, roll 1), and Miscellaneous Russian Records Collection, T 88, 3 rolls (inventory located on T 87, roll 1), National Archives, Washington, D.C. (hereafter NARS, DC). For a general discussion of captured German records, see Robert Wolfe, ed., *Captured German and Related Records: A National Archives Conference* (Athens, Ohio, 1974). Among the captured German records were also a collection of Hungarian political and military records, 1909-45 (T 973, 21 rolls); a collection of Italian military records, 1935-43 (T 821, 506 rolls); the papers of Count Galeazzo Ciano [Lisbon Papers] (T 816, 3 rolls); and the personal papers of Benito Mussolini together with some official records of the Italian Foreign Office and the Ministry of Culture, 1922-44 (T 586, 318 rolls). The story of captured Italian records is told in Howard McGaw Smyth, *Secrets of the Fascist Era: How Uncle Sam obtained Some of the Top-Level Documents of Mussolini's Period* (Carbondale and Edwardsville, Ill., 1975).

9. Herman Simon, *Das Berliner Jüdische Museum in der Oranienburger Strasse* (Berlin, 1983), 63-66; Rahel Wischnitzer Bernstein and Josef Fried, *Gedenkausstellung Don Jizchaq Abrabanel: Seine Welt, sein Werk* (Berlin, 1937).

10. Sybil Milton, "German-Jewish Genealogical Research: Selected Resources at the Leo Baeck Institute, New York," *Toledot: The Journal of Jewish Genealogy* 2, no. 4 (1979): 13-18; L. G. Pine, *The Genealogist's Encyclopedia* (New York, 1969), 155-70.

11. *Trial of the Major War Criminals before the International Military Tribunal, Nuremberg, 14 November 1945-1 October 1946* (Nuremberg, 1947-49), 31:515-19 (Nuremberg document PS 3051).

12. Cecil Roth, opening address, 11 April 1943, *Conference on Restoration of Continental Jewish Museums, Libraries, and Archives* (London, 1943), unpaginated; Philip Friedman, "The Fate of the Jewish Book," in his *Roads to Extinction: Essays on the Holocaust* (New York and Philadelphia, 1980), 88-99.

13. Hugh Gibson, publisher's note to *The Goebbels Diaries, 1942-1943,* ed. and trans. Louis P. Lochner (Garden City, N.Y., 1948), v. These diaries are located in the Hoover

Institution Archives, Stanford, California. The "rules" of Allied looting are described in Margaret Bourke-White, *Portrait of Myself* (New York, 1963), 261–63.

14. "Jüdische Kulturschätze von Worms nach Israel," *Wormser Zeitung*, 21 December 1956; "Worms jüdisches Archiv in Jerusalem übergeben," *New Yorker Staatszeitung und Herold*, 5 November 1957, 6. These clippings are located in the Worms Jewish Community Files, LBI, NY, AR 145/2 and AR 145/16.

15. Unpublished inventories available at the LBI, NY. See manuscript of the *Leo Baeck Institute Catalog: Archives*.

16. The Berthold Rosenthal Papers, LBI, NY, AR 638/II 13, contains the Green Book of Worms (349 pages transcribed) and the Worms *Judenschaftsverzeichnis*, 1515–1760 (128 pages transcribed). The Isidor Kiefer Papers, LBI, NY, AR 1895/II 1, contains the *Judenregister*, 1739–1814; AR 1894/III 126, contains administrative files of the Worms Jewish community, AR 1897/IV 1–76, contains records and photos of the Worms synagogue from the nineteenth and twentieth centuries; and AR 1899/VI 1–8, contains files of the Worms Jewish Museum. The Kiefer literary estate also includes 220 historic photos from Worms. The Fritz Nathan Papers, LBI, NY, AR 7197/IV, contains forty-two glass positive slides of the Worms synagogue.

17. Otto Böcher, *Die alte Synagogue in Worms* (Berlin, 1982). The Worms Jewish Community Files, LBI, NY, AR 145, contains clippings from March and October 1974 about the reconstruction of the Judengasse, the synagogue, and the museum.

18. Henry R. Huttenbach, *The Destruction of the Jewish Community of Worms, 1933–1945* (New York, 1981), 217–19. See also deportation lists from Jewish communities in the Palatinate, LBI, NY, AR 2039/1–3.

19. The record group, "Das Institut zur Erforschung der Judenfrage," YIVO Institute for Jewish Research, New York (hereafter YIVO) contains a file entitled "Kennkarten: Worms and Bezirk Worms."

20. For wartime reports about the German transport and evacuation of the Königsberg State Archives, see NARS, DC, *German Records Microfilmed at Alexandria, Va.*, Records of the Office of the Reich Commissioner for the Baltic States [Reichskommissar für das Ostland], 1941–45, microfilm publication T 459, especially rolls 3, 11, and 12; and Records of the Reich Ministry for Occupied Eastern Territories (Reichsministerium für die besetzten Ostgebiete), microfilm publication T 454, roll 2, frames 4907953–4907954, and roll 107, frames 1236–1238. See also Kurt Forstreuter, *Das Preussische Staatsarchiv in Königsberg: Ein geschichtlicher Rückblick mit einer Übersicht über seine Bestände* (Göttingen, 1955); Bernhart Jähnig, "Militärgeschichtliche Quellen des Staatsarchivs Königsberg (Archivbestände Preussischer Kulturbesitz) im Staatlichen Archivlager in Göttingen," *Militärgeschichtliche Mitteilungen* 16, no. 2 (1974): 173–214; and Hans Branig, Winfried Bliss, and Werner Petermann, *Übersicht über die Bestände des Geheimen Staatsarchivs in Berlin-Dahlem* (Berlin and Cologne, 1966–67).

21. Jacob Jacobson Papers, LBI, NY, AR 7002/IV.

22. Deborah Hertz, "The Varnhagen Collection Is in Krakow," *American Archivist* 44 (1981): 223–28.

23. Jewish Museum, New York, *Danzig 1939: Treasures of a Destroyed Community* (Detroit, 1980), 34.

24. For example, see Leopold Donath, *Geschichte der Juden in Mecklenburg von den ältesten Zeiten (1266) bis auf die Gegenwart (1874)* (Leipzig, 1874).

25. War Documentation Project Study, no. 1, *Guide to Captured German Documents*, prepared by Gerhard L. Weinberg and the WDP Staff under the direction of Fritz T. Epstein (Maxwell Air Force Base, Ala., 1952); and *Supplement to the Guide to Captured German Documents* (Washington, D.C., 1959). See also the seventy-six *National Archives Guides to German Records Microfilmed at Alexandria, Va.* (Washington, D.C., 1958-84); and George O. Kent, ed. and comp., *A Catalog of Files and Microfilms of the German Foreign Archives 1920-1945* (Stanford, 1962-72). A concise list of the more than thirty thousand rolls of microfilm of these captured records is found in Wolfe, *Captured German and Related Records*, 267-76. Further data are found in John A. Bernbaum, "The Captured German Records: A Bibliographical Survey," *Historian* 32 (1970): 564-75.

26. Wolfe, *Captured German and Related Records*, 267-73.

27. Friedrich P. Kahlenberg, *Deutsche Archive in West und Ost: Zur Entwicklung des staatlichen Archivwesens seit 1945* (Düsseldorf, 1972); Josef Henke, "Des Schicksal deutscher zeitgeschichtlicher Quellen in Kriegs und Nachkriegszeiten: Beschlagnahme, Ruckfuhrung, Verblieb," *Vierteljahrshefte für Zeitgeschichte* 30 (1982): 557-620. Helmut Lötzke, "Bericht über die von der UdSSR an die DDR seit 1957 übergebenen Archivbestände," *Archivmitteilungen* 10 (1960): 12-15; George O. Kent, "Research Opportunities in West and East German Archives for the Weimar Period and the Third Reich," *Central European History* 12 (1979): 38-67.

28. Henke, "Des Schicksal deutscher zeitgeschichtlicher Quellen," passim; *Guide to Captured Documents* and 1959 *Supplement*, passim; Agnes Peterson, comp., *Archival and Manuscript Materials at the Hoover Institution on War, Revolution, and Peace: A Checklist of Major Collections* (Stanford, 1978); "The YIVO Institute for Jewish Research and Its Holdings on the Holocaust," *American Committee on the History of the Second World War Newsletter*, no. 19 (April 1978): 22-24; Sybil Milton, "The Leo Baeck Institute in New York and Its Holdings on the Second World War," *American Committee on the History of the Second World War Newsletter*, no. 20 (fall 1978): 7-11.

29. Henry Friedlander, "Publications on the Holocaust," in *The German Church Struggle and the Holocaust*, ed. Franklin Littell and Hubert Locke (Detroit, 1974), 69-94; Friedlander, "The Historian and the Documents," paper presented at the annual meeting of the Society of American Archivists, Chicago, 27 September 1979.

30. John Mendelsohn, "Trial by Document: The Uses of Seized Records in United States Proceedings at Nuernberg" (Ph.D. diss., University of Maryland, 1974); Jacob Robinson and Henry Sachs, *The Holocaust: The Nuremberg Evidence—Documents, Digest, Index, and Chronological Tables* (Jerusalem, 1976).

31. Sybil Milton, review of *Guide to Unpublished Materials of the Holocaust Period*, by Yehuda Bauer, 5 vols., *American Archivist* 40 (1977): 549-51; Wolfgang Scheffler, "Der Beitrag der Zeitgeschichte zur Erforschung der NS-Verbrechen: Versäumnisse,

Schwierigkeiten, und Aufgaben," in *Vergangenheitsbewältigung durch Strafverfahren*, ed. Jürgen Weber and Peter Steinbach (Munich, 1984), 121–22.

32. Friedlander, "Historian and the Documents." See also Scheffler, "Der Beitrag der Zeitgeschichte."

33. Berlin Collection, YIVO, Record Group: 215; this document is also listed as PS 1472 in Robinson and Sachs, *Holocaust*, 140 (item 2074).

34. Walter Rundell Jr., *In Pursuit of American History: Research and Training in the United States* (Norman, Okla., 1970), 202–59; International Council on Archives, Microfilm Committee, "Recommended Practices for the Titling of Microfilm (Microfiche and Roll Microfilm) of Archives and Manuscripts," *Bulletin* (Madrid) 6 (1977): 28–33; Ernst Posner, "Effects of Changes of Sovereignty on Archives" and "Public Records under Military Occupation," in his *Archives and the Public Interest* (Washington, D.C., 1967), 168–81, 182–97.

35. Card catalog of the Hoover Institution on War, Revolution, and Peace, Stanford, California.

36. Card catalogs of the Institut für Zeitgeschichte, Munich, and the Leo Baeck Institute, New York, which cite the repository where microfilm was purchased. For example, the 260 archival and press clipping rolls of the Wiener Library Microfilm (LBI, NY, AR 7187) use the original inventory of the Wiener Library in London, including all its roll numbers. See also "The Press Archives of the Wiener Library," *LBI Library and Archives News*, no. 16 (June 1982): 6.

37. Yehuda Bauer, ed., *Guide to Unpublished Materials of the Holocaust Period* (Jerusalem, 1975), vols. 3–5, and the footnotes in all Yad Vashem publications. See particularly Chana Byers Abells, ed., *Archives of the Destruction: A Photographic Record of the Holocaust* (Jerusalem, 1981), which never cites the institution that provided Yad Vashem with its photographic duplicates.

38. Gerhard Granier, Josef Henke, and Klaus Oldenhage, eds., *Das Bundesarchiv und seine Bestände*, 3rd ed. (Boppard a.R., 1977), 661; Grete Heinz and Agnes Peterson, eds., *NSDAP Hauptarchiv: Guide to the Hoover Institution Microfilm Collection* (Stanford, 1964), 129–31, 143–44.

39. Bernard Kolb Papers, LBI, NY, AR 3959/V. Kolb was the business manager of the Jewish community of Nuremberg from 1923 until his deportation to Theresienstadt in 1941. He returned to Nuremberg in 1945 to testify before the International Military Tribunal and "liberated" more than one thousand pages of original files from the editorial offices of *Der Stürmer*. He brought these papers with him to the United States, and they were deposited as part of his literary estate at the Leo Baeck Institute. Substantial excerpts from these records have been published in Fred Hahn, ed., *"Lieber Stürmer": Leserbriefe an das NS Kampfblatt, 1925–1945* (Stuttgart, 1978). The LBI, NY, inventory is organized by locality and name of the *Stürmer* column. A similar organization is clear in the holdings of the *Stürmer* library and editorial archive deposited in the Stadtarchiv Nürnberg (Nuremberg Municipal Archives). See Arnd Müller, "Das Stürmer-Archiv im Stadtarchiv Nürnberg," *Vierteljahrshefte für Zeitgeschichte* 32 (1984): 326–29. See also

Berlin Collection, YIVO, NY, Record Group 215; and *German Records Microfilmed at Alexandria,* guide 39, which includes a seventy-seven-page fragment of Streicher and *Stürmer* correspondence with authors and illustrators during the mid-1930s, NARS, DC, microfilm publication T 174, roll 415, frames 1941149–1941225.

40. See *Trial of the Major War Criminals. National Archives Microfilm Publications,* Pamphlet M1019, which lists an interrogation report about Streicher, dated 2 July 1945, p. 85. See also Sybil Milton, "The Archival Jigsaw Puzzle: Fragmentation and Foreign Language Records of the Holocaust," paper presented at the annual meeting of the Society of American Archivists, Chicago, 27 September 1979.

41. Council of Jewish Communities in the Czech Lands, *Terezín* (Prague, 1965), 170–77.

42. Ibid. See also H. G. Adler, *Theresienstadt, 1941–1945;* H. G. Adler, *Die verheimlichte Wahrheit: Theresienstädter Dokumente.* A videotape copy of the *Der Führer schenkt den Juden eine Stadt* is available in the LBI, NY.

43. Seymour J. Pomrenze, "Protection, Use, and Return of Captured German Records," in Wolfe, *Captured German and Related Records,* 13.

44. Friedman, "Fate of the Jewish Book," 88–99.

45. Janet Blatter and Sybil Milton, eds., *Art of the Holocaust* (New York, 1981), 36–43.

46. Yad Vashem holds the records of several of these Jewish historical commissions. See also David P. Boder, *I Did Not Interview the Dead* (Urbana, Ill., 1949); and Boder, "Topical Autobiographies of Displaced People" (1950–57), transcripts of seventy interviews completed between 1946 and 1949 in the DP camps. The interviews were recorded on a model-50 wire recorder and two hundred spools of carbon steel wire and are transcribed verbatim in sixteen volumes (3,162 pages), including a detailed subject and geographical index. Boder's interviews were financed by grants from the U.S. Public Health Service and the National Institute of Mental Health. They contain detailed narratives about experiences in concentration and labor camps throughout Europe. The volumes are available in the library of the Simon Wiesenthal Center in Los Angeles and the Neurological Medical Library at UCLA, Los Angeles.

47. Rudolf Apt Papers, LBI, NY, AR 7180/II–IV.

48. Morris Vierfelder Papers, ibid., AR 7180/I–VIII.

49. Hermann Fuernberg Papers, including case files of the Gildemeester Hilfskomitee, ibid., AR 7194.

50. Heinrich Stahl Papers, ibid., AR 7171.

51. Sybil Milton, scholars' query column, *LBI Library and Archives News,* no. 19 (December 1983): 8; Milton, "The Expulsion of Polish Jews from Germany, October 1938–July 1939: A Documentation," *Leo Baeck Institute Year Book* 29 (1984): 169–99. The oral histories are an interview with Zygmund Glicksohn, September 1944 (3 pp.), Ball Kaduri Collection, Yad Vashem, Jerusalem, O 1/7; and Dr. Shaul Esch's interview of Moshe Ortner, former head of the Reichsverband polnischer Juden (56 pp.), Oral History Division, Institute of Contemporary Jewry, Hebrew University, Jerusalem, nos. 00332–00388.

52. The Oral History Program at Columbia University interviews only prominent personalities; the publications of Studs Terkel exemplify interviews with average people around certain themes, such as the Depression or the Second World War.

53. Wiener Library Microfilm, LBI, NY, AR 7187, roll 600. See also LBI Microfilm Collection, roll 239: *Anklageschrift in der Strafsache gegen Otto Bovensiepen et al.*, 1969, the indictment of the Berlin Gestapo for the deportation of the Jews of Berlin. See also transcript of an interview by Bernd H. Stappert, "Zu denen halten, die verfolgt sind!: Zeitgeschichtliches in der Lebensgeschichte der Mieke Monjau" (28 pp.), transcribing an interview broadcast on Südwestfunk, Stuttgart, 1982; typescript available through Südwestfunk.

54. Aggregate data on survival in hiding have been gathered by interviews with Berlin survivors and published in Jochen Köhler, *Klettern in der Grossstadt: Volkstümliche Geschichten vom Überleben in Berlin, 1933–1945* (Berlin, 1979); Leonard Gross, *Last Jews in Berlin* (New York, 1982); and Eva Fogelman and Valerie Lewis Wiener, "From Bystander to Rescuer: A Social-Psychological Study of Altruism in Wartime" (Social-Personality Psychology Department, Graduate Center of the City University of New York, January 1983, photocopy).

55. See Esther Katz and Joan Miriam Ringelheim, eds., *Women Surviving the Holocaust: Conference Proceedings*, Institute for Research in History, Occasional Papers (New York, 1983).

56. For an introduction to serious studies in photographic and visual communication, see Gisele Freund, *Photography and Society* (Boston, 1980); Roland Günter, *Fotografie als Waffe: Geschichte der sozialdokumentarischen Fotografie* (Hamburg and Berlin, 1977); Jean Berger and Jean Mohr, *Another Way of Telling* (New York, 1982); and Dino Brugioni, "Aerial Photography: Reading the Past, Revealing the Future," *Smithsonian*, March 1984, 150–60.

57. See Sybil Milton, "The Camera as Weapon: Documentary Photography and the Holocaust," *Simon Wiesenthal Center Annual* 1 (1984): 45–68, especially 61–63.

SELECTED BIBLIOGRAPHY

Listed here are works that have been useful in compiling this book. In addition, there are other sources that readers may wish to consult on the Holocaust in general, as well as for archival research in performance history and the Third Reich. This bibliography is by no means meant to be a complete record of all the sources available. Essays and books on the Holocaust continue to be written. Recordings and Websites are being prepared that offer readers new modes by which to research performance in the ghettos and concentration camps.

Diaries, Documents, Memoirs, Interviews, Histories by Eyewitnesses

Adelson, Alan, and Robert Lapides, eds. *Lódz Ghetto: Inside a Community under Siege.* New York: Viking, 1989.

Adler, H. G., ed. *Die verheimlichte Wahrheit: Theresienstädter Dokumente.* Tübingen: J. C. B. Mohr, 1958.

———. *Theresienstadt, 1941–1945: Das Antlitz einer Zwangsgemeinschaft.* Tübingen: J. C. B. Mohr, 1960.

Blatter, Janet, and Sybil H. Milton, eds. *Art of the Holocaust.* New York: Routledge, 1981.

Broder, Henryk M., and Eike Geisel. *Es Waren Wirklich Sternstunden.* Film. Bayrischer Rundfunk, Sender Freies Berlin, 1988.

Costanza, Mary S., ed. *The Living Witness: Art in the Concentration Camps and Ghettos.* New York: The Free Press, 1982.

Dawidowicz, Lucy S., ed. *A Holocaust Reader.* New York: Behrmann House, 1976.

Delbo, Charlotte. *Auschwitz and After.* Trans. Rosette Lamont. New Haven, Conn.: Yale University Press, 1995.

De Silva, Cara, ed. *In Memory's Kitchen: A Legacy from the Women of Terezín.* Trans. Bianca Steiner Brown. Preface by Michael Berenbaum. Northvale, N.J.: J. Aronson, 1996.

Dufournier, Denise. *Ravensbrück: The Women's Death Camp.* Trans. F. W. McPherson. London: George Allen & Unwin, 1948.

Ehrlich, Zdenka Fantlová. *Calmness Is Strength—Said Father.* Trans. Deryk Viney. Unpublished manuscript. London.

Etty: De nagelaten geschriften van Etty Hillesum 1941–1943. Amsterdam, 1991 (1986).

Fénelon, Fania. *Playing for Time.* Trans. Judith Landry. New York: Atheneum, 1977; repr., New York: Syracuse University Press, 1997.

Freeden, Herbert. *Jüdisches Theater in Nazideutschland.* Tübingen: J. C. B. Mohr, 1964; repr., Frankfurt/am Main: Ullstein, 1985.

Friedlander, Henry, and Sybil Milton. *Archives of the Holocaust: An International Collection of Selected Documents.* 26 vols. New York: Garland, 1989–95.

Friedman, Saul S., ed. *The Terezín Diary of Gonda Redlich.* Trans. Laurence Kutler. Lexington: University Press of Kentucky, 1992.

Glattstein, Jacob, Israel Knox, and Samuel Margoshes, eds. *Anthology of Holocaust Literature.* Philadelphia: Jewish Publication Society of America, 1969.

Hillesum, Etty. *An Interrupted Life, The Diaries, 1941–1943 and Letters from Westerbork.* Trans. Arnold Pomerans. New York: Henry Holt, 1996.

Die Jüdische Rundschau. "Regierung Hitler." No. 9. 31 January 1933, 1.

————. "Um die Tätigkeit des Kulturbundes." No. 63. 8 August 1933, 405.

————. Review, *Nathan der Weise.* Nos. 79/80. 4 October 1933, 624.

Katsch, Kurt. *Zurück ins Ghetto.* Unpublished memoirs, no date. Leo Baeck Institute, Doc. ME 719.

Koestler, Arthur. *The Scum of the Earth.* New York: Macmillan, 1941.

Kruk, Hermann. *Diary of the Vilna Ghetto.* Trans. Benjamin Harschav and Barbara Harshav. New Haven, Conn.: Yale University Press, 2000.

Kühn, Volker, ed. *Kleinkunststücke: Hoppla, wir beben. Kabarett einer gewissen Republik 1918–1933.* Vol. 2 (of 4). Weinheim and Berlin: Quadriga Verlag, 1988.

————. *Kleinkunststücke: Deutschlands Erwachen. Kabarett unterm Hakenkreuz, 1933–1945.* Vol. 3 (of 5). Weinheim and Berlin: Quadriga Verlag, 1989.

————. Ed. Unpublished correspondence and interviews with surviving artists who were incarcerated.

Langer, Lawrence L. *Art Through the Ashes.* New York: Oxford University Press, 1995.

Lederer, Zdenek. *Ghetto Theresienstadt.* New York: Howard Fertig, 1983.

Levi, Primo. *If This Is a Man.* Trans. Stuart Woolf. London: Orion Books, 1960.

Marette, Fanny. *I Was Number 47177.* Trans. Robert Laffont. Geneva: Ferni, 1979.

Mechanicus, Philip. *In Depot. Dagboek uit Westerbork.* Amsterdam, 1991.

Mechanicus, Philip. *Year of Fear: A Prisoner Waits for Death.* Trans. Irene R. Gibbons. New York: Hawthorn Books, 1964.

Migdal, Ulrike, ed. *Und die Musik spielt dazu: Chansons und Satiren aus dem KZ Theresienstadt.* Munich: Piper, 1986.

Mohrer, Fruma, and Marek Web, eds. *YIVO Archives. Guide to the YIVO Archives.* New York: Sharpe, 1988.

Ringelblum, Emanuel. *Notes from the Warsaw Ghetto: The Journal of Emanuel Ringelblum.* Ed. and trans. Jacob Sloan. New York: Schocken, 1958; repr., 1974.

Rovit, Rebecca. Unpublished interviews with former members of the Jewish Kulturbund, 1995–97 (including Mascha Benya-Matz and Kurt Michaelis).

————. Interview, Zdenka Ehrlich Fantlová. Tape-recording, 20 March 1998. London, Great Britain.

————. Interview, Anise Postel-Vinay. Tape-recording, 28 March 1998. Paris, France.

Spiritual Resistance: Art from Concentration Camps 1940–1945: A Selection of Drawings and Paintings from the Collection of Kibbutz Lohamei Haghetaot, Israel. Philadelphia: Jewish Publication Society of America, 1981.

Tillion, Germaine. *Ravensbrück.* Paris: Seuil, 1972; repr., 1988.

Tory, Avraham. *Surviving the Holocaust: The Kovno Ghetto Diary.* Cambridge, Mass.: Harvard University Press, 1990.

Tretayakov, Sergei Mikhailovich. *Roar China: An Episode in Nine Scenes.* Trans. F. Polianovska and Barbara Nixon. London: M. Lawrence, 1931.

Troller, Norbert. *Theresienstadt: Hitler's Gift to the Jews.* Trans. Susan E. Cernyak-Spatz; ed. Joel Shatzky. Chapel Hill: University of North Carolina Press, 1991.

Turkov, Yonas. *Yidisher Teater in Yirope twischen beyde velt-milkomes . . . Poilen.* New York: Knight, 1968.

Volvaková, Hana, ed. *I Never Saw Another Butterfly: Children's Drawings and Poems from Terezín Concentration Camp, 1942–1944.* Expanded 2nd ed. New York: Schocken, 1993.

We Are Children Just the Same: Vedem, The Secret Magazine by the Boys of Terezín. Selected and edited by Marie Rút Křižková, Kurt Jiří Kotouč, and Zdeněk Ornest; trans. R. Elizabeth Novak; ed. Paul Wilson. Philadelphia: Jewish Publication Society, 1995.

Secondary Sources

Arendt, Hannah. *The Origins of Totalitarianism.* New York: Harcourt, Brace, and World, 1973.

Bacharach, Walter Zwi. "Jews in Confrontation with Racist Antisemitism, 1879–1933." *Leo Baeck Institute Yearbook* 25 (1980): 197–219.

Benz, Wolfgang, ed. *Die Juden in Deutschland 1933–1945. Leben unter nationalsozialistischer Herrschaft.* Munich: Beck, 1988.

Bondy, Ruth. *"Elder of the Jews": Jakob Edelstein of Theresienstadt.* Trans. Evelyn Abel. New York: Grove, 1989.

Brenner, Michael. *The Renaissance of Jewish Culture in Weimar Germany.* New Haven, Conn.: Yale University Press, 1996.

Cochavi, Yehoyakim. "Kultur und Bildungsarbeit der deutschen Juden 1933–1941: Antwort auf die Verfolgung durch das NS Regime." *Neue Sammlung* 26, no. 3 (1986): 396–407.

Dawidowicz, Lucy S. *The War Against the Jews, 1933–1945.* New York: Bantam, 1975; repr., 1986.

————. *The Holocaust and the Historians.* Cambridge, Mass.: Harvard University Press, 1981.

Firner, Walter, ed. *Wir und das Theater: Ein Schauspieler-bildbuch.* Munich: Verlag F. Bruckmann AG, 1932.

Freeden, Herbert. "Vom geistigen Widerstand der deutschen Juden: Ein Kapitel jüdischer Selbstbehauptung in den Jahren 1933 bis 1938." In *Widerstand und Exil 1933–1945.* Ed. Otto R. Romberg et al. Bonn: Bundeszentrale für politische Bildung, 1986: 47–59.

———. "Jüdischer Kulturbund ohne Jüdische Kultur." *Geschlossene Vorstellung,* 1992: 55–66.

Friedländer, Saul. *Nazi Germany and the Jews: The Years of Persecution, 1933–1939.* Vol. 1. New York: HarperCollins, 1997.

Fuchs, Elinor, ed. *Plays of the Holocaust.* New York: Theatre Communications Group, 1991.

Gadberry, Glen W., ed. *Theatre in the Third Reich, The Prewar Years, 1933–1939.* Westport, Conn.: Greenwood, 1995.

Geisel, E., and H. M. Broder, eds. *Premiere und Pogrom: Der Jüdische Kulturbund 1933–1941, Texte und Bilder.* Berlin: Siedler, 1992.

Geschlossene Vorstellung: Der Jüdische Kulturbund in Deutschland 1933–1941. Catalog. Ed. Akademie der Künste. Berlin: Edition Hentrich, 1992.

Gronius, Jörg W. "Klarheit, Leichtigkeit, und Melodie: Theater im jüdischen Kulturbund Berlin." *Geschlossene Vorstellung,* 1992: 67–94.

Hartman, Geoffrey H. *The Longest Shadow: In the Aftermath of the Holocaust.* Bloomington: Indiana University Press, 1996.

Hilberg, Raul. *The Politics of Memory: The Journey of a Holocaust Historian.* Chicago: Ivan R. Dee, 1996.

Isser, Edward R. *Stages of Annihilation.* Cranbury, N.J.: Fairleigh Dickinson University Press, 1997.

Jelavich, Peter. *Berlin Cabaret.* Cambridge, Mass.: Harvard University Press, 1993.

Kaplan, Marion A. *Between Dignity and Despair: Jewish Life in Nazi Germany.* New York: Oxford University Press, 1998.

Karas, Joža. *Music in Terezín 1941–1945.* New York: Beaufort/ Pendragon, 1985.

Kater, Michael H. *Different Drummers: Jazz in the Culture of Nazi Germany.* New York: Oxford University Press, 1992.

———. *The Twisted Muse: Musicians and Their Music in the Third Reich.* New York: Oxford University Press, 1997.

Kift, Roy. *Camp Comedy.* 1999. Robert Skloot, *Plays of the Holocaust.* Madison: University of Wisconsin.

Kühn, Volker. *Die zehnte Muse: 111 Jahre Kabarett.* Cologne: vgs, 1993.

Langer, Lawrence L. *Admitting the Holocaust: Collected Essays.* New York: Oxford University Press, 1995.

Laqueur, Walter. *Weimar Germany: A Cultural History.* New York: Perigree, 1974.

Levi, Erik. *Music in the Third Reich.* London: Macmillan, 1994.

Meyer, Michael A. *The German Jews: Some Perspectives on Their History.* The B.G. Rudolph Lectures in Judaic Studies. New York: Syracuse University Press, 1991.

Müller-Wesemann, Barbara. *Theater als geistiger Widerstand, 1934–1941.* Stuttgart: M & P Verlag, 1997.

Presser, J. *The Destruction of the Dutch Jews.* Trans. Arnold Pomerans. New York: E. P. Dutton, 1969.

Reinharz, Jehuda, and Walter Schatzberg, eds. *The Jewish Response to German Culture.* Hanover, N.H.: University Press of New England, 1985.

Richarz, Monika, ed. *Jewish Life in Germany: Memoirs from Three Centuries.* Trans. S. Rosenfeld. Bloomington: Indiana University Press, 1991.

Rosenfeld, Alvin H. *Double Dying: Reflections on Holocaust Literature.* Bloomington: Indiana University Press, 1980.

Rovit, Rebecca. "Collaboration or Survival, 1933–1938: Reassessing the Role of the *Jüdischer Kulturbund.*" In *Theatre in the Third Reich, The Prewar Years, 1933–1939,* ed. Glen W. Gadberry. Westport, Conn.: Greenwood, 1995: 142–56.

Schumacher, Claude, ed. *Staging the Holocaust: The Shoah in Drama and Performance.* Cambridge: Cambridge University Press, 1998.

Schwertfeger, Ruth. *Women of Theresienstadt: Voices from a Concentration Camp.* Oxford: St. Martin's, 1989.

Skloot, Robert. *The Theatre of the Holocaust: Four Plays.* Madison: University of Wisconsin Press, 1982.

———. *The Darkness We Carry: The Drama of the Holocaust.* Madison: University of Wisconsin Press, 1988.

Spiegelman, Art. *Maus I: A Survivor's Tale.* New York: Pantheon, 1986.

———. *Maus II: A Survivor's Tale, and Here's Where My Troubles Began.* New York: Pantheon, 1991.

Steinweis, Alan E. *Art, Ideology, and Economics in Nazi Germany: The Reich Chambers of Music, Theater, and the Visual Arts.* Chapel Hill: University of North Carolina Press, 1993.

Stern, Fritz. *Dreams and Delusions: The Drama of German History.* New York: Alfred A. Knopf, 1987.

Taub, Michael, ed. *Israeli Holocaust Drama.* New York: Syracuse University Press, 1996.

Young, James E. *The Texture of Memory: Holocaust Memorials and Meaning.* New Haven, Conn.: Yale University Press, 1993.

Zortman, Bruce H. "Theater in Isolation: The *Jüdischer Kulturbund* of Nazi Germany." *Educational Theatre Journal* 24 (1972): 159–68.

Selected Archives

Stiftung der Akademie der Künste, Berlin

Federal Archives of Germany: Bundesarchiv, Koblenz; Potsdam; Außenstelle III Zehlendorf, Berlin

Centre de Documentation Juive Contemporaine, Paris, France
The Jewish Museum, Prague, Czech Republic
Leo Baeck Institute, New York (partner in the Center for Jewish History [New York], spring 1999)
Patmáník (Monument) Terezín and Terezín Museum, Czech Republic
U.S. National Holocaust Memorial Museum, Washington, D.C.
Wiener Library (Institute of Contemporary History), London
Wiener Library at Tel Aviv University, Sourasky Central Library
Yad Vashem, Jerusalem, Israel
YIVO Institute for Jewish Research, New York (partner in the Center for Jewish History [New York], spring 1999)

Selected Discography and Websites in Progress

Professor David Bloch (Tel Aviv University) is producer and artistic director of the Terezín Music Anthology by KOCH International Classics Series. This is part of The Terezín Music Memorial Project, sponsored by Vaclav Havel and the Czech Republic. Among the compact discs that have been produced are: selected cat. no. 3-7109-2H1, vol. I, Viktor Ullmann: piano sonatas 5-7 and string quartet no. 3; No. 3-7230-2H1, II, Gideon Klein: string, chamber music, piano sonata, choral works. No. 3-7151-2H1 III, Hans Krása: chamber music, songs, orchestral *Brundibár*. Bloch also has created a Website related to this project: www.tau.ac.il:81 /~ bloch2/terezin

Professor Joshua Jacobson (Northeastern University) produced *Hear Our Voices: Songs of the Ghettos and the Camps,* HaZamir HZ-909, HaZamir. Distributed by Transatlantic Music Publications, New York. HaZamir Recordings POB 126, Newton, MA 02159.

Music of Terezín: Victor Ullmann: "The Emperor of Atlantis." Arabesque Recordings Z6681. 1996.

"Der Kaiser von Atlantis" *and the Hölderlin Lieder by Ullmann.* Gewandhaus Orchestra, Leipzig. London 440854-2.

Volker Kühn has produced the double CD of original recordings, *Bei uns um die Gedächtniskirche rum, Berlin Cabaret: Friedrich Hollaender und das Kabarett der zwanziger Jahre in Originalaufnahmnen.* Berlin: Akademie der Künste, 1996.

Beit Terezín, Israel: www.cet.ac.il.terezin bterezin@inter.net.il This is the site of the Theresienstadt Martrys Remembrance Association.

United States Holocaust Memorial Museum, Washington, D.C.: www.ushmm.org

CONTRIBUTORS

REBECCA ROVIT (editor) is a scholar and theater historian who has held fellowships from the American Council for Learned Societies (1997–98), the Memorial Foundation for Jewish Culture (1997–98), and the American Philosophical Society (1996) for her work on the Jewish Kulturbund theater in Nazi Germany. She is preparing a monograph on the Kulturbund and representation. Dr. Rovit has published articles and book chapters on the Kulturbund and essays and reviews on German theater, the Holocaust, and performance history in such journals as *American Theatre, Theatre Survey, TDR,* and *Contemporary Theatre Review.* She has taught theater history at Illinois State University, having received her doctorate in theater history from Florida State University. Her e-mail address is rrovit@juno.com.

ALVIN GOLDFARB (editor) is Provost and Vice President for Academic Affairs and Professor of Theater at Illinois State University. Dr. Goldfarb has served at Illinois State University as Dean of the College of Fine Arts (1988–98) and department chair of Theater (1981–88). He has published articles, notes, and reviews in such journals and scholarly anthologies as *Theatre Journal, Performing Arts Journal, Journal of Popular Culture, Theatre Survey, Southern Theatre, Exchange, Tennessee Williams: A Tribute,* and *American Playwrights since 1945: A Guide to Scholarship, Criticism, and Performance.* He provided an annotated bibliography of Holocaust dramatic literature for the anthology *Plays of the Holocaust* and *Staging the Holocaust: The Shoah in Drama and Performance.* He co-authored *Theater: The Lively Art* and *Living Theater* and *Anthology of Living Theater* with Edwin Wilson. A member of the Illinois Arts Council, Dr. Goldfarb has won awards from the Illinois Alliance for Arts Education and the American College Theatre Festival.

SAMUEL M. EDELMAN is a professor of rhetoric and intercultural communication in the Department of Communication Arts and Sciences at California State University–Chico. He also founded the program in Modern Jewish and Israel Studies. He has been a consultant in public speaking and has lectured on Jewish rhetoric and taught courses on the Holocaust. He is preparing a co-edited collection of essays and survivor testimony on cultural resistance during the Holocaust.

M O S H E   F A S S is an Israeli scholar who now works at the Rothberg School for Overseas Studies at Hebrew University, Jerusalem.

D O N   G I L Z I N G E R   J R . is a professor of English at Suffolk County Community College, Selden, New York. He is currently writing a bio-bibliography of Aaron Kramer. He also writes on the Canadian-American science fiction writer William Gibson.

J O Ž A   K A R A S was born in Warsaw, Poland, as a Czech national. He graduated from the State Conservatory of Music (violin) in Prague and the Hartt School of Music of the University of Hartford. He has been a violinist with symphony orchestras in Prague, Medellin, Colombia, and Hartford, Connecticut. He has taught at the University of Hartford and Yale University, while authoring many articles on Czechoslovak music as well as on the Violin Method. His *Music in Terezín 1941–1945* (New York: Beaufort/Pendragon Press, 1985), published in several languages, has been revised for publication in summer 1999. Karas discovered more than fifty original scores composed in Terezín. He founded the Karas String Quartet in 1979 to perform such compositions. He conducted the North American premieres of the children's opera, *Brundibár,* in Czech and in English. He also conducted the recording of the opera for Channel Classics, Amsterdam.

R O Y   K I F T trained as an actor at the London Drama Centre, is a translator of stage plays, and is a contributor to theater magazines. He has been a full-time playwright since 1972, winning several literary awards, including the Thames Television (Stage) Dramatists Award (1974), the *Förderpreis* of the *Württembergischen Staatstheater Stuttgart* for a libretto, "Joy" (1984), and a Berlin Writer's Award (1987). His play on Kurt Gerron and the cabaret artists of Theresienstadt, *Camp Comedy,* is forthcoming in *The Theatre of the Holocaust, Volume Two,* ed. Robert Skloot (University of Wisconsin Press, 1999). He plays the narrator in Ilona Ziok's documentary film, *Kurt Gerrons Karussell* (1999). He currently lives in Castrop-Rauxel, Germany, and is working on a screenplay based on the experiences of a jazz musician in Theresienstadt and Auschwitz.

A A R O N   K R A M E R (1921–97) gained national prominence with *Seven Poets in Search of an Answer* (1944) and his work on Heinrich Heine (1948). He was a leading resistance poet throughout the McCarthy era. As a professor for English at Dowling College, Oakdale, New York, he also co-founded *West Hills Review: A Whitman Journal.* In addition to his numerous scholarly studies on American poetry, he published his own poetry. His translations include *A Century of Yiddish Poetry* (1989) and his most recent *The Last Lullabye: Poems of the Holocaust* (Syracuse University Press, 1998). He pioneered the therapeutic use of poetry for the disabled.

V O L K E R K Ü H N is a German stage director and author whose productions, including cabaret revues, have been produced all over Germany. He has worked for television and written television documentaries on cabaret in the concentration camps and entertainment in Nazi Germany. His published contributions to cabaret literature include his five-volume anthology of cabaret texts from modern Germany, including the Third Reich (Quadriga Press, Berlin). He has also written on Friedrich Hollaender (Weidle Verlag, Bonn, 1996) and produced an exhibition at Berlin's Akademie der Künste on Berlin cabaret of the 1920s (1996). His own *Banker's Opera* premiered in April 1998 at the Düsseldorfer Schauspielhaus.

S Y B I L H . M I L T O N is an independent historian, currently serving as vice president of the Independent Commission of Experts: Switzerland-World War II. Dr. Milton was previously senior historian at the U.S. Holocaust Memorial Museum, Washington, D.C., 1988–97, and chief archivist at the Leo Baeck Institute, New York, 1974–84. Her publications include co-editing the twenty-six-volume *Archives of the Holocaust,* as well as *Art of the Holocaust* (1981). Her forthcoming book on the photography of the Holocaust as historical evidence will be published by University of North Carolina Press.

A L A N E . S T E I N W E I S is Associate Professor of History and Judaic Studies at the University of Nebraska–Lincoln. He is the author of *Art, Ideology, and Economics in Nazi Germany: The Reich Chambers of Music, Theater, and the Visual Arts* (University of North Carolina Press, 1993) as well as numerous articles relating to Nazi Germany, German antisemitism, and Holocaust pedagogy. His current research explores the creation and uses of knowledge about Jews and Judaism in Nazi Germany.

CREDITS

The following publishers have generously given permission to reprint copyrighted works: From *The Leo Baeck Institute Yearbook,* 1993, Steinweis, "Hans Hinkel and German Jewry, 1933–1941," reprinted by permission of the Leo Baeck Institute. From *Theatre Survey* 35, no. 2 (1994), Rovit, "An Artistic Mission in Nazi Berlin: The Jewish Kulturbund Theater as Sanctuary" reprinted by permission of *Theatre Survey.* "Zores Haben Wir Genug." Copyright 1992 by Volker Kühn; translated with permission of the author. Permission by the Akademie der Künste Berlin to translate and reprint documents from the Jewish Kulturbund collections: Fritz Wisten (FWA) 74/86/995, 1002, 1021; 74/86/5001, 21, 23, 75, 102; 74/86/5102; FWA 74/86/053; SJK Edith Eisenheimer 1.53.55,2; SJK Martin Brandt 1.56.66; Kurt Singer Archives 1.53.36.1,2. "S'Brent" reprinted by permission of Joshua Jacobson. From *Jewish Social Studies,* Fass, "Theatrical Activities in the Polish Ghettos During the Years 1939–1942." Copyright 1976 by JSS. Reprinted by permission of Indiana University Press. From "Theatre and Concerts from the Ghettos and Concentration Camps" from *Theatre between the Two World Wars* by Yonas Turkov. Copyright by Knight Publishing 1968. Translation of extended citations permitted by the Congress for Jewish Culture. From *Performing Arts Journal,* material for Alvin Goldfarb, "Theatrical Activities in the Nazi Concentration Camps" and Mirko Tuma, "Memories of Theresienstadt." Copyright by *Performing Arts Journal* 1, no. 2 (1976). From *The Publications of the World Union of Jewish Studies.* Copyright 1986 by The Publications of the World Union of Jewish Studies (Jerusalem) for Samuel M. Edelman, "Singing in the Face of Death: A Study of the Jewish Cabaret and Opera during the Holocaust." From *A Holocaust Reader,* ed. Lucy S. Dawidowicz. Copyright 1976 by Behrman House, Inc. Reprinted by permission of Neal Kozodoy. From *Surviving the Holocaust: The Kovno Ghetto Diary,* by Avraham Tory, Cambridge, Mass.: Harvard University Press, copyright 1990 by the President and Fellows of Harvard College. Used by permission of the publisher. From *Belsen.* Copyright 1957 by Irgun Sheerit Hopleita Me'Haezor, Tel Aviv. Reprinted by permission of the World Jewish Congress, Jerusalem, for Samy Feder, "The Yiddish Theater of Belsen." For cabaret sketches (Leo Strauss), *Einladung* and *Theresienstadt Fragen,* permissions by translator Roy Kift and editor Ulrike Migdal. From *Letters from Westerbork* by Etty Hillesum. Copyright 1986 and permission extended by Pantheon. From *Waiting for Death* by Philip Mechanicus. Copyright 1968 by Calder & Boyars. Excerpt reprinted by permission of Marion Boyars. From *The Scum of*

INDEX

Note: Page numbers in **boldface** refer to documents in the text. Page numbers in *italics* refer to illustrations.

Library of Congress Cataloging-in-Publication Data

Theatrical performance during the Holocaust : texts, documents,
memoirs / edited by Rebecca Rovit and Alvin Goldfarb.
p.   cm. — (PAJ books)
Includes bibliographical references and index.
ISBN 0-8018-6167-5 (alk. paper)
1. Jewish theater—Europe—History—20th century.   2. Holocaust,
Jewish (1939–1945) Personal narratives.   I. Rovit, Rebecca.
II. Goldfarb, Alvin.   III. Series.
PN3035.T485   1999
792'.089'924—dc21   99-29416
CIP